# Shyton United

STANLEY GOBSEN

Heads or Tales Press
ISBN: 978-1-912704-32-3

# DISCLAIMER

This is a work of fiction. Any names or characters, businesses or places, events or incidents, are fictitious. Any resemblance to actual persons, living or dead, or actual events is purely coincidental.

# DEDICATION

For

All Football Fans

# Contents

# ACKNOWLEDGMENTS

Cover designed by Mihailo Tatic

<u>**Prologue**</u>

4th May, 2013. This date is important. This was the date of the most important day in Shyton United's, and indeed Shyton town's, history; the day that changed everything.

Shyton. My home. It was where I was born, where I was raised, and where I quickly left when opportunity arose. It's a grim former industrial town that used to be surrounded by smoke-spewing factories, manufacturing anything from plastic switches for vibrators to plastic toilet roll holders.

To the untrained eye just noticing Shyton's rolling green hills, the occasional flock of sheep, the two-up and two-down red brick houses and a permanent grey sky that refused to let in the sunshine; it could almost seem quaint. There's grime in the air and in your lungs. It's the kind of place The Smiths would've sung about and the perfect setting for a Ken Loach film.

The population the other day was 52,000, but having spotted yet another family hatchback with a roof-rack full of luggage, I had no doubt that the population had yet decreased... by four.

Yes, it's hard to believe that this town in the north of England used to be an industrial powerhouse... a town that once rivalled Oldham. How times have changed, much like the A160 connecting the A180 with Immingham Docks is about to.

One of the former factory owners, one of the factories that made those little black switches for vibrators, was a fella that went by the name of Jack, nicknamed 'Huge Jack' as he was a big lad. You couldn't miss him as he drove a yellow painted Rolls, wore a sheepskin coat much like my good friend, John Motson, smoked Cubans and had a handlebar moustache. The handlebar moustache made him look a little like a porn star, quite similar to Hugh 'Le Coq' Mongous. He certainly was larger than life. When Shyton could no longer compete with Taiwan in the competitive plastic-switch-for-vibrators market, the masses fled. Today, the high streets looked like the streets in a nuclear test town, and not far off Chernobyl. The shops were abandoned, terraced buildings boarded up, and outside every other block a tramp could be seen begging for some rope. Seeing as hardly anyone wandered the streets, you wondered why tramps even bothered to beg there. The only remaining shops were a butcher's selling meat only fit for dogs, a Greggs selling its normal depressing fare only fit for dogs, and a sex shop—the best in the north of England and owned by Huge Jack.

Huge Jack was now 55, and wore a toupee that the character Morris from the Martin Scorsese flick *Goodfellas* would've been proud of. Huge Jack was one of the biggest makers and distributors of amateur porn in the country, just a few leagues behind Dirty Desmond. Huge Jack was the man behind such titles as *'Shyton Me', 'Shyton: When the Curtains Close'* and *'Shyton Housewives: Whenever, Wherever'*. Yes, the amateur porn industry in Shyton was thriving like the blind army ants in southern California, and was one of its few big success stories. Huge Jack's film *'Shyton Me'* even won a *'Hardie'* for best film, and the town itself had been honoured with having the highest rate of teenage pregnancy in England.

The other surprising success story of Shyton was the town's football team, Shyton United. Having made its way up the lower leagues, the team was now in the Championship battling Wolves for second place and automatic promotion to the Premier League. Its home was Creek Alley, a 20,000 all-seater football stadium mostly financed by Huge Jack and the rest of Shyton's porn industry.

Interestingly, the site of Creek Alley dates back to Celtic times when it is believed it was the site of a popular brothel. Then, when the Romans invaded, a fierce and bloody battle took place. The Romans won and turned it into an even bigger brothel. In the year 1850, a Roman coin was discovered. According to calculations, it became the price of a Roman era hand-job. Depravity ran through the streets and veins of Shyton.

Years later, the site was turned into a fudge-wrapping factory, hence Shyton United's nickname, *'the Fudge Packers'*.

And it's this football team that has heralded my return. My name's Stanley Gobsen, though certain friends called me 'Gobby', not just because of my name but also because I could half prattle on. Friends and uncles would quite often stick a red ball in my mouth and leave me prone in the basement for days on end, I prattled on that much.

Gobsen is a Danish name and all my Danish ancestors were fisherman, of trout specifically. They say that in our family we just needed to hold our hands out over water and fish would jump into them—our family had even been compared to Jesus Christ as we could get a load of fish with very little bait. In fact, the real secret behind our family's success with the chickens of the ocean—and something I'll reveal here even though it could mean my head—was that we'd soak the bait in a cocaine solution. It drove the fish batty to try and get the bait, it was easy pickings from there.

When the Gobsen clan migrated to England sometime in the 19th Century and settled in the north because of the familiarity the cold brought, it was not long before they took up their rods, their nets, their cocaine and established a fishing empire that stretched 35 miles Eastwards from Goole all the way to Spurn Head. Fishing remained big in my family (and subsequently cocaine, though for very different reasons), even when my father brought my mother inland to Shyton and set up Shyton's premier fishmonger's. With daily imports of semi-fresh junky fish delivered by his brother Brian, the business flourished; though mother was none-too-happy, complaining of the smell of fish, spending two hours a day scrubbing her hands and threatening to leave father for the butcher, who had been making advances, as well as the best pork and apple sausages north of Birmingham.

When I came of age, I was expected to take over the fishmonger business by first spending a couple of years with Uncle Brian and his crew out at sea or on the river. I steadfastly refused as I was never one for fishing (too many days at sea with a bunch of horny men with nobs like frozen fish fingers). Frozen fish fingers + horny men = frustrated, pissed out of their heads fishermen. Though this upset my father and uncle, I was a firm believer in choosing our own destinies and clean, non-fishy hands. Plus I was pretty sure that the Narcs were onto them. No, what I was interested in were documentaries and that was one of the reasons why I didn't linger in Shyton (apart from father and uncle threatening to stab me with fish hooks), and instead went straight to Manchester. Not much call for documentarians in Shyton, pornographers though was another story.

With my Danish hair, I was ripe for the visual medium. I was the Steve Ryder of documentaries long before Steve Ryder became a household name on BBC Sport. After leaving Shyton I made numerous award-winning documentaries that were the toast of film festivals of cities such as Hull, Gdasnk and Torquay. Perhaps you've seen *Hamsters: Man's True Enemy*?

With Shyton United on the brink of achieving promotion to the Premier League however, I thought it was time to make my return to my hometown and chronicle, if they made it, their first season in the top flight of the English football league structure. The club were also very willing for me and my top snooper, Bob, to document their historic first season in the English top flight. Even more so as one of their players was, like me, born and bred in Shyton and had almost single-handedly dragged them up from non-league obscurity.

Of course, I was talking about local bad boy Tommy 'Machine' Gunn.

With unprecedented access, and through recordings made by me and Bob, extracts from blogs, Twitter, round-the-clock illegal surveillance, and interviews, we were able to document their story, warts and all. What we documented was without precedent, in both sporting and legal history. So, sit back, unzip and enjoy, as there really was only one 'Shyton United'.

<u>**2<sup>nd</sup> May, 2013**</u>

Two days before that most pivotal and important turn of events, I went to visit Tommy Gunn at his flat situated on a rundown council estate located in inner Shyton. There was graffiti on the walls, and the garage doors were spray-painted with words such as 'I WOZ 'ERE… UN4TUNATELY'. Kids kicked an empty Coke can around in a car park where the best car was a red 95 Fiat Punto—good car.

Tommy's flat was straight out of an IKEA catalogue (if everything in the catalogue was chipped or had dried red alphabet spaghetti over it), and had colourful plastic toys strewn everywhere. There were framed photos of a younger-looking Tommy on a sideboard. A couple of them showed him being arrested by the local constabulary—in one of said photos, he was giving a copper the finger whilst giving it large.

Tommy's now 26, though by the thinning and receding hair on his noggin you'd think he was older. The temples of his head throbbed when he chewed gum or when he was trying to solve complex equations such as the amount of change he'd get from a quid when purchasing a pint of milk. There he sat sprawled, legs as wide apart as though he were visiting a gynaecologist, across a dirty white sofa in nothing other than his Union Jack British Bulldog boxers. Here's a transcript of my interview:

**STANLEY:** You come from a broken home, is that right?
**TOMMY:** It was broke, so what? Windows, plumbing, fuses kept blowing.
**STANLEY**: I meant your family.
**TOMMY:** Bastard dad left us when I was a kiddie, so I had to make some bread anyway I could.
**STANLEY:** Could you shed some light on why you were first sent away?
**TOMMY:** Hang on, I'll switch the light on.
**STANLEY**: No, no, I meant could you tell us what you were sent away for?
**TOMMY:** I stabbed my bastard uncle in the leg with a pocket knife cos he was eating my doughnut.
**STANLEY:** You'd been in and out of Shyton young offenders' institute since you were eleven. It was whilst there that you were

spotted by a Shyton United scout. Can you tell me about that?

**TOMMY:** Bren! Get me a cuppa! You want something, Stan?

**STANLEY:** I'm good, thanks.

**BRENDA (shouting from the kitchen):** Get it yerself! I'm feeding the kids.

**TOMMY:** Fuckin' kids.

**STANLEY:** So, my question?

**TOMMY:** This is what happens when you get kids. Missus can't even make you cups of tea. You got kids?

**STANLEY:** I had a vasectomy. How did it come about that Shyton United spotted you?

**TOMMY:** I was playing for Shyton's Young Offenders' youth team, and a scout, Funny John spotted us. By the following week I was on trial, then the week after being cleared, I was on a football trial, and by the end of that month I was in the match day squad.

**STANLEY:** Why's he called Funny John?

**TOMMY:** Cos he's a bit funny, innit? Always cracking jokes… like the one when he sits down and accidentally gets a cock up his arse.

Tommy kept touching his hair just like that member of One Direction, Harry Styles when the lads appeared on *James' Corden's Carpool Karaoke*. What was that about?

**STANLEY:** You signed your first professional contract at 18. You're now 26, never wanted to move?

**TOMMY:** Yeah... I mean, nah!

**STANLEY:** You've had numerous offers to join bigger clubs over the years and you've rebuffed every offer...

**TOMMY:** Yeah, I rebuffed them. If it wasn't for United, I'd still be banged up. Owe them, innit?

**STANLEY:** It's a bit surprising that with your club on the brink of promotion to the Premier League—the most lucrative and richest football league in the world—you still live on a council estate.

**TOMMY:** Team's had to do it on a shoestring budget.

**STANLEY:** The other members of the squad own their own houses.

**TOMMY:** Well, cos I'm from Shyton I've had to represent and sacrifice.

**BRENDA (from the kitchen):** Dontcha listen to him! He's a spineless coward that doesn't have the balls to ask that Maury for a rise.

**TOMMY:** That does it.

Tommy disappeared from the lounge and into the kitchen, at which point there was the sound of a load of plates being smashed, as though they were recreating a Greek wedding. Bob and I headed away sharpish.

We then went to pay a visit to the managing director of Shyton United, Maury Git'a at his office at Creek Alley Stadium.

Maury's office had a framed black and white photo on the wall that showed a muddy pitch with an old man and his dog watching classic Shyton United. It brought back memories. The black and white days of defenders 'Prick' Johnson and 'Mental' Jimmy, goalie 'Potato' Patrick, winger 'Tricky' Dixie and forward 'Mahogany' Dave. Maury Git'a wore a suit that looked Zara but spoke Burton. He had a late 80s five o'clock shadow and a mane of great silvery hair as 'Father Ted' was described in the episode, *'A Christmassy Ted'*. Maury was often referred to as 'The Silver Ghost' or 'That Git with the Silvery Hair'.

**MAURY:** You see Stanley, unlike the town, the club's founded on a sure financial footing. We think long-term. That's why Tommy's tied down to a 20-year contract.
**STANLEY:** Bit excessive?
**MAURY:** The contract is merely a reflection of our mutual admiration for each other. Thanks to my strategy of prudence, and under the magnificent stewardship of Sid Chesterton, I'm just a step away from achieving history.
**STANLEY:** If Shyton United does get promoted to the Premier League, which route will you go down? QPR's, 2012-2013, go for broke—overspend on a load of past-it players and still get relegated or Derby's, 2007-2008, hardly spend a penny and hope for the best but get relegated anyway with a record low points total?
**MAURY:** We shall probably follow Derby's example but perhaps buy the odd exceptional player here or there, nothing too extravagant... And not get relegated! We shan't become another Leeds, mark my words.

A day before the crucial match against Crystal Palace, I met up with Shyton United's manager, Charlie Greencock at his office at the club's training ground. His office was littered with framed, signed photographs of him and many famous footballers, as well as numerous trophies and awards that looked as though he'd got them made himself. Sitting behind his desk fiddling with a gold pen, the forty-two year old had a bright orange complexion—a sign that he'd spent too long at a tanning salon, and admired Donald Trump a bit too much. He was a snazzy dresser in his Armani suit, and for some reason he still had his hands-free headset on. He exuded confidence, and Tommy Hilfiger cologne—I wasn't sure if the over-confidence was merited… nor the Tommy Hilfiger cologne.

**STANLEY:** You've chopped and changed your team a fair amount this season. With one game left, do you even know your best team?

**CHARLIE:** I know my best team, but my best team has got 15 players in it. However, sometimes it's not easy because as supreme leader it's vitally important that you make decisions. So it's my job to not always put square pegs in square holes, but sometimes put the odd square peg in a round hole. And at the moment we're knocking on the door of success.

**STANLEY:** Who would you say has been the real driving force behind your promotion push this season?

**CHARLIE:** Myself.

**STANLEY:** With regard to the playing staff.

**CHARLIE:** Well, Tommy would be the fans' choice. Tommy is, without a shadow of a doubt, a player.

**STANLEY:** Which means?

**CHARLIE:** That's not important. What is important is that you win games at any level.

**STANLEY:** How are things coming along for the big game tomorrow?

**CHARLIE:** The plans we put in place this week have gone according to plan. We'll be ready for Palace tomorrow. Palace is just another step. You know if we stand still, we're going backwards. We've got to keep moving forward and appear to be moving forward.

**STANLEY:** It's quite a miracle that you've gotten this far after black November when Shyton couldn't buy a win.

**CHARLIE:** Don't know what you're on about. In November, we got 8 points from 4 games. That's automatic promotion form.
**STANLEY:** Sure it is.

At which point I left out of fear of being even more confused. Tomorrow was the big day and I needed to get ready.

From the Twitter account of @JoeMeek, President of Fudge Packer for Life (FPL) supporters club: *'Biggest game of season. Biggest game ever! Get down & support Shyton. #PLHereWeCome #FPL'*

It's match day, the day of the biggest match in Shyton United's history. If they won against Crystal Palace, they'd finish second and automatically get promoted to the Premier League. We were in the Creek Alley Stadium's rather small changing room that had just a few wooden benches, a few hooks, a couple of showers and Old Sally, Huge Jack's buffer. Charlie Greencock, with his ever present hands-free headset, delivered a lecture from his whiteboard that displayed a 4-4-2 formation. By his side, as always—like a resident sidekick—was assistant manager Ben 'Mystic' Twaddle – a shaggy-haired guy in a brown and white Shyton United tracksuit. Speaking of shaggy, he did look a bit like Shaggy from *Scooby-Doo*. Mystic always either had his hands clasped together in prayer or would move into a Muslim prayer position. Which deity he prayed to wasn't clear… If it was a deity. He may have worshipped William Shatner for all anybody knew.

Sixteen or so footballers, all wearing their fudge-brown Shyton United football kits with white trim, sat glued to the gaffer's every word… or were just numb from having listened to him all season. I wasn't sure. My brain was still numb from yesterday.

**CHARLIE:** Alright, you talentless no-hopers. Thanks to me and my enormous tactical brain, we're a win away from automatic promotion.
**BEN:** Heed Charlie's words. The force is strong with him.
**CHARLIE:** Listen up, if you score first, you have a 75 per cent chance of not losing the game. It doesn't take a brain surgeon to work out that you have to get off to a good start and score.

Shyton United owner, Sid Chesterton stormed into the changing room like that X-Men character whose name I've forgotten. There he was smoking a cigar and wearing a John Motson-style sheepskin coat— almost the exact same as Huge Jack's. They must've shopped at the same place. They also looked an awful lot alike. I had heard they were cousins but many wondered whether they were in fact twins who had been separated at birth because of the expense, with one of them having been offloaded to an aunt. Alongside Sid was Maury Git'a, like a creepy shadow—a creepy Robin to Sid's retired Batman.

**SID:** Alright laddies. Final and biggest game of season, nay, biggest game in club's history. I want you to show them true Shyton grit that only a fudge-packer can stand.
**TOMMY:** Come on boys!

Shyton United headed out of the changing room. Tommy head-butted a wall, then charged out. James 'K-Y' Black, the lanky goalkeeper head-butted the same wall and collapsed. I helped him back up and he thanked me by calling me Tony. I corrected him. I managed to get a quick word with Tommy.

**STANLEY:** Tommy, you're not too fond of Charlie Greencock, are you?
**TOMMY:** The gaffer's a complete cock. Cock by name, cock by nature. I'm gonna nut him one of these days.

I didn't doubt him.

There was a vociferous sell-out crowd cheering on their heroes, Shyton United. The crowd chanted 'C'mon you fudge-packers!' It did bring a tear to this documentarian's eye and not much makes me tearful—except for when Captain Kirk allowed Edith Keeler to die. The town had suffered so much, what with the chlamydia epidemic, and now here was a ray of light.

The first half saw Shyton United try shot after shot at the opposing team's goal without success. It got to a point where Tommy tried to be fancy and lob the goalkeeper only for the ball to be just tipped over.

**TOMMY:** Fuck a pig in the arse and call it barbecue!

He was evidently frustrated. I wasn't sure if that could ever be considered barbecue. Anyway, by half-time it was still 0-0 and the gaffer wasn't happy as he tried an alternative pep talk by conducting it in the centre circle with the Shyton United team seated in it. It was more awkward and embarrassing than when Pip Turner had publicly stated he'd beat me in the short best documentary award at the

'Doccos', only to be soundly beaten.

**CHARLIE:** That was fucking pathetic! If I had been out there we'd be 5 nil up already. Get down the flanks and shoot on sight, you bunch of pussies! Jesus, that's a lot of hard work gone under the water, under the bridge.

Charlie stomped off the pitch like a child who had just discovered that he was adopted and his biological parents had been country bumpkins and first cousins.

**BEN:** Feel the ball into their net, my brothers. Let the force of Christ Our Saviour guide you.
**TOMMY:** Shut it, Mystic.

Ben clasped his hands together and skipped away to the touchline. That was not unusual for him as he had once auditioned for The Royal Ballet.

**TOMMY:** Alright, we can do this. Ignore that orange turd.

The second half got underway and Tommy straight away powered forward towards the penalty box when he was on the receiving end of a late tackle. It looked pretty tasty did that tackle. The referee signalled for a free kick on the edge of the penalty area. It was Tommy that was going to thump it. He stepped up and hit a screamer into the top corner. What a thumper!

The fans went wild, waving plastic turds in the air - plastic turds, which symbolised Shyton United and their fudge-packing history. Tommy celebrated by pretending to 'machine gun' the fans. He mouthed something but I couldn't quite catch it.

The match finished 1-0 to Shyton United, which meant they'd secured 2nd spot and automatic promotion to the Premier League—The bestest league in the world. The Liverpools, the Manchester Uniteds, the Chelseas, the Arsenals, and now the Shyton Uniteds. Shyton had earned the right to be in that class.

After the match, the champagne was overflowing in the changing room as the team celebrated. I caught a few words with the gaffer.

**CHARLIE:** What can I say? I've done it. We gave ourselves a hill to climb and we climbed it.

Sid threw open the door with Maury following, dusting down Sid's coat like he was his own personal servant. It looked like Maury would do anything for that man. Anything.

**SID:** Lads, lads, lads. You done me and Shyton proud. Now settle down for a bit, I got some news I need to get off me big, hairy chest.

The team sat on the benches, still downing bottles of Asda's finest sparkling wine, as it turned out to be.

**SID:** I been with club when we was just a non-league outfit with a stolen park bench for a stand and today, eight year on, we made it to Premier League.

A huge, deafening cheer went up.

**SID:** But for me, that ride is over. I gone as far as a son of a butcher's son can.
Butcher's son? The same fella?

**SID:** With that said, I sold club.

There was an awkward tense hush like when I shoved my 'docco' in front of Pip Turner's face. Could Sid really have sold Shyton United?

**SID:** Now, don't be getting nervy. New owner promised me he'll keep you all and make Shyton United one of biggest clubs in Premier League, something I could never do. So, up the fudge-packers!

Sid didn't hang around and he scarpered along with his sidekick Maury. There was stunned silence except for Tommy who was head-butting 'K-Y' Black's upper arm.

**K-Y:** Stop it, Tommy! Boss!

From the Twitter account of @JoeMeek, (FPL): *'Yes! Shyton United promoted! @TomMachineGunn legend! #PLHereWeCome #FPL'*

<u>**5<sup>th</sup> May, 2013**</u>

The following day, having had a night to contemplate this devastating news, I visited Tommy Gunn and his wife, Brenda at their home. This was the first time I had really gotten to talk with Brenda. She was not your typical WAG, (wives and girlfriends), as she wore an oversized jumper to conceal her own layers, leggings that showed off a much unwanted camel toe, and well, for lack of a better word, she looked frumpy. She actually resembled that Flump with the woolly white hat from the children's TV show *'the Flumps'*.

Tommy was yet again sprawled on his sofa just wearing his Union Jack British Bulldog boxers. Did he have any other clothes? Could he not afford them? Must he advertise his chappie to me?

**TOMMY:** Man, this blows more than Sharon Dobbs.
**STANLEY:** Who's Sharon Dobbs?
**TOMMY:** Some slag who does it behind the KFC.
**BRENDA:** How'd you know?
**TOMMY:** *(Cough)*. Shinji lad told me.
**STANLEY:** With a new owner coming in, maybe this is the opportunity you need to secure a new contract.
**BRENDA:** He won't secure nothing. Only thing he's apparently secured is free blow jobs from some slag behind the KFC.
**TOMMY:** It was the Japanese lad!
**BRENDA:** He's nothing but a gutless wonder.
**TOMMY:** Oi! Watch it! Shinji ain't gutless.
**BRENDA:** Take no notice of him, Stan. For all those years that he's been with that
team and look at the pigsty we're living in! The manager of the Co-Op earns more than him.
**TOMMY:** Steve's got a GCSE!

Fearing another fight was brewing and more plates would soon be flying, I left in a jiffy.

<u>**6<sup>th</sup> May, 2013**</u>

A press conference was called. Sid Chesterton and Maury Git'a faced the frenzied pack-of-hungry-wolf-like press.

**TABLOID JOURNALIST:** Sid, why are you selling now?
**SID:** For the benefit of club. Only so far I can take it.
**TABLOID JOURNALIST:** You've owned the club for years, you're Shyton born and bred, why not stay now that they're in the Premier League?
**MAURY:** I believe he's already answered that question. For Shyton United to move forward the club needs massive investment, how else will they compete with the super-rich, allegedly FFP-flouting clubs of Manchester City and Chelsea? Sid has done a marvellous job to get us this far.
**SID:** It's time someone else took reins.
**TABLOID JOURNALIST:** Who is the new owner?
**MAURY:** That'll be announced in due course.
**JOE MEEK:** How could you, Sid! You're meant to be one of us! You've sold us out!

A bunch of burly security men then led Joe Meek, the Twitterer—a Michelin Man lookalike with steak & kidney pie stain on his Shyton United top—out of Creek Alley's conference room.

From the Twitter account of @JoeMeek: *'Cant believe Sid sold club. #Traitor! New Owner wont know the meaning of being a fudge packer. #SellOut #DarkDays #FPL'*

A new owner had been announced and the squad gathered at Shyton United's training ground, Bluewood, for a meet and greet. You could cut the tension with a Gobsen trout. All the main players were there in the changing room, as well as Mystic. Maury was out in front next to a small table, which had an iPhone on it connected to some JBL Bluetooth speakers, retailing at a hundred smackers from your local Curry's. Tommy, looking agitated, kept fidgeting and patting his ever-receding hairline; it seemed like he was about to nut someone. K-Y glanced over at Tommy nervously, seemingly fearing it would be him. Better him than me.

**TOMMY:** Get on with it!
**MAURY:** It is my honour to present to you, the great new owner of Shyton United, Mr Chen Hu. Everybody stand and bow!

Nobody stood up and bowed. Maury pressed play on the iPhone and the Chinese national anthem played. In walked a tall Chinese man looking richer than Mark Zuckerberg and wearing a suit that glistened and said, 'I cost ten grand'. Chen Hu cut an imposing, stern-looking figure that made me feel a little unhinged. K-Y visibly gulped—though he did that a lot as if he always had something thick stuck in his throat. Another Chinese guy also walked in, a smallish man called Wang Yong who was Chen Hu's interpreter and his Maury. Maury stopped playing the Chinese national anthem and bowed to greet Chen Hu. Maury sucked up more than a Dyson.

**CHEN HU'S WIKIPEDIA PAGE, A SUMMARY:** *Mr Chen Hu, billionaire entrepreneur. Factory owner—maker of mobile phone cases & plastic switches. As of May 1<sup>st</sup>, 2013, there have been no allegations of corruption for 20 days.*
**CHEN HU (Chen Hu only spoke Mandarin but I later got everything officially translated):** Congratulations on promotion to the Premier League. I can't wait to exploit you all.
**WANG YONG:** Mr Chen Hu wishes to congratulate you on winning promotion to the Premier League.
**CHARLIE:** It was nothing, really. When you have a football brain like mine, piece of piss.
**CHEN HU:** Are they all here?

**WANG YONG:** Mr Chen Hu wishes to know if they are all here.
**MAURY:** Yes, except for Shinji Takamoto, whose wife just gave birth.
**CHEN HU:** Shinji Takamoto? Japanese?
**WANG YONG:** You have Japanese player?
**MAURY:** Absolutely. We're a forward thinking club.
**CHEN HU:** Japanese!

Chen Hu then, oddly, spat on the ground. That's a sure way to spread tuberculosis.

**CHEN HU:** Bring out Li Bang.
**WANG YONG:** We have surprise for you. Li Bang! May I present to you, first new signing of this new era. China's number one player.
**MAURY:** Excellent, Mr Chairman, sir.

Li Bang, a young Jet Li lookalike already dressed in a Shyton United kit, came in, head bowed like the subservient person Chen Hu liked. Maury later nicknamed Li Bang 'Marketing Gold Mine'. All of a sudden, Li Bang broke out into a quick breakdance with Chinese pop music emanating from a mobile attached to his shorts. He jumped up.

**'MARKETING GOLD MINE':** Li Bang!

Wasn't expecting that!

There was an understandable uncomfortable uncomfortableness in the room. A few players shifted uncomfortably. It was even more uncomfortable than when I inserted my docco up Pip Turner's channel tunnel. That kind of uncomfortable behaviour might not sit comfortably in very normal Shyton.

**CHARLIE:** One second. Why wasn't I consulted? I'm in charge of this team.
**CHEN HU:** Wang.
**WANG YONG:** Mr Charlie, you are fired.
**CHARLIE:** What! You can't do that. My players won't stand for it.
**TOMMY:** Think again.
**CHEN HU:** Wang.
**WANG YONG:** You are all fired except Mr Tommy and Mr James. We give you five minutes to get off premises.

**K-Y (whispers to Tommy):** Lucky for us, eh?

Maury opened the door for Chen Hu, then followed him and Wang Yong out of the door, scurrying after them like a loved up rat. Wouldn't be surprised if Maury polished their shoes, and polished other things too.

Charlie and the team were dumbfounded, except K-Y who had a big grin splashed across his face. Not even K-Y could explain why he was retained.

<u>**10<sup>th</sup> May, 2013**</u>

From the blog, Fudge Packer for Life, Joe Meek wrote:
*'…Seriously need to question the decision to sell to billionaire Chen Hu. Yes, he's a billionaire and can take Shyton all the way to the top but how did he get his billions? From exploitation of the masses and through dodgy deals! I checked into his past and there's been a ton of allegations levelled at him, he seems shady to say the least. Could he be leading Shyton United down an unfamiliar, alternative dark alley?'*

A week later, I visited James 'K-Y' Black's home, situated in the suburbs of Shyton where there were tree-lined streets, freshly-cut lawns, and houses with their own gates and driveways. It was pretty and perfect. A really good location for *'The Real Housewives of Shyton'*, if ever it was going to be made. It was a stark cry from where Tommy resided, for certain.

Shyton United's long-standing goalie was signed 6 years ago, after being spotted playing for Saint Paul's Catholic boarding school. From his Catholic boarding school's Facebook page, I was able to find a Catholic Priests' football team photo with a spotty teenage James Black in the middle, surrounded by various priests of different ages all leering at him. Cosy.

K-Y showed us into his house, where all the lights were off and just a few candles were lit.

**K-Y:** This is my humble abode.
**STANLEY:** Why do they call you K-Y?
**K-Y:** Funny story. It's because I normally almost always have lime-flavoured jelly as part of our pre-game meal.
**STANLEY:** Why are the lights off?
**K-Y:** We're big environmentalists. Honey? Great news! Babe, what you doing in the conservatory with the lights off? They won't be able to see you! They're shy.
**STANLEY:** I see.
**K-Y:** It's finally happening. I'm going to be a huge star. Soon, I'll be England's number one goalie!

I could make out the footsteps of K-Y's partner walking away. Wasn't able to get a visual.

**K-Y:** Camera-shy. Bless.
**STANLEY:** What was your background like?
**K-Y:** Well, I'm from a tiny village where my dad's a priest—pretty conservative background. Got sent to a Catholic boarding school, which was tough. Those nuns and priests hated kids. Not all of them, some were quite loving.

**STANLEY:** Loving?

**K-Y:** Yes, went above and beyond. Comfort us when we got homesick, help us with our homework, made sure we washed inside and out. There was one, Father Victor O'Reilly who was a right meanie though. Any excuse to smack us, tap our knees and take liberties with rulers.

**STANLEY:** What kind of liberties?

**K-Y:** You know, what priests do with rulers and pens… Prodding, poking and stuff. Backsides didn't half hurt sometimes.

<u>**22<sup>nd</sup> May, 2013**</u>

I happened to be in Maury's office waiting to interview him as he chatted on his mobile. I noticed that he continually shifted uncomfortably, looked uneasy and had the air of corruption all about him. He looked shiftier than one of the tradesmen Del Boy would no doubt do business with.

**MAURY:** Not over the phone!

Maury slammed down the phone and smiled at me. What was he hiding? At that moment Tommy burst through the door like a trapped fart finally escaping the clutches of Johnny Vegas. He didn't look happy… Tommy, not that tiresome Johnny Vegas.

**MAURY:** Tommy! Our star player!
**TOMMY:** Exactly! Cos of me we're in the Premier League. I want what's due.
**MAURY:** And you have security for twenty years!
**TOMMY:** I live on a fucking council estate!
**MAURY:** Which endears you to the fans even more! Makes you one of them. We need that connect.
**TOMMY:** I am one of them. I'm their neighbour!
**MAURY:** Tommy, you're the soul of this club. You can't put a price on that. Some things are worth more than money.

Maury's mobile rang again and he briskly got up and left his office.

Tommy sat down and rubbed his face, then turned to me. He was most definitely not a happy chappie.

**TOMMY:** I'm gonna add him to the sods-to-nut list.

Tommy then got out his mobile and started typing.

**STANLEY:** What are you typing?
**TOMMY:** Just said. I'm adding that fucking Maury to my sods-to-nut list.

I tried to check to make sure my name wasn't on there. Couldn't see it.

<u>**23<sup>rd</sup> May, 2013**</u>

The following day I got to spend more time with Tommy and his family in his council flat. I drank a mug of Twinings's English Breakfast tea—the best tea—whilst in their kitchen. At the kitchen table Brenda fed Lidl' apple puree to their baby daughter, Shannon. The apple puree didn't look good. Sweet mush. Their toddler son, Luke was playing with his Matchbox Mini in his rice pudding. I found it most off-putting and wanted to remonstrate when I realised I wasn't at some fine-dining establishment. There was rice pudding on the floor and on the walls. I was careful not to step in it.

Tommy was noshing on some bangers and mash that though seemed relatively tasty, seemed a bit too heavy for a top-flight footballer. Brenda started introducing me to their kids. She apparently forgot that she had already done that the first time I met them.

**BRENDA:** That's Luke. Say hello, Luke.
**LUKE:** Willy!
**TOMMY:** Boy's got an obsession.
**STANLEY:** With?
**TOMMY:** Toy cars. Maybe he'll be the next Lewis Hamilton.
**BRENDA:** And our Shannon. Just two for now as it's all we can afford! Isn't that right, you bastard?
**TOMMY:** Shut it. If they get rid of me, I'm gonna nut someone.
**STANLEY:** Mr Chen Hu seems like a reasonable man. I'm sure he won't dispose of anybody else.

<u>**30<sup>th</sup> May, 2013**</u>

The following week Bob was carrying out his usual duties of visiting the club's training ground, installing surveillance gadgets in the main players' houses, bidets and doing other general spying stuff when he spied Tommy entering a cosmetic surgery clinic. It was a clinic for a whole range of aesthetic, superficial treatments from laser hair removal to Botox treatments and the like. I assumed that Tommy had gone in to get a quote for Brenda's much needed cosmetic surgery and liposuction but he was in there a long time. Bob called me on the blower and so I ventured down. We waited outside for Tommy to emerge, munching on a couple of Gregg's sausage rolls while we waited. Half an hour later he did.

**STANLEY:** What kind of treatment is Brenda after?
**TOMMY:** Err… what you doing here?
**STANLEY:** Nose job is it?
**TOMMY:** Err… yeah.

I was about to ask another question but then Tommy cleared off sharpish. I suspected Brenda was actually after the works including liposuction… and a face-lift… and a boob job.

<u>**24<sup>th</sup> June, 2013**</u>

A few weeks had passed without much at all happening. Most of the remaining staff and squad had time off and were on their hols. I myself went to a comic-con and got Robert Llewellyn to sign my special edition Red Dwarf DVD. I also had a week at home watching every series of Red Dwarf. It was 'smegging' great.

Tommy, Brenda and the kids had a weekend in Blackpool. They didn't enjoy it. I wouldn't be surprised if their marriage was at breaking point. Straight after the Blackpool trip, Tommy was, rather mysteriously, summoned to London for a week.

Whilst Tommy was summoned to the bright lights of London town, Brenda summoned me to her grotty digs.

**BRENDA:** We get Blackpool and Tommy's off to London. Why didn't we go to London?
**STANLEY:** I'm sure it's football-related business.
**BRENDA:** Something's up, I can tell.

Something was up. Brenda still looked the same and I got no hint that an appointment with a cosmetic surgeon was in the pipeline. It was getting desperate for her.

When everybody was back, including Tommy, a team meeting was called at the club's training ground.

I hadn't seen Tommy since before he was called to go to London and so I tried to catch up with him before he joined the others for the meeting. He pulled up in his clapped-out old banger and got out and… WAIT! Tommy had new hair! Yes, new hair had been implanted.

**TOMMY:** What yer looking at?
**STANLEY:** So, Brenda's not getting a tummy tuck?
**TOMMY:** Fuck off.

It's not often that I'm shocked but that was such a time. Of all the people to get something like that done, Tommy was the last person I'd have thought of. I wondered what Brenda thought of it.

In the changing room Tommy sat next to Li Bang. Li Bang had just come back from winning the breakdancing freestyle championship in Shanghai. There was no sign of K-Y or Shinji Takamoto. At least with Tommy you had the nucleus of the team there.

There were occasional glances at Tommy's hair but then he stared back with a look that could kill and the glances glanced away.

Mystic yet again had his hands in a prayer position. He was alongside a tubby and balding man with a dyed-black goatee who looked suspiciously like famed Spanish coach, Juan Lopez. On closer inspection and then having to ask who he was as he didn't like me closely inspecting him, he did indeed reveal that he was Juan Lopez, former manager of Spanish La Liga team, Villareal.

**'SPECIAL' JUAN LOPEZ:** Hello. I am 'Special' Juan Lopez. I am a very proud man today because all managers like to arrive at the best clubs, and we know Shyton is one of the most important clubs in the world.

A few of the players started laughing.

**TOMMY:** You went too big there, mate.
**JUAN:** I like to play a very sexy game. I want the ball like it's woman's nipples.
**TOMMY:** What did you say, you nob?
**'MARKETING GOLD MINE':** He say ball is nipple.

Chen Hu, Wang Yong and Maury breezed in like a breezy breeze.

**MAURY:** Shinji's dead.

Chen Hu spat at the ground, as jaws dropped to the floor except Li Bang's as he didn't know Shinji. The silence was crispy.

**MAURY:** Tommy, outside in 5.

Chen Hu, Wang Yong and Maury marched out. There was the sound of a toilet flushing, then K-Y came in from a different door.

**K-Y:** What did I miss?

Nobody answered. K-Y sniffed the air.

**K-Y:** What? It's the curry I had last night. Christ, it ain't that bad. Get over it. It's not as if someone died.

I sneaked out after Tommy had left the changing room and caught him outside in a secluded part of the training ground near the changing room building. He was with Maury. Tommy's face was as red as a lobster's, he looked as though he were steaming… like a just cooked lobster. Maury was shaking his fist and pointing his finger at Tommy like he was a naughty schoolboy. What was that about and why hadn't Tommy head-butted him?

I went out into Shyton town centre to grab a bite to eat. I had wanted to find out if food had gotten worse or better since I last ate out in Shyton back in 1993. As I was out I bumped into Joe Meek, dressed as always in his Shyton United top. He was gulping down a can of Shyton bitters.

**JOE:** This ain't Spain. This ain't the glamour of Madrid or Barcelona. How's this Spanish fella gonna handle managing club like ours? It's a whole kettle of other fish. Shyton fish. And Shyton fish ain't like other fish. It ain't for human consumption.

I could attest to that.

**STANLEY:** He's won league titles, surely this shows Chen Hu's intent?
**JOE:** I got my doubts. You sees what happened to Brum, and before that Man Citeh.

I took a couple of steps back, as his breath was making me drunk. Did passive drinking exist?

**JOE:** Stan, I just worry about club's future.

On that note I thought it was time I visited Maury again, this time at his house. I took my 2008 Ford Focus hatchback in mint green and drove to Maury's house, a charming cottage with a thatched roof out in the smoggy Shyton countryside. As I was on my way there I had my car radio tuned into the local Shyton news when I heard the announcement as read by local DJ, DJ Mike.

**DJ MIKE:** New Shyton United owner Chen Hu has been charged with corruption and fraud back in China.
**STANLEY:** Crikey!

I parked my 2008 Ford Focus hatchback in mint green with extra legroom and faux mahogany dashboard and proceeded up the winding path to Maury's cottage. As I proceeded, a *'Shyton Daily'* newspaper went flying past me, thrown by some hooligan newspaper boy, and landed on Maury's doorstep. I picked up the newspaper and read the headline. 'Scandal hits Shyton United'.

**STANLEY:** Indeed it has.

I made a mental note of the headline, then rang Maury's doorbell. Maury showed me into his lounge, where numerous framed university and college certificates adorned the walls. They all bore Maury's name. I tried to do a closer inspection of each, only for Maury to usher me away.

At a coffee table was a pot of tea. He poured me a cup. The tea was not good, and certainly a world away from the surprising good tea I was served at Tommy's. I then presented Maury with *'The Shyton Daily'*. He tossed the paper aside.

**STANLEY:** How will these charges affect Shyton United?
**MAURY:** I wouldn't worry about it. It's just a misunderstanding. Mr Chen Hu is a billionaire, so naturally there are a lot of jealous people out there. I can guarantee you that Mr Chen Hu is one hundred per cent committed to Shyton United.
**STANLEY:** At the moment he's being held in jail. How will he be able to run the club now?
**MAURY:** Well, he was never involved in the day-to-day running of Shyton United per se, he was more of a behind-the-scenes money man rather than a hands-on owner.
**STANLEY:** He seemed pretty hands-on from what I saw.
**MAURY:** Not at all. Nothing will change, mark my words. I prefer to look at the positives. We have a brand new manager, new team…
**STANLEY:** With Shinji dead you only have three first team players, and one of them, Li Bang, seems more preoccupied with breakdancing than football.
**MAURY:** Li Bang is and will be an incredible player. Mark my words.
**STANLEY:** You have to admit that things have got off to a pretty bad start.
**MAURY:** Sometimes you have to take the rough with the smooth. Take a battering from tsunami-like waves before it goes plain sailing. The foundations have been laid and Mr Chen Hu is in this for the long term.

Whilst Tommy was out I popped round to their place hoping to catch a quick word with Brenda. She opened the door with Luke in her arms.

**BRENDA:** What you want? Tommy ain't here.
**STANLEY:** I know…

I could sense that Brenda was super pissed about Tommy's new hair.

**BRENDA:** This is about Tommy's fucking hair, ain't it?

I may have uttered a few grunts. She slammed the front door in my face regardless.

<u>**28<sup>th</sup> June, 2013**</u>

In what was once Charlie's office but which now belonged to Juan, I got to know 'Special' Juan Lopez. Posters of glamour models were plastered all over the walls of his office as well as managerial awards, and photographs of him with some sexy-looking, bikini-clad women. This guy had class.

**STANLEY:** I've followed your career from when you first started out in Segunda La Liga.
**JUAN:** Haha, yes I was much slimmer then. Winning trophies has made me put on weight.
**STANLEY:** What attracted you to Shyton United?
**JUAN:** When I see the supporters of Shyton and how the club works, it is like a religion to them. It's beautiful. We will try to do our best to bring trophies for them. And look at my office. My office here is thirty metres long and ten metres wide, it is bigger than the Oval Office in the White House. I can see the training grounds and it is incredible.
**STANLEY:** How different do you think football is here to how it is over in Spain?
**JUAN:** In England sometimes the other team starts with the long ball and that makes life difficult. I will try to make Shyton play beautiful football but keep the ball on the ground. Like Justin Timberlake once sang, I'm bringing sexy back.

<u>**1ˢᵗ July, 2013**</u>

To prepare for Shyton United's first ever Premier League campaign, the gaffer ordered his team back early for pre-season training and Juan was already hard at work sticking up posters of bikini-clad Spanish glamour models all over the walls of the training ground's changing room.

Mystic was doing some Tai Chi mixed in with Jedi knight movements, whilst Tommy, K-Y and Li Bang did some more traditional stretching exercises. Juan was whispering to himself. I managed to stick my iPhone closer to him to pick up what he was saying. It was odd.

**JUAN:** Dip it into sugar then put it into the mouth.

It looked like Juan was salivating much like Homer Simpson did when thinking of food. I was disturbed.

Maury then walked in with an Arab-looking fellow who was wearing a headscarf and white attire. He looked like a sheikh. My deductions proved correct.

**MAURY:** Everybody, please welcome our billionaire new owner, Sheikh Abdullah Hassan XII.

Later I did some research (typing his name into Google, basically) into Sheikh Abdullah Hassan XII and discovered that he was a very wealthy individual, as most of them seem to be, and along with his family owned numerous companies including an airline, an energy business, hotels and a mysterious media company that I could find little information on except for one particular nugget which I'll divulge later. He also had a reputation of being a playboy. At the time of publishing this book he had 4 wives, and had more children than Marlon Brando.

**SHEIKH ABDULLAH:** Please, don't stop what you are doing, you naughty boys. I promise exciting times and...

Sheikh Abdullah turned to Maury with a look of shock upon his face.

**SHEIKH ABDULLAH:** We only have three players?

Maury shrugged. I would've expected that due diligence had been carried out and that this would be known. Still, with such an abundance of wealth it probably did not matter one jot. He could probably buy anyone.

**SHEIKH ABDULLAH:** …And a magnificent new, complete team that meets the criteria of any 11-a-side league. This is a bold, new era! Viva the Shit…on!

Sheikh Abdullah inspected one of the posters featuring a glamour model.

**SHEIKH ABDULLAH:** I know this one. She is very bendy.
**JUAN:** Gigantic, mucho, mucho nipples.

Afterwards I talked with Maury in his office at Creek Alley Stadium.
**STANLEY:** How can a local adult film company possibly sponsor Shyton United for 10 years at the tune of £100m?
**MAURY:** They're a very successful adult film company. They have a website and even a Facebook page!
**STANLEY:** Isn't Huge Jack Off Productions bankrolled by Hush Hush Enterprises, which is a subsidiary of Sheikh Abdullah's OppressCo Holdings Ltd?
**MAURY:** They made 50 films last year.
**STANLEY:** It seems as though you've managed to sell the club from one dubious individual to yet another dubious individual.
**MAURY:** There is nothing at all dubious about Sheikh Abdullah.
**STANLEY:** His country has an appalling human rights' record. Journalists and bloggers are heavily censored, and when they do speak out they're routinely arrested and flogged. Women are treated as second-class citizens and are arrested if they drive.
**MAURY:** That's not the Sheikh's fault. What can he do? He himself has spoken out against many of these things but he's just one little voice. Change is gradual except at Shyton United where with the Sheikh at the helm we shall make giant strides, mark my words.

**<u>2<sup>nd</sup> July, 2013</u>**

I stopped by Tommy's flat. Brenda was feeding Luke and Shannon. Both appeared to have gained weight. Medicine balls sprang to mind. Tommy and Brenda were having yet another barney, no doubt partly fuelled by Tommy's recent expenditure.

**BRENDA:** Did you know he had a secret stash?
**STANLEY:** Drugs?
**BRENDA:** No, you wally, cash! All this time I've been scrimping and saving, even cutting open the used toothpaste to scrape it all up and this bastard's gotten a nice little nest egg hidden away. Look at me!

I tried not to. She looked awful. A bloated, saggy lamb dressed up as mutton.

**BRENDA:** I deserve nice things and instead I shop at Primark. And this arsehole spends what we do have on his fucking shitty hair.
**TOMMY:** Stop having a go at my hair.
**BRENDA:** Selfish cunt!

Brenda got right in Tommy's face.

**BRENDA:** I gave up my figure and career as a hairdresser. Least you could do is give me something. You got more hair, I want more.
**TOMMY:** But your hair's fine, you silly cow.
**BRENDA:** You have a new billionaire owner! Gimme!
**TOMMY:** More kids?
**BRENDA:** More everything. More, more, more! Get that new contract! I'm not waiting another 8 years!
**TOMMY:** You don't understand!

Tommy then stormed out, head-butting a wall on the way. I presumed Tommy had suffered more concussions than a heavyweight boxer.

**BRENDA:** That's it. You and your hair fuck off.
**STANLEY:** You and Tommy were childhood sweethearts, right?
**BRENDA:** Yeah. And look where it got me! Two boys were chasing me, Tommy and Gavin. Gavin's living in Liverpool now and has got two cafés. He treats his missus like a princess—holidays in Benidorm

every summer and fake tans all year round. I heard he's even got a timeshare. Look what I've got with this loser.
**STANLEY:** I'm sure in time Tommy will get the contract he deserves.
**BRENDA:** I'm not holding my breath. My mum and dad warned me. Tommy acts hard on the pitch but he's such a pussy. A pussy with new pussy hair. Real men don't get hair transplants.
**TOMMY:** I heard that!
**BRENDA:** PUSSY!

I feared for the kids. Should I contact social services?

Later that night I got a tip off from an anonymous source that I shan't name who said something was going down outside the Creek Alley Stadium that very night. I went down there by car, incognito, and used special night goggles—the ones James Bond might have used—as well as a microphone that could pick up conversations on the moon.

Outside the stadium was Sheedy Dovani, a short, sly middle-aged super agent. He also had the best lisp ever. If he were to enter a lisp contest against Chris Eubank then Sheedy would win hands down. Everything looked even more suspicious as he wore a beige raincoat. And who was with him? Maury Git'a. That guy was as straight as an arrow if the arrow had been bent into a triangle. Here's what we picked up:

**MAURY:** And I'll get 10% from each transfer?
**SHEEDY:** Indeed, Mr Maury. I'll make a special transfer to your nominated Swiss account. No one knows a teeny, tiny thing. Now, which clients do you like? Paolo Liago?
**MAURY:** Come on, Sheedy. Everybody knows you don't sign Brazilians after they reach 28 and become fat pigs. I know who we want.

They then nodded to one another and parted ways. Shifty characters.

# 9<sup>th</sup> July, 2013

A week later, the remains of what was left of the team—which had been as decimated by Chen Hu as a victim of a serial killer who had an obsession with acid—had a light training session before discovering some exciting news.

Tommy practiced taking penalties with K-Y—he had such a powerful left boot. One went in, then another and another, bursting the net. I feared for Shyton if they were ever to concede a penalty or free kick, but I feared for the opposing goalie when facing Tommy. Mystic performed some Bruce Lee kung-fu moves, badly, while Li Bang also did some kung-fu (but like a master) and he performed an incredible 360 kick that accidentally clipped Mystic on the chin and knocked him into the middle of the week after next. Hopefully we'd all be spared Mystic's morning sermons from now on.

Maury and Juan then arrived, out of the blue, with six spanking new first team players. Both were licking their lips and looked like the cat that had not only got the cream but a whole cow as well.

**JUAN:** Tommy, Bang Bang, Anal. See our sexy new team.
**K-Y:** What did the gaffer call me?
**TOMMY:** Shut it, Anal.
**MAURY:** Allow me to introduce the fellas who are going to propel us into the Champions League. First, Sao Columbus.

Sao Columbus, or 'Photographic' to his friends was a defender with cornrow hair and an attitude that screamed chilled. He was a stylish, cultured player who could bring the ball out from defence much like a Glenn Hoddle in his sweeper days playing for Swindon. He also had a penchant for all things bling. Clothes, jewellery, his car was even featured on MTV show, *Pimp My Ride'*.

**SAO:** Where am I?

He also had a bad memory. Sao wandered off aimlessly, muttering to himself. Confused boy.

**MAURY:** Somebody get him.

K-Y grabbed Sao but Sao slipped through his hands. This really didn't bode well for the season.

**MAURY:** Ronnie Morrison. Our new captain!

Ronnie Morrison was a mean-looking, towering presence in defence. A tough tackler and a real general – or in other words, a mouthy git. His family were all notorious criminals from the East End of London and used to break legs for money as well as luck. The crime rate went up at whichever club he played for. Reminder: Buy a new, extra large, extra secure safe. Carry mace.

**TOMMY:** What? You can't do that, you cunt! I'm the captain, the lifeblood of this team!

**MAURY:** Tommy, relax. It's just for publicity.

**RONNIE:** Easy boy. Have you led teams to Premier League titles, cup finals? Nah, thought not. I was born to lead. Now, fall into line.
**TOMMY (under his breath but nothing escaped my mics):** I'm gonna nut him.
**MAURY:** Dwayne Ford.

Dwayne 'Suspect' Ford was twenty-seven years old and was like beige, unseasoned wallpaper—bland in every way—and the complete opposite of Sao Columbus. His memory was long, sharp and detailed and his attitude was edgy.

**DWAYNE:** If I catch anyone looking at my wife, they're dead!

He was also known to be extremely protective of his wife.

**MAURY:** England left back, Sonny Jackson.

How the hell did they get all these players?

Sonny Jackson was nicknamed 'Doughboy' after the character in the film *'Boyz in da Hood'* as portrayed by Ice Cube, in one of his finest roles. He was quite chunky, also like Ice Cube in *'Boyz in da Hood'*. I would've nicknamed him doughnut, personally. He had gold teeth too, not like Ice Cube in *'Boyz in da Hood'*. Too OTT for my liking.

**SONNY:** Yo! What up dawgs!

**MAURY:** Brazilian international, Bombalbo.

Financial Fair Play was out the window, then. How could they afford all these?

Bombalbo 'Gordito' was one of the star strikers of the Brazilian national team and at 26 it was quite a mystery why he was at Shyton United. With a shaved head and buckteeth, he reminded me of somebody else. I shall rack my brains later.

**BOMBALBO:** What's that in the sky?
**JUAN:** They call it a cloud.
**MAURY:** And finally... Ricardo Bombalbo.

I nicknamed him 'Flash Harry'. Even as he was introduced he was posing in the same position as Michelangelo's David. What a poser! His slim, toned body with perfect bronze skin did nothing for me, despite a tingling. I bet most Shyton women would prefer more normal blokes than his chiselled body and model-like looks. And apart from tons of cash, private jet, garage full of sports cars, what else could he offer?

**MAURY:** And about ten extras over there.

Maury pointed at about ten nondescript football players kicking a ball around on an adjacent pitch. They were all kitted out in Shyton colours. I didn't recognise any of them, and shan't describe them as they just won't feature prominently and I'd rather watch reruns of *'You've Been Framed'*. The nondescript football players stopped playing and waved. I waved back.

From the Twitter account of @RB9 (Ricardo Bombalbo): *'This place is disgusting. Ricardo hopes there's an Armani nearby. #Lucky2HaveMe #MirrorMirror'*

<u>**12<sup>th</sup> July, 2013**</u>

The transfer business didn't end there however, as Maury called a press conference to unveil yet another new player. Every fee had so far been undisclosed. It was as fishy as one of my ex-girlfriend's nether regions—and believe me that was so fishy that I was forced to open all the windows and the front door whenever she visited. It also made me ponder whether she had been born in the sea and been captured by Uncle Brian. I should've drug-tested her.

Between Maury and Juan was Bombinho, another Brazilian forward who also had buckteeth. And they said British teeth were bad! He also had curly hair that was as greasy as a chippy's fryer. The grease was literally dripping onto the floor. The cleaner would have a long night, no doubt. Bombinho even owned his own hair product company called Bombinho Juice. That must've been the stuff dripping from his hair.

**MAURY:** It's my honour to present Shyton United's latest acquisition, João Antonio Cesar Rodrigo Flavio Santos de Lima Luís Arantxa Sánchez da Silva. Also known as Bombinho.
**BOMBINHO:** It was always my dream to play for United. So I am very happy to be here at Manchester.
**MAURY:** You signed for Shyton United.
**BOMBINHO:** Who?
**TABLOID JOURNALIST:** How much did he cost?
**MAURY:** I can assure you that he represents great value for money.
**TABLOID JOURNALIST:** How are you paying for all this, Maury?
**MAURY:** This press conference is over!

Maury sprung up and ushered Bombinho and Juan away. Bombinho looked incredibly disappointed and already had his mobile out. I guessed he was phoning Sheedy, his agent.

Translated from the Twitter account of @BombinhoJuice: *'What have I done? #MyAgentMustDie'*

<u>**15<sup>th</sup> July, 2013**</u>

I went again and paid a visit to Brenda and Tommy. When I say paid, I mean paid. As Tommy was still not earning much, Brenda demanded a fee each time we interviewed them. I slipped her an envelope when Tommy wasn't around.

They were at the table in the kitchen. Brenda looked, as always, terrible. She also looked less than pleased as she fed her fat kids. She did however seem to have gotten over Tommy's hair.

On the table was a local newspaper with Shyton United being featured on the front page.

**BRENDA:** Sixteen new players!
**TOMMY:** I know, I know.
**BRENDA:** One of them apparently cost £50m! Grow some balls will you. Luke's got bigger balls than you.
**TOMMY:** No, he doesn't!
**BRENDA:** If you don't march into his office right now and get that new contract, don't bother returning home.
**TOMMY:** See what I have to put up with, Stan? Not only have I lost the captain's armband, I've lost all respect in my own house.
**BRENDA:** What's he on about? You never had any respect in his house. Now clear off and get what you're owed or the captaincy and respect won't be the only things you'll have lost.

Tommy started sulking and wandered off. This was awkward. Why did I bother coming? I needed to break the tension.

**STANLEY:** Kids are looking healthy.
**BRENDA:** Fuck off.
**STANLEY:** Right.

Knowing that Maury wasn't in his office, unlike Tommy who was most likely searching for him there, I arrived at Maury's new home having been given clear directions to get there and not to tell Tommy. When I arrived, I was most impressed with his new abode.

Maury then showed me around the grounds of his large farmhouse with its flock of sheep and solitary cow that he called 'Leah', named after an ex-wife.

**MAURY:** It was a snip, really. I had to upgrade, I'd been in that cottage for far too long and well, have to look the part. Don't want to be seen as the poorest director in all of the Premier League. That wouldn't do the club any favours. Image is everything.

Maury pointed at a barn.

**MAURY:** You see that barn? I'm thinking of converting it into a stable and breeding racehorses. I even thought I could let little retards come and ride here some time.
**STANLEY:** That's not appropriate.
**MAURY:** You can't say that, Stanley. Even little retards should be allowed to ride horses. Really, would've expected more from you.
**STANLEY:** That's not what I meant. I meant…
**MAURY:** Yeah, I bet I could make a mint out of the local children's hospital. And best of all, plebs will think I'm some kind of saint.

Maury had obviously forgotten that I taped all conversations.

From the blog, Fudge Packer for Life, Joe Meek wrote:
'…*Loving all these new players. Finally, we got a team that can compete with the best and a team that actually has the required numbers. Though having read the papers it does seem suspect. How we paying for all these? They better not raise ticket prices. Already gone up. Soon your average Joe Meek won't be able to go. Don't trust that Maury fella as far as I can throw him either but at least we won't embarrass ourselves against the top teams. Could we challenge for Champions League places? Shyton United vs. Real Madrid. Could it happen?*'

From the Twitter account of @RonniesCheapGoods: *'In town now! Get your bargains! Red hot sales! Top quality merch from a man you can trust. #RonniesMerch'*

The next day Tommy finally tracked Maury down. Tommy had spent the night in his car. He was unshaven and smelt of used Fiat Punto. It wasn't nice. Tommy stormed down the corridor and burst into Maury's office. Maury was on the phone and looked a little bit startled, as you'd expect. I just caught him say:

**MAURY:** 231250. By Monday, right?

Maury then slammed down the phone. When listening to that number again, I worked out that it was an account number. My sleuthing skills were top-notch.

**MAURY:** Tommy! You can't buy your passion.
**TOMMY:** My wife's making me go loopy.
**MAURY:** You should've gotten yourself a servile, little Asian woman. If you'd like me to set you up then I can. An associate has an agency and before you know it we can get one of them giving you some 'suckee, suckee' in no time.
**TOMMY:** You've spent £400m!
**MAURY:** One moment.

Maury picked up the phone and dialled a number.

**MAURY:** The numbers were meant to be undisclosed!

Maury hung up the phone.

**MAURY:** Exactly! £400m! Sheikhy's broke now. You wouldn't ask a penniless man for money now, would you? Would you ask a tramp for his last sip of cheap Scotch?
**TOMMY:** His Bentley's made of gold!
**MAURY:** He's keeping up appearances. Stanley, do you mind giving us a few minutes?

Maury then ushered me out of his office and closed the door. Being a rather suspicious documentarian, I lingered outside and did the kind of eavesdropping any old woman from the North East would be proud of. I could hear murmurings and more murmurings. A moment later and Tommy emerged. He was not a happy chappie. I opened my mouth to say something, then thought better of it and watched as Tommy looked at me then the wall then me again then the wall before head-butting the wall. I was relieved. The wall, not so much.

I could only speculate as to what they had discussed. I doubted it was about three-legged kittens. I once had a three-legged kitten. Named him Lex. He died.

When I got home, I went online and researched all the new players, gathering as much info as I could. I stumbled across Bombalbo's blog, a blog dedicated to food. I checked it out. His last entry was for coxinha, a croquette, a popular Brazilian street food:

<u>Coxinha</u>

*Ingredients:*
*600g chicken breasts.*

*10 cups of chicken stock.*

*Two large carrots.*

*Four tablespoons butter.*

*Four onions.*

*Four bay leaves.*

*Four cloves of garlic.*

*The juice of two limes for zesty flavour.*

*500g soft cream cheese.*

*Six cups of flour.*

*Four large eggs.*

*Five cups of finely grated bread crumbs.*

*Vegetable oil to fry the coxinha.*

*Salt and pepper to taste.*

*In a large shallow pot, cover the chicken breasts with the stock… This is making me hungry. Now I saliva on my keyboard. Find another blog to make to learn how to make yummy coxinha. Chef! Coxinha! Now!*

That was the end of the entry. Bombalbo's obviously a real foodie. A demanding, insatiable one who's oblivious to typing what he says out loud.

45

<u>**17<sup>th</sup> July, 2013**</u>

With Maury's help and a nice backhander that would probably help furnish his next lounge, I managed to secure interviews with the majority of the new players at the club's training ground.

First up was Sonny. Slouched on the bench, jeans hanging from below his waist and boxers way up, cap at a jaunty angle—rather uncouth.

**SONNY:** Dawg, I was raised in Peckham, innit? By Auntie M and 'im.

I later learnt that 'dawg' was a term of endearment rather than Sonny mistaking me for being a canine.

**STANLEY:** Where were your parents?
**SONNY:** Died before I was born, yer get me?

This was rather shocking and nonsensical.

**STANLEY:** Both?
**SONNY:** Yo dawg, yer deaf or summat?
**STANLEY:** So how did your mother give birth to you?
**SONNY:** Yer tryin' be clever? All that matters is Aunt M and me, innit? Yer get me?
**STANLEY:** And your uncle?
**SONNY:** Don't go messin' wit da past. Past is past and dats truth. Yer hearing me or yer me go gangsta on yer ass?
**STANLEY:** Why don't you want to discuss your past, specifically your uncle?

At which point Sonny got to his feet, swaggered (or maybe jived?) over and started to remove an object from between his boxers.

**SONNY:** Yo, I'm gettin' pissed, dawg.

I didn't think 'dawg' was a term of endearment any longer. I did think he looked rather threatening and I immediately shifted and closed my legs.

**SONNY:** I'm gonna shut your motor.

**STANLEY:** But that's outside and I need it to get around.

He then pulled the object out. It was the latest iPhone.

**SONNY (into mobile):** Yo dawg, this dawg sucks yo. I'm outta here.

Sonny then flicked his gold chains in my direction and went away. It was all very real and very 'gangsta' as he said. I guessed his uncle really fucked him up… somehow.

Next up was an interview with Sao. Unfortunately, the interview never took place as Sao either forgot or well, forgot. I called him on the number he gave me but ended up speaking to somebody from American Express. Now waiting to be authorised.

When Sao failed to show I sat down with Ricardo 'Flash Harry' Bombalbo who had his smartphone out and was using a mirror app. He didn't look at me once.

**STANLEY:** Bit surprising you chose to play for a small town team from the north of England.
**RICARDO:** The whole world and its slums needs to see Ricardo.
**STANLEY:** That's very nice of you.

I layered that sentence, no I dipped it, no, I battered it in thick, excessive amounts of sarcasm.

**RICARDO:** People tell Ricardo that Ricardo is a super cool guy.

The sarcasm missed him by a wider margin than an American missile on its intended target. And why did he keep talking about himself in the third person?

**RICARDO:** Ricardo gives because Ricardo can.
**STANLEY:** What do you hope to achieve at Shyton United that you could've more easily achieved had you joined Chelsea or Manchester United?
**RICARDO:** In years to come, the people will remember that Ricardo, on his own, took a small team and made it Ricardo fantastico.
**STANLEY:** Could you tell us about your background?

**RICARDO:** It was a very beautiful background. All around Ricardo is beauty. Even the shit I did this morning was beautiful. Would you like to see it?
**STANLEY:** How is it?
**RICARDO:** Supplements and a beautiful bacteria I had inserted in my anus. Beautiful shit.
**STANLEY:** Your parents must be exceedingly proud of you.
**RICARDO:** Ricardo's papa died when Ricardo was a young handsome boy. Ricardo doesn't talk. Bye. Ugly.

He then winked… at the mirror app and went on his way. Ronnie then stormed in, slamming some lockers shut on the way, and sat down. He looked like he was in a huff.

**RONNIE:** Alright, I'm 'ere. Spit it out.
**STANLEY:** Thanks for…

Ronnie checked his gold watch.

**STANLEY:** I'm just trying to find out a little bit about each…
**RONNIE:** You got the Internet? Cos if you don't I got a mate who can set you up.
**STANLEY:** I have use of wireless communications.
**RONNIE:** No idea what you said but if you've got Internet then you can find out about me for your thing.
**STANLEY:** I read on your Wikipedia page that your dad was in and out of prison when you were growing up.
**RONNIE:** So what?
**STANLEY:** And your mum was in and out of prison as well.
**RONNIE:** And?
**STANLEY:** And your older brothers were in and out of prison.
**RONNIE:** What of it?
**STANLEY:** You were sent off to live with your uncle but he was also in and out of prison.
**RONNIE:** And what?
**STANLEY:** So you were raised by a neighbour for a lot of your childhood. Must've been tough.
**RONNIE:** Nah. What makes that?

Ronnie pointed at my watch.

**STANLEY:** Longines.
**RONNIE:** Fuck that shit. I can get yer a sweet Rolex. Dead cheap.
You want it?
**STANLEY:** No, I – I…

Ronnie then got up and went, slamming more locker doors on the way.
These weren't going well, so I packed up and went home. I ate a Linda
McCartney cottage pie for dinner. Quite tasty.

During this period Shyton United went on a pre-season tour of Iceland, which seemed rather odd as Iceland only had about two teams, (update: 79 according to Wikipedia). Most of the team, management and Maury flew on a specially chartered flight. For some reason Tommy was made to fly Easyjet. On their pre-season tour they visited the hot springs, a school in Reykjavik, the birthplace of Bjork, a pub and ate some preserved shark meat that caused a number of the team to miss training. For those not ill in bed, they did some running around near the base of the volcano that caused Europe so many problems a few years ago.

Juan Lopez made numerous changes for his two matches, some shark-preserved enforced, giving playing time to every available Shyton United player. He also used a number of different formations as well. They didn't call him the tinker man for nothing. Shyton United lost both matches, 3-1 and 2-0 respectively.

**JUAN:** You must wait until the end. At the end of the season, you can say whether it's a good or bad season.

While having another dinner (of non-preserved fish) at a cosy Icelandic restaurant with a fireplace by every table, I questioned Maury over a nice slab of mutton head.

**STANLEY:** Why do a pre-season tour of Iceland?
**MAURY:** We wanted to get the Latin players familiar with colder conditions.
**STANLEY:** According to Bombalbo, all the foreign lads wore thermal underwear, tights and gloves, and by the end were hotter than a nuked McDonald's apple pie.
**MAURY:** Aha. I didn't know Brazilians had a sense of humour.
**STANLEY:** So, where next for pre-season? Siberia?

Maury tapped his nose.

**MAURY:** More ice wine!

From the Twitter account of @JoeMeek: *'Whats the point of playing in*

Iceland? How is kicking a ball around in a frozen food supermarket gonna help? #Wasteoftime #WhateverHappenedtoBeejams'

<u>22<sup>nd</sup> July, 2013</u>

Bad news for Shyton United fans as the club announced via their website that they would be raising ticket prices for the forthcoming season by 20% across all categories but a 10% discount for those not yet conceived and for those who had recently passed on.

From the Twitter account of @JoeMeek: *Fears have come true. We want our club back. How are we gonna afford this? #FootieForTheMasses #FPL*

I caught up with Joe at his favourite local, The Fudge & Wrapper. He sipped from a pint of best, whilst I had a shandy. I did indeed get some unwanted attention. Ladies' drinks weren't commonly drunk by men around these parts.

**JOE:** Tickets were already dear for people on low incomes, no incomes like myself, the pensioners and the kids, so how are we going to go now? I'll have to scrimp and save every dole cheque, and just come to my local almost every day. They don't think about us.
**STANLEY:** Couldn't you watch the game on the telly?
**JOE:** Nah, not the same. Besides, seen how much Sky is? Might as well go and watch Shyton live.
**STANLEY:** Still, I suppose if you want the best players and you want to be competing with the best, this is the price you pay.
**JOE:** I was quite happy with our lot, I think the majority were. Whether we had the Bombinhos here or not we'd still be going to matches, doesn't matter if we're in the Premier League or the Conference League North. And we wouldn't be owned by no foreigners then, or paying a fortune to watch our team.

The next stop on Shyton's pre-season tour saw them go to the home country of Sheikh Abdullah—Saudi Arabia. All players were on the same flight this time, although Tommy was forced to sit at the back in economy next to the toilets. Bombalbo had an iffy tummy all throughout the flight due to the preserved shark meat he'd taken a liking to back in Iceland. Ben 'Mystic' Twaddle wasn't granted a visa due to his unknown religious beliefs and so didn't travel. Instead he went on a retreat in the middle of Epping Forest with a few of his lads.

In stifling heat that reached the high 40s they played three games in a week. Each game lasted a lot longer than 90 minutes due to the amount of frequent rehydration breaks. Tommy had drunk so much water that it was a surprise that Saudi Arabia wasn't a real dry state. During the tour Juan's team managed to get one draw thanks to a fluky goal scored by Ricardo Bombalbo when Tommy smashed the ball at him for waving to his adoring public, (they weren't waving at him though) the ball cannoning off his head and looping over the stranded goalkeeper. Aside from that moment of good fortune (not so much for Ricardo), Shyton managed to come away from Saudi Arabia avoiding a whitewash but with plenty of heatstroke. Still, with such high temperatures it's a miracle that they didn't come away with a few dead bodies as well. This documentarian was quite glad to be sitting in an air-conditioned press box, although getting to and from the stadia proved tough. How anybody could ever contemplate playing football at that time of year was beyond perplexing. I would imagine anybody deciding to play football in this region at this time of year either put no thought into it, didn't care or had some other incentive. I decided to put this to Maury as we sat in the press box whilst Shyton United got hammered by Al-Qin… Bombinho was crying on the pitch, with his tears immediately evaporating upon leaving his eyes.

**STANLEY:** What were you thinking of taking in Saudi Arabia for some pre-season games? Most of your players have lost a stone each and I'm pretty sure I saw K-Y melt a little bit, as there's now something distinctly raw about his forehead.

**MAURY:** Do the marines or the SAS or the foreign legion train in namby-pamby, air-conditioned conditions? No, they're trained in the toughest environments imaginable to make them real men. That's what we're building here, a team of real men to prepare them for the tough season ahead.

**STANLEY:** It's got nothing to do with Sheikh Abdullah wanting to show off his new team to his family?

**MAURY:** Absolutely not. We'd never do anything to the detriment of the team.

**STANLEY:** Even Juan's slimmer.

**MAURY:** We've helped many during this trip.

**STANLEY:** But it's a football team! It's not a crack-commando unit. How will this stifling heat help them when they're playing away to Stoke on a Monday evening?

**MAURY:** Because they'll have balls of sand.

**STANLEY:** Sand?

**MAURY:** Toughest stuff in the world.

**STANLEY:** Not steel?

**MAURY:** You can bend steel. You can't bend sand.

**STANLEY:** Seriously, there can't have been much planning to stage a pre-season tour of Saudi Arabia. Didn't you or anybody else know how hot it could get?

**MAURY:** Have you seen the hotels here? How's your room? I made sure you had a Jacuzzi in yours.

Maury then checked his gold Rolex. It looked new, expensive and made me envious. A servant came over to our table.

**SERVANT:** Your Bentley Continental GT is waiting, sir.

**MAURY:** Right you are.

After the match all the players were taken to the hospital and had IV drips attached and were given rehydration tablets. They were then ambulanced back to their hotel where more drips were waiting for them. Collectively they had lost the weight of an entire League Two team.

Still the Sheikh made sure they had some entertainment and ordered belly dancers to put on a show for them, followed by a grand spectacle of the public flogging of a blogger who had the temerity to write that women should be allowed to drive. Unfortunately, most of the players were unconscious and didn't get to witness the spectacle. I will never view BDSM in the same light again.

From the Twitter account of @JoeMeek: *'And now Saudi Arabia? Shyton United are really screwing this up. @MauryShytonUtd #WhatYouThinking'*

From the Twitter account of @RB9: *'I don't think these Saudi women can really enjoy looking at Ricardo with a black cloth over their eyes. #MirrorMirror'*

## 7<sup>th</sup> August, 2013

It's just ten days until Shyton United's first game of the season away to Sunderland. The players had all gone under intense rehydration therapy, although Tommy thought that meant spending all day in a pub and had to be dragged out. Juan, having lost some of his ample frame, spent a good few days eating lots of paella and having no sex.

**JUAN:** I can do it!

From the Twitter account of @JoeMeek: *'Good to have the team back. They've shown true Shyton grit after 2 wasted trips. @MauryShytonUtd Knob'*

From the Twitter account of @Bombalbo: *'Happy to be back in my kitchen. Can't wait to make some more coxinha. #MissedMyBrazilianFood'*

Whilst the team were away on these two trips, a number of the team's houses were burgled. Police were investigating.

<u>**8<sup>th</sup> August, 2013**</u>

I met Joe Meek at his local who gleefully showed off his season ticket.

**STANLEY:** I thought it was too expensive.
**JOE:** It's Shyton, I can't not go now, can I? It's in the blood. So I'll have one less pint of best a week, see the kids less often and no more cheese crust pizzas on Sundays, small price to pay. We're in the Premier League for fuck's sake!
**STANLEY:** So, is that it? Accept the increase in prices?
**JOE**: Nah, we're mobilising and we'll speak with the club about it. As long as there's no more increases. Like you said, sometimes you got to pay the price if you want to watch the Bombinhos of this world. Roll on Sunderland!

<u>**17<sup>th</sup> August, 2013**</u>

It's the first game of the season away to Sunderland and the team was in the changing room in their Shyton United kit. They all looked remarkably well and seemed back to pre-pre-season tour physique. 'Special' Juan Lopez gave the team one last talk. He had a 4-1-3-2 formation up on a whiteboard and made thrusting motions towards it with his hips. The sexual deviant.

Tommy flicked through a Spanish-English dictionary. I was impressed. I didn't know Tommy could even read in English. Bombinho meanwhile sobbed like a little girl, which made Tommy start growling at him.

**JUAN:** I want you to penetrate their box again and again like you're on a meter with a prostitute. Ricardo, slip inside, feel around, and shoot. Everybody, shoot. Shoot everywhere!
**BEN:** May the force be with you.
**TOMMY:** Shut up, Darth.

Tommy pushed Mystic, who made the sign of the crucifix.

**BEN:** The power of Christ compels you!

What denomination was Mystic? Or perhaps he was part of some cult? Must investigate. The team headed out to a rapturous reception. Of course the reception was for Sunderland. There were a number of Shytonites in the Stadium of Light, waving their plastic turds in the air and cheering for their heroes—their new heroes. Most of them hadn't seen the likes of Ronnie Morrison, Sao Columbus or Ricardo Bombalbo play for their team yet. Bombinho continued his ritual of crying whilst Ronnie Morrison continued to look at everybody as though they were a potential burglary victim—allegedly. As with each pre-season match K-Y had to lead Sao Columbus to the pitch in case he got lost on the way. During one of the games (for some reason I neglected to mention this in my previous entries—I hope Sao's memory issues aren't contagious), in Saudi Arabia Sao had somehow managed to get lost just prior to a game and he ended up in Doha, Qatar. Of all the countries to end up in, he ended up in one that had no football history.

Sunderland looked fit, lean and as though they hadn't been foolish enough to have spent a week in a sauna. They were ready but were they a match for Shyton's own 'galaticos'? On paper Shyton United should destroy Sunderland but during their pre-season matches Shyton United looked as cohesive as a bunch of alpha male lions ready to spread their seed.

Shyton United kicked-off their first ever Premier League game.

I had managed to sneak the tiniest of microphones onto all their kits, and picked up in-game conversations so that, like never before, we could hear what went on during a top level Premier League encounter.

Tommy had the ball and surged forward in characteristic fashion with the Sunderland fans roundly booing him. Not sure why. Perhaps it's because he once said that all people from the North East were scum. Needed to verify that.
So, Tommy was surging forward when:

**RICARDO (in Portuguese):** Pass to Ricardo.
**'MARKETING GOLD MINE' (in Mandarin):** Over here!
**BOMBINHO (in Portuguese and whilst sobbing):** Pass!
**SONNY:** Motherfucker! Gimme the motherfucking ball, yo motherfucking bitch!
**TOMMY:** I don't understand!

Tommy whacked the ball, it swerved viciously and burst into the opposition's goal.
He went over to the Shyton United fans and pretended to machine gun them.

**TOMMY:** I'd do it too!

Bombinho hugged Tommy, crying. He must get incredibly dehydrated. How was he at funerals?

**BOMBINHO:** I'm very happy.

The match ended with Shyton United beating Sunderland AFC 1-0;

their first win in the Premier League. What a start!

From the Twitter account of @JoeMeek: *'Get in! Great result. Tommy 'Machine' Gunn does it again. #FPL #EuropeHereWeCome'*

After the team had gone over to the fans to celebrate with them (except Bombinho who seemed more sad than happy), they continued celebrating in the changing room; giving each other high-fives and bear hugs to K-Y. Ben Twaddle got down on his knees and started, it seemed, worshipping them. Ricardo stood in front of Ben, then held out his hand.

**JUAN:** Fantastic win. Tommy, I loved how you stuck ball into their net. Reminded me of when I stuck my balls…

Bombinho, not crying for once, stepped out of a shower stall with a towel around his waist. His hair was ultra-shiny and it dripped continuously—it looked like there had been an oil spill in that particular shower stall. K-Y, also with a towel wrapped around his waist and another around his head, then stepped into the same shower stall.

**K-Y:** Looks like you went for a swim in the Gulf of Mexico. What is that on your hair?
**BOMBINHO:** 'Bombinho Juice'. Gives hair shine, silkiness and, how you say, spunk.
**K-Y:** Spunk, eh? Sounds nice.

Bombinho strolled away. K-Y shut the shower stall door, then all of a sudden there was a loud thud and a shriek. K-Y told me he had landed right on his arse. I thought it must've been painful, but he said it wasn't at all.

Li Bang and Sonny were the last ones in the changing room. Li Bang was wearing a plain shirt and jeans whereas Sonny was kitted out in his full bling attire. I didn't think Sonny owned a mirror.

**SONNY:** Li Bang. We need to do something about yo threads, man.
**'MARKETING GOLD MINE':** We do?
**SONNY:** Fo' shizzle. We gotta bling you up and pimp you out, yer

know what I'm saying?
**'MARKETING GOLD MINE':** I'm sorry, my English is not good.
**SONNY:** Come with me, cuz. Yo bitch ain't gonna recognise.
**'MARKETING GOLD MINE':** But I no have dog.

<u>**18<sup>th</sup> August, 2013**</u>

In Tommy and Brenda's council flat, Brenda burped the very round and podgy Shannon. Luke flung a bowl of food away from him with his stubby hands. He seemed to know better than his mum. Let's hope he did that at every mealtime.

Tommy told me beforehand that he'd try a new tactic to appease his unhappy wife. He waved a contract in her face. That was probably not the best start.

**TOMMY:** I've got it!

Brenda snatched it from him, though. She might not know much about nutrition or motherhood but she wasn't all that dumb.

**BRENDA:** What's this?
**TOMMY:** What do you think? It's papers for our divorce!
**BRENDA:** What? Really?

Brenda was smiling. Gullible fool.

**TOMMY:** Course not, dopey.

Brenda glanced at it. The smile vanished quicker than one of my ex-girlfriends' upon discovering that I enjoyed wearing ladies' underwear.

**BRENDA:** This is one of those DIY contracts, isn't it? It's even in your own handwriting!

The tactic had failed.

**TOMMY:** I scored a goal.
**BRENDA:** You're a Premier League footballer now! When are you gonna make me a Premier League wife?
**TOMMY:** I don't do miracles.

Tommy then started raging.

**TOMMY:** You don't understand!

Tommy head-butted a wall, which already had a hole in it.

**BRENDA:** And stop head-butting the walls. We ain't got money to fix them.

Again feeling awkward, I made my excuses and left. One of these days I will finish a cup of tea at Tommy's house.

<u>**19ᵗʰ August, 2013**</u>

Tommy was at the end of his tether and his tether wasn't that long to begin with. Feeling exasperated and seemingly unable to go to Maury, Tommy went to see the gaffer at his office at the training ground. Tommy hoped through Juan things could be resolved.

**TOMMY:** You gotta do something, gaffer. My ball and chain's driving me barmy and I can't do Jack.

Juan flicked through an English-to-English dictionary.

**JUAN:** Maybe buy some wine and chocolates for Jack?
**TOMMY:** What?
**JUAN:** You cannot ask Mr Maury?

Tommy rose up and head-butted a wall, causing a hole in one of Juan's glamour model posters.

**JUAN:** Not Maria!

**TOMMY:** You don't understand. No one understands. Maury's got me over a fucking barrel.

Juan raised his eyebrows.

**JUAN:** Does he? Mm, never tried that. You must be patient, little bee, like my wife when she's waiting at a restaurant for our anniversary dinner and I'm in hotel room banging hot young girl who could be my daughter.

Tommy grabbed Juan by the scruff of the neck. Tommy looked like a rabid dog. I would've stopped him but I had woken up with a bad back… and I feared his wrath.

**TOMMY:** Do something or I'll lipo your fat Spanish arse.
**JUAN:** I'll see what I can do.

Tommy stormed out.

**STANLEY:** Are you okay, Juan?

Juan was rubbing his chubby neck, which was now sunburnt red.

**JUAN:** You know, if you can understand Tommy you can understand anyone. I understand him.

From the Twitter account of @RonniesCheapGoods: *'Brand new kettles. Mint condition. Boxes damaged. Low prices! #RonniesKettles'*

<u>**24<sup>th</sup> August, 2013**</u>

It was time for the second match of the season and the first at home for Shyton United. And it couldn't get much tougher, unless perhaps it was Manchester United or Manchester City or Chelsea or Tottenham… as they faced Arsenal. Arsenal were 11-time league title winners and one of the most successful during the Premier League era. Shyton fancied their chances though after their thrilling, easy victory away to Sunderland. Could Shyton continue that rich vein of form and really lay the marker down and strike fear amongst the traditional elite of English football?

Shyton United featured a full-strength team with Bombalbo and Bombinho in attack, Ricardo Bombalbo on the wing, Tommy in central midfield alongside Dwayne 'Suspect' Ford and all the other less usual suspects. Many considered Shyton United to have the most fearsome attack in the land and be able to outscore any team. Unfortunately, they went down 3-1 at home to Arsenal. The fans applauded them off at the end. True Shytonian manners.

In the tunnel at the end of the match, a clearly frustrated Juan Lopez said this to me:

**JUAN:** I need to know why after all the problems in the game there were only three minutes added. Answer me that! Only good thing is that my 22-year-old cousin is at a nearby hotel.

The gaffer wandered off muttering something in Spanish. I guessed they were numerous expletives. Perhaps I should consider learning Spanish?
Were referees already against Shyton United? Was there a vendetta against them? There were some iffy decisions in that game. Typical Arsenal.

<u>**27<sup>th</sup> August, 2013**</u>

Just three days later, Shyton United were in action in the league cup away to lowly Burton Albion, a team so low that most readers won't have a clue as to which league they're in. Therefore, I shan't waste too much time on them here. As it was such an easy game, most of Shyton United's first team were given time off to relax at home, take a quick break, visit Shyton's many brothels and generally recuperate for the bigger game at the weekend away to Newcastle.

**JUAN:** I don't think I am underestimating this team at all.

Juan and I spoke on the team bus on the way to Burton.

**JUAN:** A football player cannot play 40 plus games in a season. It's too much. I need a squad of sexy boys and I need to use them all as I wish.
**STANLEY:** The 'cupset' is a common occurrence. A defeat and exit from one of the tournaments you'd have a good chance of winning could severely damage morale.
**JUAN:** Come on, my sexually inhibited friend. We are playing a team that nobody out of… What are they called again?
**STANLEY:** Burton.
**JUAN:** Where is Burton? Are we playing the clothes shop that I've seen on many streets in your cold, wet country?
**STANLEY:** I see that you've decided to keep Tommy and K-Y in the team.
**JUAN:** They're my engine. We need some experience. Besides, the Premier League is my oxygen, this cup is just an unnecessary aphrodisiac.

The team bus pulled into Burton Albion's stadium.

From the Twitter account of @JoeMeek: *Just seen team for @BurtonAlbion Criminal! Lack of respect. #Cupset is on the cards. #JuanDontGetIt'*

Fielding just two regulars in—Tommy and K-Y—with the likes of Bombinho, Ronnie, Sonny, Dwayne et al left at home to enjoy Shyton's impressive red-light district, Shyton United's team of reserves, youths and the third kind put in a solid effort against a team they had been widely expected to trounce. Shyton United took the lead in the first half only to be pegged back in the 2$^{nd}$ half, then they again retook the lead through a Tommy Gunn thunderbolt. Burton Albion, the lions of their respective league, roared back again to draw level and take the game to extra time – not something that would've pleased Juan Lopez who found these kind of fixtures an unwelcome distraction from the bread and butter of Premier League football.

In extra time there were no more goals, just a few more crunching tackles from the Burton Albion team and so the match went to penalties. K-Y wasn't known for his penalty saves, or even for his competent goalkeeping and yet much to everybody's surprise he pulled one off leaving Tommy, captain for the day, to take the final penalty. Could Tommy yet again be Shyton United's hero and pull them through? He placed the ball on the spot then eyed the goalkeeper with a look that said, 'I'm going to kill your mother, rape her then carve her up and feed her to your children' and, rather audaciously, chipped the keeper; much to the home support's anger. Tommy raced over to the twenty Shytonians who made the trip and did his machine gun celebration uttering words that any true psychopath would've been proud of. Shyton through on pens 5-4.

<u>**31<sup>st</sup> August, 2013**</u>

That weekend Shyton United were away to Newcastle United. Newcastle was home to some of the most passionate supporters in the land who were as well supporters of one of the least successful sides in the last 40 years. What troopers they were. The home crowd were passionate, jeering the owner and yet another inept manager as Shyton were cruising at two goals to nil.

During the game and unseen by the referee, Tommy made a nasty challenge on one of Newcastle's French players. The player writhed around in agony as though he'd just been bitten by a walker from the TV show *'The Walking Dead'*. Play however continued with Sao picking up the ball.

Sao played it forward to Tommy, who did a one-two with Ricardo before laying off for Bombalbo to swivel, shoot and score. What a team goal! What play! What a necessary foul by Tommy. Marvellous. Final score: Newcastle United 0 Shyton United 3. Get in!

Despite the excellent win, controversy surrounded the incident involving Tommy Gunn and that tackle on the French garcon. In the Shyton United changing room at St. James Park (insert current name here), I asked Juan about it.

**JUAN:** Well, I didn't really see it. It's hard to see from the dugout area and it was quite a way from me, plus there was a beautiful young girl behind me and...
**STANLEY:** Oh really?
**JUAN:** Oh yes indeed. Big boobs! Besides, Tommy is not that type of player.

Tommy then barged past us, even managing to make Juan stumble to the side. The gaffer's sheer weight made him seem pretty immovable.

**TOMMY:** Where's that whingeing French pussy? I'm gonna finish him off!

Tommy disappeared out into the corridor, with Ronnie Morrison and others trying to stop him.

<u>**1st September, 2013**</u>

I was finally welcomed around Ronnie's 'gaff' the following day. It was another huge mansion with fountains, and marble and granite everywhere. Ronnie himself welcomed us into his home and showed us around. Oddly, most of the rooms were filled with unpacked boxes. The outside looked like a home, the inside more a goods warehouse.

**RONNIE:** Still unpacking.

A lot of the boxes apparently contained new televisions, fridges and computers.

**RONNIE:** We're holding a raffle.

Ronnie's mobile then rang.

**RONNIE (into mobile):** Yeah Ma?

Ronnie turned away from me. I looked at the boxed items. They were top of the range goods that would fetch a pretty penny along the Tottenham Court Road. Ronnie went over to a corner and whispered.

**RONNIE:** No, Ma. Can't do this weekend. Home. Alright, Ma. Yeah, I know… I miss Uncle Reg too.

Ronnie hung up as I was checking out a Samsung 64" LED TV. Nice model.

**RONNIE:** That's a sweet model.
**STANLEY:** I've been looking to upgrade.
**RONNIE:** I can let you have it on the cheap. It'd be like you're robbing me blind.
**STANLEY:** Don't you need it?

Ronnie then showed me into what I thought was his dining room where there were loads more TVs. Boxes of wall-to-wall TVs, in fact.

**RONNIE:** Nah, I'm alright for TVs.
**STANLEY:** Why do you have so many?

**RONNIE:** Little hobby of mine, like stamp collecting. Also love eBay, you know? Like a family business.

**STANLEY:** Was it a tough decision to move to Shyton away from London?

**RONNIE:** Nah, mate. With eBay, you can live anywhere and still trade.

**STANLEY:** Settled in okay?

**RONNIE:** Yeah, lots of business this way. Now. Anyway, you want this TV or not? You won't get a better price, my son.

Ronnie put an unwelcome arm around me. I could only have been more uncomfortable if it had been K-Y's arm.

**RONNIE:** Trust me mate, *it's a steal.*

Ronnie winked at me. Why did he wink?

**STANLEY:** I'd better ask the wife first. She holds the purse strings.

I wasn't married. Deciding that all this stuff was probably hookey, I thought I had better move away from this subject.

**STANLEY:** How chuffed were you when you were made Shyton United captain?

**RONNIE:** Meh.

**STANLEY:** There's been some notable tension between you and Tommy.

**RONNIE:** He's a bit of an ungrateful cunt, innit?

**STANLEY:** He'd been captain almost ten years.

**RONNIE:** Then players of my calibre come along, should be more appreciative. Anyway, 'bout the TV, you want it or not?

I then made my excuses, as I feared being roughed up and given a thorough pasting. Should I go to the police with my suspicions?

Later that night I got a text from Tommy asking me to go round his place sharpish. I went and when he opened the door he thrust a videotape in my face.

**TOMMY:** What the fuck is it?

The tape was labelled 'play me'.

**STANLEY:** Play it and find out.
**TOMMY:** Play what?
**STANLEY:** The videotape.
**TOMMY:** The what?
**STANLEY:** The videotape you're holding.
**TOMMY:** What's a videotape?
**STANLEY:** That thing you're holding is called a videotape.
**TOMMY:** What's it do?
**STANLEY:** It's like a DVD but on videotape.
**TOMMY:** You're no good.

Tommy then flung the videotape out the door and over the balcony to the street below. I heard a scream. When I went downstairs people were gathered around the videotape asking what it was. This was one of the reasons why I left this town.

From the Twitter account of @JoeMeek: *'Cant stand international break. Two weeks of no Shyton. What am I gonna do? #PissedOutOfBrain #DrinkMore'*

Whilst all the players were away playing for their respective countries, I got down to compiling my notes, catching up with *'The Walking Dead'* TV show, writing my mini-biography of Bill Oddie, and visiting my family. I again was reminded why I left Shyton—not just for documentarian reasons but also to get away from those fishing-obsessed, fish pie-eating bastards.

I finally met my sister's sprog; ugly little thing. Many folds of skin, slept a lot, burped, vomited, ate, then went number two—which my sister assured me was adorable. It was a little bundle of smells and unfortunate liquids.

Juan and Mystic were also around in Shyton. They both spent time fine-tuning their tactics and their training regimes. Juan was a busy-beaver, going from house to house like he was delivering milk. Not sure what he was actually delivering, although I suspected it was indeed something creamy. Mystic spent a lot of time at the local church, then the local mosque, then at the nearby synagogue, before attending a local sci-fi convention in which Anthony Daniels (C3PO from Star Wars) was making an appearance.

At that very convention held at the local town hall (the only space big enough for conventions in Shyton), I caught up with Ben 'Mystic' Twaddle.

**STANLEY:** Ben, which religion do you follow?
**BEN:** I am one and yet I am all. I'm like Pi from Yann Martel's *Life of Pi'*. I embrace all religions, beliefs and philosophies whether it's of a Jedi nature or not.
**STANLEY:** So you're not a monotheist?
**BEN:** There is only one God!
**STANLEY:** Which one?
**BEN:** May peace be with you and you return to the hellfire in which you were spawned. Hare Krishna.

He then danced away like a Morris Dancer, as he had little cymbals on his knees and bells on the palms of his hands. What an odd fellow.

Breaking news from the BBC website: *'Sao Columbus, central defender for Shyton United and England, has gone missing in action whilst overseas on duty for England. England, who are due to play Portugal later today, announced that Sao was last seen training with the England team and his whereabouts are as yet unknown...'*

And the BBC weren't done there. More breaking news from the BBC website: *'The police are treating as suspicious the death of a young man from Reading. The exceedingly young man was last seen getting into a lift at a top London hotel with Shyton United owner, Sheikh Abdullah Hassan XII. More to follow.'*

I called Maury about the Sheikh but he refused to discuss it.

<u>8<sup>th</sup> September, 2013</u>

Breaking news from the BBC website: *'Sao Columbus, the England and Shyton United footballer, has been found wandering the streets of Berlin. He appeared unfazed, though rather perplexed as to why he was in Berlin and as to why he was wearing football boots. Once he was reminded that he was a professional footballer, all seemed to come flooding back and he has since returned to England for a thorough check-up at Shyton United's medical facility.'*

<u>**14<sup>th</sup> September, 2013**</u>

The Premier League was back in action and Shyton United were at home against West Bromwich Albion, a team that's comparable to Shyton in its size, roots and history. It was also a team that they'd no doubt be like come the end of the season; a team fighting to stay in the Premier League.

Whilst the team got ready in the changing room I saw Maury approach Tommy, who was doing some stretching exercises.

**MAURY:** Understood?
**TOMMY:** Fuck off, will ya? Just leave me alone.
**MAURY:** Good, glad the videotape was clear.
**TOMMY:** Videotape?
**MAURY:** The videotape.
**TOMMY:** What's a *'videotape'*?

Tommy and the rest of the team left the changing room and went out to meet a capacity crowd. Maury was left scratching his head. Still, a videotape in this day and age?

Shyton were attacking with a relentlessness not seen since last season, leaving West Bromwich Albion a giddy wreck. Shyton won 3-1 and went 2<sup>nd</sup> in the league! What a super start to the season.

In spite of their good performance against West Bromwich Albion, the gaffer had called in his team for some early-morning practice. I waited for Tommy to arrive at the training ground car park. All around were premium and exclusive cars—it was like being in a car dealership in Mayfair. There were Lambos, top of the range Mercs, Land Rovers and Aston Martins; what a life! Then Tommy arrived in his dented Fiat Punto.

I observed as Tommy stepped out of his car and looked at all the expensive vehicles. I think I heard him growling, and before I could say hello he had stormed off to the changing rooms.

I waited to see who would arrive next, and soon enough a pimped-out saloon was driven in. Its hydraulic suspension made the car bump up and down in time with the pounding hip-hop blasting out of the car. It pulled into a parking space. I naturally assumed it was Sonny Jackson, so I was rather surprised when Li Bang got out wearing shades and dressed to the nines in bling.

From across the way, and with Sao by his side, Sonny then called out. I hadn't noticed him arriving.

**SONNY:** Yo! My nigga!
**'MARKETING GOLD MINE':** What up, my nigga?
**SAO:** What'd he say?
**SONNY:** Li Bang is part of the Shyton posse now. Ain't that right, Li Bang my man?

Li Bang approached them both and gave each of them a fist bump.

**'MARKETING GOLD MINE':** Fo' sho'.

I had to Google these expressions to make sure I'd spelt them correctly. I wasn't really up-to-date with today's lingo.

As I was about to enter the entrance of the training ground complex, another car pulled up; and this one was chauffeur driven. It was an executive saloon BMW 7 Series with blacked out windows. Dwayne stepped out with what appeared to be a glamour model. Blonde, a chest that would make the Himalayas envious, and a smile that was like a powerful fridge magnet. I was drawn to her, then I realised where I'd seen her before. It was Cheryl Ford, former Page 3 girl, the girl voted as the one most British men choked their chickens to. I couldn't help but notice that Dwayne's eyes darted this way and that like a very suspicious-looking person. What was he looking for? My god, she was hot. My little sailor was definitely standing to attention and ready to sail the seven seas.

**STANLEY:** Everything alright, Dwayne?
**DWAYNE:** Someone's looking. I can feel it.

Later, upon returning home and uploading all the film and audio myself and Bob had collected, I found that Bob had picked up some audio of Ronnie Morrison who had been kicking balls at K-Y. The audio was picked up at the time Dwayne arrived. Of the film footage we had gotten at that precise moment, I noticed that not only were Dwayne's eyes acting strangely, Cheryl's eyes were seemingly locked on something.

**RONNIE:** Cheryl! Sweetheart!

Yes, Cheryl Ford was once Ronnie Morrison's childhood sweetheart.

Back in the car park as Dwayne was attempting to plant a blubbery wet kiss on Cheryl's cheek, her gaze remained transfixed on Ronnie's.

**DWAYNE:** What's the matter?
**CHERYL:** Nothing.

Dwayne eyed her suspiciously then turned around even more suspiciously before turning back to her super suspiciously. This guy was even more paranoid than the Mexican musical group, *'Los Paranoias'*.

**DWAYNE:** Go straight home.

Cheryl got back into the car. How could she be married to such a guy? I wondered if I could grab a few moments with her.

**DWAYNE:** Don't forget to clock in!

As she was driven away, she glanced at Dwayne with the kind of look you'd give a turd you had just discovered was on your shoe.

Back to the footie training, Juan had decided that it was time his Shyton United team learnt the most valuable lesson in football.

**JUAN:** What is most important thing in modern football?
**TOMMY:** Tackling, and threatening people with a nutting.

Tommy started head-butting the air. He was a bit of a psycho, was Tommy.

**JUAN:** Wrong.
**DWAYNE:** Keeping possession.
**RICARDO:** Looking good.
**JUAN:** No, no, no. Tricking the referee. Look at the greatest players, all could fall in the box and win a penalty. This is the best skill. Ben?

Mystic had been kneeling down in a south-easterly direction and praying. Was he now a Muslim? Upon command he got up.

**JUAN:** Ben, show us.

Ben strode into the penalty area, skipping like a male ballet dancer, he leapt like a dolphin then dropped to the ground as though he were a sack of spuds. He writhed around in pain like he'd been shot more times than Zed in the movie, *'Killing Zoe'*. I was a film buff and you'll find plenty of movie references within.

**BOMBINHO:** I know this already.
**JUAN:** But not in England. Here, only the English can do it.
**RICARDO:** It's true. Ricardo dives and Ricardo's a cheating foreigner. Tommy dives and it's because he's learnt it from Ricardo.

Tommy squared up to Ricardo and got so much in his face, it was hard to tell where each person began.

**TOMMY:** Listen here, Ricardo Bomba... Blomba...
**K-Y:** Bombalbo.
**TOMMY:** Bomba... Bombalomba... Bombaleeno... When was the last
time you saw me dive? Eh?

Tommy then did the unthinkable and head-butted Ricardo on the
nose. Ricardo fell to the floor like Ben had demonstrated before and
writhed around in pain.

**JUAN:** Yes, that's it. Excellent Ricardo. You do it like professional,
better than Ben.
**RICARDO:** My beautiful nose!

It did look rather bloody. K-Y vomited. Poor boy. I guess he was not
used to seeing bodily liquids coming out of orifices.

Later that day, Tommy was summoned to Maury's office at Creek
Alley Stadium. Maury looked royally pissed off. If he'd been Yosemite
Sam, he'd have steam coming out of his ears.

**MAURY:** You're lucky we convinced him not to press charges.
**TOMMY:** He's a pussy.
**MAURY:** He's a famous pussy. Do you know how bad this could've
made Shyton look? Thank god the media believed that hair dryer crap
again. Look Tommy, do you want to return to prison?

Tommy ground his teeth. I'm sure I saw specks of white coming out of
his mouth. He would've made a good black pepper grinder.

**MAURY:** So fall into line. Get out.

I could tell that Tommy was very close to head-butting Maury, and
everything else around him. I took a few steps back just in case.

Extract from Bombalbo's blog, Food with Bombalbo...
*'After training I went out into Shyton town centre hoping to sample some local
Shyton specialities. I carried with me a tourist brochure with many places where I
could taste tasty food. I was super excited. I really hoped to find something as good
as coxinha. I made my way to an English fish and chip shop where in the window
they advertised something called a 'deep-fried Mars bar'. I did not know what this*

*is so I went and ordered four. Then ordered four more. Super tasty.'*

News from the BBC website: *'Sheikh Abdullah Hassan XII, the Saudi owner of Shyton United, is no longer a suspect in the mysterious death of Gavin Jones, a known rent boy from Reading. According to the coroner, the 18-year-old died from asphyxiation following an apparent sexual act that went wrong. Footage of Mr Jones entering a lift with the Sheikh has mysteriously gone missing. A statement from his solicitors has been released stating that the Sheikh was out of the country when the incident took place.'*

Power and wealth saves the day again.

From the Twitter account of @RonniesCheapGoods: *'Rolex watches. Just come in. Get one while stocks last! #Rolexes #NotFakes #SmokingHot'*

<u>**18<sup>th</sup> September, 2013**</u>

While I was settling down for the evening with a bowl of microwaved spaghetti carbonara, my mobile rang. It was Tommy. He'd been sent another package. As we spoke I kept looking at my ever-cooling carbonara.

**STANLEY:** Could you not open it?

He then raged at me, nothing of which I understood so I went round to his flat. Tommy slammed the front door shut behind us and punched the wall before thrusting the package into my chest.

**STANLEY:** You didn't open it?
**TOMMY:** What do you think?

I opened the brown-padded envelope and took out a DVD. Tommy snatched it from me. He held it up and read the label.

**TOMMY:** 'Put me into your DVD player and play me'. Eh?

Tommy went into his lounge where many DVDs were scattered around his massive TV, the DVD player and on his floor. He put the DVD onto the floor then turned on his TV and DVD player. When he went to pick up the same DVD he quite unwittingly picked up a different DVD and put it into the DVD player.

**STANLEY:** Err… Tommy?
**TOMMY:** Shut it. I'm watching something.

The scene of the girl climbing out of the well from the film *'The Ring'* played. Tommy screamed, heaved up the TV and tossed it across the room then grabbed me up by the throat.

**TOMMY:** I'm going to die!

As I was choking I couldn't respond. He then let go of me and before I could stop him he had raced out of the flat. I went after him in my car, him in his and followed him to Creek Alley Stadium.

Tommy headed straight for Maury's office and burst in as Maury was about to tuck into a meatball Subway sandwich. I'd kill for one of those right about now.

**TOMMY:** I gotta get out of the country.
**MAURY:** Why?
**TOMMY:** That film. It's real. She'll get me! Someone sent me a DVD and...
**MAURY:** Hold on. Did you watch the DVD?
**TOMMY:** Yes, you fucktard. I gotta get out. Not much time.

Tommy glanced at his watch. Should I have intervened? Nah, too much fun.

**MAURY:** I sent you that DVD.

If Tommy had been a boiling kettle then he'd have whistled, popped and then exploded. In fact he did sort of explode as he charged around Maury's desk and slammed Maury against a wall.

**MAURY:** You keep this up and you'll be right back behind bars. Would you mind?

I reluctantly left Maury's office as what we were recording was gold. I waited outside his office then Tommy eventually emerged, calmer and more subdued.

**STANLEY:** Well?
**TOMMY:** I'm not gonna die.
**STANLEY:** Course not. That was the movie, 'The Ring'.

Tommy then stared right through me, causing my knees to tremble and knock together. I smiled and beat a hasty retreat. Crazy dim-witted footballers.

Bob and I received a tip off that there might be a possible meeting between two people that perhaps shouldn't meet. We went to Dwayne's luxurious gated home, which had cameras everywhere and a security guard outside. Fortunately, we had a pair of powerful binoculars, and a microphone that could pick up chatter emanating from Alice Springs, Australia.

I spied and saw Dwayne chilling on a La-Z-Boy chair as Cheryl handed him something, a drink. He then motioned with his hand and she moved. Maybe she was blocking his view of the TV. A short time later, and Dwayne had dropped his drink and wasn't moving at all. Cheryl left him, got into her Porsche Boxster and sped away. The security guard was snoring his head off. Dwayne would not be happy about that.

We got into our car and followed her.

After driving here and there, she finally came to a stop along a high street. When she got out, she was like a new person; a badly disguised new person. She was wearing a headscarf and a ginger wig. Didn't do anything for her. Bob and I then put on our superb disguises – fishing hats and anoraks. I also put on a fake moustache – perfect. We were like a couple of Inspector Clouseaus—the superior Peter Sellers version.

Cheryl Ford looked around before entering into a busy Starbucks coffee shop. We followed and lo-and-behold, she sat down at a table where none other than Ronnie Morrison was seated.

The place was full of people sipping coffee, munching on sandwiches and reading papers. This didn't seem like the wisest place to meet. We plopped ourselves down at a nearby table that was within earshot of everything.

Ronnie was wearing a tracksuit with his name emblazoned on the back of it. They hadn't thought this through very well.

**RONNIE:** Got you your fave. Passion fruit frappe.

Ronnie slid the frappe over to Cheryl.

**CHERYL:** You remembered. So sweet, babes. But what if someone sees us?

Bob and I both looked around and there was nothing to worry about as literally everybody in the coffee shop stared at them. Most were loudly whispering 'Look, that's Ronnie Morrison…' and, '…isn't that Dwayne Ford's missus?' 'What are they doing together?' 'He's fucking Ford's wife!' and so on.

**RONNIE:** Relax, no one's gonna notice us.

He reached out to touch her hand but she retracted it.

**CHERYL:** Stop, I'm with Dwayne now.
**RONNIE:** Why are you with that turd for? You're better than that.
**CHERYL:** When I heard that Dwayne was going to sign for Shyton, I thought I could handle seeing you again.
**RONNIE:** I can feel your fire.
**CHERYL:** Oh Ronnie!
**RONNIE:** Remember what we did in KFC?
**CHERYL:** I can't believe where you dipped those boneless dips. So hot!
**RONNIE:** Finger lickin' good.
**CHERYL:** Oh yes, KFC never tasted so sweet.

They caressed each other's fingers. Ronnie licked his lips then he suddenly looked over at Bob and I. I had to do what I could and show that we weren't at all interested in them, so I grabbed Bob's reluctant hand and started caressing then licking it. That made Ronnie (and Bob) shudder, and they looked like they'd both imminently heave. Either way, it had the effect of repulsing Ronnie and making him return his attention to Cheryl and forget about me and Bob. Once we had had enough, Bob went to the toilets and spent an hour washing and scrubbing his hand clean. We then popped into Boots and he bought some hand sanitizer. I thought he went a bit overboard.

Afterwards, I went to pay Maury a visit. He wasn't at home. In fact, he would never be home again at that address, as somebody else answered the door. I was told that Maury had sold the place to him and that Maury had moved elsewhere. I got on the blower to Maury who then gave me directions to his new house – a mock-Tudor house with manicured lawns. It was like something out of a Merchant Ivory film.

Maury showed me around yet another brand new house of his. I hated moving. Not sure how he could do it so often. He took me around the back, (no giggling) to his huge outdoor pool and Jacuzzi.

**STANLEY:** Beautiful.
**MAURY:** I had to move. The last one was too far away and the commute was killing me. With this house, I've saved ten minutes on my journey. Think of all that petrol money I'm saving the club! Now that's business sense.
**STANLEY:** How much did this house cost?
**MAURY:** That's right! Ten minutes!

He wasn't going to give me a straight answer.

**STANLEY:** What did you say to Tommy last time?
**MAURY:** Oh that. That was just a misunderstanding.
**STANLEY:** Something's fishy.
**MAURY:** My chef is preparing us some sushi.
**STANLEY:** Oh, that must be it.

From the Twitter account of @JoeMeek: *'Huge game away at Stamford Bridge. These are the moments you live for. Never thought I'd see it. #ShytonTheBlues'*

From the Twitter account of @MauryShytonUnited: *'Chelsea vs. Shyton United. First time meeting in the league. First of many! #HistoryInTheMaking #ShytonUnited'*

From the Twitter account of @BombinhoJuice: *'Why aren't I playing for Chelsea? #KillMyAgent #MonsoonTears'*

Shyton United were back in league action away to Chelsea, one of the biggest games of their season and an incredible moment for all Shyton supporters. Ricardo was declared fit to play despite having a plaster on his nose. Brave lad.

And it was Ricardo 'Flash Harry' who was involved in most of the action in the first half. Sticking to the wing, Ricardo took on the fullback by doing step-over after step- over after step-over.

**BOMBALBO:** Pass!
**BOMBINHO:** Pass!
**SAO:** Pass that... thing... round... white and... ball!

Ricardo still had the ball and was still doing his step-overs. He kept on going, beyond the goal-line, beyond the pitch, past the stewards, past the away end, down a tunnel and then he stopped when he noticed that he was now in the car park.
After a brief delay to retrieve both the ball and Ricardo, the match resumed, in the stadium, with the score delicately poised at 0-0.

Bombinho had the ball and was performing some amazing tricks (unlike Ricardo he was doing it on the pitch), when he got into the box and was fouled by a gangly defender who was nicknamed 'Groot'. Clearly a penalty, the referee had to give it. The referee waved play on though, and Sonny won the ball back by doing a hard but fair tackle on an opposition midfielder. He slipped it through for Tommy who skipped past one challenge and into the box. Tommy was about to shoot when a defender slid into tackle, pulled out at the last moment and didn't make contact. Tommy dived like a male ballet dancer as Mystic demonstrated in practice. The referee blew his whistle and pointed to the spot. Very controversial decision there.

**BOMBINHO:** I go down and nothing.

Bombinho wept a solitary tear as Ricardo snatched the ball from Tommy.

**RICARDO:** Ricardo's taking it! Ricardo, Ricardo, Ricardo! Get out of here you pasty white, Mars-bar-eating slobbadee doo. Ugly man!

The whole stadium could hear Tommy growl, and growl more impressively than the MGM lion. Ricardo placed the ball on the spot. He nonchalantly tried to chip the keeper, then wheeled off to celebrate; not realising the goalkeeper had caught it. The goalkeeper hoofed the ball up-field.

**JUAN:** Arrogant, beautiful bastard!

The long ball evaded Ronnie and went to an opposition striker who struck the ball with venom. The shot lost its venom when it hit Sonny full-on on the arse and the ball dribbled towards K-Y. Easy collect. K-Y went to pick it up but the ball slipped through and trickled over the line. K-Y buried his face in his hands before examining the turf for any bobbles. The turf was as smooth as baby's apple sauce puree.

**RONNIE:** You berk!

Shyton lost the match 1-0, dropping to 5th. There'd be many questions that would need answering. I spoke to the cause of the 1-0 defeat outside Shyton's changing room.

**K-Y:** It's a new ball. Definitely something's up with that. Also, the pitch. I mean it bobbled. New groundsmen here probably, so it was them too. And there was this mysterious gust of wind...

Maury strode past up to Juan.

**MAURY:** Juan, just the man. Unfortunate defeat today.
**JUAN:** Yes, it's a bad defeat but I'm sure we are improving. And it was away to Chelsea. Most difficult match.
**MAURY:** Yeah, but most managers could've predicted the impending calamity that is James 'K-Y' Black.
**JUAN:** But he's so agreeable and, how you say, accommodating.
**MAURY:** Yeah, you're fired.

Maury marched away, leaving the gaffer gobsmacked. It was an awkward moment, so I backed away from Juan before he started sobbing or raging or trying to do something else to me that I wouldn't like… at first.

I immediately went up to Maury's office to seek answers about Juan's strange sacking. Maury had his feet up, smoking a cigar and looking at the newspaper, *'The Shyton Daily'*.


**STANLEY:** Juan's taken you to 5$^{th}$ place!
**MAURY:** I know. Terrible, isn't it?
**STANLEY:** Who gave the order?
**MAURY:** Have you seen this?

Maury slid the newspaper over to me. I perused the headline that read, 'Chen Hu dies at 50.'

**STANLEY:** Crikey. Says he may have been executed by firing squad.

The door burst open like a watermelon in a vice, and in charged Bombinho.

**BOMBINHO:** I want more money! If I stay here, here in this primitive shit…

Bombinho started crying again and through his tears mustered up a few more heartfelt words. Was he the second coming of Oliver McCall?

**BOMBINHO:** I want more money.

Sheedy appeared in the doorway, like that old WWE wrestler, *'the Repo Man'*.

**MAURY:** Sure, why not?

Maury got the club's chequebook and wrote out a sizeable cheque. He handed it to Bombinho who snatched it from him. Sheedy slithered away with Bombinho following, still crying for some reason.

**BOMBINHO:** Perhaps a new LaFerrari will make me feel better.

Bombinho was gone… to the Ferrari showroom.

**STANLEY:** Just like that?
**MAURY:** Sure, why not? We're a very giving club and like to reward when a reward has been earned.
**STANLEY:** Hasn't Tommy earned some of these rewards?
**MAURY:** Tommy's a special case. He's beyond rewards, as nothing is better than the reward of the public's admiration and adulation as well as knowing you're doing something for love rather than money.
**STANLEY:** Who gave the order to sack the gaffer?
**MAURY:** Juan is headstrong, a loud-talker – he'll get over it.
**STANLEY:** Who gave the order? I know it wasn't you.

If you hadn't noticed, I was embodying Michael Corleone from *'The Godfather Part II'*.

**MAURY:** Then let it go. This is the business we have chosen, so don't ask who gave the order because it has nothing to do with business. People come and people go, it's the way of the game.

Was Maury doing Hyman Roth from *'The Godfather Part II'*? He was even spitting his words out like Roth did at that hotel in Cuba. Were we having a Godfather Part II face-off? Excellent movie, though I prefer the first.

I was out in Shyton town centre with Tommy, who had been sent out to get the cheapest pizza he could find. He was dressed in a shell suit that looked like it had been specially transported from 1980s Liverpool. Tommy had already been to a number of new pizzerias and discovered that they didn't offer any combos, when he finally plumped for a frozen double pack ham and cheese pizza from the supermarket. He was growling but it wasn't through his mouth. We passed an upmarket bistro, *'The Fat Mongrel',* where we spotted most of his teammates dining out.

Inside the bistro having a lavish dinner and a joyous time (despite the fact that Juan had just been sacked and that an important league cup game was just a couple of days away), were Dwayne, Cheryl – who sat adjacent to Ronnie, Li Bang, Sonny and his lingerie model girlfriend— Marie, Bombinho and Ricardo. Bombalbo was at his own table with a load of food in front of him. That guy sure could eat. Sao was meant o be there but had gotten lost and ended up at the home of a Mr and Mrs Shaw. The elderly couple let him stay for his tea.

The rain started coming down, sizzling upon Tommy's face, raging as he was. He marched off. I on the other hand fancied a bite to eat, and I didn't quite fancy Tommy's deluxe ham and cheese pizza—that no doubt came from ham that was originally not ham but horse.

Dwayne, Cheryl, Ronnie, Li Bang, Sonny and Marie – Ann Summers summer catalogue page 23, Bombinho and Ricardo made a toast. Where was K-Y?

**ALL OF THEM:** To money!
**DWAYNE:** Ownership!

Bunch of overpaid prima donnas. I sat at a nearby table so I could capture everything on my iPhone. I was alone, of course. Bob had become quite wary of spending time with me. I looked over and saw that Bombalbo was really devouring his food like a champion pie-eater. Was he a real life version of Homer Simpson?

Bombinho did quite the opposite, as he played with his filet mignon then signalled to a waiter by clicking his fingers.

**BOMBINHO:** You call this medium rare?

Bombinho tossed the plate against a wall. Were all these footballers raised by wild animals? Where were the manners? The etiquette? The humble working class background that should be a part of them all? Scumbags!

**BOMBINHO:** Get me another!

Bombinho started sulking, resting his chin on his palms. Bombinho juice dripped down the side of his curls.

**SONNY:** Hey Li, check out these pics of my latest bitch.

Sonny showed Li the photos of Marie on his phone. I peered over and managed to get a good look. Large screen mobiles were superb.

**MARIE:** What did you call me?
**SONNY:** Nothing, ho.

He really did say that. Marie went back to her salad as though no insulting words were uttered. The times we lived in. If Tommy had said that to Brenda then he'd have no more teeth. I never could have said that to my Danish relatives. Danish women had fiery tempers, worse than Nigerian women, and would have turned me into bait for the next time their hubbies went fishing.

A dapper-looking gent in his 70s wearing black sunglasses and sitting at a table across from them caught Dwayne's attention. Black sunglasses? Inside? Maybe he was a retired rock star.

**DWAYNE:** Who's he looking at?
**CHERYL:** Who?
**DWAYNE:** That old geezer. Staring at you since we got here. Old perv!
**RONNIE:** Calm down, Suspect.

Dwayne charged over to the table where the old gent sat with a petite woman, a third of his age. 'Well done, my son' is what I would've said if I'd been from certain parts of London. Dwayne grabbed the old gent by the scruff of the neck.

**DWAYNE:** You eyeballing my missus?
**PETITE WOMAN:** Please, my grandfather's blind!

Ronnie and Sonny managed to pull Dwayne off the old gent who then collapsed back onto the chair. Ronnie dropped a few £50 notes onto their table to pay their bill. That was decent of him.

**PETITE WOMAN:** You okay, granddad?

I went over and checked the old gent's pulse. Probably most action he'd had in a while. He seemed okay. I explained to her that they were all footballers. She understood immediately. Everybody knew about footballers being a bit special. Though her sympathy could also have been the few hundred quid that she'd already spent at Miss Selfridge. She declined the offer of my phone number.

The manager told them they were all banned. The ban was immediately rescinded when the manager realised how much the bill was and how prompt they were to pay it. Money made everything okay.

**<u>23<sup>rd</sup> September, 2013</u>**

I got wind that Juan was going to Shyton United's training ground to say his goodbyes and pack his things. I caught up with Juan at his office as he took down his much-loved posters of glamour models in tight, revealing bikinis.

**JUAN:** It's not a big problem. A big problem would be if I go all night and Freddy Chorizo cannot be milked. So they don't want me, not a problem. I go France, Espanà, Italia – many possibilities.
**STANLEY:** You're not a little peeved off as it's only September and you're 5th, having won three games, which is great for a newly-promoted side. Not to mention that you made it through to the next round of the league cup.
**JUAN:** Listen bumblebee, I had three-year contract. I'm going now on year-long trip to pollinate all that I can.
**STANLEY:** With Mrs Lopez?

Juan laughed a huge belly laugh.

**JUAN:** With, without, Juan is never alone. So, you think I'm angry? As Michael Jackson sang, *'I'm a lover, not a fighter'*.

From the blog, Fudge Packer for Life, Joe Meek wrote:
*'This is all going tits up already. I had my doubts about Juan Lopez but he proved a pretty reasonable manager. We won 3 games for fuck's sake! Why sack the gaffer? And sack him just before a big cup game! What's Maury playing at and what's he trying to achieve? Club needs stability, hope the next manager will get a fair crack of the whip and have the chance to build something long term. See you, Juan. Thanks for the wins, could come in crucial at the end of the season.*

*Job seeker's allowance is a joke. Any less money a week and I'd barely be able to eat at local Harry Ramsdens. No jobs, no money – who's with me? Least I've got Shyton United – my life.'*

Manager-less Shyton United were away to Everton in the league cup third round. Not a massive trip to make but a massive hurdle if Shyton United were to make it to the fourth round of the league cup for the very first time. Everton had been going great as of late, as they continuously strove to get out of Liverpool's shadow and no longer be known as a poor man's Tranmere.

On the team bus on the way to Goodison Park I caught a few words with Maury.

**MAURY:** I know some clubs and managers don't really give much thought to the league cup, and would rather not be in it; but I think Shyton need to go for these competitions as they will help establish Shyton United as a major force.
**STANLEY:** Sacking Juan Lopez right before this pivotal tie was not the best idea then.
**MAURY:** Stanley, one must move on. Juan Lopez is the past, I live in the future; that's where my mind is always focused. I see Wembley, I see trophies, I see a bigger house, and I see us getting a reaction from the players and getting a result at Everton.
**STANLEY:** With Ben Twaddle in charge?
**MAURY:** Ben's an able individual. I, along with the board, have the utmost faith in Twaddle.

The team arrived at Goodison on a gloomy weekday evening and got ready in the changing room. Ben Twaddle had selected a fairly attacking team with Bombinho playing as a false nine, Ricardo playing as a false eleven and Bombalbo playing as a false ten. I had no idea what any of that meant.
Mystic attempted to give a rousing speech to the troops before they went out onto the battlefield.

**BEN:** My Christian crusaders, believe in yourselves like I believe in you and like Krishna believes in you. Do not forget the words of Spock, *'When you eliminate the impossible, whatever remains, however improbable, must be the truth.'*
**TOMMY:** Shut it, Mystic.
**BEN:** Do not fear the opposing team; we are greater and we will win

with courage, skill and the power of a million gods behind us pushing us forward.

**K-Y:** I'm not sure if I like a million behind me pushing me forward. Could be too many for me to take.

The teams went out, Everton in blue and Shyton in their changed colours of cream with brown trim. It was a tight first half, with Everton enjoying more possession than Dwayne Ford; and Shyton United quick on the counter thanks to balls to Ricardo, who tested the fullback time and time again. There was more of the same in the 2$^{nd}$ half with Shyton United emerging as winners by three goals to nil. Surprising.

As the team celebrated, Ben Twaddle sat on a rug in deep meditation chanting *'om'* until the team picked him up and threw him in the bath. Maury came down to congratulate him as well.

**MAURY:** You see Stanley! A reaction! 3-0 and we're in the next round. Mark my words, we're going to Wembley and that sacking will be considered the greatest stroke of genius since something else amazing happened.

<u>**25<sup>th</sup> September, 2013**</u>

The next day and despite Ben Twaddle's success at Everton, the press gathered to witness the unveiling of Shyton United's new manager, Luis Jalapeno. Sheikh Abdullah and Maury hadn't just hung around, they had scoured Europe for their man. They had tempted a manager famed for his bitterness, his outspoken nature, and his notoriously unhappy demeanour. A man sneered at as much as he was also revered for his incredible success. The new gaffer was certainly going to bring a vibe different from that of Juan Lopez.

Luis was as tanned as that guy from that auction programme, and he had streaks of grey hair, which gave him a George Clooney look. He forever wore a smug facial expression and an attitude like he was too good to be here. The Sheikh must've been paying him a King's, (or Sheikh's) ransom. Cameras flashed as Luis took some questions.

**LUIS:** My record speaks for itself. Every team I've managed has won trophies. There is only one Luis Jalapeno. If Juan was 'special', I wouldn't be here.
**TABLOID JOURNALIST:** Juan's record was pretty impressive for the short time he was here, considering it's a newly promoted team, lots of new signings, new league and country for a lot of them, himself included. How are you going to better what he achieved?
**LUIS:** Because I am Luis Jalapeno. I do not need to answer this question. What have you done? You just write stories. Me? I win leagues and you write stories about me winning leagues. I'm not answering this question.
**TABLOID JOURNALIST:** Controversy has followed you everywhere you've gone. Do you really think you'll be the stable influence Shyton United needs?
**LUIS:** I bring trophies and success. That's all that matters. I am Luis Jalapeno, I don't change. I arrive with all my qualities and my defects. I'm tired of this. I'll let my results speak for me…

Time would tell if that appointment would prove to be a success or more aggro than it was worth.

From the Twitter account of @JoeMeek: *'I rate Luis Jalapeno but his teams play some shite football. Not the Shyton way. #SexyFootball'*

From the Twitter account of @BombinhoJuice: '*Maybe playing for Shyton United won't be so bad now. #HappyJalapeno*'

From the Twitter account of @Bombalbo: '*I like Jalapeno… especially on pizza. #SpicyPizza*'

From the Twitter account of @RonniesCheapGoods: '*New gaffer coming in. He'd better not take away my captaincy or he's a dead man. #TopQualityMerch*'

<u>**28<sup>th</sup> September, 2013**</u>

In Luis Jalapeno's first match in charge, Shyton United were at home to Cardiff City – *the Red Bells*. Luis was busy at his whiteboard drawing up his formation whilst Mystic, dressed as a Morris dancer, did a little dance in front of Ricardo. Ricardo looked as baffled as Tommy was when he opened that package and found the videotape.

**RICARDO:** What are you doing?
**BEN:** Finding peace in dance.

Ricardo started poking him. Did he think Ben was some kind of piñata and that he would soon get some sweets?

**BEN:** I cannot be ruffled. I am harmonious.

Luis finished drawing up his formation of 9-0-1 on the whiteboard. He'd already instructed the team numerous times, but he evidently didn't trust them and so felt an extra drilling was appropriate.

**LUIS (to Ricardo):** What are you?
**RICARDO:** Beautiful left winger.
**LUIS:** No, defender! You?

Luis pointed at Tommy.

**TOMMY:** Central midfielder.
**LUIS:** No! Defender!

And so on and so on... With only Bombalbo playing up front as a forward and the rest not just parking the bus but parking an Airbus A380. How were they going to concede? How were they going to score!

There was yet another vociferous, capacity crowd. Shytonians were the best. However, the mood soon changed and as the away fans booed Shyton's tactics the home fans joined in, agreeing with their Cardiff counterparts. Typical fickle Shytonians.

Shyton eventually had the ball back after playing 'keep the ball away from our penalty area as maybe it's a bomb not a ball' with yet another unseen crunching foul by Tommy. Tommy was getting a reputation. Ricardo broke forward and dribbled past the opposition's defence. He then unleashed a screamer into the top corner that almost burst the net. Ricardo celebrated by performing muscle poses as Luis screamed from the bench.

**LUIS:** Defend! Defend!

Shyton then spent the rest of the match forming a wall in front of their penalty area and repelling everything Cardiff launched at them. Bombalbo gained weight just standing in his own half near the centre circle, and he told me later that he had come up with a new recipe that he'd get his chef to make later that evening. By the end of it, Cardiff had run out of ideas and just tried pot shots that were either blocked, easily saved, or shots so bad that the fans behind the goal were more in danger. By the end of the match most fans, Shyton's as well, had left; with Luis still shouting at his team to defend. Shyton United won 1-0.

After the match I visited Luis Jalapeno in his office at Creek Alley Stadium. His office was decorated in photographs and portraits of himself. Was he related to Ricardo?

**STANLEY:** Exciting match.
**LUIS:** I could crush you. Teams are remembered for what they've won. This team will win.
**STANLEY:** Don't fans have the right to be entertained?
**LUIS:** I hear Shyton has many establishments where you can be entertained. Try there.
**STANLEY:** Moving on. Tommy Gunn was yet again involved in another nasty challenge, which resulted in the opposing player being in some agony. Any comment?
**LUIS:** Where did this take place?
**STANLEY:** Around your penalty area.
**LUIS:** And how far is that from the dugout? Too far away for me to comment.

Luis then looked down at a notebook in front of him on his desk.

**LUIS:** He's not that type of player.

**STANLEY:** What is that type of player?
**LUIS:** You see their player dived, you say nothing.

Luis yawned. I was losing him. As a documentarian it was important to antagonise but not to the point that you risk losing your subject.

**STANLEY:** Are you at all worried about the sack considering Shyton United have already gotten rid of two managers within the space of a few months?

Maybe that was too antagonistic as well.

**LUIS:** I was fired once. The owner is now eating creamed corn through straw. You like creamed corn?

I thanked him for the interview then exited sharpish, not before congratulating him on a well-deserved victory. Us Danish have superb teeth, which must be preserved at all costs, much like Icelandic shark meat.

<u>**29<sup>th</sup> September, 2013**</u>

The following day I went to visit Tommy and Brenda. Somehow they were still together, despite Brenda's numerous threats and Tommy's hair. I guess she really did love him deep, deep, earth-core deep down.

Tommy sipped an energy drink and yet again had his legs spread apart with only his boxers on. I felt as uncomfortable, awkward and yet strangely tantalised as the characters were in the film *Basic Instinct*', when Sharon Stone's character crossed then uncrossed her legs.

**STANLEY:** Where's Brenda?
**TOMMY:** Welfare office, I think.

The front door opened and closed. Brenda came in carrying groceries—mostly frozen microwavable dinners (Tommy was some diet-conscious athlete). She unpacked no-frill item after no-frill item then joined us and slammed a document down in front of Tommy. I liked feisty women. I wondered whether she could be a dominatrix. Some men would pay good money for her attitude. I could've suggested it to her, as I'm sure she could do with the extra dough.

**BRENDA:** Tommy's merchandise is the biggest seller, again!
**TOMMY:** Nice to be popular, innit?

Brenda disappeared then returned carrying Luke, who was wearing a badly handmade Shyton United top with Tommy's name on the back. Cute, fat baby.

**BRENDA:** See that T-shirt Luke's wearing? I made it. Me.
**STANLEY:** I can tell.
**BRENDA:** That's right. We can't even afford to buy one of Tommy's own football shirts!

Brenda put Luke down and his shirt ripped to pieces. Times were tough. I hoped they wouldn't try asking me for some more money. Perhaps I should shorten the amount of time I spent with them? Tommy swept up the document and pointed at me.

**TOMMY:** Drive me to the stadium. I'm gonna see Maury.

I tried to say 'but'.

TOMMY: Wanna save fuel.

I drove Tommy to Creek Alley Stadium and we went up, (I went up, Tommy stormed up like a tornado), to Maury's office. He burst in as he always did, then did a Brenda and slammed the document right on Maury's desk. Maury wasn't in the office though. That was some wasteful, needless slamming.

TOMMY: Where's that tight bastard?

A toilet flushed and in walked Maury. I hoped he had washed his hands.

MAURY: Gentlemen.

Tommy picked up the document and re-slammed it onto the desk.

TOMMY: My shirts are still the biggest seller! I want a new contract now and for everything to be wiped!

I didn't notice at the beginning, as he moved like a shadow and with such stealth he seemed to be wasted as a super agent, but Sheedy slipped into the office like a penis that had been heavily lubricated.

MAURY: Alright, alright. You've got your new contract.

I thought I spotted Sheedy wink and nod as Maury slid over to Tommy what looked like a contract. I didn't get a chance to peruse it.

MAURY: Just sign there.

Tommy signed two copies quicker than Robbie Williams had signed his contract with EMI back in the day. What a dumb move that was by EMI!

TOMMY: Woohoo!

I thought this was all rather suspicious, Tommy I guessed didn't. He charged out in jubilation, hands waving in the air and shouting a series of 'woohoos' that were quite out of character for Tommy. In one of his hands he held a copy of the contract. I followed hoping to get a look at it. We walked down the corridor and then Tommy hugged Sao and Sonny. I'd never seen Tommy so happy.

**TOMMY:** I'm rich!

Tommy rushed away, smiling from ear to ear.

**SAO:** Who was that?

I drove Tommy home. Brenda was again feeding the semi-obese kids. I was pretty sure Shannon was pushing the food away as though she was genuinely full. I feared that at some point I would witness spontaneous self-combustion. We should put hidden cameras in their house. We had? Oh, good.

Tommy slammed his new contract down in front of Brenda.

**TOMMY:** Look!

Brenda glanced at it.

**BRENDA:** This is a 25-year contract! And for the same money!

Tommy then did the best impression I had ever seen of an angry King Kong, head-butted the kitchen door and charged out of the flat pulling me along with him. I was an unwilling puppy.

In no time at all we were back in Maury's office at Creek Alley Stadium.

**TOMMY:** You screwed me! Again!

Maury waved a videotape in front of Tommy. Should he be doing that in front of me? I needed to see what was on that tape. Note: Find a way.

**TOMMY:** What's that?

Maury groaned as he put down the tape and then waved a DVD in front of him.

**MAURY:** Any more complaints and you know where this is going.

All the wind in Tommy's sails seemed to leave and he looked as deflated as one of Huge Jack's non-inflated blow-up sex dolls. He left in a whimper and I took him home where he collapsed face down onto his sofa.

**BRENDA:** Pathetic!

Tommy jumped up like a flea and started thumping his chest and giving a roar that King Kong would've been proud of. Maybe I should start calling him that?

**TOMMY:** I've had it with you, Maury, all of youse. If you ain't happy then sod off!

Tommy rampaged his way upstairs, causing the mini-blimps to cry. Brenda looked in so much shock that I'm pretty sure my fist could've fitted inside her mouth. Tommy returned.

**TOMMY:** And stop feeding the kiddies so much. They look like… they look like… they're fucking hairless apes!

Bravo! Tommy then disappeared. Not wanting to be left alone with Brenda, I scooted off.

Finally we were back in league action and a huge and exciting game against a team that could arguably be called the Barcelona of the Premier League – Stoke City. A home game too, so Shytonians were hoping/praying for a classic, with smooth crisp passing, and sublime skills to woo the crowd.

From the Twitter account of @JoeMeek: '*Hope our players get out of this one uninjured. #SUFC/SCFC*'

From the Twitter account of @BombinhoJuice: '*Home to a team called Stoke City. Glamorous game. I'm so happy. #SexyFootball #Fear4Life*'

From the Twitter account of @MaurySUFC: '*Forget your El Classicos, this is real football right here. Shyton vs Stoke. #RealFootball #TicketsStillAvailable*'

And the game lived up to its billing and everybody's expectation with Jalapeno parking the Airbus and hoping to sneak a goal, with Stoke 'tackling' and closing down space sharpish. It was beyond dull. It was like watching slow-drying paint dry. Fans of both sides, and there weren't that many fans, chanted 'boring' and I joined in as well until…

Ronnie Morrison cleared the ball to Bombinho who raced through on goal, beating two Stoke defenders who had tried sliding in with tackles that looked like they were intended to maim. Though of course, I'm sure the Stoke boss would've issued the typical 'they're not that type of player' line. Bombinho scored and the fans offered a sort of golf clap – the fans that were awake that is. I was pretty sure I saw most of the fans yawning, sleeping and snoring. At one point free cups of coffee laced with Red Bull were being handed out.

Stoke later equalised and I was told it finished 1-1. I didn't want to dwell on the match for too much longer as otherwise I would've killed myself. However, I did have a quick word with Luis Jalapeno after the match.

**LUIS:** You cannot play football against team like that. They're killers not footballers. My team try play good football but that team, we're lucky nobody is in hospital.

**STANLEY:** Aren't you over exaggerating a bit?

**LUIS:** Did you watch this match?

**STANLEY:** I nodded off.

**LUIS:** If I want wrestling I watch WWE, this is not football. I think only one team came to play. Pele once called football *'the beautiful game'*. I think Stoke City never heard this.

**STANLEY:** There have been accusations of diving against some of your players.

**LUIS:** When someone is coming at you to injure you, do you just stand there and take it or do you try to avoid it? Bombinho and Ricardo need to protect themselves and jump out of the way when people are coming to injure them.

The following day I was surprised to discover that I had been invited round to Bombinho's place where we were to have coffee. I had hoped to spend a day with some of the players in their homes and get to know them better and see what made them tick. Money, I had guessed.

I pulled into the entrance of Bombinho's gated mansion, gave my name to the security guard then drove up to a mansion that could've been mistaken for the White House.

One of Bombinho's man servants was there to greet us, and ushered us into a lounge that was bigger than my pad, my old pad and the pad I first got upon leaving home – combined. Marble, granite and the finest craftsmanship were everywhere. Unfortunately, we came on a day Bombinho and his wife were having a right old barney.

Dressed in a white dressing gown, Bombinho was on his hands and knees, and in tears. Was he ever not in tears? As we entered, his blonde bombshell of a wife who can't have been more than 24 and with boobs as big and as natural as Jordan's, was heading out. A small part of me wanted to head out with her.

I had noticed a limousine waiting in the driveway but had just assumed that was one of their many cars.

Fearing issues with language I had an interpreter with me who was able to translate the barney as it took place.

**MRS BOMBINHO:** I hate this big, luxurious house. I hate the Olympic-size swimming pool. And the masseuse is shit.
**BOMBINHO:** Don't leave, baby.
**MRS BOMBINHO:** This place is so horrible we are forced to take the helicopter to
London to do our shopping.
**BOMBINHO:** I'll do anything. I'll move Shyton closer to London.
**MRS BOMBINHO:** This is no life! We'll be in our villa in Malaga.

A young nanny who was pretty damn sexy as well, carried a toddler and ran after Bombinho's wife. Mrs Bombinho then snatched the toddler away and jumped into the limousine. Bombinho looked at me, I looked at him. The Clash's song, *'Should I Stay or Should I Go?'* entered my head.

**STANLEY:** Everything alright?
**BOMBINHO:** My life here is terrible! I'm living like a peasant! And now my wife… You just can't understand. Who will I sleep with tonight?

He cried some more then untied his dressing gown, took it off and stepped over to his indoor swimming pool. He dived in. Poor fellow.

We left, the interpreter and I going our separate ways like ships in the night.

<u>**7<sup>th</sup> October, 2013**</u>

I went with Bob over to Dwayne's mansion that was just down the road from Bombinho's. The house was almost a replica of George Harrison's home, Friar Park. Absolutely sumptuous. This house had a couple of security guards outside, a gate and more cameras than a Big Brother house. When I finally got clearance, which involved facial recognition software, my fingerprints being scanned and a background check to make sure I wasn't a womaniser, I was allowed in. Thirty minutes later I got to meet Dwayne in his lavish lounge where there were even more cameras. One of the security guards then told me that I mustn't make eye contact with Cheryl, or Dwayne would go ballistic. I promised I wouldn't.

**STANLEY:** I see you've got quite a few surveillance cameras around the place.
**DWAYNE:** You can't be too careful. Lot of untrustworthy people about after all my possessions.

Cheryl then walked in. She was looking more gorgeous than ever but I quickly averted my gaze when Dwayne began to eyeball me.

**CHERYL:** Drink, babes?
**DWAYNE:** Sure.

Cheryl went over to fix him his screwdriver. Out of the corner of my eye I spotted her adding some white powder to his drink.

**DWAYNE:** You want one too?
**STANLEY:** No, I'm fine.
**DWAYNE:** Suit yourself. Cheers then.

Dwayne gulped his drink down as Cheryl disappeared out of the room. On the mantelpiece was a framed photo of an adolescent Dwayne, face red with rage, anger and raging anger. A middle-aged man stood behind him with his arm around a woman similar in age to him wearing a tight-black dress. His other arm was around a much older woman with grey hair and wearing a knitted jumper. Both of this man's hands were worryingly close to the women's breasts. Another man in the photo had his arms resting on a woman sat next to Dwayne. The man seemed to be pulling her back towards his crotch. I guessed it was his mum. A rather odd photo.

**DWAYNE:** That's my family, I keep it there to remind me that nobody can be trusted.
**STANLEY:** Who's in the photo?
**DWAYNE:** Well, me, my dad, mum, uncle Derek, auntie Rachel and gran.
**STANELY:** That's your mum sat down next to your right?
**DWAYNE:** Yeah.
**STANLEY:** And the man behind her with his hands on her is your dad?
**DWAYNE:** No, uncle.
**STANLEY:** Oh. And the other man?
**DWAYNE:** My dad.
**STANLEY:** Close family. Lots of good times were shared… amongst other things?
**DWAYNE:** What?

Dwayne blinked again and again then staggered a bit.

**STANLEY:** Close family.

He yawned then went over to the sofa.

**DWAYNE:** Bit cream-crackered.
**STANLEY:** It's just after midday.
**DWAYNE:** The gaffer's got us doing lots of train…

He nodded off. I had to find Cheryl. I knew what she was up to but even though it was damaging to Dwayne it would just be gold for the documentary. The sound of Dwayne's snoring echoed in my ears to the extent that I wondered whether he had a medical problem.

I already had Bob on the case and he followed Cheryl to Shyton's premier hotel, the three star Shyton Inn which was as bland and as sterile-looking as a Travel Lodge. Parked across the road with his secret agent-style microphone and camera, Bob caught Cheryl exiting a black cab disguised as a Muslim woman – hijab and all. Those Islamic dresses really did make for excellent disguises, plus you could eat as much as you want and nobody's none the wiser! Cheryl fled to the safety of the hotel. A couple of minutes later another black cab pulled up and out stepped Ronnie Morrison wearing no disguise at all. Ronnie was shaking his fist at the cabbie.

**RONNIE:** D'yer know who I am? I'm Ronnie Morrison, you twat! England defender! Shyton United captain! M-O-R-R-I-S-O-N!

Ronnie then tossed some £20 notes at the cabbie before storming off into the hotel as well. There'd be some loving there that afternoon. Rough, angry loving, which lasted about 30 minutes before they both departed separately. I guessed Ronnie was saving himself for his next match.

Translated from the Twitter account of @BombinhoJuice: *'Bombinho is empty and dry. My love has gone! #FillMyHeart #ShareMyBed'*

The following day Bob and I met up and went round to pay K-Y a visit. He was also having issues at home.

K-Y chilled on the sofa, two mugs of tea in front of him on the coffee table. He looked tentative, slightly agitated, hands together. His partner was nowhere in sight.

**STANLEY:** How long's it been since you first applied?
**K-Y:** Two years back. Seems like they don't want people like us to have kids.
**STANLEY:** Have your teammates been supportive?

K-Y gulped down some of his tea like a pro.

**STANLEY:** When's their next visit?
**K-Y:** Tomorrow lunchtime.

The next day, K-Y and his partner were again rejected to adopt. The world could be a cruel and unfair place sometimes—especially for minorities, which I'm fairly certain K-Y and his partner would be categorised as. If only there were more honest footballers.

It was another boring international break, which meant no Shyton United. Still, Bob and I managed to sort through what we'd recorded and compile everything. Should make for a cracking warts and all doc; my fishermen ancestors would be proud… not!

I met a lady friend during this time. She happened to be Maury's secretary and as I had become a frequent visitor of Maury's, we'd gotten to know each other fairly well. We'd already been out for dinner and cups of tea though we had yet to get further than the peck on the cheek stage. I wondered whether I should push it more and try to be more forward and more manly, however, I didn't want to frighten her off. She was pushing 40 and perhaps women of that age liked to take things more slowly… Although having said that, time was not on their side so perhaps they would be more eager, and to put it how Tommy would've no doubt said it, they would be gagging for it. Next time I visited with her I'd take her to the *Horse & Cart* pub and get her plastered.

From the blog, Fudge Packer for Life, Joe Meek wrote:
*'As it's internationals and more raised expectations from England who'll no doubt qualify then get shown up come major tournament time, it's time all Shytonians looked at the performances of Luis Jalapeno's team. I was no fan of Juan Lopez but in comparison to Luis Jalapeno he was a god of sexy football and the reason why Pele called the game 'the beautiful game'. The football being played at the Alley is utter dross that would bore the shit out of fans watching a Sunday League game. It's time we showed our disapproval and dissatisfaction with performances by using our feet and stamping very often to the tune of The Smiths' 'Heaven Knows I'm Miserable Now'. On another note, my benefits came through so me and the family went out to celebrate at T.G.I. Fridays. Top night out.'*

With most of the Shyton United squad now returning or having just returned from international duty with their respective countries, it was difficult to meet up with any of them; except for one notable exception – Bombalbo. Bombalbo was dropped for the Brazil national team due to a perception that he wasn't fit enough and that he was getting a bit porky. The tabloids and sports magazines in Brazil displayed sneaky images of Bombalbo in his speedos (not a pretty sight) whilst he relaxed by his family's swimming pool in the opulent area of Leblon in Rio de Janeiro. His national team coach was furious and when the team met up for training, threw a whole load of coxinha at him—which had an effect on Bombalbo similar to what the donuts did on Homer Simpson when he was in the Hell Labs Ironic Punishment Division. Bombalbo was sent back to Blighty in disgrace, occupying two seats on the plane. So I paid him a visit at a local café for some eggs, coffee, pastries, back bacon, fried bread, few more eggs and some black pudding that he'd acquired a taste for.

**BOMBALBO:** My father was a baker and my mother was a baker. My father's father had a food stall and my mother's father had another food stall. They fought a lot, then became friends, joined forces and had a very large food stall making the best coxinha in all of Rio de Janeiro. Then my father and mother took over the food stall and later got a bakery. Food is in our blood.

Bombalbo showed me a photograph of his parents and grandparents. It was like looking at a photo of the Brazilian version of Eddie Murphy's *The Klumps*. Bombalbo tucked into his eggs and other foods whilst chatting to me. It was like interviewing Roald Dahl's *Mr Twit* what with the bits of food flying about.

**BOMBALBO:** After my career in football is over I will go home and take over the family business. Maybe I will expand and open a few Brazilian eateries here.
**STANLEY:** Why did you pursue a career in football instead?
**BOMBALBO:** Only thing more in my blood other than food is football.
**STANLEY:** Really?
**BOMBALBO:** You do not believe me? Besides, I also dreamed of

trying all the foods of the world.
**STANLEY:** I believe that.

I started feeling nauseous so I decided to leave the 'professional athlete' to his first breakfast of the day.

A day before Shyton United's big game at the Palace I met Ricardo 'Flash Harry' Bombalbo, back from international duty and at home in his palace of a home that was like a shrine to him. In fact, there were shrines in Thailand that were less 'worshipping'. Statues of Ricardo were all around both inside and out, statues not too dissimilar to Michelangelo's David. There was also a fountain out at the front with him in a goal-like celebration; on his knees, with hands raised to the skies.

Ricardo sure did have a chiselled physique which I saw first-hand while he chilled on his cream leather sofa, with only a luxurious white towel around his waist. Now, I was without doubt a heterosexual man but on occasion you did meet a fellow that you wouldn't mind bumming. Ricardo wasn't just chilling, he was actually posing for yet another portrait. All around his house were paintings depicting Ricardo in a variety of poses and states of dress and 'undress'. In fact, he had had so many portraits done that artists from all over the country flocked to Shyton to seek work. It had become the 3rd biggest industry in Shyton after unemployment and pornography.

**STANLEY:** Impressive.
**RICARDO:** Yes, fortunate ladies tell Ricardo this often.

**STANLEY:** The paintings.

Ricardo pointed to a painting that parodied the album cover of Michael Jackson's *Thriller*.

**RICARDO:** I especially like this one with Ricardo and the tiger cub. Look at his toned butt, it's beautiful.
**STANLEY:** I suppose. Why do you continually speak in the third person?
**RICARDO:** What third person? He is Ricardo.
**STANLEY:** Is there a special someone?
**RICARDO:** Yes, of course. Ricardo. Ricardo is special in many people's lives. When Ricardo was a little Ricardo at school in Funchal, Madeira people would always say little Ricardo was special and give him a hat. Little Ricardo would always bring smiles and tears to

people's faces… so happy to watch little Ricardo.
**STANLEY:** You're little Ricardo?
**RICARDO:** I am big Ricardo. Want to see how big?

I shuddered. I couldn't take it any longer so I made my excuses and left.

It's an away game at Crystal Palace, a place famed for their cheerleaders, their eagle and the best, loudest fans of any yo-yo club. As it's Shyton United visiting and their now renowned style of football of don't pass, don't move, lump it forward and tackle hard not many Shytonians made the trip south. Even some Palace fans were reluctant to come so prices were slashed and the latest Dwayne 'the Rock' Johnson action/comedy/crap/kids' movie was played before and during the game. Even so, it still wasn't a sell out and a lot of the fans used the time to play *'Candy Crush'* on their mobiles.

In the changing room, Luis Jalapeno gave some further instructions. You could imagine what they were.

**LUIS:** Defend, block, suffocate this team of all their breath then when they start planning their evenings and what they'll have for dinner, we hit them!

A few of the players that were awake nodded. Most were already snoring and a few yawned, fighting to stay awake.

**BEN:** Energise and reawaken and thou shall emerge from the valley of death a learned man.
**TOMMY:** This ain't Charlton we're playing, you wally.

The team headed out and returned with a scrappy, dire 1-0 victory thanks to a fine volley from the man mountain, Bombalbo. Nothing else happened. Most of the players did feel quite well rested afterwards though. Shyton United up to 3ʳᵈ!

The Palace manager had to be restrained numerous times and even tried to throttle one of Shyton's players – he was that infuriated. He also refused to shake Luis Jalapeno's hand and called him a purveyor of boredom to the Match of the Day reporter. I spoke to Luis Jalapeno afterwards to get his views.

**LUIS:** Who won? We won. More points on the table. I do not care what coach of failing team thinks of me. I just care about my team and getting results. I remember when I was 9 or 10 years old and my father was sacked on Christmas Day. He was a manager, the results had not been good, he lost a game on December 22 or 23. On Christmas Day, the telephone rang and he was sacked in the middle of our lunch. Results are all that matter.

Luis then wandered off, clearly reminiscing about the past and more determined than ever to make sure Shyton United won games and that they'd never feature last on Match of the Day.

Later, I caught up with Tommy and drove him home. We're either becoming mates or he now sees me as his recognized free chauffeur. When we entered his home we could hear tears coming from the master bedroom upstairs.

The room was cosy (a word estate agents used often when describing a room or property that was bloody small) and warm, with a large collection of teddy bears.

**STANLEY:** Nice collection of teddy bears.
**TOMMY:** Ta.
**STANLEY:** Brenda's built up a nice collection.
**TOMMY:** Nah, *she* ain't.

Brenda was sobbing as she stared at her reflection in a tall wardrobe mirror.

**TOMMY:** What's matter?
**BRENDA:** Look at me!

Tommy checked her over like he was a photocopier scanning a document.

**TOMMY:** What?
**BRENDA:** I'm so fat and ugly but we're too poor to get plastic surgery!

I looked at Tommy. Something changed in him, I could tell. I guessed that seeing Brenda in that appalling state hit a nerve, sensitive nerves Tommy never knew he had… nor me for that matter.

**TOMMY:** Oh.

He now realised how much he'd neglected her. Tommy left the bedroom then returned, head-butted the door and left again. I dreaded to think how many times he'd suffered a concussion. I was left alone with Brenda, who was still sobbing. It was an uncomfortable situation and I got the feeling that Brenda didn't care for me. I left sharpish, then got some Ben & Jerry's ice-cream. Cookie dough, in case you were wondering.

From the Twitter account of @JoeMeek: *Worrying news I'm hearing about Sheikh Abdullah. Finally got stability now this? #RocktheShyton'*

In the last day or so, there had been startling revelations in the media that alleged a number of transfer fees had been left unpaid which put another question mark over owner, Sheikh Abdullah Hassan. The other question marks regarded his suitability, being from a country that openly oppressed women and freedom of speech. There was also his alleged participation, despite 'evidence' to the contrary, in a homosexual act that resulted in a young Englishman's death.

I needed to get the story from Maury, so I made my way down to Creek Alley Stadium where I spotted Maury getting out of his £150,000 Aston Martin… a car that made me drool. No idea why he got it in orange, though.

**STANLEY:** Maury! Is it true that the club is up for sale?
**MAURY:** Not at all, Stanley. The Sheikh's one hundred percent behind us.

Maury then went swanning off, so imagine how flabbergasted I was when a press conference was called half an hour later.

In front of a hastily gathered press pack of reporters and Joe Meek, Maury read a statement, a slew of microphones before him. I, like many others, was on the edge of my seat. There was a tense hush in the room and more flashes than a Tory MP on Clapham Common had ever witnessed.

**MAURY:** To reiterate, all transfers have been paid and accusations that they weren't are just slanderous lies.

That regular tabloid journalist stood up like a shot and called out.

**TABLOID JOURNALIST:** Has the club been sold?
**MAURY:** I can confirm that an Arab businessman, who wishes to remain anonymous, has successfully bought the club from Sheikh Abdullah Hassan XII.

**JOE MEEK:** Fucking hell.

**TABLOID JOURNALIST:** Who is this businessman? Does he have confirmed funds?

**MAURY:** All I can say is that he's wealthy, with substantial assets in the Middle East.

There were even more flashes from cameras and questions being thrown left, right and centre.

**MAURY:** There'll be no more comment at this time.

He was going to give me a comment, I was damn sure about that.

A successive away game, and this time Shyton United travelled to Southampton – one of the few success stories of clubs promoted to the Premier League, and a model for all, including Shyton United. A team that played good football and a club that developed excellent players. A profitable club that bought players cheap and sold them high, and the only team whose fans had every right to sing *When the Saints Go Marching In'*. Shyton United had their own version but it was titled, *'When the Fudge Packers Go Marching Out… then In'*.

With Shyton United close to the top of the table, this was a monumental game against a team that matched their ambitions and were surely one of their main competitors, especially if Shyton United kept their good form going.

Luis Jalapeno kept an unchanged line-up, which wasn't difficult as his team wasn't the biggest and so this meant a forward line of Bombalbo… The Saints' fans urged their team on as they pressed and harried the Shyton United team. But with Shyton United players like Bombinho and Ricardo able to hold onto the ball using their trickery and ball possession skills, it was only a matter of time before Shyton were able to break the Saints' hearts. Tommy drove from midfield, being supported on the flanks by Sonny Jackson and Suspect, with Li Bang running free from midfield (or as Jalapeno called it, 2<sup>nd</sup> line of defence). Tommy threaded a ball through to Li Bang who squared it to Bombalbo who then let rip a shot that burst the net like the alien did to Ripley's stomach. Shyton United won 1-0 and they had a new chant.

*'One nil to the Fudge Packers…'*
The Saints fans and players booed Shyton United off whilst Luis Jalapeno had a smug look upon his face. His team were inching closer to the top of the mountain.

In the changing room Luis Jalapeno was trying to cheer up his players who all looked as though they'd been beaten. He patted each player on the head and gave them a hug and kiss, only K-Y went over to Luis and did the same to him. I grabbed a few words with Luis.

**LUIS:** It's us against them. You've seen how teams and opposing fans treat us. Teams diving or trying to injure our players. Even the F.A. is against us! Two successive away games! There's conspiracy. They don't like the fact that Shyton are breaking status quo. They see us as Yoko Ono of football teams, as they can't bear for Francis Rossi and Rick Parfitt be separated. This is truth. We are Shyton, we don't care!

Luis turned to his team hoping they'd repeat it. They didn't.

<u>**27<sup>th</sup> October, 2013**</u>

Well, Maury's a slippery fellow and my assuredness that I'd get a comment was somewhat misplaced. He was being more difficult and harder to pin down than a former female gymnast covered in oil. I persevered however, calling him on his mobile, his landline, calling his secretary at his office, emailing, Facebooking and Tweeting. I even wondered whether I could still send a telegram. None of it worked until I picked up *'The Shyton Daily'*, and after drinking shots of Irish coffee, I called him again and got through. He agreed to meet at his office and answer all my questions.

**STANLEY:** You're a hard man to get a hold of.
**MAURY:** As it's so big, is what the ladies say.

I was pretty sure that the ladies would say the opposite, although I wasn't exactly sure what he meant.

**STANLEY:** The club was sold to an anonymous businessman in the Middle East.
**MAURY:** That's right.
**STANLEY:** Who has just sold it to a Russian oligarch.
**MAURY:** Mr Alexander Kovich.
**STANLEY:** Is this any way to run a club?
**MAURY:** It's *a* way.
**STANLEY:** What happened to the other owner?
**MAURY:** Sheikh Abdullah?
**STANLEY:** No, the other one. The one we know nothing about.
**MAURY:** It's business. He spotted an opportunity and took it, then decided it wasn't for him and sold it to Mr Alexander Kovich for a sizeable amount.
**STANLEY:** Are you seeing any of this sizeable amount?

Maury coughed a few times and then I caught a glimpse of a brand new diamond-studded watch.

**MAURY:** Not at all. I'm just the custodian, as it were. I act, as always, in the best interests of Shyton United. Not hard to get buyers in this economic climate.
**STANLEY:** Seems easy for you.

**MAURY:** Yes, I have a talent.

**STANLEY:** Don't you think this club needs stability? Since Sid Chesterton sold up, this club has had four owners.

**MAURY:** Shows how much this club is valued and wanted by the elite.

**STANLEY:** Instability breeds instability.

**MAURY:** Rubbish. We have the same players and have had the same manager for about a month now. We're as stable as any other club, like Portsmouth were, Cardiff City, Leeds United, QPR, Fulham… More stable in fact. And look where we are in the league! Look at Arsenal, same manager for years and hardly any trophies since the mid-2000s. Then look at Chelsea, higher turnover of managers than McDonalds' but loads of trophies. Your *instability* breeds success. Now, it's time for my press conference.

We made our way to the conference room and Maury sat before yet another slew of microphones in front of a salivating media scrum. Maury was loving this, I could tell.

**MAURY:** First of all I would like to state that it is utter nonsense to suggest that Alexander Kovich has links with the Russian underworld.

**TABLOID JOURNALIST:** The Russian Government themselves have labelled him a criminal.

**MAURY:** Because he's a political dissident. Are you siding with Putin? *'Ya tivayou mait yeball.'* Mr Kovich is a fine upstanding businessman who's one of the world's biggest contributors to ending diarrhoea.

If only Mr Kovich could help Maury's verbal diarrhoea. I wanted to find out more about Maury and how he became the man he became. I paid a visit to his elder sister, Rose, who lived in a charming cottage in a small village ten miles east of Shyton. She served teacakes and tea. I should've visited her more often. She was about five years Maury's senior and had a fuddy-duddy way about her as though she were actually much, much older. The years had not been kind… in fact, they'd been pretty devastating.

**ROSE:** Did Maury tell you about our broken family?

**STANLEY:** Maury doesn't discuss his personal life too much. I've just experienced his many new houses and new toys.

**ROSE:** Yes, he loves his toys and spending money. I suppose he's never been content to settle for less… always wanting more. I think our parents' divorce when he was a wee nipper and our mother's constant whoring had an effect on poor Maury.

**STANLEY:** Constant what?

**ROSE:** He's always sought shelter and affection in money. Has a great mistrust of people.

**STANLEY:** You don't say.

**ROSE:** I do say. When our dad failed to pick us up for our weekly visit, we never saw him again. From then on, I'm sure that Maury felt that he was on his own and had to look out for himself, and making money helped.

**STANLEY:** Making money at the expense of others? Amassing a fortune apparently through illegal means?

**ROSE:** I don't think our Maury would do that. He loves his money but he'd never do anything unscrupulous.

I started to leave…

**ROSE:** Stepdad after step-dad used to pick on Maury telling him he was useless, hitting him with their shoes. One stepdad used to play Frisbee with Maury in the garden, then put the Frisbee down and throw his shoe instead. A lot of right-footed shoes ended up in our neighbour's garden. Our neighbour turned the shoes into a kind of garden sculpture – like in *The Wicker Man*.

I made my excuses and left, leaving Rose in her fantasy world where bunny rabbits talked, little hobbit-like creatures lived in mushroom houses, bears really did eat honey and Maury was a saint. She'd find out soon enough.

<u>**28<sup>th</sup> October, 2013**</u>

I was still troubled by the Tommy situation. I knew Maury had something on Tommy, and that was why he treated one of his star players like used chewing gum. I went round to Tommy's to investigate. It would take all my tact and powers of persuasion to get to the bottom of this.

**STANLEY:** What's Maury got on you?
**TOMMY:** I can't tell youse.
**STANLEY:** C'mon.
**TOMMY:** No!
**STANLEY:** C'mon!
**TOMMY:** Leave off.
**STANLEY:** Remember when you asked for more per interview?
**TOMMY:** Maury's got something and if I step out of line I'd be banged up again.
**STANLEY:** What is it?
**TOMMY:** Can't say.

I changed tact and started pouting.

**TOMMY:** What you doing?
**STANLEY:** Pouting.
**TOMMY:** What-ing? You coming onto me?
**STANLEY:** No!
**TOMMY:** You'd better pay me a lot fucking more if you're into that!
**STANLEY:** Are you renting yourself out?
**TOMMY:** I ain't a house.

The conversation was getting me nowhere. I sweated so much my brow and forehead could've been confused with the brows and foreheads of an out-of-shape fun runner that just completed the London Marathon. I wiped away the sweat then got up and, in jest, punched Tommy on the upper right arm.

**TOMMY:** What you doing?
**STANLEY:** Just joking.

Tommy gave me a penetrative stare that made me feel so

uncomfortable and guilty that it was as though I were passing through an American airport.

I thanked Tommy and went on my way, taking my car to Crabby Bridge—a well-known attempted suicide spot. Attempted, as it crossed over a stream and the height from the stream to the bridge was only around 4 feet. Had I become a terrible interviewer? Were my days as a documentarian numbered? Should I have become the cocaine-fuelled fisherman my parents had wanted me to be? I called Bob and he came and got me. We went back to my place, stopping to get some fish and chips on the way. Shyton did do the best fish and chips in this part of England, between Liverpool, Manchester and Hull. Bob got a saveloy, which I had a bite of. He felt up my hand and then I was reassured.

<u>**29<sup>th</sup> October, 2013**</u>

Luis Jalapeno lectured his team in preparation for a fourth round league cup
game away to Leicester City.

**LUIS:** Remember, defend, defend, defend. Then, when they are bored and frustrated you go up the other end and score. We're playing a small-time team who'll never achieve anything. We can beat them with little effort.

Tommy was shaking his head, at which point a few strands of hair fell off. Poor workmanship.

**TOMMY:** This is shite.
**BOMBALBO:** No, no. This is ShytOn.
**TOMMY:** Why don't we just play our normal game? We'd beat them easy.
**LUIS:** Tommy, do not concern yourself with my strategy, maybe spend more time concerning yourself with your hair.

Alexander Kovich was seated in the directors' box, taking in his first match as Shyton United owner. Little known fact about Alexander Kovich was that he liked to breed Havana and Standard Chinchilla bunny rabbits. Dressed impeccably in a priceless silk suit, he had an old bullet wound scar on his neck and a deep cut running down from his left eye. As I gazed at him, getting the full picture, a 6ft blonde-haired model sat next to him. That must've been Ivana Kovich, his ice queen.

I studied Alexander's expressions throughout the match. I spotted quite a few frowns, what I thought were groans and then him resting his chin on the palm of his hand looking most unimpressed. The football on display by Luis Jalapeno's team was worse than dire—worse than Danny Dyer.

Bob had managed to fit a few gadgets beneath the seats in the director's box so we could pick up some audio. The following was what we captured.

**MAURY:** Anything wrong, master? More champagne?

There was some grunting that I guessed was Alexander's way of saying yes.

On the football pitch, the whole of the Shyton United team were defending in or around their penalty area. I wasn't sure if they had ever gotten out as I kept an eye on Alexander throughout. I then witnessed him smashing his champagne flute to the floor. It wasn't long before Alexander angrily departed.

Translated from the Twitter account of @BombinhoJuice: *'Our football lacked passion, spunk, sexiness… I want to go home!' #MyAgentMustDie'*

I paid a visit to Luis Jalapeno at his office to talk about the league cup match against Leicester City.

**STANLEY:** Last night you played a game many expected you to win, yet you got trounced 4-0. Do you think you got your tactics wrong and showed the league cup a lack of respect?
**LUIS:** You don't tell me how to manage my team. I am Luis Jalapeno, who the hell are you? Get out!

Luis shoved and pushed me out of the office. Luckily I was in a tai chi moment.

Before the big home game against Manchester United and following the disastrous result at Leicester, Luis Jalapeno quite uncharacteristically allowed his team to have a night out on the town; not just allowed but organised. Luis Jalapeno was not normally one for allowing such nights during the season and usually demanded his players return home, lights off at 9. He himself was a man with staunch Catholic beliefs who had already scared the bejesus out of boys who came to visit his daughters—even if his two daughters had only just started primary school, as had the boys. The little boys were quite dumbfounded when Luis asked them what their intentions were. The parents assured Luis that their children only wanted to play with their Lego, some video games and perhaps dress up, after which the play date was cancelled and the boys sent home crying.

I did however theorise that Luis's organisation of the night out at Shyton's newest, trendiest and only nightclub, *Essence*, was because he feared a player rebellion due to his boring tactics and his enforced playing of players out of position. I guessed he hoped it would boost morale following the disappointing exit to Leicester in the league cup. He then convinced the core of the team—Ronnie Morrison, Sao Columbus and Sonny Jackson—for them to band together to help team morale, and of course, get the other players onside.

A red carpet was lain out with burly bouncers in tuxedos keeping paparazzi at bay. Out of a limo, Dwayne and Cheryl stepped; both dressed to impress. Dwayne then shook his fist at everybody, shaking Cheryl's fist too, as they were handcuffed together.

**DWAYNE:** Don't you look at her!

A burgundy, 90s Datsun mini-cab pulled up and out stepped Brenda, looking like shit dressed as shit with a dress straight out of a 1980s nightmare. Tommy was in his best Top Man suit. I watched on, in amongst the paparazzi as they both headed to the entrance, when their path was blocked by one of those burly bouncers.

**BURLY BOUNCER:** Can I help you?
**TOMMY:** I'm Tommy Gunn!

**BURLY BOUNCER:** This is a private party for Shyton United players.
**TOMMY:** I play for fucking Shyton United.
**BURLY BOUNCER:** You don't look Premier League. More League Two.

Despite all the commotion and noise of the paparazzi I could still make out Tommy's growl as the burly bouncer checked his list.

**BURLY BOUNCER:** Alright. Use the side entrance.

The other humongous-sized bouncer 'ushered' them over to it. I then made my way in, doing a *'Goodfellas'* and walking in through the kitchen then making my way into the happening nightclub where scantily-clad women were dancing in cages and the bar seemed to go on forever.

The party was under way as Brenda and Tommy went to a table. The rest of the Shyton United team were with their respective model-like WAGS, and were looking so fancy that I was sure the whole of Bond Street was out of stock. The champagne was flowing and the glasses were clinking.

Bob and I had both put cameras and microphones all around the place, having made a deal with Huge Jack—the owner of *Essence*; The deal being that we'd do a documentary on him at a later date. It never happened.

**BRENDA:** Look at all these gorgeous women. They're so glamorous. Look at me!
**TOMMY:** You're still gorgeous.
**BRENDA:** I'm disgusting!
**TOMMY:** You're not. You're my doughnut.
**BRENDA:** What? I'm a doughnut?

Brenda fled to the ladies.

Meanwhile in the gents, as Bob and I later viewed from the footage we'd gotten, K-Y and Dwayne got to know each other while they used the urinals.

**K-Y:** Nice.
**DWAYNE:** What!

K-Y stuck his phone up, which displayed a photo.

**K-Y:** Our new Chihuahua.
**DWAYNE:** Your 'partner' not here tonight?
**K-Y:** Nah, you'd know it if my baby was here, Suspect.
**DWAYNE:** Why do people keep calling me that?
**K-Y:** Everybody's got a nickname.

They headed to the sinks and washed their hands.

**K-Y:** Cheryl's looking gorgeous.

Dwayne then grabbed K-Y by the scruff of the neck and slammed him against a wall. Tiles cracked.

**DWAYNE:** You look at her again and I'll rip your balls off, stick them in a blender and piss on them.

What a bully! I'd keep that footage. Meanwhile back in the club, Bob and I both noticed that Ronnie and Cheryl couldn't keep their eyes off each other. Even when Ronnie danced close to a leggy brunette with his hands groping her arse, his eyes were locked onto those of Cheryl's; I bet the arse he was moulding was in his mind Cheryl's voluptuous rear. Ronnie had better watch it, as Dwayne was more paranoid and suspicious than ever. I sat nearby as Cheryl sipped a cocktail through a straw then played with the straw with her tongue. I was aroused and felt the sergeant major spring to attention. Li Bang joined Dwayne next to Cheryl. I hadn't heard much from Li bang, I hadn't even bothered interviewing him yet, as I suspected his English was limited; and besides, a football-playing, breakdancing, hip-hop wannabe Jackie Chan had little interest for me.

**'MARKETING GOLD MINE':** Dwayne, why you so paranoid over Cheryl?
**DWAYNE:** I'm not paranoid!

His English was better than expected.

Dwayne put his hand onto the table, which meant Cheryl's hand was also on the table as they were again handcuffed together.

Remember the photograph of Dwayne with his 'close' family? I did some further digging and it turned out that when Dwayne was a teenager he once came home early from school and caught his dad in bed with his auntie. The following week he caught his mum in bed with his uncle and sometime after that caught his dad in bed with his granny. No wonder he became so paranoid, suspicious and a complete bastard.

Back on the dance floor, Sonny broke out some moves, and then started grinding with a young shapely Samantha Fox-lookalike. He spanked her playfully. I worried that my sergeant major would never be at ease again. Whilst I struggled with my steel rod, Bob was at the bar where Bombalbo happened to be.

**BOMBALBO:** Give me all you got.
**BARMAN:** Alcohol?
**BOMBALBO:** Food!

With his stubby finger, Bombalbo pointed at some salt & vinegar crisps.

**BOMBALBO:** Give me one.

The barman handed over a packet of salt & vinegar crisps.

**BOMBALBO:** Box!

In a corner of *Essence* Bombinho was sobbing at a table despite being with four hot young honeys that could've graced any FHM magazine cover. They were caressing him, nibbling at his ears and no doubt fondling his nether region. Was this a club or a brothel? The poor bastard then pulled out a huge clown-like handkerchief and blew his nose. The honeys, their breasts looking as though they were all trying to escape forwards, continued fawning over him and treating him like a sex god. Why hadn't I become a footballer?

I couldn't take it anymore; even Li Bang had a honey with him! I signalled to Bob and we got out of there. We'd seen enough to make it through the night.

Here it was, one of Shyton United's biggest games of the season against the biggest club in the country, Manchester United. The stadium was half-empty and dead quiet. Fans considered Shyton United so boring that the majority of the fans who did attend their games were tired-looking mothers with young babies, rocking their sprogs to sleep, and old-age pensioners trying to get a good kip in before tea.

It's a sad state of affairs when you couldn't sell out against Man United. Man United sold out all the time. How was this going to affect Maury's business plan, if he had one? I very much doubted he had a business plan at all. Still their new Russian owner, Mr Kovich who we hadn't yet heard a peep from, wouldn't have been happy at this.

Even though it was Manchester United and you wouldn't expect Shyton to be all gung-ho, you would at least expect some effort, considering the talent Shyton United possessed. Their players were more restricted and constrained than Jack Nicolson's character towards the end of *'One Flew Over the Cuckoo's Nest'*. The Shyton United players battled bravely but after wave after wave of Man United attacks, their resolve was finally broken. After going a goal down, Shyton tried to be a bit more attack-minded, which left them exposed and allowed Man United to get the killer second goal. And when Shyton did attack it was a shambles, as Shyton had quite forgotten how to attack.

At the end of the game when the referee was about to blow the final whistle, all the mothers in the crowd collectively shushed him. So the referee used his hands to signal the end of the match rather than blow his whistle.

**5<sup>th</sup> November, 2013**

We had surveilled Bombinho's house, as Bob and I both found him hilarious. Who knew what would happen next and what hotties might just be roaming around in the buff in his palatial mansion? Bob had fitted the latest hi-tech gadgetry guaranteed to capture HD quality footage complete with Dolby surround sound. We had the popcorn and a packet of Kleenex ready.

Bombinho came down his grand staircase wearing a silk dressing gown; nothing to get excited about at the moment. He picked up the post.

**STANLEY (V.O.):** Bombinho has discovered another letter from the local constabulary regarding numerous speeding incidents.

[Bombinho's dialogue was mostly in Portuguese but we've had it translated so that you needn't copy and paste on Google Translate, which is abysmal anyway]

**BOMBINHO:** What the fuck is this?
**STANLEY (V.O.):** The poor sod is confused.
**BOMBINHO:** Con? Con - with? Constab? Stab? Stab...u? Stab you.

Bombinho's eyes widened. A shock was coming.

**BOMBINHO:** Somebody wants to stab me?

He screamed then scrunched it up and chucked it aside.
**STANLEY (V.O.):** He later found out that nobody wanted to stab him... except maybe his wife.

Shyton United were at Anfield to play the mighty reds. Liverpool was known for the Beatles, their footballing tradition as well as success, being the European Capital of Culture in 2008, Scousers' sharp wit and intellect, and for their low car insurance premiums. It was a daunting place to play, with the Kop renowned throughout the land as being passionate and thunderous, how would Shyton United cope with it? Liverpool themselves were in a good run of form, scoring goals at will. This would surely prove to be the Fudge Packers' defence's (whole team) biggest test ever.

And so it proved. Shyton United lost 4-0 in no small part, thanks to a truly inept performance from James 'K-Y' Black. I caught a word with K-Y after the game.

**STANLEY:** Are you a bit worried about Luis? He looked to be steaming.

K-Y visibly gulped. He was a good gulper.

**K-Y:** I'm sure it'll be fine. The gaffer understands. Besides, they just gave me a new 3-year contract.

I hadn't known that. Why would they give K-Y a new contract with all the mistakes he kept making?

**STANLEY:** Do you think your performances justify a new contract? All four goals were directly or indirectly your fault.
**K-Y:** That's a bit harsh. I'm trying my best!
K-Y broke down in tears and ran away like a little girl with pigtails holding her favourite dead hamster – a sick, twisted girl. (Okay, maybe K-Y wasn't a sick, twisted girl).

From the blog, Fudge Packer for Life, Joe Meek wrote:
*Well, that was just diabolical, and not just the keeper's performance. I knew Anfield would be a tough place to go but to lose 4-0 and not put up a fight is just not the Shyton United way. Shytonians have always struggled, fought and resisted getting stuffed. That team just bent over and took it like a ravenous ladyboy who'd been paid top-dollar. If the gaffer's plan was to defend and grind out results then it's*

*all gone up Fudge Packer creek. When what he's known for is keeping a tight ship and then that fails, what else is there? Time for a change of tactics or a change of manager!'*

<u>**11ᵗʰ November, 2013**</u>

At training, a visibly riled Luis Jalapeno berated the players like I'd never witnessed before. It was the rant of all rants that not even an Alex Ferguson could beat. Here's a brief transcript to summarise what he said:

**LUIS:** You're all shit!

For most of the training session Luis resembled a boiling pot that nobody had removed from the stove. After the strenuous workout that the gaffer gave them (he really put them through their paces), Sao, calm as you like, jive-walked past Luis. He had some balls, or the most carefree attitude ever – I wasn't sure.

**LUIS:** Sao. Do not forget, you have a drug test in half an hour.
**SAO:** Yeah, yeah, yeah.

I visited the medical centre at Shyton's training ground to witness first hand one of these drug tests. Sao was due to be here for his test. I waited, along with the drug tester. I knew she was the tester because she wore a white uniform, checked her watch every 30 seconds, had a tablet with Sao's name on it and told me:

**DRUG TESTER:** I'm the official drug tester.

When Sao didn't turn up, and when my chat up line failed to work on the curvaceous drug tester, ('you like your eggs over easy or fertilised?'), I ventured over to Luis' office at the Shyton United training ground to have a chat with the pleasant one.
**STANLEY:** How do you answer critics who say you play anti-football?
**LUIS:** I say, 'shove it up your ass'.
**STANLEY:** Don't the fans deserve attractive football rather than your negative, defensive kind?
**LUIS:** I am in the results-based business. Sexy football might win a cheap boyfriend but plain Juanita gets a big house and a fifty-year marriage with a rich accountant.
**STANLEY:** People pay good money to watch these games. Already this season, prices have gone up from £20 for a standard ticket to £40.

You could at least entertain them.

**LUIS:** It's not important how we play. If you have a Ferrari and I have a small car, to beat you in a race I have to break your wheel or put sugar in your tank. Anyway, we're third in the league, what do you want? If you want entertainment, go to Silvio Berlusconi's house.

**STANLEY:** There are murmurings that Alexander Kovich isn't happy either.

**LUIS:** It's not a problem if the club sacks me. In two months I get a new job. Everybody wants Luis Jalapeno.

**STANLEY:** So you're not worried that your time could soon be up?

**LUIS:** You know what else is up? This interview!

Luis rushed over to me and pushed me out of the door again. It was becoming a familiar habit. Bastard.

Bombinho's house wasn't the only house Bob had bugged. Tommy's council flat was also targeted. Not because I particularly wanted to watch Tommy getting jiggy with his ball and chain (the very thought gave me the willies though it gave Bob something else), but because I feared for the children's safety and was sure that at some point social services would have to be called.

While Bob and I watched from the safety and privacy of my home/surveillance unit, Tommy returned and spotted another package on the floor by his front door.

**STANLEY (V.O.):** This should be interesting, Bob.

Tommy opened the package and removed a DVD. He played it. Least he knew what a DVD was.

**STANLEY (V.O.):** Amazing, Bob. It's showing Maury getting a much younger Tommy drunk by slyly filling up his glass of cola with pills and vodka! Tommy's fast-forwarding the DVD now. Hmm, Maury's egging him on to open a safe and remove a briefcase. Why I never! What's that noise? Sounds like a bear growling? Ah, it's Tommy.

Tommy burst out of his living room and bolted out of his flat.

**STANLEY (V.O.):** He's off! I'd better get to Maury before he does!

I raced to Creek Alley Stadium and got there just before Tommy did. I happened to live within earshot of the stadium, so by the time I turned up ready for all hell to break loose, I instead found myself getting a cup of cocoa from the dispenser then waiting for a good ten minutes.

Tommy finally arrived and burst somewhere else, in this case into Maury's office. I followed. Maury's expression was priceless. Aghast was a word I'd use to sum it up.

**TOMMY:** It was you!

Tommy went round and grabbed Maury by the neck. Few more

minutes of this and I'd have to call the police, an ambulance, and a lawyer to explain why I didn't call immediately rather than a few minutes later.

**TOMMY:** I got proof that it was you. You set me up!
**MAURY:** What proof? How?

Good, Maury could breathe. Tommy's vice-like grip wasn't too vice-like after all, though Maury's voice was bordering on screechy.

**TOMMY:** Don't know but I got a DVD and I've made copies!

Had Tommy made copies? How had he? Did he know how to copy DVDs? If he did then he'd gone up by one IQ point in my estimation.

Super-agent and all-round creep, Sheedy slinked in and nodded. To paraphrase *'He-Man'*, 'he had the power'.

**MAURY:** I'll give you a new contract.
**TOMMY:** I want out!

Tommy then stormed out, almost knocking me over in the process. I also left Maury's office but kept close so I could do some expert eavesdropping. Sheedy had a breathy, slithery, demonic kind of voice. He reminded me of the shadow of Gary Oldman's Dracula in the 1992 film, *'Bram Stoker's Dracula'* directed by Francis Ford Coppola. Worldwide gross of over $215m.

**SHEEDY:** Mr Maury, engineering a move away, maybe to City, might be a good idea.
**MAURY:** But he's the pride of this club. This is going to cost us.
**SHEEDY:** But he's English. English players are overpriced and can get top-dollar! Alternatively, we could make him want to stay.
**MAURY:** How?
**SHEEDY:** Put a spin on it, Mr Maury.

I didn't like how Sheedy kept referring to Maury as Mr Maury – very Peter Sellers *'The Party'*. I myself, doing my best Sheedy impersonation, then slinked and slithered away.

Shyton United faced a home game against Swansea City, the Welsh Wizards, another team that Shyton United should try to emulate. Swansea were a well-run club from top to bottom and it didn't seem to matter who managed them, as the structure was already in place. Could Maury replicate Swansea's system of having a sound financial platform, a playing system and a team of coaches and scouts who were in-sync and all knew their roles? I doubted it. I asked Maury about it.

**STANLEY:** Is Swansea a club that Shyton United should try to emulate both on and off the field?
**MAURY:** No.
**STANLEY:** Why not?
**MAURY:** We don't emulate we innovate!

Certainly the way he managed the club's books was innovative. Back to the game and it was another snooze-fest, as Luis' team kept it tight at the back and tight in the middle. The strikers were so tight that they were like super virgins. Alexander Kovich had his feet up and was catching forty winks. He'd even had a new La-Z-Boy chair installed to make his naptime during games that much more comfortable – it was the envy of all us spectators.

Somehow though, despite Shyton United only venturing forward when Swansea had gotten bored of passing it around, they scored a goal. The goal woke everybody up and gave one 80-year-old a heart attack. Mr Chapman would be dearly missed. Donations should be made out to his widow, Louise Chapman of 82 Collingworth Road, Shyton.

Bob and I were sat in our mobile recording unit, my hatchback, to capture any of the goings on with the Shyton United players.

Needing a breath of fresh air, Bombinho strangely elected to venture out into Shyton town centre, the place with the least amount of fresh air; thanks to years of industrial abuse. In fact, according to GreenerWorld.com, Shyton was the most polluted place west of China.

It would appear that Bombinho was sobbing again. I went in for a closer look.

Bombinho was plodding along the deserted high street looking in a right sorry state. I approached, recording device in hand.

**STANLEY:** Bombinho, what's wrong?
**BOMBINHO:** Look at this place. It's worse than where I'm from, the favelas of Rio. She was right to leave.
**STANLEY:** Doesn't your reported £200,000 a week wages make it a little bit easier?
**BOMBINHO:** No! I'm a slave on a three-year contract. Like that beautiful Blatter said.
**STANLEY:** What made you want to become a footballer?
**BOMBINHO:** I had no education, just football. I love football. I would play for free. It's not like now. Kids grow up, not for the love of football but for the love of the fast cars, the beautiful women and the money. The soul has left football.

Bombinho spotted and pointed at a homeless man whose smell might have been the cause of 25% of Shyon's pollution.

**BOMBINHO:** He should not be in my view!

Bombinho clicked his fingers and a charcoal grey Lambo arrived. Where did that come from? They must've been tailing him.

**BOMBINHO:** Get out! I'm driving! My car! My car!

He then sped off, leaving his minder behind. He looked at us to give him a lift. Told him to bugger off. What? We're not Uber.

Next up for Shyton United was an away game at West Ham United, their 13<sup>th</sup> league game of the season. Thirteen was considered an unlucky number. In Chinese culture, four was considered unlucky; as the sound of the word was similar to the Chinese word for death. I was not a superstitious chap and didn't go in for all that mumbo jumbo. All I wanted was a good match; but with Luis Jalapeno 'King of Boredom' at the helm, that seemed as unlikely as one of Bombinho's floozies ditching him for
yours truly.

The Hammers' fans sang *'I'm Forever Blowing Bubbles'* as the Shyton United fans fluffed their pillows, ready for a good snooze. In fact, Shyton's games were becoming so infamous for boring football that doctors were recommending insomniacs go watch their games for a chance of a kip. Because of this, every Shyton game, home or away, was now sold out.

The match got underway with the away side rushing back, as per instruction, around their penalty box. The West Ham team were pretty bemused by it.

**LUIS:** Get back! Back! Further! Great Wall! Great Wall!

Thankfully, through a bit of individual skill from Ricardo, Shyton United got the goal they so deserved in their only attack and shot of the game. 1-0 to the Fudge Packers!

Afterwards I caught up with the gaffer and asked him about how lucky he was to have an individual like Ricardo who could win you games even if your team played poorly.

**LUIS:** I hate to speak about individuals. Players don't win you trophies, teams win you trophies, squads win you trophies, Luis Jalapeno wins you trophies.
**STANLEY:** Aren't you afraid of the future?
**LUIS:** I know all about the ups and downs of football. I know one day I will be sacked.
**STANLEY:** You don't fear the sack?

**LUIS:** No, I fear for the person that sacks me.

He then went off, full of confidence and making me feel that I'd never want to cross paths with him.

Games were coming thick and fast. We found ourselves already in December in Shyton's first season in the Premier League. In league game 14 they would face Tottenham, the most successful football team… of 1961. Tottenham were known for their flair as well as for producing great players for other clubs.

It was another home game for Shyton United, and I noticed that Alexander Kovich wasn't in his usual place in his La-Z-Boy chair in the directors' box. I found out later that he had to attend a bunny rabbit competition, 'Shyton's Hottest Bunny'. Alexander's bunny, Rexovich, came second. The judges were declared missing the following day.

Tottenham fielded a strong line-up, as did Shyton United who had been remarkably lucky so far with injuries. From the off it was the usual offering from Shyton—sideways passing, pass back to the keeper to hoof it forward, argue with the ref, argue with the linesmen (I refuse to call them assistant referees), and feign injury. But the worst one that Luis had instilled/instructed his players to do was to whisper in the opposition players' ears that they fancied them and hoped that they could go home together afterwards for some rumpy pumpy. This had the effect of the opposition players running away from the Shyton team, and consequently the ball. It had the desired effect in this game as well. Despite Tottenham spraying the ball beautifully all over the pitch like a water sprinkler, whenever a Shyton United player got near they'd give them all the space and time in the world. Shyton United won 4-0 and moved up to third!

From the Twitter account of @JoeMeek: '*How much can a Fudge Packer take? I'm full of this s***. #BringBackHonestFootball*'

A little bird had told us that something might be going on that very evening between Ronnie and Cheryl. So Bob and I took the Bugmobile (our new name for my car) out and followed Ronnie, as he drove his brand spanking new Aston Martin to a beauty spot in the Shyton Hills. The secluded spot was also known by its more elegant name 'Screw Spot', and was surrounded by big bushy trees. There were rolling hills and a vale beyond. The position offered a great view of all of Shyton. You could see Huge Jack's film studios, as well as his old factory, and Creek Alley Stadium. You could also see a thick layer of smog that had yet to be fully broken down and identified by scientists, nor had they been able to give a timescale before a mass evacuation would need to be called.

We parked quite a way from Ronnie's car, but using our special night vision goggles we got a good view of Ronnie's smiling face. Whatever was going on I'd never seen him happier. His mouth was doing a goldfish impression… What was he mouthing? It seemed like he was saying, *'ooh ahh Cantona'*. I got Bob to scribble that one down. Cheryl's head then popped up. That explained everything. Question was, how did she get away from Dwayne?

We checked my iPad and brought up the cameras that had been installed in Dwayne's house. We had to go through many cameras before we found him in his very own state-of-the-art surveillance room. Wasn't quite up to what Bob and I had created but it certainly would have worked in keeping tabs on Cheryl.

On a computer labelled CHERYL TRACKER, Dwayne tracked Cheryl. He had a joystick and there was a red light flashing on the screen in front of him. He was sipping on what looked like orange juice. He leaned back and yawned then said,

**DWAYNE:** Got you.

And just like that, Dwayne crashed and fell asleep. Had his drink been tampered with? It looked like Ronnie was about to be on the move so Bob and I got out of there before he would notice us. We drove home to analyse our footage.

Games truly were coming thick and fast, as just several days later they had a game with Aston Villa, a team that you just felt in a couple of years would achieve great, wondrous things. As a Shyton United supporter, I hoped that this imminently born-again powerhouse wouldn't rear its ugly head during this game! Aston Villa was probably the most fearsome team in England; they weren't nicknamed 'Villans' for nothing.

However, Aston Villa's form hadn't been up to much. They'd secured a notable opening day victory but since then had slipped away. Perhaps they were like a caged tiger waiting to be released. I spoke to Luis Jalapeno to find out if he would change tactics due to the fact that, going by form, Shyton should easily dispose of Aston Villa.

**LUIS:** No.
**STANLEY:** Why not?
**LUIS:** I think you're like a voyeur, no? I bet you stay awake at night abusing two pillows and calling them Shyton and United.

He stormed off. That was a lie. One pillow was enough.

True to his word, Shyton didn't change—much to the joy of the insomniacs in the crowd who'd gotten the best kip they'd had in a long while. Shyton went on to win 1-0. Mark my word though, I saw great things in that Villa team. Onwards and upwards, Shyton United marched! You might not have liked the gaffer's methods but they were winning.

<u>**14<sup>th</sup> December, 2013**</u>

Shyton United faced a daunting trip to Goodison Park, the home of Everton Football Club. With the weather going from nippy to frosty, and with so many lads hailing from more exotic climates, was it a worry that they wouldn't be able to do it on a chilly day in the North West?

**MAURY:** Not at all. We bought players with balls. Come rain or shine, our players will perform. Once the referee blows his whistle, the lads will be warmed up in no time.

I then got a quick word with K-Y before he went into the changing room. Training with the foreign lads every day, he'd surely know whether they could handle it.

**STANLEY:** I just asked Maury if the weather could affect some of the foreign lads and he said that they had courage, they had balls and it wouldn't affect them. What do you think? Won't it have an impact on players like Bombalbo, Bombinho and Ricardo Bombalbo?
**K-Y:** No, I'm in full agreement with Mr Git'a. These players have balls. I've seen those balls, and they're impressive balls. You talked about Ricardo, he's got the best set of balls of all of them.

With Alexander Kovich still absent from Shyton United games, Luis Jalapeno could play the dour football he'd come to be known by and not have his boss literally looking over his shoulder. And dour football was indeed served up by both teams. With Shyton United happy to sit back and soak up the pressure and Everton also in a 'I need a big stomach to make room for all that turkey so I'd better not do much running' frame of mind, it was a bore draw of the ultimate kind. 0-0. Yawn.

Despite the result and the negative football, Shyton United remained in the top four and on course for an unlikely Champions League spot. However, there was a long way to go, and anything could happen.

From the Twitter account of @RonniesCheapGoods: *'Samsung 50" LED TV. £399! Can't beat it. #RonniesGoneDiscountCrazy'*

Translated from the Twitter account of @BombinhoJuice: *'I'm so lonely. Only 3 girls with me tonight. #SexyNights'*

<u>**17<sup>th</sup> December, 2013**</u>

Much to my surprise because they'd kept it so hush-hush, I was invited to the brand new opening of Shyton's latest nightclub, 'Jackson Bang's Phat Hos'. The nightclub was a joint venture of Sonny Jackson and Li Bang, with a little assistance from Huge Jack—who seemed to have his fingers in everything. As you could guess by the name, it was a rather sleek, stylish, Chinese/Western fusion joint with scantily clad females (both Chinese and western) dancing on platforms. It had loud hip-hop music and everything else that was required of a nightclub.

I met with Sonny and Li upstairs in their office on opening night to find out more about the business, and themselves. Even in the office the music was thumping, causing everything to vibrate, including my lone kidney.

**SONNY:** Welcome cracker, to da lab.
**STANLEY:** Whose idea was 'Jackon Bang's Phat Hos'?
**SONNY:** Fo' shizzle it be ma nizzle 'ere.
**STANLEY:** What did he say, Li?
**'MARKETING GOLD MINE':** Yo homie, it be my baller ass.
**SONNY:** Fo' sho, we got da cake, clucker!

I wasn't getting any of this. Maybe I should speak to their partner, Huge Jack.

**STANLEY:** Is Huge Jack about?
**SONNY:** That wanksta baller? Yo, you be trippin'?
**STANLEY:** Err… what?
**SONNY:** Yo homie, you ain't got the 4-1-1.
**STANLEY:** I don't? Do I need to have it? Is that like a P45? Listen, would it be possible to speak in plain English? Li Bang, why did you get Sonny Jackson as an English tutor?
**'MARKETING GOLD MINE':** Don't be a hater, homie.
**SONNY:** Yo, we can kick it back at da crib.
**STANLEY:** Kick what?

Sonny's parents dying really had a huge impact on the way Sonny spoke. Could it be true of Li Bang too? I asked.

**'MARKETING GOLD MINE':** No, my parents live in Shanghai.

Sonny elbowed Li Bang.

**'MARKETING GOLD MINE':** Yo, they be in da Eastside ghetto, yo punk-ass buster.
**SONNY:** CREAM, mofo, CREAM.

I'd had enough. I had no idea what these two playas were going on about so I left with Bob, not before memorising every curve and detail of May Li, one of the semi-naked dancers at the club. I'd be happy visualising that later in the night.

With just a few days before Chrimbo, Shyton United faced a massive test with a home game against Manchester City – the new Manchester United. It was a capacity crowd of yawning fans, along with the surprise return of Alexander Kovich. Alexander Kovich looked super cute in his PJs, all snug like a slug in a rug. It looked like his blonde bimbo, I meant wife, was snuggled up to him in what looked like… a bed? Yes, they had a bed in the directors' box. This was all very John and Yoko. Cashmere blankets, a fire burning, perhaps Alexander had never slept better than when he 'watched' Shyton United play.

If Shyton were to win, they'd go second in the league. It was a meteoric rise and fully deserved.

The match was on! In one of Shyton's many attacks (this wasn't true but I occasionally found myself creating imaginary football matches where Shyton United played like Brazil 1970), Ricardo rounded the opposition goalkeeper and played a slide pass to Bombalbo who just failed to reach the ball by a matter of… yards. Christ! How fat was this guy now? He'd put on at least ten more pounds. I needed to get him on the scales!

Bombalbo was left huffing and puffing after that attack. He did not look good.

After the game had finished I went into the Shyton United changing room at Creek Alley Stadium. The Shyton United team were gathered together. They were as quiet as some very frightened mice that had just discovered that the family cat they'd been tormenting had miraculously evolved into a mouse-obsessed lion. And they should've been frightened as Shyton lost the game two nil, putting under-pressure-manager, Luis Jalapeno under even more pressure. Alexander Kovich hated the football being served up.

Luis paced up and down, then kicked over a bin. He shook a fist at the bulging Bombalbo.

**LUIS:** You are meant to be a striker! Zero, zero. You are fat shit.

The fat bastard Bombalbo had tears in his eyes, then got out a Mars bar and scoffed it down. He then brought out a tub of Ben & Jerry's Cookie Dough ice cream and started scoffing that down too. His sugary tears fell into the tub of ice cream but that didn't deter him from eating more. He got out a bag of salt & vinegar Monster Munch, crushed the packet, then sprinkled the contents onto his ice cream. He devoured the concoction like a starving bear tasting flesh for the first time. Maybe he was pregnant?

Luis pointed at K-Y next.

**LUIS:** Who are you?
**K-Y:** I'm the goalkeeper.
**LUIS:** No! You are shit! Super shit! Who trained you?
**K-Y:** Err…
**LUIS:** Shit trained you, shit!

I hadn't noticed because of Bombalbo's eating, (was it making me hungry or sick?) but Mystic was dressed as a Catholic priest.

**BEN:** You're all going to burn in eternal damnation! Thor, the god of thunder, will thunderise your houses!

Mystic was a very confused wally.

It was time for the Shyton United Christmas party. The party was to be held at the conference room in Creek Alley Stadium because Maury wanted to save money. He had hoped to show Alexander Kovich how frugal he could be, and he'd heard that this kind of behaviour often led to goodwill from Kovich—Goodwill that might result in a brand new Porsche 911.

Word on the grapevine was that Bombalbo was to play Father Christmas. Maury reasoned, again trying to get into Alexander's Porsche good books, that they could save money on buying a Father Christmas fat suit if Bombalbo did it. Bob and I were both excited to see Bombalbo as Santa Claus, so we both sped along to the stadium to find the car park deserted and nobody home. There was a notice on the door to the Creek Alley Stadium's reception. It read:

> *'Party cancelled. No more fun till team play better foot*ball. Alexander 'Mr Bunny' Kovich.'

Mr Bunny? We went round to Maury's house (house no. 3? I'd lost track) to find out what was happening.

**STANLEY:** Doesn't seem as though Alexander Kovich has much goodwill at the moment?

Maury was roasting marshmallows over a log fire. They were burning.

**MAURY:** I'm sure Mr Kovich has plenty of goodwill and Christmas cheer in him. There are 911 reasons for good cheer.

**STANLEY:** Should I call 999?
**MAURY:** 911? This is not America, you Carrera.

The marshmallows were now on fire. Maury was lost in his Porsche dreamland.

**STANLEY:** Maury, we'll be going now.

Bob and I got out of there and headed away from any potential explosion. My face was much too precious to be damaged. Maury didn't die and there was no fire as one of his servants put out the marshmallows before it was too late. The servants sent Maury to bed daydreaming of a winter Porsche land. Sounded good when I wrote it.

From the blog, Fudge Packer for Life, Joe Meek wrote:
*'Heard the Christmas party was cancelled. Good. Hope the gaffer finally gets the message and changes style of play. This might be Shyton's best Christmas present ever. Get to work, you lazy overpaid bastards! Right, that's enough of that. Now I have to take my laundry to mum's. Why the old mare can't pick it up I've got no idea.'*

## <u>25<sup>th</sup> December, 2013</u>

It was the 25<sup>th</sup> of December, and you know what that meant? That's right, coming up with excuses not to spend it with the family. Bob and I had spent the whole of Christmas Eve and the following morning coming up with great big whoppers of excuses. 'Dog died', 'got severe case of the runs', 'my love daddy has handcuffed me to the bed', 'I've just been saved by Jesus and have gone to the Congo to save their souls' etc… In the end Bob told his family he was busy and I told my family I couldn't leave Bob alone—because he was suicidal ever since his pet tarantula copped it in an accident involving my size 12 shoe. What was it doing out of its tank?

So, we were self-invited to some of the players' houses to see how they spent their Christmases. First up was Bombalbo. His house was basically like a huge kitchen, pantry and dining room – it was more restaurant than house. He may have had the biggest private kitchen and pantry in the world.

Bombalbo was sat at a huge oak dining table with the biggest roast turkey I'd ever laid eyes on. It was the size of a newborn calf! With it were so many side dishes, at least a hundred. And joining him in this feast was precisely nobody. I licked my lips. The turkey looked so juicy and succulent.

**BOMBALBO:** It is a Chester Turkey.

Also on the table were a stuffed pork leg, tropical fruits, and some kind of dessert that looked like bread pudding.

**BOMBALBO:** That's Rabanada, it's like French toast. Bread and cinnamon, covered in a thick syrup made from port, honey and cinnamon.

The spread was causing my saliva to go into overdrive.

**STANLEY:** Could we have some turkey?

Bombalbo wrapped his arms around the prized turkey. Then with a mouthful of stuffing and turkey meat, spurted:

**BOMBALBO:** No! My turkey, my turkey!

Selfish bastard.

**STANLEY:** Are you happy to be alone on Christmas Day?
**BOMBALBO:** I'm not alone. Look at the turkey. His name is
Rodrigo.

Bombalbo carved up more of Rodigro.

**STANLEY:** Don't you miss your family at this time?

Bombalbo responded but I had no idea what he said, as it was
completely indecipherable due to him scoffing down his food. Bits of
turkey and potato went flying out of this mouth. Yuck. It reminded me
of Mr Creosote from *'Monty Python's Meaning of Life'*, which was
probably inspired by the scene in *'Magical Mystery Tour'* when John
Lennon shovelled spaghetti onto Aunt Jessie's plate.

**STANLEY:** Have you ever thought that perhaps you eat too much? Is
food your friend?
**BOMBALBO:** Food doesn't call Bombalbo names like 'Spotty
Bomba', 'Blobalbo' or 'Slobalbo'. Food just listens and makes me
happy.
**STANLEY:** Bullied as a child?

Tears welled in his eyes as he shovelled food into his gob. Anyway, it
was getting vomit-inducing watching the tub of goo, so we left and
went to K-Y's house to see what he and his mysterious partner were
up to.

Again, K-Y's house was super dark, only illuminated by his fireplace.
K-Y was wearing a woolly jumper with reindeer embroidered on the
front. It was the kind of jumper your granny would've knitted, in fact
my own gran did knit one for me when I was a nipper. Why K-Y was
wearing one, who knew? From the kitchen we could hear the sounds
of pots and pans being put hither and thither.

**K-Y:** They've been busy in the kitchen all day.

K-Y was busy roasting his chestnuts over the fireplace. I got a feeling of déjà vu. Hopefully he'd not set these alight like Maury did his marshmallows. Ouch.

**STANLEY:** What does Christmas mean to you, K-Y?
**K-Y:** Oh Christmas is a wonderful time. I remember the priests used to give us lots of extra stuffing on Christmas. It's a time for family, for togetherness. We hope to have our own family one day.
**STANLEY:** Trying are you?
**K-Y:** Oh yes, every night but it's fruitless.
**STANLEY:** Why is that?

Maybe I'd finally get to the bottom of all this and find out the true… Suddenly from the kitchen there was the sound of a lot of pots and pans crashing to the floor.

**K-Y:** Sorry Stanley.

And K-Y up and left to see what the commotion was. Mystery: unsolved.

Next up was a trip to see Ben Twaddle who we were informed was at his local Anglican church. We arrived at the 18th century church with its grand spires, its stained glass windows and its crumbling gravestones to hear from the Vicar:

**VICAR:** Sadly, Ben has since departed us…
**STANLEY:** From this world?
**VICAR:** From this church. You may find him with that Krishna sect.

We made our way down Shyton High Street where we spotted such a sect. A group of chanting, singing Hare Krishna devotees with their shaved heads, orange bed sheets and little cymbals clanging together. Bob and I asked them if they had seen Ben Twaddle. They had! He was at the Hare Krishna temple. He certainly seemed more Krishna than St Peter so we popped along there. After being force-fed rice by the bowl and some vegan cheesecake (no idea how they did it but it was good), we discovered that Ben was no longer there and had moved on. This was getting to become a story in itself – *The Trail of Ben*

We got out our tablet and searched on a popular monopolising search engine for all the religious institutions in Shyton. It had already been a surprise that there was a Hare Krishna community in Shyton, so we were dumbfounded to discover that there were around one hundred other religious groups in the town. Where had they all sprung up from? They were worse than Starbucks. I hadn't even realised that Shytonians were religious – they always seemed to me to be the least religious, most sinful people in the country. They did after all have the second highest divorce rate, second highest rate of teenage pregnancy, second largest crystal meth industry, and the second biggest porn industry in the country. First in the UK was of course Swansea.

We decided to check the local synagogue whose rabbi said that Ben had been there but had since moved onto the mosque—at which point the rabbi told us to tell Ben that he was no longer welcome on their territory. He wasn't at the mosque either, nor was he at the Hindu temple where we were told he'd just left. Then, then we found him. He was smartly dressed in black trousers, a white shirt and black tie standing outside a new modern, white as white church, along with a couple of young blue-eyed Americans. They all carried little books and wore name badges. As we approached, they, including Mystic, turned in unison and smiled, encouraging us to come nearer.

**STANLEY:** Bob, they're Mormons! He's a Mormon! About turn, about turn!

Bob and I hightailed it out of there before they could try to convert us. We went to the local kebab shop and ordered the Christmas kebab special.

As I chowed down my halal Christmas lunch, I remembered something odd about Mystic.

**STANLEY:** Bob, did Ben have Vulcan ears?

My mobile then vibrated with a text message from Ronnie. It read:

*'Get your arse down here pronto. Got turkey with all the trimmings. Ma did it.*

Turkey with all the trimmings? Would beat the crap we were eating, even if it meant having to buy something from Ronnie. I ditched Bob who pleaded for me to stay, as he didn't want to be alone on Christmas Day. For you see, it was on Christmas Day that his wife ran off with one of Huge Jack's in-house movie directors, Big Jim Pussyfucker. Incidentally, Big Jim was the director of one of Shyton's biggest pornographic successes *'Biggest Potholes of Shyton: Sink then Swim'.*

Once I managed to extricate myself from Bob's vice-like handgrip, I went over to Ronnie's gaff where he had the biggest Christmas tree I had ever had a butcher's.

**RONNIE:** I can let you have it for three score.

Beneath the tree and laid out from there to the kitchen were present upon present (or perhaps they were just goods).

**STANLEY:** Got lots of people coming over this year?
**RONNIE:** Hopefully. I put the word out.
**STANLEY:** Got a big family, have you?
**RONNIE:** Why you asking?

He then rolled his sleeve up to reveal five gold Rolex watches.

**RONNIE:** What do you think of these babies? Two grand each, or I'll let you have the lot for eight.
**STANLEY:** Didn't you say there'd be turkey?

My stomach was rumbling. My stomach hated rumbling. Just then a shrill voice called down. The voice sounded familiar.

**SHRILL VOICE:** Ron! Hurry up and come back upstairs. Miss Strawberry needs her cream.

I shuddered. But wait, that was Cheryl! Dwayne's Cheryl. She was upstairs and getting the Ronnie Morrison hard tackle.

**RONNIE:** Give us a bleeding minute! I'm doing business. She ain't

been here five minutes.
STANLEY: Was that Cheryl?
RONNIE: Nah, mate. Seven grand, final offer.
SHRILL VOICE: But I'm cold, and fluffy panda is getting Sahara.

Ronnie shook his head.

RONNIE: That Dwayne must've been as empty as Stevie G's Premier League medals' cabinet.

He bolted upstairs, not before turning and pointing what must've been an exhausted finger.

RONNIE: Tomorrow morning, car park. Bring the dough for those Rolexes.

Before I had a chance to tell him that I wasn't interested he had disappeared. Where was I going to find seven grand? Where was my turkey with all the trimmings? From upstairs, sex groans and other pleasurable noises emanated.

CHERYL: Oh Ronnie.
RONNIE: Oh Cheryl.

Was Dwayne passed out again? If not, his Cheryl tracker needed fixing. My stomach was not only rumbling, it was grumbling. It was grumbling more than Tommy did leaving a meeting with Maury. I needed stuffing and not the kind K-Y was probably talking about. Was Tommy's worth a try? They might only be eating a tin of Heinz baked beans with turkey bits. Did I dare it? I considered that I should probably get something for the kids so I went on my way and visited the first Muslim corner shop I could find. There wasn't much to buy but I managed to pick up something.

Tommy opened the door. His hair was looking magnificent.

TOMMY: What do you want?
STANLEY: I got the kids something.

I gave it to Tommy, whose little rascal son, Luke was clinging on to his leg like Winnie the Pooh to his last jug of honey.

**TOMMY:** Dairylea?
**STANLEY:** Christmas is a time for sharing. You can share those.

I wandered into the flat after Tommy gave Luke the Dairylea. Luke took them, then started spreading the contents all over the walls. The boy must've hated the sight of food now.

To my surprise, the flat was decorated quite nicely in tinsel, with a big artificial tree with artificial snow on it, and quite a few wrapped presents under it. But why were they still wrapped?

**BRENDA:** Because they're just boxes! Nothing's in them!
**TOMMY:** The kids have been playing with the boxes all day. Kids love boxes.

Brenda was looking beefier than ever. I had to hope that Tommy would soon get a new contract and do something about her. Maybe trade her in for a newer model?

**STANLEY:** Having the traditional Christmas? Had your turkey lunch yet?
**BRENDA:** Turkey? Don't make me laugh.

Brenda handed me a tub of KFC chicken.

**BRENDA:** That was our Christmas lunch.
**STANLEY:** I didn't know KFC was open on Christmas Day.

I took out a leg and started munching on it.

**BRENDA:** That was from last night.

I shrugged my shoulders and kept munching anyway. As long as I ate something that was white meat on Christmas Day, then I was happy. I planted myself down onto the sofa as Tommy went back to watching the alternative Christmas message, and Brenda went back to eyeballing Tommy. Luke had found a new box to play with and just about hid himself in it. The box was tight, bits of his flab came bulging out, then the box exploded open and Luke rolled out. Anyway, the tension was unbelievable. I had to break it.

**STANLEY:** Maybe with it being Christmas, Maury will follow in the footsteps of Scrooge and offer that new contract?

Nothing.

**STANLEY:** So, Tommy, huge away game at Norwich tomorrow. Ready for it?
**TOMMY:** I'm trying to watch Ant & Dec!
**STANLEY:** Right, well…

Without anything else being said, I departed. I tried to pop round to Bombinho's place as I thought he might be alone this Christmas Day, what with his wife having left. However, nobody answered the door. I checked my iPad and connected to one of the cams in Bombinho's lounge. I needn't have worried about his mental wellbeing, as he was well taken care of by at least three buxom young ladies. Bastard. Feeling randy yet frustrated, he headed to one of Huge Jack's massage parlours for the Christmas special. One-hour Swedish massage, small Sherry with the ladies, then a half an hour rubdown. Cheered him right up.

It was Boxing Day – the time of year to go shopping and for foreign footballers to rejoice at plying their trade in England. This year saw Shyton United away to the home of the Canaries; Norwich City. Shyton United were hoping to turn the gas way up on this bunch of canaries.

Norwich – known for its mustard, its turkeys, and its famous mustard turkey sandwiches, was perhaps most famous for knocking out Bayern Munich in the second round of the 1993-1994 UEFA Cup. Would a shock be on the cards that night? Shyton United were riding high in the league playing the dourest football since Greece won the European Championships in 2004. Could they see off yet another Premier League lightweight?

Luis Jalapeno dropped Bombalbo to the bench. Of course they no longer had benches in the Premier League, they had those comfy leather chairs that could comfortably sit an average-sized human being. An overweight Brazilian was another matter, and therefore Bombalbo was forced to watch from the changing room. Subsequently, they had Bombinho leading the attack with Ricardo in a false nine position. I caught up with those two as they arrived outside of Carrow Road stadium. Both of them were wrapped up as though they were about to attempt to cross the Antarctic, more Captain Scott than Roald Amundsen. They shivered and their teeth chattered.

**STANLEY:** Bombinho, you'll be leading the line for Shyton against Norwich City. Ready for the challenge of one of the league's tightest defences?
**BOMBINHO:** It's Christmas. Why am I here in this freezing country? I should be home with replacement wife. This is football, not snowball.

Bombinho hurried away to get some heat.

**STANLEY:** Ricardo, I hear you'll be playing in a false 9 position.
**RICARDO:** There is nothing false about Ricardo. Ricardo is true and beautiful. Why you say false, you fishy finger?

Ricardo pranced and danced away shaking his head. I then checked my body odour. Adidas fresh. He was mistaken!

Shyton United went on to win the match 1-0 thanks to a pearler from Tommy Gunn with the outside of his left foot. Was there no stopping the boredom that was Shyton United?

From the Twitter account of @RonniesCheapGoods: *Boxing Day sales!! Top of the range microwaves, teles, you name it we got it! Hottest goods, best prices. #BoxingDayBargains #RonniesMerch'*

From the Twitter account of @MarurySUFC: *'My last tweet. Twitter's become a place of hate. Shall not be a target 4 trolls! #UpTheShyton For cheap Shyton tickets: MauryCEO@shytonunited.com'*

Much to the delight of the foreign players as well as the England national coach, the Shyton United players were taken away from their families and loved ones yet again to travel the not-so-great distance to the wonderful city of Hull – most well-known for its top university, and the *'Only Fools and Horses'* episode, *'To Hull and Back'*. In that episode, poor old Denzil kept hearing and seeing Del Boy and believed he was going mad. Classic.

Unfortunately, they were without Bombinho for the match. Bombinho had impressed all the team by managing to hold onto the handle of his front door despite quite a few of them trying to pull him away and get him on the coach. He stayed at home, was fined a week's wages and said it was the best thing he'd ever done.

Shyton United was also missing Bombalbo, who literally couldn't get onto the coach because he couldn't squeeze through the coach door. Luis had tried to load Bombalbo into the luggage hold but was advised by Maury that this might not be a good idea on health and safety grounds. So it was decided to leave him behind. Sources told me that instead of going home he went to the local chippy and ate five chip butties.

So, with a depleted line up and a limited attack, instead of opting for his normal 9-0-1 formation, Luis chose a 10-0-0 formation. Ricardo was tasked with breaking out from the penalty area, and trying to score a goal anyway he could. He didn't. Tommy couldn't make any driving runs, Li Bang's forays forward went no further than the halfway line and the rest of the team just formed a wall to repel any Hull attack. Final score: 0-0.

Rumours were abound that Tommy Gunn was poised to join Manchester City in the January transfer window. It was in the local rag, *'The Shyton Daily'*, on various football websites and it was on Reddit—which meant it must be true. It was time to hear it from the horse's mouth so I paid Tommy a visit.

Tommy was standing outside his council flat looking like he was about to explode like a suicide bomber. The outside of his flat had been vandalised with graffiti. 'Scum', 'leech', 'traitor', 'money-grabbing bastard', and 'you're shit in bed' were amongst the many things spray painted on to his walls, door and windows.

**TOMMY:** What the fuck?

As I was about to talk to Tommy, his mobile phone rang to the tune of Beethoven's 9th. I hadn't expected that.

**TOMMY:** What? … I'm not going to City. … I didn't fucking hold the club to ransom … Fuck off, you wanker!

Tommy hung up his cheap Virgin mobile phone. I think it was a Sony Ericsson. He couldn't even afford a good phone!

**TOMMY:** Fuck!
**STANLEY:** An angry supporter? How'd they get your number?
**TOMMY:** Yeah, my dad. Fucking wanker. No idea how he keeps getting hold of my number. Bren probably gave it to him. He can fuck off. And she can fuck off. And you can fuck off. Fuck. That Maury bastard. I'm gonna fuck him off right now!

No idea what he meant by that, but I drove him to see Maury who was in his office, no doubt wheeling and dealing, like a certain former Pompey manager might have done.

As Tommy and I broke in like a couple of 'bad-ass' cops from a 1970s TV show, Maury was just finishing a phone conversation.

**MAURY:** Monaco's a good place.

Maury slammed down the phone. Monaco? That would need investigating.

**TOMMY:** It's you spreading these lies about me to the press!
**MAURY:** Calm down.
**TOMMY:** Why does everybody think that I wanna go to City? They all think I'm a traitor now.
**MAURY:** Relax. It wasn't me, okay? These things have a habit of occurring. Look, this is easily resolved.
**TOMMY:** How? Even my ma wants me dead now.
**MAURY:** Well, she always had a bit of Norman Bates about her. Anyway, why not prove to everybody your heart belongs to Shyton by signing a new contract?
**TOMMY:** I did sign a new contract and it was worthless! All you're gonna do is screw me again and I don't like getting screwed; not even by Brenda!
**MAURY:** I swear on the soul of my dead wife, you'll have parity with the other Shyton players. All I need are all those copies of that DVD. We got a deal?

Had Maury been married? Whatever happened to Mrs Git'a then?

Anyway, cue for Tommy to go mental (a happy kind of mental), throw his arms up in the air, dance around the room (I think he attempted the locomotion), then go zooming out of the office and all the way home like that little piggy. I myself took my reliable Bugmobile, drove past Tommy, then waited for him at their flat, sipping on a mug of tea I had managed to get from Brenda. She charged me £1.50 but that was to be expected. Tommy finally arrived home, out of breath, red-faced and panting harder than a lion forced to copulate with the entire harem because they were all in heat at the same time.

His two kiddies, Luke and Shannon, were rolling around on the floor playing… although, they might not have been playing but just rolling around unable to stop due to the roundness of their figures. In fact, they were both sobbing and neither seemed pleased at the situation. I was going to pick them up and sit them down but my arms were tired. Good thing Tommy had returned home, as I didn't think I could stomach watching another TV show about cosmetic surgery. Brenda was obsessed and it was the only thing she ever watched now. It was putting me off my tea.

Luke managed to stop rolling for a moment, and put a hand down to stabilise himself as Tommy came into the living room.

**LUKE:** Judas!

Tommy presented his new contract to Brenda. She initially refused to take it. She'd been there before and assumed that Tommy had been screwed over again. He kept dangling it in front of her eyes, yet she somehow managed to ignore it and continue watching TV. Was her eyesight able to circumvent objects?

**TOMMY:** Read it!
**BRENDA:** Fine!

She perused it, dropped her mug of tea to the floor and passed out. It must've been a good contract. Tommy had a gleaming smile plastered across his face. Today he had become a man.

From the Twitter account of @RB9 (Ricardo Bombalbo): '*Why Ricardo has to play so many games? Ricardo should be on beach, girls looking at Ricardo's sexy body. #FindaWay #MirrorMirror*'

With New Year fast approaching and a new game just a couple of days away, the foreign players gathered to protest to Maury about the situation. They decided beforehand not to speak to Luis about it as he too was a foreigner, and also because they feared him. Maury on the other hand was a pussy cat, a pussy cat that liked to give out money.

Into Maury's office did storm Bombinho, Ricardo, and Li Bang, while Bombalbo came in on a specially designed electric wheelchair with a special robotic feeding arm for when two hands weren't enough. It took a bit of time for Bombalbo's custom wheelchair (decorated in the Brazilian flag) to fit through Maury's office door but after a while they managed to squeeze him in. So much for the storming, anger and passion that they had wanted to show on a united front.

**RICARDO:** Hey you, pasty one. Ricardo not like playing so much footieball. Ricardo's hair, Ricardo's skin, Ricardo's testículos won't be good after all this.
**'MARKETING GOLDMINE':** Yo playa, yo be trippin'. I ain't down wit no soccer every break o' dawn. Yer get me?

Bombinho was in tears, naturally.

**BOMBINHO:** I'm just a poor boy from the Favelas of Rio. All I wanted to do was play football everyday and now in this country, you make me play football everyday and for so much money, don't you care? Why is there no Christmas break?
**RICARDO:** Ricardo needs time for healing.
**BOMBALBO:** I need time for eating.

Maury held his hands out to placate them.

**MAURY:** Lads, lads, lads settle down. It's in your contracts to play— even when it's Christmas and New Year. If the gaffer selects you then you have to.

The foreign lads faced each other and formed a huddle. There were whispers in Portuguese. Li Bang was nodding away for some reason. I was pretty sure he spoke no Portuguese and did not hail from Macau.

Bombinho then broke from the huddle and stood face to face with Maury. He emerged as the leader of this rebellious faction. His face was stern, determined and he had not a single tear in sight. What speech was he going to give? How was he going to persuade Maury to let them off so that they wouldn't have to travel to Stoke on New Year's Day. Most sane people would do anything to get out of playing Stoke City. Most sane people would do anything to get out from having to travel to Stoke on a freezing New Year's Day. Most sane people would castrate their own fathers to avoid doing both of those horrible things.

Bombinho's mouth opened. Were we going to experience a Churchill 'we'll fight them on the beaches' moment? The anticipation was greater than when I was 21 and got down on one knee at Mr Jolly's Circus to propose to Maureen. She said no.

Bombinho took a deep breath then spoke:

**BOMBINHO:** No.

That was the biggest disappointment I'd experienced since I got down on one knee at Shyton Roller Park, and proposed to Lyn. She said no. I must stop making those analogies.

Maury held up contracts, one for each of the players present. How he managed to get them into his hands so quickly, I had no idea. Perhaps Maury practiced the black arts? With him working so closely to Sheedy, it was certainly possible.

**MAURY:** These are your contracts and they stipulate that you must play when fit and if selected.
**BOMBINIIO:** No!
**MAURY:** I've give you each a New Year's Day bonus to play Stoke.
**RICARDO:** How much you pay Ricardo?
**MAURY:** Twenty thousand each.

The foreign players turned to each other and nodded.

**RICARDO:** Okay, pasty man. We play Stoke.

The foreign players departed.

**STANLEY:** Twenty thousand to play Stoke City?
**MAURY:** Yeah, I think I got a bargain there. I would've paid double that.

Misguided fool.

Translated from the Twitter account of @BombinhoJuice: *'More cash means more love for Bombinho. #MoneyMakesTheWomenComeRound'*

It was New Year's Eve, which meant it was time for a right old knees-up. Bob had deserted me for some bird he'd met online – she had three kids and a Fiat Panda 4x4. However, I had high hopes that Alexander Kovich wouldn't cancel the party this time round because even though they had a game the next day away to Stoke, it was only Stoke. Stoke were a team with a sometime unwarrantedly fearsome reputation of being hard to beat, whereas the main worry should have been whether you'd leave Stoke walking or by wheelchair. Anyway, that match was to come. It was New Year's Eve and it was time to boogie.

Word around the campfire was that there'd be a big bash at Jackson Bang's Phat Hos nightclub. I put on my tuxedo, last worn in 1985, with its pink frilly shirt, and made my way to the club. I saw plenty of the club's players piling in along with their WAGs, it was sure to be a special night. I couldn't wait to get loose, let my hair down and party like it was 1989.

I pulled up, got out and did my best John Travolta *'Saturday Night Fever'* walk. The bouncers glared at me, but it was me, Stanley Gobsen, official documentarian.

**BOUNCER:** Name?
**STANLEY:** Stanley Gobsen.
**BOUNCER:** Your name's not on the list.
**STANLEY:** Check again. I know all the players.

I spotted Sao jive-walk past and head towards the entrance near me. I waved at him.

**STANLEY:** Hey! Sao!
**SAO:** Who's that?

Sao entered the club.

**BOUNCER:** Not on the list. Step aside, sir.

I turned away and went back to the Bugmobile. I munched on a packet of KP dry roasted and put the car radio on. *Dancing Queen'* by ABBA was playing. No Bob, no wife, no lap dance… 2013 was ending at the bottom of the slide like Paul McCartney sang in the Beatles' song *'Helter Skelter'*, except was I to go back to the top of the slide and do it again? How would 2014 fare? And what was to happen to Shyton United? There were still a couple of hours to midnight. I checked the glove compartment – no alcohol. Still, KP dry roasted, can't be all bad. I went and got a kebab, then made my way home to review the latest footage and other recordings. That was how I spent New Year's Eve 2013. Thoughts returned to the Crabby Bridge.

Despite everything, including the threats, most of the Shyton United team were available for the treacherous game away to Stoke City. Ricardo was there, less than happy, though his agent and bank manager were 20,000 times happier. Luis even fielded Bombalbo. Luis had spent most of his post-Christmas sticking his fingers down Bombalbo's throat, making him vomit most of the Rabanada he had eaten.

Back to the match, there was widespread anticipation that Shyton would maintain their impressive winning form and keep up the push for a Champions League spot. Stoke meanwhile also had aspirations of pushing for a top ten league finish—heady times for Stoke City fans.

The match was underway and Ricardo had the ball on the wing, hugging the touchline like a modern day Stanley Matthews or a John Barnes. Shyton United actually ventured into an opposition half for only the 5<sup>th</sup> time in 4 games. Ricardo charged towards an opposing fullback. The beautiful one stopped and feigned many step-overs, then did more step-overs and more feigning. And more. Something was wrong, the narcissist couldn't stop. It was like he was on automatic step-over mode. The players stopped playing and the opposing fullback scratched his head.

Tommy and Ronnie chatted together in the centre circle.

**TOMMY:** I think he's stuck.
**RONNIE:** Happened to my bruv once. His hand had a tendency to grab stuff from a shop and stick 'em in his pocket over and over again. Couldn't help himself. Even did it at ma's dinner table.

The fullback stopped scratching his head and nicked the football from between Ricardo's feet. Ricardo continued feigning step-overs. Eventually the ref halted the match and allowed Mystic and the physio to come onto the field. Along with Tommy they helped Ricardo off it. Ricardo continued doing his step-overs even when his feet were no longer on the ground.

Despite Shyton's victory, (they had won with an injury time header from Ronnie Morrison), the mood was sombre after Ricardo's bizarre injury. The Shyton United team filtered in, with Luis patting each of them on their bottoms.

K-Y stopped at Luis after he had had his bottom patted. Did he want another?

**K-Y:** How's Ricardo, boss?
**LUIS:** Bad. They say he might not make it.
**SONNY:** Yo gangsta, yo saying he might kick da bucket?
**LUIS:** No, it's worse. In his head, he might forever be playing Stoke City.
**BEN:** Master Yoda!

That was indeed horrific news, perhaps the worst news anybody could ever hear, ever. The players and management didn't utter another word for the entire journey home.

With a new year comes new possessions, and for Tommy and Brenda that meant a sparkling new house after he had gotten his long overdue new contract. And not just a house but a bona-fide mansion! It was a definite upgrade from the council flat they'd lived in, which was now being occupied by a bunch of squatters who planned to protest the new Hi-Speed rail link that threatened to destroy most of Shyton's appalling countryside.

Tommy's new house had a lavish garden with an immaculate lawn, the kind that you'd enjoy tea on. They also had their own gardener called Tom. The lushness was out of this world. Petunias, nightshade, oak trees and manicured lawns as far as the eye could see… if you were short sighted—about an acre, in all honesty.

I visited with them and spent time upstairs in their wall-to-wall marbled bathroom with its gold-plated taps, his and hers bath robes and personalised soap. Tommy and Brenda were in a Jacuzzi, sipping champagne. All those years of nagging and shouting and threatening Tommy had finally paid off for Brenda.

**BRENDA:** More champagne and strawberries!

Brenda shouted at a butler who was standing by the door. Brenda then turned to me. Would I get a glass of champagne too?

**BRENDA:** We got our very own slave.
**STANLEY:** You must be proud.
**BRENDA:** What? You think we don't deserve it? You think we should be in the gutter our whole lives?
**STANLEY:** No, no. I'm very happy for you guys.
**TOMMY:** D'you want me to nut him, Bren?

Brenda squeezed him… I dreaded to think where.

**BRENDA:** No, hon. Your nutting days are over. The butler can do it. Jeeves! Collins!

I doubted the butler's name was Jeeves or Collins but I was not staying to find out. I departed their mansion like a shot. Their mansion with its walls painted in pink, portraits of the family as if they were a Lord and Lady, and other decorations that wouldn't have looked out of place in a Barbie house.

It was FA Cup weekend and Shyton United faced another daunting trip to Norwich City. Unfortunately, Ricardo was still in a catatonic state and hadn't yet recovered from the shock of playing away to Stoke so was unavailable for this match. This meant that, with an unhappy Bombinho still weighed down with the separation from his wife, and Bombalbo weighed down due to fat, Shyton United would have a less than intimidating attack. However, with limited options Luis would be forced to play the 'unhappy one' alongside the 'fatty one' and hope that somehow they'd get the goal that would see them through… or that their defence would be able to stay strong, resolute and tight in the face of the fearsomely prolific and deadly Ricky van Wolfswinkel.

The FA Cup was the oldest football competition in the world and was revered from Ho Chi Minh City to Slough. It was a competition that everybody wanted to win. It was a trophy that had eluded some of the game's greats like Brian Clough and Robert Rosario. Would Luis Jalapeno show the competition respect and go all out to try and win it? It was a competition, along with the league cup that was attainable for a club of Shyton's size and with Shyton's squad.

However, in a surprise move, Luis Jalapeno dropped everybody, leaving behind most of the first team squad, with a few exceptions. I asked Luis about this.

**STANLEY:** Luis, you've only kept Bombalbo, K-Y and Li Bang in the team, why?
**LUIS:** I don't answer to you. I answer to the man upstairs. But I don't want you reporting lies. Bombalbo plays because he's fat, K-Y plays because he needs practice and Li Bang plays because I don't have anybody else. Premier League is priority, I decide what is best.
**STANLEY:** The FA Cup is the oldest competition in the world. Don't you think it deserves more respect?
**LUIS:** It's a cup competition. Premier League and Champions League is where the money is, and where I'm taking Shyton United.
**STANLEY:** Is it not too big a risk to play so many youth team players?
**LUIS:** Young players are a little bit like melons. Only when you open and taste the melon are you 100% sure that the melon is good. Now, I

have a bunch of boys to get ready who today will become men. Get out of my way, you masturbator.

Luis pushed me out of the way and got his team of reserves and youth team players ready for their first ever outing for the Shyton United first team. How could this team ever hope to stop somebody like Ricky van Wolfswinkel? Shyton United had to hope that K-Y didn't drop any clangers and that Bombalbo could focus on putting the ball into the net rather than what he'd want to eat for that night's dinner.

Despite the youngsters and reserves putting up a fight, Norwich ran out 4-1 winners. It could have been less but for K-Y putting in a performance that could best be described as calamitous. And it could have been more if Ricky van Wolfswinkel hadn't had a rare off day at the office.

**K-Y:** It's not my fault. You know, I heard that Norwich City practice black magic. I mean, Delia Smith! She must be some kind of witch. She's got them all at it and that's why these strange things happened. I mean, I never dropped a cross and threw it into my goal before.
**STANLEY:** You did that three times. The other goal went through your hands and legs when Li Bang passed it back.
**K-Y:** Black magic. I'm going to go up to Delia's box and see the doll she's been sticking things into. I bet it's a doll of me!

K-Y went away looking for Delia Smith's box. I doubted he'd find it. He wasn't good at finding those kinds of things.

From the blog, Fudge Packer for Life, Joe Meek wrote:
*That was just pathetic. Fudge Packers have respect and put up the best resistance to defeat and battle on till the end. No fight, no desire, no passion and no respect for oldest cup competition in world. Luis, you destroyed our team with your horrible brand of football and now we're out of the cup because of you. We could've won this. It's time for Luis to say sayonara and feck off back to foreign land.'*

From the Twitter account of @RonniesCheapGoods: *'I got a set of hot wheels. An Enzo Ferrari has just fallen into my lap. Must go! PM 4 info. #HotHotHot #RonniesMerch'*

After the horror of getting knocked off the FA Cup, even worse because it was Norwich that did the knocking, Luis summoned in his team early to do some extra training. Even though the majority of the first team hadn't been involved due to Luis' arrogance/blind faith in the reserves and youth team, he brought them in early anyway.

**LUIS:** They all need extra practice. If reserves and youth play more with first team then this kind of result will never happen again! I trust too much, this is my problem.

I headed away from Luis as he got to work. Maury had asked me to visit him at his new house. Yes, another new house. I was about to get into the Bugmobile when I spotted Sao walk away from the training ground and towards his turbo-charged sports car with all the extras, and extras for the extras. I was pretty sure he shouldn't be leaving training already, because training had just begun. Also, he had another drug test to do following training.

**STANLEY:** Forgotten something, Sao?
**SAO:** Don't think so. Oh yeah, stupid me. Gonna go and buy a new Lambo, innit?

He face palmed his forehead and I then did the same. Stupid boy.

Sao got into his sparkling sports car that he can't have had for more than a couple of months, revved up the engine and sped away.

**RONNIE:** Stanley!
**STANLEY:** Uh oh.

Ronnie came charging over with a brown leather briefcase. He slapped the briefcase on to the top of my Bugmobile and opened it up. It was full of Rolex watches.

**RONNIE:** How many you want?
**STANLEY:** Thing is, I'm a bit short at the moment.
**RONNIE:** I'll put you down for five, alright? Give us the dough.

I fumbled through my pockets for some cash.

**STANLEY:** Sorry, I don't have that kind of cash on me.

I needed security.

**RONNIE:** I accept credit cards.

He got out a portable credit card machine. I reluctantly got out my Visa and gave it to him. I selected five Rolex watches as he charged me, then he left, with most of my savings as well as my soul. Perhaps I could sell these watches?

I postponed my meeting with Maury, choosing instead to spend the next couple of days locked away in my bedroom sobbing away.

Bob managed to raise me out of my stupor by reminding me of the documentarian oath, and we made our way over to an extremely extravagant three-storey mansion which featured a fountain outside. I loved fountains. I often imagined dancing around, splashing the water and getting all silly. Maybe it was the Danish fisherman ancestry that was coming into play there.

We entered through the huge door into the mansion, which was a good 30-minute drive from Creek Alley Stadium. Maury really was every estate agent's dream. A butler showed us into a grand palatial ballroom where Maury was sat in an ostentatious throne that the Queen herself wouldn't have felt out of place in.

**MAURY:** This was a bargain. And one not to pass up.
**STANLEY:** Where does the money come from?
**MAURY:** Prudence and sound financial planning.

Sheedy slithered in from the shadows to slip a wad of cash into Maury's pockets.

**MAURY:** Not now, Sheedy.

Maury grinned then showed us around his lovely home. Despite the furnishings, it didn't feel like a home at all. Where was the noise, the chatter, the warmth and the people? It was just a shell without its hermit crab.

Maury showed me his kitchen that could make food for a hundred guests. Stainless steel this, granite top that, it was truly top of the line.

**STANLEY:** Are you happy, Maury? All this money, these houses, does it make you feel good at night?

For the first time I could sense something wrong with him. His bottom lip quivered for a brief moment.

**MAURY:** Of course I'm happy. Let me show you the conservatory! Perfect for the summer.

Following the shock cupset against Norwich, there was a home game against perennial yo-yos, Sunderland. The Black Cats (more domestic than panther) were once again struggling in the league and waiting till closer to the end of the season to start playing well and then miraculously survive—it was a strange club.

Ricardo was still absent and was being attended to by the renowned psychologist Dr Crimson de Marnier. The team hoped to have his flair, skill and narcissism back soon because Shyton United were in dire need of something.

Even despite two early exits from domestic cup competitions, they were riding high enough in the league for everybody to be optimistic. Could their league momentum continue at home against Sunderland? I had a chat with Luis Jalapeno before the match.

**LUIS:** We have no Ricardo due to his fear of Stoke, no Bombalbo due to his fear of not eating, and now no K-Y.
**STANLEY:** Fear of being a goalie?
**LUIS:** I drop him because he's shit.

You couldn't argue with that logic.

**LUIS:** The transfer window is open. I need more players. How can I compete against teams that spend much, much more money? I speak with owner tomorrow. Today is not a good day to speak with him.

The owner, Alexander Kovich made a surprise return to watch Shyton United play. Though I had yet to speak to the man, I had guessed that he wasn't a happy bunny—not that you could tell as he was actually dressed in an Easter Bunny costume. What was going on? Was this why Luis had said it wasn't a good day to speak with him? He had fluffy pink fur, big ears – the works! Alongside him was his wife, who was dressed quite normally and looking rather pissed off about her husband's bunny fetish. Very strange couple.

Shyton United had been made favourites to win this match mainly because of their league form, Sunderland's woeful league form and the

fact that Shyton's first team cost about ten times more than
Sunderland's. However, as mentioned earlier, Shyton United were
without two of their biggest attacking players, and subsequently
struggled to break down a Sunderland team that had decided to park
the bus. Final score 0-0.

I caught a word with Luis after the match.

**LUIS:** As we say in my country, they brought the bus and they left the
bus in front of goal. Now I must go and speak to Bugs. It cannot wait.

I was curious about the condition of Ricardo and wanted to pay a visit to him while he was having a session with Dr Crimson de Marnier. Bob managed to arrange for me to be in the room when Dr Crimson was having his private session with Ricardo. Obviously, this was completely unethical and breaking every rule, so without no one knowing, Bob snuck me in by claiming he was from a laundry company, and hid me in a laundry bin that had been accidentally left behind in Dr Crimson's office. I managed to capture the whole session on film – some of which will be made available on YouTube whilst the rest will be available on eBay for the highest price. No timewasters.

**DR CRIMSON:** Tell me about your childhood.
**RICARDO:** Ricardo was a happy boy.
**DR CRIMSON:** Playing Stoke City away is not the reason for this. Tell me about your childhood.
**RICARDO:** Ricardo was a happy boy.
**DR CRIMSON:** What did young Ricardo do?
**RICARDO:** Ricardo was always bouncing.
**DR CRIMSON:** What do you mean, 'bouncing'?
**RICARDO:** Bouncing knee to knee. Ricardo bounced.
**DR CRIMSON:** Whose knee?
**RICARDO:** Little Ricardo was bouncing. Bouncing. Bouncing on his uncles' knees.
**DR CRIMSON:** Which uncle?
**RICARDO:** Uncles. Twenty uncles, Ricardo was bouncing.
**DR CRIMSON:** Then what happened?
**RICARDO:** Just little Ricardo was bouncing.
**DR CRIMSON:** Just bouncing?
**RICARDO:** Bouncing. No more bouncing. Stop the bouncing. Ugly, fatty and spotty Ricardo. Stop bouncing.
**DR CRIMSON:** Who called you ugly and fatty?
**RICARDO:** Bouncy, bouncy! Bounce, dough ball, bounce. Bounce on the floor, bounce like basketball.

So, Ricardo was a porker. And apparently so rotund that he could be used like an oversized basketball. Least it explained his insane narcissism.

**DR CRIMSON:** You can conquer these fears. You're not a dough ball anymore. You are not a basketball. Repeated: You are not a basketball. You are Ricardo Bombalbo – beautiful soccer player, sexy and strong and supple… and did I give you my home number, Facebook and Grindr username? You can achieve anything.

Ricardo broke down in tears.

**DR CRIMSON:** Relax. You're safe. You're in a good place and you're free of bouncing on your uncles' knees. There'll be no more bouncing… unless you want to bounce on me later?
**RICARDO:** Ricardo doesn't want bouncing any more. No, no more bouncing.

At which point I fell asleep. Thankfully, Bob returned and picked up the laundry and we analysed the footage. Apparently at the end Ricardo had overcome his fear of an uncle's knee, and bouncing on any uncle's knee, and more importantly, he'd also overcome playing Stoke City. Dr Crimson got paid but didn't get laid. Anyway, how Ricardo managed to equate Stoke City with being bounced on the knees of twenty uncles I had no idea. Still, with doctor-patient confidentiality I guess we'd never know.

*BEWARE OF YOUR UNCLE'S KNEE!

<u>15<sup>th</sup> January, 2014</u>

Tommy and Brenda invited Bob and I to a lavish dinner they were hosting, to which all of the Shyton United team were invited, as well as Maury, Alexander Kovich, Huge Jack and other eminent Shytonians. Notable by his absence was one Luis Jalapeno… Even Ben Twaddle was there, though he used the occasion to spread his (unknown) religious beliefs and gave out pamphlets containing many Vulcan proverbs.

Back to the dinner, and it was a chance for Brenda to finally play the role of hostess, a role she'd hoped to play ever since she was a wee girl and had played the game with her little friends.

For the dinner they had gotten the well-known catering company, Shyt Food, to do the food. Bombalbo wrote a blog about the dinner and an extract will follow this.

I arrived in my finest tuxedo and was greeted by Tommy, dressed up in his own tuxedo. He fidgeted throughout and you could tell he wasn't comfortable wearing it. Brenda was sporting a Vivienne Westwood gown – if only she had the body and looks of Thandie Newton (Thandie tempted me with her seductively innocent and coy smile). However, Brenda wasn't the most odd-looking person there, as Alexander Kovich showed up in his bunny rabbit suit, alongside his disgruntled wife. Again, we're not talking Playboy bunny outfit but real Easter bunny. Obviously his brain had gotten damaged at some point in the recent past.

Once dinner was served, Ronnie got up to toast Tommy and Brenda and their new-found wealth. Bob and I weren't allowed at the main table as we weren't Premier League, and had to sit at the children's table.

**RONNIE:** Tommy, Brenda, with this new home and your new weekly wage, you're now a Premier League couple. Everybody, join me in saying, 'one of us'!
**SHYTON UNITED TEAM:** One of us! One of us! One of us!

It was like a cult. I didn't join the toast as Luke and Shannon were throwing their peas at me and my eyes were too busy trying to look up Cheryl's dress. Being at a table half the size of the main dining table had its advantages.

Brenda truly excelled as hostess. She may not have had the body of the other WAGs, or the face of the other WAGs, or the personality of the other WAGs, or the style of the other WAGs, or the body of the other WAGs, (though Tommy assured me that she had numerous appointments in Harley Street the very next week), but in her mannerisms and attitude she was born to be the hostess with the mostest – direct quote from *This is Spinal Tap*'. It was almost like a happy ending. Of course it wasn't, as it was only January.

Extract from Bombalbo's blog, Food with Bombalbo…
*'Dinner at new player Tommy Gunn's house was most delicious. There was an entire roast pig stuffed with a stuffing of apple, sausage, chipotle and cabbage – I ate two fifths of it myself! There was also pheasant done five ways, tasty black tie scallops, black cod brûlée, moist lobster ravioli, foie gras stuffed escargot, quail egg sitting on a crest of lemongrass with a raspberry duck confit, rubber tyre covered in a chocolate ganache and caramelised fingertips, and so much other food that I need to eat right now! Go away. I'm eating! Hello? Domino's?'*

<u>**18<sup>th</sup> January, 2014**</u>

Shyton faced a difficult away game to Arsenal. Shyton's recent form had been less than stellar, and with rumours that Kovich was about to bring the axe down upon Luis Jalapeno's tenure as Shyton United manager, there was a noticeable tension in the air.

The match was underway at Arsenal's huge library and Shyton United were under intense pressure from the off, as the Premier League champions of 2004 tried to find a way through. Arsenal; the team that Barcelona most feared playing; played slick pass after slick pass and yet nothing could penetrate this resolute Shyton defence until Ronnie played a back pass to K-Y, which slipped through K-Y's hands and dribbled into the goal. Disaster!

Ronnie rushed up to K-Y in a noticeable rage.

**RONNIE:** You first class plonker!
**K-Y:** Wasn't me! The ball hit a mole. I think he's been living under the penalty area for a long time. He's got furniture!

Tommy restrained Ronnie from doing any damage to K-Y.

Shyton United lost the game 3-0 in what could best be described as a woeful and inept performance. Shyton were lacking in passion, lacking in creativity, lacking in ideas, lacking in a game plan and were showing all the hallmarks of a Luis Jalapeno team.

Alexander Kovich's reaction to the performance wasn't exactly subtle. He let off some steam by smashing up the furniture in the directors' box with a cricket bat. It was funny to watch a man dressed up as a bunny rabbit smash up glass tables and bottles of liquor. Maury looked on approvingly. He was such a stooge.

From the Twitter account of @RB9 (Ricardo Bombalbo): *'To Ricardo's fans and lovers, Ricardo is back. Stoke is in the past. Ricardo is future. #LifeIsBeautiful #LifeIsRicardo #MirrorMirror'*

<u>**20<sup>th</sup> January, 2014**</u>

After reading Ricardo's tweet that he had finally recovered from playing Stoke City, we went to his house to pay a visit. As well as the numerous portraits of Ricardo, the home was now like a house of mirrors but with more mirrors than a house of mirrors because there were mirrors on the ceilings and the floors too! No wonder the owner of the local mirror shop, (who was affectionately known as 'Man in the Mirror'), had recently been able to purchase a brand new four-storey townhouse.

In Ricardo's lounge that was more a shrine to him than a lounge, Ricardo posed in the buff for yet another painting. He had a crown of leaves on his head and a single leaf covering his gentleman. He lay on a Roman style couch as a curly-haired artist added the final touches to a canvas.

**STANLEY:** Do you consider yourself a narcissist?
**RICARDO:** No, no, no. What's a narcissist?
**STANLEY:** Having excessive interest in oneself.
**RICARDO:** Ricardo loves himself, what's wrong with that? If you don't, who will? When Ricardo was a young Ricardo, Ricardo was spotty this and fatty that.
**STANLEY:** Yes, we heard… porker.
**RICARDO:** What you say?
**STANLEY:** Nothing.

I later found a photo of a teenage Ricardo and he was indeed spotty and chubby. Not sure if he could've been bounced around but he could've been worth a try. Ricardo was getting emotional and the artist wasn't happy with me either.

**RICARDO:** Daddy Ricardo even said Ricardo's penis would never be as big as Rocky the Chihuahua!

Ricardo ran out of the lounge in tears. I turned to the artist to apologise.

**ARTIST:** I've seen his penis. It's tiny.

There you had it. Ricardo's penis would've been intimidated by a Chihuahua's.

Oddly, I was summoned to meet Maury at Creek Alley Stadium and brought into Luis Jalapeno's office. Luis eyed me suspiciously and I assumed he was just as confused as to why I was there. I had been tempted to do some more probing when Luis spoke up. He looked agitated. The whispers around the training ground, the Creek Alley staff and the fans was that Luis was headed for the chopping block any day now.

**LUIS:** You again.

Luis glared at me. I felt like the audience member given the Lionel Blair stare treatment.

**LUIS:** I think you are obsessed with my team, no? I bet you lie awake at night getting turned on by thinking up stuff about them.

Luis may have been half right but I daren't say.

**MAURY:** Luis, you're sacked. May I introduce our new manager, Oren Goldman!

A timid-looking, mole-like chap (think of Hans Moleman from The Simpsons) was pushed into the room by unseen hands. Whose hands? And why were hands pushing him into the room? When I saw him I immediately thought of the word 'tool'. It was not a word I used often, it was not a word I used at all; yet it seemed the most appropriate word to describe him.

**LUIS:** What! I am Luis Jalapeno!

Maury then shouted.

**MAURY:** Security!

A couple of big burly security men came racing in. They were the kind of men you'd cross the street to avoid. They dragged Luis away.

**LUIS:** I have won championships all over the world. You have not heard the last of me!

His voice trailed off like the last guitar chord in a song.

**STANLEY:** Mr Goldman, welcome to Shyton. What's your approach to the game?

Oren tapped his ear. He had some earpiece in there, but why?

**OREN:** ... I will play, or rather my team will play, entertaining football and...

Oren again tapped his earpiece.

**OREN:** Score lots of goals.

I looked at Maury, who grinned a huge grin. This was all rather iffy. Oren was a puppet and I could only guess who was pulling his strings.

<u>**23<sup>rd</sup> January, 2014**</u>

I found myself in K-Y's kitchen. It was decorated in a floral pattern and was all very summery and gay (meaning happy). However, K-Y was anything but gay, as he seemed rather downbeat after shipping a number of goals in the last few games.

I had caught K-Y as he was preparing a light supper. He wore a flowery apron that complemented his kitchen and was standing over a bowl with a whisk.

K-Y's partner was in the pantry with the lights off and tossed him an egg, which he dropped. I could just make an outline of a person. They were slightly on the heavy side, but then a lot of Shytonian women were.

**K-Y:** First they bring out a new ball. Another egg, babes.

Another egg was thrown which he again dropped.

**K-Y:** Then we get new groundsmen who cut the grass all wrong. Another, darling.

Another egg was thrown and dropped, smashing to the floor.

**K-Y:** Then we start playing and it gets windy. Another...

An egg was thrown and he again dropped it. The floor was getting ready to become an omelette.

**K-Y:** And now some footballers are wearing specially designed boots that can help them kick a ball really hard. I mean, so hard it hurts the hands. Another egg.

I stepped in and took an egg from the outstretched hand of K-Y's partner. I carefully put it into K-Y's hand yet he somehow fumbled and dropped the egg. This was ridiculous.

**K-Y:** I'm sure someone's been sabotaging my gloves making them slippery. Another, hon.

In a flash and while my back was turned, K-Y's partner stomped out with feet so heavy that it sounded like a herd of elephants trying to escape from a ravenous lion. They then spoke in a voice that reminded me of Christian Bale's voice as Batman.

**K-Y'S PARTNER:** Here! Take your fucking eggs!

K-Y ducked as a carton of eggs was hurled at him.

His partner was gone. Should I have followed them to discover their identity? K-Y then slipped on the egg-covered floor and landed on his back. Ouch!

The wolfish press gathered in the conference room at Creek Alley Stadium to witness the unveiling of Shyton's first January signing, as well as see Oren Goldman for the first time. 99% of the press didn't care about the presence of Oren Goldman. Then again, I didn't think Oren cared whether he was there or not. He appeared to be trying to hide.

I couldn't spot this new signing. The usual people were there – Maury, Oren (okay, he wasn't usual as he'd just been installed as manager), and there was some tiny, emaciated Indian chap who was wearing a T-shirt with the words 'No Money No Honey'.

**MAURY:** Thank you for gathering here today. I'm delighted to announce Shyton United's first January transfer window signing… our new nimble goalkeeper, Jay Patel. Jay is the best goalkeeper in all of India. His athleticism is beyond compare. Watching him dive for a ball is like watching Superboy!

Had never heard of that superhero character. How would he be able to cope with the six-footers of the Premier League? At the back of the room, I noticed K-Y was there. I watched as he crushed a plastic cup filled with bubbling hot chocolate. He screamed in agony, the whole room turned to face him, and then they took photos. It wasn't a good day for K-Y.

I had to find out what Maury was up to, so following the press conference I went to his office and asked him straight out.

**STANLEY:** Will you come out with me for a glass of Shiraz?
**MAURY:** No.
**STANLEY:** Okay. Jay 'Beanie' Patel is unheard of outside of his native India, and indeed, in his native India – a strange acquisition?
**MAURY:** Not at all, think of the Indian market! More than a billion people. With an Indian player, we'll be number one.

Why did that sound reasonable to me? This was all very unreasonable.

With Shyton United so far only making one January acquisition, the pressure was on Jay 'Beanie' Patel to impress. He was put through his paces in his first training session. However, not only was it his first training session, it also looked to be his first time on a football pitch. He came across like a lost puppy and cut a lonely figure standing in goal.

Bombalbo, Bombinho, Ricardo, Tommy, Sonny and Dwayne then took shots at him like they were firing a machine gun. Jay didn't move an inch. Oren jogged over to him and spoke his own thoughts for the first time.

**OREN:** You have to stop the ball.
**JAY:** Okay, sir.

Tommy powered another shot straight at Jay, the force of which sent Jay flying into the back of the net. K-Y came over and squatted next to a winded, gasping-for-air Jay. Our mini-microphones in the goal could pick up anything.

**K-Y:** You better keep playing like that, sweet cheeks.

Sweet cheeks? Was K-Y trying to come on to him? Jay got to his feet then another Tommy thunder buster flattened him. This was not looking good.

After training had ended, Tommy was in the changing room getting dressed into his new Armani silk outfit when Sao came in wearing his large Dr Dre Beats headphones. I didn't get the fuss about them.

**SAO:** Hear you're off to City.

Was that old chestnut circulating again?

**TOMMY:** What?

Tommy stormed out as only Tommy could. Sao continued to bob his head to the music. Mystic, dressed in The Matrix-style clothing, tapped

Sao on the shoulder. Sao removed his headphones.

**BEN:** Sao, you have missed another drug test. If you miss another, they say they will ban you. Be at one with the test, like I am with the trees.
**SAO:** Yeah, yeah, yeah.
**BEN:** Another coming is scheduled. Please, twinkletoes, do not be led astray by the dark side.

Sao put his headphones on again and carried on his way. How was he not banned yet?

Bob and I left the changing room and went looking for Tommy. We found him in a deep discussion with Sheedy, in a secluded spot next to the changing rooms. What was that about?
**28<sup>th</sup> January, 2014**

It felt like it had been ages since Shyton United's last game and so it was good to get back underway and into what we were all here for — the football. We weren't here for the scandals or the innuendo, it was the football and Shyton United faced a stern test against the biggest team from Wales — Swansea City.

Since the last game there had been massive upheaval at Shyton United, new manager in Oren Goldman and new number one goalie in Jay Patel; yet the Shyton first team still seemed incredibly short on options. If they suffered a series of injuries then their first team would be obliterated.

The big bonus was that Ricardo was back in the first team and he replaced the humongous Bombalbo. The new gaffer had decided it would be better for Ricardo to lead the attack, and even decided to drop Bombinho to the bench. Perhaps Oren Goldman wasn't as weak as I had suspected. He had balls but these were balls that K-Y didn't like. Oren's big balls of course dropped K-Y to the bench and handed a first team debut to Jay Patel. I still didn't understand Maury's thinking about this move. This was a keeper who could end up sending Shyton United down the wrong end of the table. I went searching for Maury and headed down the tunnel where in the distance I spotted Maury with the debutant himself, Jay. It looked like Maury was holding a needle behind his back. Using our best stealth techniques, we got super close and were able to record the audio with our super microphone—the kind the CIA used. Was Maury going to give Jay a confidence booster before the match?

**MAURY:** Ah, Jay, just the man.
**JAY:** Mr Maury, I don't think I can play.
**MAURY:** Nonsense. Oh my God, there's an image of Ganesha etched on the floor.

Lame. However, the gullible fool Jay bent down for a closer inspection and Maury rammed the needle into Jay's puny buttocks.

Disgusted, we left and headed to our usual position to cover the match.

The game was underway and that confidence booster had done the trick. Jay Patel was a beast! Early on in the game, an opposition striker approached Jay's goal:

**JAY:** Come on, sisterfucker!

Jay dived at the striker's feet and grabbed the ball. Jay was like a Mexican jumping bean as he repelled shot after shot raining down on his goal.

**RONNIE:** He's the dog's bollocks.
**TOMMY:** A Chihuahua's bollocks. Must be the kinda guy who's shit in training and turns it on match time.

K-Y, in the dugout, was the only one not happy about Jay's incredibly natural performance. He crushed another plastic cup filled with bubbling hot chocolate. He screamed again. Idiot.

Into the second half and finally, Shyton United had a chance with a fantastic pass by Tommy played through to substitute Bombalbo. Any other striker would've been clean through and had an 80% chance of scoring. Unfortunately, Bombalbo was not the same Bombalbo at the beginning of the season, he was at least twice the man now; literally. Bombalbo huffed and puffed but couldn't reach it and the ball trickled its way to the keeper. Tommy was pissed off, as you'd expect.

**TOMMY:** I've played two through balls to you, can't you run anymore?

**DWAYNE:** Do you want to cause a fucking earthquake in Wales?

In the directors' box at the Liberty Stadium, Maury and Sheedy relaxed in reclining leather armchairs drinking fine Scotch whisky aged 25 years.

**MAURY:** Why is Bombalbo so fat? He's 26, you said we had 2 years before he'd get fat.

Sheedy shrugged his shoulders. Something was amiss.

**SHEEDY:** His wife has a bun in the oven.

**MAURY:** Looks like he's got a bakery in his.

Game finished 0-0, disappointingly. However, with that point gained, Shyton United were now over the famous 40-point mark, generally considered to be the number needed to guarantee safety and stave off relegation. Shyton United would at least be competing in the top flight next season.

Translated from the Twitter account of @BombinhoJuice: *'It's so cold, I hate it here! I hate it, I hate, I hate it. #MyAgentMustDie #CarryMeHome'*

<u>**30<sup>th</sup> January, 2014**</u>

I was driving Tommy back to his mansion. Why I was still his designated driver, I had no idea. A few days ago, he had purchased several new cars, including a Ferrari, Ranger Rover, something pink for the missus and a Bentley Continental, which was the car he had me driving him home in.

He sat in the back and poured himself a brandy. Before I had gotten into the car he'd made me put on a chauffeur's cap and a jacket. It was imperative that as soon as I got the chance I informed him that I already had a vocation as a documentarian, and that I had no wish to be his official chauffeur. If I chickened out of doing that, then I'd need to ask the obvious – what did the job pay and was there a pension?

We pulled up onto his gravel-laden driveway and went into his house. Brenda had requested that he come home immediately after training had finished. She said she had a surprise for him, which was the reason he'd knocked back at least three brandies. He was worried that she had another bun in the oven – the thought of that process happening put me off my dinner.

Tommy rushed upstairs to their bedroom and I must say, what a bedroom. It was utterly awful – large, gaudy-looking bedroom with pink wallpaper, a chandelier, distorted mirrors everywhere and a huge surround sound entertainment system.

**TOMMY:** What's the surprise? Where you been? What's happened?

Brenda was facing away from us at her dresser. She had a pink Barbie robe on and was brushing her hair. Was I intruding? Had I gone where no documentarian had gone before? Then, without warning, Brenda swivelled around.

**BRENDA:** What do you think?

Both Tommy and I jumped back many feet. We hit the wall.

**TOMMY:** Fuck! Who hit you?

She chucked a pink bottle of perfume at him, which hit me square on the forehead. I think it was a bottle of Britney Spears' 'Fantasy'. I slumped to the floor.

**BRENDA:** Nobody hit me!
**TOMMY:** But your lips! They're swollen.
**BRENDA:** I got them Botoxed, you idiot!

Tommy looked confused and Brenda went back to admiring her disaster of a face. I passed out.

<u>**31<sup>st</sup> January, 2014**</u>

After regaining consciousness and making my way to A&E and getting a quick onceover from the doc, I made my way home and went to sleep. When I woke up, I discovered it was now the 31<sup>st</sup> January; a momentous day, as it was transfer deadline day and where better to spend it than with Maury at his office at Creek Alley Stadium.

**STANLEY:** Can we expect any late transfer deals?
**MAURY:** No.

We waited and waited. All evening, Maury and I sat staring at each other, just waiting for the phone to ring or for him to pick up the handset and make that last minute deal, and also to break the incredibly awkward tension. It was the longest night of my life. Midnight was fast approaching when the telephone rang. Maury answered.

**MAURY:** Yes… Yes… Good. Okay.

Maury hung up.

**STANLEY:** Who was that?
**MAURY:** We just signed two Russian players.

I had just been about to complain about how understrength this team was, and now it seemed Maury had been working on a couple of deals all along. Who were these Russian players? Where did they play? Would they suit Oren Goldman? Did he even know about this?

**STANLEY:** Who are they?

Maury checked his watch.

**MAURY:** Oh, is that the time? There just aren't enough minutes in the day. I haven't even had my special night time massage. Bye!

The transfer deadline passed.

<u>**1st February, 2014**</u>

Without hesitation, I immediately went around to Maury's house and was let in by the butler. Maury was having a continental breakfast which included freshly baked croissants and a pot of coffee—all smelt mighty fine.

**MAURY:** Morning Stanley. Care for a croissant?
**STANLEY:** Yes, no. Wait, those two Russian players you bought…
**MAURY:** They're still warm.
**STANLEY:** They've gone already!
**MAURY:** What? The croissants? No, they're still here in this basket.
**STANLEY:** I mean the Russians. They were bought last night, then you loaned them to Zenit Saint Petersburg and Spartak Moscow, respectively.
**MAURY:** Alexander wanted to help out a couple of struggling Russian clubs, what's wrong with that? He's got a huge wallet, that man.
**STANLEY:** This is very fishy.
**MAURY:** That'll be the kippers. Care for one?

I did a Tommy and stormed out. Nothing was right. Nothing was right at all!

There was a match that day but I wasn't in the mood. I could see my club going down a slippery, murky path. The kind of path I suspected K-Y went down most nights. I didn't want my beloved Shyton United stooping to such levels of depravity.

I'll let Joe Meek tell you what happened in the match:

From the blog, Fudge Packer for Life, Joe Meek wrote:
*'…Southampton came to pay us a visit. With Luis Jalapeno gone because of his shite football and ultra-defensive tactics we all expected a massive difference in performance. Well, we ain't seen it yet. Gotta give the gaffer time but how much time can a Fudger give? Yeah, beating the Saints 1-0 is good and we'd have bitten your hand off beginning of season to be where we are in the league but where's the fun? Where's the sexy football? Got to say, I miss Juan. Best manager we've had to date.'*

Bob and me were at Shyton's training ground car park about to witness another Oren Goldman training session when we spotted Ronnie thumping the steering wheel of his Bentley. I always wondered whether Ronnie owned a Bentley, because he was a bit bent. Bob and I used our ninja skills and got in closer. He had the *'The Shyton Daily'* newspaper in front of him.

Bob zoomed in on his camera and managed to capture the front-page headline:

*'SEXUAL LIAISONS AT UNITED'*

Ronnie got out his mobile then jumped out of his car and shoved us aside.

**RONNIE:** Get the fuck out my way!

Behind us with a long zoom camera, the kind that made Bob salivate, was that Shyton Daily reporter who was sole reporter on all things Shyton United. He wasn't of my ilk but he was competent none the less. Ronnie spotted him and thrust the newspaper into the reporter's chest.

**RONNIE:** How do the press know that I'm shagging a teammate's bird?

Well, if it was just conjecture before, it was bloody fact now. What was Dwayne going to say? This could very well destroy morale and the entire Shyton United team. Cue dramatic music. Ronnie turned to us.

**RONNIE:** Clear off!

We did as we were told. However, being true documentarians we holed up in the Bugmobile until Ronnie left the car park. In true detective/stalker fashion we followed him, trying to be as inconspicuous as possible. Ronnie drove to a large warehouse in the industrial area of Shyton United then stopped his Range Rover. A hefty-sized WWE-type muscle freak that made Bob tremble, got into

Ronnie's car. They then drove off. What was happening? What was Ronnie up to? We kept following them as they drove down a residential tree-lined street. Ronnie parked his car tight to the kerb then there was nothing. We waited a few cars down. Then that reporter from earlier strolled past us, munching on a hotdog. He soon reached Ronnie's car. Ronnie and his heavy rushed out of the car, grabbed the petrified hotdog chewing reporter and bundled him in. The hotdog didn't make it and was left by the kerb. There was a brief kerfuffle, a rumble, then quite oddly the reporter got out of the car and he was all smiles! He didn't even care about the half-eaten hotdog that was left to go to waste on the side of the street. The reporter had a bounce in his step and I thought he was going to start dancing all the way home.

Ronnie pulled away in his car and drove off. I was going to find out what was happening! We followed and once Ronnie was safely inside his house, we charged up to his door and rang the doorbell. Ronnie greeted us and showed us inside. There were even more boxes, as well as crates.

**RONNIE:** Primo wine, straight from Chile. Want some? 12 for the price of 18!
**STANLEY:** What happened with the reporter?
**RONNIE:** What you mean?
**STANLEY:** At the training ground car park then after?

Ronnie eyed me suspiciously. Fiddlesticks, I hoped his heavy wasn't around.

**RONNIE:** That was nothing. Minor misunderstanding about me and some unknown childhood sweetheart whose name begins with a 'C'.
**STANLEY:** That reporter's well-known for printing sensationalist stories.
**RONNIE:** Don't worry about it, bruv. There's thirty-thousand reasons why you shouldn't. Now, how about that wine?

Bob and I left carrying a crate of wine that was sure to last until the end of the season. Bob was a Guinness man, whereas I was more of a sweet sherry man. Still, the wine would come in handy for dinner parties and other such events we never hosted or were invited to.

I was eager to find out if Dwayne knew anything about what his missus was getting up to, so Bob and I left early and went round to Dwayne's gaff hoping to catch a few words. We arrived at about 10am after getting held up by the school run mums in their SUVs, and then realised we hadn't had any breakfast yet. So we spent a considerable amount of time at Joe's Café stuffing our faces with a full English each. It took us a while to get moving after that so that's why we didn't arrive till late. We'd also stopped off to get a copy of *The Shyton Daily*. There was nothing on the front page about Ronnie and his escapades. We had expected a follow-up story yet there was nothing. The thirty thousand reasons did the trick.

So, we rang Dwayne's doorbell and Cheryl answered wearing a fairly see-through dressing gown. It was quite open and her ample cleavage was showing. She had black underwear beneath her gown and we both immediately forgot why we'd gone there.

**CHERYL:** Yes?

I was never normally a mumbler or a stutterer but I could barely get anything intelligible out, as my eyes remained transfixed on what I thought were 36B breasts. I could certainly see why Ronnie was risking it all to be with her.

**CHERYL:** Yes?

A few minutes had clearly passed and Cheryl was getting agitated. The morning air was making her nipples go erect, which only exacerbated the problem of us not looking at Cheryl in the eye or being able to properly answer her. Something had to be done as she grew impatient and our choppers grew ever longer and excited for a first bit of action since I was at the massage parlour and Bob was… well, who knew with Bob. So, as hard as it was, (and it was very hard), I closed my eyes then answered.

**STANLEY:** Is Dwayne about?
**CHERYL:** He's sleeping. Why are your eyes closed?
**STANLEY:** Saving energy. New technique. Didn't Dwayne just get

back from training?
**CHERYL:** That's why he's sleeping. He's tired. What do you want?
**STANLEY:** Did Dwayne see the newspaper yesterday?

And just like that the door was slammed in our faces. We could open our eyes again. Well, that didn't go well. Bob and I were heading away when he pointed at some of the rubbish bins. We went over and saw a ton of shredded newspapers.

**STANLEY:** She shredded every copy of *The Shyton Daily*! She'd better hope they've removed the story online. Hey Bob, do you think Dwayne's only ever awake now for training and matches? I never ever see him otherwise.

As we contemplated that, we got a tip off that something was going down at Tommy's place so we headed a few houses down to Tommy's mansion.

Tommy was just arriving home in his brand new Ford Mustang. It was blue with a white stripe down the middle. As he returned, and as we also witnessed, his humongous kids were being taken away by two suited and booted people. The two of them heaved and pulled Luke and Shannon towards a specially reinforced Ford Focus. Tommy jumped out and blocked them before they could go any further.

**TOMMY:** Who are youse? Gimme my kids back!

Tommy tried picking up Shannon but couldn't lift her either. Brenda was at the front door looking rather impassive, dressed in her dressing gown and smoking a cigarette. She ventured a bit further out onto the porch. I then noticed that she had a large bandage on her nose. How would she look a year down the line? One of the strangers spoke up.

**STRANGER 1:** We're from social services. We have a court order to remove these 'children'.

The social services woman even used air quotations when she said children. Could they have been dwarves all along?

**TOMMY:** What youse talking about?

**SOCIAL WORKER (formerly stranger 1):** Your children are medically obese!
**TOMMY:** Luke! Shannon! My tubsters!

The social workers dragged the hobbits to the waiting car. Tommy went over to Brenda. A barney was about to ensue.

**TOMMY:** Look what you've done, you crazy cow!

She slapped him full power across the face.

**BRENDA:** Stop calling me fat!

Brenda then disappeared inside. Tommy looked around and spotted us being nosey. He came for us.

**STANLEY:** Depart! Depart! He wants to head-butt us!

We managed to flee the scene before any head-butting could take place. A lucky escape.

Extract from Bombalbo's blog, Food with Bombalbo…
*'I don't know why but club has ordered me to join a fat camp. I tell them, this is not fat, this is well-fed man with the tastiest flesh ever. I go to Fat Camp but I sneak in lots of fabulous treats like the deep fried Mars bar from Shyton, as well as tasty Brazilian treats like pao de queijo (cheese bread balls), brigadeiro (chocolate treats) and bolinho de chuva (yummy donuts)… I must stop writing. Saliva on keyboard. But, I try lose weight and maybe eating Brazilian treats I succeed.'*

<u>**5<sup>th</sup> February, 2014**</u>

The next day I went looking for Tommy. Brenda had called me and through slurred speech and Botoxed lips had managed to say that Tommy had been gone all night. I searched high and low for Tommy, then went to the one place I knew he would be, Shyton Hills, or to be specific 'Screw Spot', the very place where Tommy's first born child was conceived. I was not wrong as I went over to Tommy who was sat perched on the edge, overlooking the smog of Shyton.

I plopped down beside him, continuing to record everything as was my duty as a documentarian with Danish ancestry. Tommy didn't look like a happy chappy.

**TOMMY:** They took me kids.
**STANLEY:** Yep.
**TOMMY:** My kids. I might not be world's greatest dad or even Shyton's greatest dad but I love them kiddies.
**STANLEY:** So you've got to fight to get them back.
**TOMMY:** I can't get my head round what that cow did.
**STANLEY:** I'm sure it's all the medication she's on.
**TOMMY:** She didn't give two shits, Stan. She's a monster.

It was hard to argue that point. She looked like one too.

**STANLEY:** But I think now's the time to focus your energy on getting your kids back, as well as trying to get Shyton's season back on track.

I had £25 on Shyton United finishing in the top four so it was bloody imperative that Tommy played and played well.

**TOMMY:** My head's not in it.
**STANLEY:** So that's it? You're giving up?
**TOMMY:** What's the point? My wife's nuttier than a bag of KP and has less love in her than Cersei from *'Game of Thrones'*. Least Cersei loved her kids! My kids are gone and Shyton United is run by muppets with a bunch of shitty muppets in the team.

The bugger had a point.

**STANLEY:** Didn't know you liked *'Game of Thrones'*.
**TOMMY:** Yeah, I like that Jon Snow.

I'd got him.

**STANLEY:** Would Jon Snow give up?
**TOMMY:** I'm not Jon Snow.
**STANLEY:** No, you're Tommy Gunn. Hardest nut in the league. You've injured more players this season than even Ryan Shawcross.
**TOMMY:** That's right.

Tommy's chin rose up. I could see the passion and violence re-emerge in his eyes.

**STANLEY:** Jon Snow wouldn't take it lying down. He'd fight, he'd fight all of them.
**TOMMY:** Yeah! I'm getting my kids back!
**STANLEY:** And you'll make Shyton win again and finish in the top four?
**TOMMY:** And yeah! Shyton gonna win!

Tommy went raging back to his car and sped off. He got a ticket for speeding but he didn't give a flying fugu. Maybe my bet was going to pay off after all.

Outside of Creek Alley Stadium, a most unusual event was occurring. I had heard about this rumour for a quite a few weeks but I just put it down as that, a rumour. It was sort of along the lines of Michael Jackson sleeping in an oxygen chamber, there being plans to put a Michael Jackson statue outside of Craven Cottage, and Michael Jackson having had plastic surgery – hogwash. However, to my surprise when arriving at Creek Alley, I saw that many local dignitaries as well as the press had gathered for an unveiling. An unveiling of what? The unveiling of a new statue and you wouldn't be surprised to hear who the statue was of. I'd advise having a bucket on hand in case you felt that vomiting might be imminent.

Maury, Alexander (not dressed as a bunny this time) and Oren were on a podium in front of the 10-foot high statue, which was underneath a white sheet.

**MAURY:** I have the great honour to officially unveil this statue in honour of the man who has rescued our club from the brink…

Rescued this club from Maury Git'a!

**MAURY:** This man, this man with a heart of gold, this man that has done so much for this club, for me…

For your bank account…

**MAURY:** The very humble, the rabbit loving, rabbit caring, rabbit breeding, rabbit wearing, rabbit eating, Mr Alexander Kovich.

The stern-looking Alexander Kovich pulled a string and unveiled a bronze statue of Alexander, looking stern yet piggy-eyed and wearing a bloody bunny rabbit costume. The man was mental!

Alexander grunted his approval.

**MAURY:** I also have the pleasure of officially announcing a change of name for Creek Alley. From this day forth, it shall be known as 'The Cutesy-Wootsy Fluffy Bunny Stadium'.

I needed a bucket… and a shot of something - maybe a bullet.

Maury pressed a button, which revealed the sign bearing the new, sickening name. I was going to confront Maury there and then but I was seething. I'd had enough. I headed for the local and drowned my sorrows with a sherry and a pickled egg. I was then sick for two days.

It was time for a huge away game at everybody's second favourite club, Manchester United. United had been having a bad time of it of late, and trailed the top four by a fair few points. However, they were sure to break back into the top four with Division Two winning manager David Moyes at the helm.

The Theatre of Dreams was a magical place, much like the theatres in London's West End. Lots of great acting by the regular players, gourmet sandwiches served for the true loyal fans, encores (or Fergie time as it was known here) a given, and a history of prima donnas. It was truly a place favoured by those wishing for Manchester United to remain top of the tree.

Could Shyton United topple them and knock them off their perch? With Oren Goldman managing and Moyes in the opposing corner, the two clubs had two of the finest tacticians the game had ever seen.

Bombalbo was still away at fat camp, so it was up to Bombinho and Ricardo to lead the attack. Tommy was in the side despite his recent family problems, but after our little talk he was fired up and looked as though he was up for maiming a few players.

In fact it wasn't too long into the action when a United player rather callously mistimed his tackle on Tommy, causing Tommy some considerable discomfort. However, Tommy, being the warrior that he was, got back to his feet and glared at the United man who had been laughing at Tommy. He'd regret that. A few minutes later, he did regret it as Tommy went through the United player like a hot knife through butter.

**TOMMY:** Take that, you cunt!

The referee deemed the challenge tough but fair, inexplicably. The United man was carried off on a stretcher and was never to be seen or heard from again. The match finished 1-1. Shyton United had now gone 4 games without a win and had plummeted to 10<sup>th</sup> in the league.

After the match I caught up with Tommy to ask him to explain himself.

**TOMMY:** He shouldn't have laughed, should he? I have no remorse. What goes around comes around, and for me, it's an eye for an eye.
**STANLEY:** An eye for an eye and the world will soon be blind.
**TOMMY:** Fuck off.

Tommy pushed me away. I grabbed a quick word with Oren Goldman.

**STANLEY:** Oren Goldman, any comment on the tackle by Tommy? The injury looks incredibly serious, maybe career threatening.
**OREN:** I assure you, Tommy is not that type of player.
**STANLEY:** No, no, I think he is that type of player whatever that type of player is.
**OREN:** No, he's not that type of player. He's a good boy.

Tommy then came charging up to Oren and dragged him away.

**TOMMY:** Hurry up, we's waiting for youse. I got a fucking meeting to get my kids back after this. Nothing's gonna stop me!

I was with K-Y as he returned home. He was carrying a bunch of artificial flowers. Why he couldn't fork out for real ones I had no idea.

**K-Y:** These will last longer. I'm hoping that these will brighten the mood.

We arrived outside his front door. It was drizzling and the air was cool. It matched the pain and feelings within him, I sensed.

**STANLEY:** So what happened, K-Y?

K-Y turned to me with a solemn expression plastered across his face. You couldn't help but feel touched and feel pity for him.

**K-Y:** Our application to adopt a kid was turned down.

We entered his house. He threw his jacket onto the sofa.

**K-Y:** Honey? Babes?

We followed him into the kitchen. There was a note on the kitchen table. K-Y picked it up with dread etched on his face.

**K-Y:** They've left us.

The flowers suddenly drooped, as did K-Y's face. Had he bought clown flowers?

**STANLEY:** Magic drooping flowers?
**K-Y:** Yes, got them from the magic shop in the high street.

This was getting depressing, so we left K-Y alone with his loneliness and suicidal thoughts, and headed home. An hour later we got a tip-off that K-Y was at Rainbow Bridge. We sped along in the Bugmobile to the bridge and sure enough, saw a depressed and alone K-Y sitting on the edge of the railing of the bridge. This was becoming an increasingly popular hangout in Shyton, with it overlooking a dual carriageway; a dual carriageway that offered two inviting escape routes out of Shyton. I had taken the same route many years ago.

K-Y leaned further forward, keys in hand.

Bob and I got out of the Bugmobile and approached. Nobody else was about, except a passer-by who hid behind a tree. Maybe he was the tip-off. I called out to K-Y.

**STANLEY:** Don't do it, K-Y.
**K-Y:** Why not? Lost everything, even my place in the team.
**STANLEY:** Maybe you should talk to someone. C'mon, get down lad.

K-Y threw his car keys in the air...

**STANLEY:** Don't!

K-Y caught his car keys. Surprising.

**K-Y:** What? Safe as houses with these hands.

K-Y gazed at his hands then dropped his car keys, which hit the windscreen of an oncoming car. The car swerved and crashed into the side of another car, causing a pileup of old bangers. There was carnage and potatoes everywhere. A lorry carrying potatoes had been involved too.

K-Y stared at me and I stared back. He climbed down then fled. I hopped back into the Bugmobile and was away quicker than you could say baked.

Liverpool were the visitors to Creek Alley Stadium this time, and it was set up for a cracking game. Liverpool had had an incredible season so far and were flying high, playing the most entertaining football seen for a long time. Though Oren Goldman had been manager for a couple of weeks, the football on display hadn't changed that much and the influence of Luis Jalapeno was still very much felt throughout—in the style they played and the way they dived, feigned injuries and so forth, wasting time at every opportunity. This game really did represent a true contrast in styles – Liverpool's fast-flowing attacking gung-ho style to Shyton's 'defend at all costs and who gives a shit if we score a goal' style. What was going to happen in this contest between the two surprise heavyweights of the 2013-2014 season?

Bombalbo once again didn't feature because he was at the fat camp, and, by all reports had gained weight. We'd visit him in the following days. Therefore, it was pretty much the same team with Jay Patel at the back and flying around in goal like a juiced-up dragonfly.

The match was underway and Shyton United again carried out their usual appalling tricks. Dwayne 'Suspect' Ford asked the Liverpool players if they knew where their WAGs were and maybe they should install their very own trackers (pretty sure that Dwayne had a financial interest in the company behind those Cheryl trackers); Tommy Gunn scythed down every opposing player he could; Ricardo dived but wasn't rewarded with a single free-kick or penalty; Ronnie Morrison got the home addresses of all the Liverpool players and management as well as their schedules for the upcoming week; and so on. Still, the standout player once more was Jay Patel who managed to repel almost every shot that came his way from this rampant Liverpool side… every shot but the three goals he conceded. Shyton United 0 Liverpool 3.

**STANLEY:** Oren, disappointing result and that's now 5 games without a win. Can you turn it around?
**OREN:** I believe so.
**STANLEY:** You sound confident. Liverpool are in serious form at the moment and have surprised many this season.
**OREN:** Yes, Liverpool are a very good team and will win many games. They have a very good manager in Brendan Rodgers who

makes his team play nice football. I hope Mr Kovich's team can also play nice football that entertains Mr Kovich.

**STANLEY:** Do you think Liverpool will win the league and not slip up?

**OREN:** Yes, I would put my house on it. With Brendan Rodgers, they have a manager who knows which team to play and how to play. I believe he will leave no stone unturned in his quest for the title.

**STANLEY:** Turning to Shyton, apart from Jay Patel, it wasn't a very good performance.

**OREN:** I thought we were outstanding for most of the match except for the moments when Liverpool scored three goals.

Oren's mobile rang.

**OREN:** Mr Kovich… Yes, sir… right way, sir…

Oren then hurried away like an eager guinea pig. Shyton United were doomed with this double act. In the changing room the team were nattering amongst themselves. There was an air of defeat in the err… air. I was about to interview some of the players when Oren was almost thrown back into the changing room. His cheeks were red, as were his eyes. If I didn't know any better I'd say he'd been crying after getting a right rollicking from Kovich.

Oren coughed and tried to get the attention of the players. They all ignored him.

**OREN:** It is a very disappointing result and is not good enough.

Oren stamped his foot down, which was more Riverdance than Alex Ferguson. I suspected that Kovich was behind Oren's attempts to stamp his mark on this team.

**OREN:** Now, I am afraid, I must warn all of you, if you do not improve, I might be forced to maybe drop one of you.

A football boot went flying in Oren's direction and hit him on the head. He almost dropped, he swayed then he regained his composure and picked up the boot, cradling it like it was a precious artefact.

**OREN:** Somebody's boot came off. May I return it?

The team headed to the showers.

**OREN:** So, we are agreed that next time you will all play better?

Mystic got in Oren's face.

**BEN:** Grow some balls, you infidel!

Mystic twirled around, banging his cymbals, then he performed a Jedi knight pose.

Alexander, who I guessed had been listening outside, stormed in with Maury. The players stopped in their tracks and stared at Alexander's open mouth. In hushed tones and one by one in the sound of a choo-choo train, and as if it were a build up to an epic musical number:

**TOMMY:** He's going to speak.
**RONNIE:** He's going to speak.
**DWAYNE:** He's going to speak.
**K-Y:** He's going to speak.
**RICARDO:** He's going to speak.

Then in a rather surprising operatic voice, Li Bang sang,

**'MARKETING GOLD MINE':** He's going to say something!

Alexander had a shockingly thunderous voice for a man-rabbit (a mabbit?)
[Alexander spoke in Russian but I had it translated]
**ALEXANDER:** If you lazy pigs do not start playing well and win, I will use a nail gun on your scrotums and a sander on your helmets then make rabbits' droppings out of all of you!

Alexander pointed at all of them then left in a huff.

**RONNIE:** What did that commie say?
**'MARKETING GOLD MINE':** I did not say anything.

The team had gathered together at Shyton United's training ground for some quite expected news. It was Mystic who would break the news, with Oren standing timidly behind like a little boy lost in the woods. Who was the manager?

**BEN:** My happy little elves, Sao's been banned for nine months for again failing to attend a drug test.

Mystic's voice then took on a demonic tone. Had he suddenly been possessed? This guy was scary and it was no wonder that Bob had refused to be anywhere that Mystic was. This proved troublesome as Mystic was assistant manager of a team we were making a documentary of.

**BEN:** And he'll go straight to hell and burn and suffer insufferable...

Thankfully Tommy came to our rescue and head-butted Mystic, knocking him out. Oren scampered away on all fours like a puppy, and even made yelping noises like a hurt puppy might.

After hearing the completely unsurprising news, I went round to Sao's house. It was my first time visiting Sao at his home, as we could never locate it due to the confusing directions he'd always give us. It again proved difficult, as the directions he gave us sent us to numerous places around Shyton. Ordinarily I'd assume that the person doing that was trying to have me merked, but this being Sao and with him probably suffering from an undetectable form of Alzheimer's, I expected these problems and was much more tolerant and patient than usual.

I eventually found his place after contacting his mother, and arrived at a house that didn't quite look right. There were half-finished projects and renovations everywhere: A partially finished driveway, a garden lawn that had only been mowed a quarter of the way, tiling that was incomplete, holes in the ceiling, and a kitchen that had a phone in it upon a small round table, with various takeaway menus next to it.

Sao was poolside in his board shorts, drinking a glass of milk through a straw. He had an assortment of drinks on a table next to him and he was drinking from them randomly. I guessed he couldn't remember what he wanted to drink so he had a bit of everything; from a hot filter coffee to an iced tea, to a cola, an orange juice and something green.

**STANLEY:** What will you do now?
**SAO:** I'll carry on. Play footie.
**STANLEY:** You can't. You've been banned.
**SAO:** First I've heard of it. Doesn't mean I can't play for Shyton though, does it?
**STANLEY:** Well, it does. That's what a ban means.
**SAO:** I'll play somewhere else then, stupid.
**STANLEY:** It's international.
**SAO:** I'll go Spain. I'm cultured.
**STANLEY:** Just because you're an English defender who can pass the ball doesn't make you cultured, nor does it make you unique in Spain. It's common there. It's called being a footballer. Anyway, you can't play in Spain.
**SAO:** Barcelona will take me.
**STANLEY:** That's in Spain… for now.
**SAO:** PSG might take me.
**STANLEY:** Sao, the ban is in force across the world. You can't play football anywhere.
**SAO:** How about if I drop down a league to say, Everton.
**STANLEY:** Everton plays in the Premier League.
**SAO:** You sure? Didn't notice them.

I had long since mused as to why Sao was the way he was. I knew he had been raised in an orphanage, but I wasn't sure if something had occurred there that had made him so mentally damaged. He had a brain of a 30-something wrestler who had had an earlier career as an NFL player.

**STANLEY:** Sao, what do you remember of the orphanage?
**SAO:** What orphanage?

It was worse than I thought.

**STANLEY:** Your parents died when you were just a babe in arms. As

you had no other family, you were raised in a non-secular orphanage.
**SAO:** Sister Bernie never did nothing down there.

Crikey.

**STANLEY:** Bernie? Down where, Sao?

Poor blighter was now in tears.

**SAO:** Just 'cause she had a tache, and was nicknamed the 'Beer Guzzler' don't mean she was a bloke in nun's clothing.
**STANLEY:** She was a bloke?

Sao's memory had just gotten a whole lot better. Bugger wasn't so traumatised after all, or was he?

**SAO:** Who told you about her and her ruler?
**STANLEY:** Her ruler?
**SAO:** My oven!

Sao rushed into his house like he was running away from a fire.

**STANLEY:** You don't have an oven!

Poor sod. Seemed like that orphanage had really fucked him; literally. I was also worried about his health and safety. If he didn't die in some brutal fashion, then I was pretty sure he'd be the guy that would get others to die in that brutal fashion. He reminded me of the cartoon character Mr Magoo. I scampered off before anything bad happened to me, leaving him with his happy/sad/selective memories.

<u>**15<sup>th</sup> February, 2014**</u>

It had been a while since I had chatted with fellow Shyton United fan Joe Meek, so I popped off to the Fudge and Wrapper pub and got a round in as Joe hadn't gotten his dole money yet. By the way, if you fancied a cool, smooth tasting ale, then Shyton's ales were some of the best in the region, particularly Shyton Brown Ale Pulpy, Shyton Mild (had a nutty flavour) and Shyton IPA-DB (India Pale Ale - Delhi Belly). Shyton's ales were noted for their distinct brownish colour, pungent aroma, salty flavour and sour aftertaste that remained for days afterwards. This was probably due to the water which came from Shyton Spring, which was uncomfortably close to Shyton's sewage treatment plant, as well as Huge Jack's Film Studios.

We sipped our beers, the courtesy buckets by the side of the table in case we needed to spit out or vomit up the beer.

**JOE:** A great many fans are right unhappy with how things are going. Ticket prices are up and entertainment is down, even if we are doing well in the league for a team expected to be rock bottom. Having said that, form has been shite recently. Five games without a win? Knocked out of both cups? The way we're going, we'll be just above relegation zone and ready for the drop next season.
**STANLEY:** Sounds like you don't have confidence in Oren Goldman.
**JOE:** Do you have confidence in Oren Goldman? Man's a puppet for that rabbit we've got as an owner. And what the fuck is up with that? We're fudge packers, not rabbits!
**STANLEY:** So you want Oren out?
**JOE:** Amount of money we've spent on transfers last summer window and wages—which must be bleeding us dry—it's fucking necessary as fudge we get into Europe.

We'd better hope Maury's plan, if he had a plan, would work.

After spending the last couple of days compiling footage, sprucing-up audio, saving files and shredding tax documents, Bob and I decided to take a long overdue visit to Bombalbo at his fat camp. He had been ordered to go to fat camp by the club, and despite his initial reluctance had decided to give it a try when 12 armed and muscular security personnel broke into his house at 6am and dragged him out of bed, put him into a van then took him to fat camp.

The fat camp's motto was 'new mind, new body, new life, new lifetime membership only £429 a year'. The counsellors and experts at the fat camp weaned their clients, as they called them, off a variety of food vices and helped with their eating disorders. They made their clients eat healthy meals plus do a regular assortment of exercises to stimulate them physically and mentally, they as well coached them psychologically to get to the root cause of their clients' overeating. 9 out of 10 times their methods worked, it was a shame therefore when we caught up with Bombalbo in his room and saw no real difference.

**BOMBALBO:** I do not know why I am here.
**STANLEY:** Because you're fat?
**BOMBALBO:** In my country, people who look like me are not fat. We're respected.
**STANLEY:** You have to play Premier League football, but you can't if you have a frame better suited to sumo wrestling.
**BOMABLO:** Football is not just about speedy people. Football is vision, timing, touch. I don't need to be skinny, hating-food person. I can be me and still score lots of goals just like fatty Ronaldo, fatty Kaka, fatty everybody.
**STANLEY:** You've been here at the Shyton Fat Camp for a short while, and the counsellors have told me that in that time you've put on weight rather than lost it. How is that possible?
**BOMBALBO:** I am a, how you say, foodie? A gourmand, nobody gets between my food and me.

Bombalbo got out a tin of caviar and some blinis.

**STANLEY:** Is somebody aiding you? Smuggling in food?

Bombalbo eyed me suspiciously. He got up and headed backwards.

**BOMBALBO:** Why are you here?
**STANLEY:** I'm making a documentary.
**BOMBALBO:** Who sent you? The food is mine! I am Bombalbo and I will eat!

Bombalbo charged out. I contacted Maury who then contacted the fat camp who then contacted the security personnel who nabbed Bombalbo and took him home. The fat camp had been a failure. Shyton United would have to accept Bombalbo as he was.

I had been invited round for dinner at Ronnie's gaff. It was nice to get invited anywhere these days, as the players were getting more and more suspicious of me. Of course, I myself had been suspicious of Ronnie's motives at inviting me, as I was sure he'd try to flog me something.

We were at his dining table, where some fancy bone china was laid out. There were boxes of crockery to the side. How much was this going to cost me?

**RONNIE:** See you got your eyes on the china.

I should wear sunglasses whenever I met with Ronnie.

**STANLEY:** Yes, very nice.

Well, what else was I going to say?

**RONNIE:** I got a load in, dirt cheap.

He took out a case with a whole dinner service.

**RONNIE:** Can let you have this for two score.

His mobile rang, thank god!

**RONNIE:** Yeah Dad? … Yeah, this weekend's pukka. Big cup game in London. Tell Ma to get ready.

Ronnie hung up.

**STANLEY:** What was that about? Something exciting?
**RONNIE:** Never you mind, son.

There was the sound of footsteps coming down the stairs, we both turned. The feet were at the end of some nicely-waxed, smooth, golden, long naked legs… Cheryl's legs. Before I saw what the legs were at the end of, Ronnie coughed.

**RONNIE:** Company, filming, nosey-parker…

I was not a nosey-parker! Respected documentarian more like! The feet did an about turn and ran upstairs.

**STANLEY:** Who was that?
**RONNIE:** Ma.
**STANLEY:** Your mother? Your mother's got sexy legs.

Ronnie then grabbed me by the throat.

**RONNIE:** Why you looking at ma's legs? You some kind of perv?

Through strained gasps I managed to eek out,

**STANLEY:** Sorry, I know that they're not your mother's legs. They looked familiar.

His grip tightened.

**RONNIE:** You don't look at Cheryl's legs neither! Now you cough up forty quid, take your dinner service set and clear off.

He let me go and I coughed up the forty pounds. He handed me the case containing the dinner service set.

**RONNIE:** Want a bag?
**STANLEY:** Sure.

He bagged it up for me.

**RONNIE:** Alright, come again tomorrow and I'll have some spanking new crystal glasses in. For you mate, I'll do a special price. Visit **www.RonniesBargains.com** for the best deals. Now fuck off, you perv.

He slammed the door in my face. I wasn't liking him at all.

<u>**21<sup>st</sup> February, 2014**</u>

There was a big game this weekend, and to get the players up for it Oren Goldman's master made the decision for his team to stay overnight in the glamour town of West Bromwich. Shyton United hadn't won for quite a few games, so perhaps this get-together would do them the world of good.

At the plush five-star Hilton hotel in the heart of downtown West Bromwich, I caught up with Oren in the lobby.

**OREN:** Mr Rabbit said we needed to do something so he said I should take them away from Shyton and maybe they can bond.
**STANLEY:** Can they be trusted to behave?
**OREN:** They are good boys.

Bob and I went nosing around down the corridors of the Hilton, with its various portraits of local West Bromwich Albion hero Bryan Robson adorning the walls. We reached one of the suites, where loud noises and groans were coming from. It was Sonny Jackson's suite.

**SONNY:** That's it, suck it bitch.
**ANGRY FEMALE:** What'd you call me?
**SONNY:** Nothing, bitch.
**ANGRY FEMALE:** Don't you be calling me no bitch.
**SONNY:** I ain't calling you bitch, bitch.
**ANGRY FEMALE:** You just called me bitch then, you wanker.
**SONNY:** Don't be calling me a wanker, bitch. Now just get down and suck it, bitch.
**ANGRY FEMALE:** Suck what? There's nothing there, little bitch.
**SONNY:** Bitch, don't be cussing my dick.
**ANGRY FEMALE:** I've seen more meat in a vegetarian restaurant, you little pussy bitch.

There was some loud sobbing. Sonny was crying!

**ANGRY FEMALE:** Oh what's wrong? Did mummy hurt little bitch's feelings?
**SONNY:** I just wanted you to suck my dick, bitch. Why you gotta be hating?

**ANGRY FEMALE:** Suck your dick? And take away your mummy's job?

Sonny was now wailing.

**ANGRY FEMALE:** Oh stop your crying, you big baby bitch.

There was a loud slap.

**SONNY:** My mummy used to beat me, don't go beating Sonny. Don't beat sonny, don't beat baby. Nobody puts Sonny in the corner.
**ANGRY FEMALE:** She beat her little bitch because he had a small dick? Did you wish for a big dick and instead you became a big dick?

Somebody was coming to the door then it swung open and Sonny ran out, a bright red hand mark on his cheek. The sultry voluptuous black female who'd put Sonny in his place came chasing after him. She was in some sexy black lingerie that made my chipolata stand to attention. I loved a dominant woman.

**ANGRY FEMALE:** Where you going, bitch? That's what you get for mistreating women! If you can dish it out, you can take it, now get your arse back here.

Sonny cowered in a corner, with the rather frightening woman advancing on him like a carnivorous animal about to capture its defenceless prey. She grabbed him by the ear then dragged him back to the room. Reminded me of my old headmistress. She used to give me the cane everyday then sneak off to the ladies afterwards.

**ANGRY FEMALE:** I'm going to teach this bitch a lesson.

The door slammed shut and we heard screams. Sonny's screams. That boy was going to get it. We didn't stick around.

Here was the match against the mighty West Bromwich Albion, a team that struck fear into the opposition and was feared the world over. Albion – a word that hardly any football fan knew the meaning of. Due to the previous night's beatings, Sonny was considered psychologically unfit for the match, and the pussy chose to remain at the hotel, cowering in the shower wasting water.

It was a capacity crowd in this charming part of the Midlands and yet again, Shyton played in a very lethargic manner. Bombinho gave the ball away repeatedly, Bombalbo failed to get on the end of anything, and Ricardo spent more time diving and failing to win anything. It was only Tommy who seemed to have any real drive or motivation to win the match. He had real Shyton grit inside him.

Second half and Tommy won the ball back with a nasty-looking challenge and passed it to Li Bang who was easily dispossessed. The ball was hoofed forward and a West Brom striker had a clear chance at goal. But for the heroics of a pumped up Jay Patel, he would've made it 1-0 to West Brom. Tommy had had enough.

**TOMMY:** What's wrong with you bastards?
**RICARDO:** Relax, we're just playing a stupid small team. Ricardo will do something magical and win game.
**TOMMY:** Small team? They've been around for ages. They're a big club, third biggest in the area! And for your information Ricardo, we ain't won a fucking game all month.
**RICARDO:** Stop worrying, you'll get wrinkles.

Then, in a moment reminiscent of Vinnie Jones and Paul Gascoigne, Tommy discreetly grabbed hold of Ricardo's crown jewels and gave a not so gentle tug.

**TOMMY:** Listen princess, either you start playing well or I'm going to make you my bitch for the rest of the season.

Ricardo nodded and soon was playing the best football he'd played since his last club. The message from Tommy soon got round the team and they all began playing much, much better. Oren Goldman was standing proud on the touchline like he'd just pulled off a masterstroke.

**OREN:** The Oren magic has worked again.
**STANLEY:** You didn't do anything.
**BEN:** No, but we all know who did. The great Bumba in the sky.

Mystic got down on his knees and started worshipping the mythological African god, Bumba.

With Tommy leading the charge and even Bombinho putting in a shift, Shyton scored three goals without reply, one of which was a real peach of a goal – Tommy had skipped past one challenge then played it out wide to Ricardo, who whipped in a cross. Ronnie headed it down to Tommy who struck a thunderous shot, but the shot was going wide until it cannoned off Bombalbo's gut and almost burst the net. Priceless.

Shyton United finally got their long overdue win. Could they make those Champions League places yet?

In the changing room while all the players and management celebrated, Ronnie was in a corner, speaking in hushed tones on his mobile. Alexander then arrived, with Maury playing the Russian national anthem on an iPhone.

[Again I was kind enough to get it translated from Russian]
**ALEXANDER:** Better.

Alexander Kovich left. Articulate chap.

The team, and everybody associated with the team, then made the return trip to Shyton. Ricardo was still a bit fearful of Tommy wanting to turn his gonads into little boxing speed bags, so I accompanied him home to make sure he was safe. As we returned, Ricardo had an almighty shock. Ricardo's house had been ransacked. All his paintings were gone, as were the statues depicting him in Ancient Greece Olympian style poses.

**RICARDO:** Ricardo's beautiful paintings!

Ricardo collapsed to the floor and wept.

**RICARDO:** Why!

Ricardo threw his hands up in the air. I doubted the paintings of him were worth much.

**RICARDO:** That bastard will pay!
**STANLEY:** Who?
**RICARDO:** Tommy!
**STANLEY:** You think Tommy did this? I hardly think Tommy would stoop so low… plus he was playing a football match today, with you!
**RICARDO:** You saw how he touched Ricardo's precious balls. Ricardo shall get him back.

It took me a good few hours to convince Ricardo that Tommy wasn't behind the mysterious disappearance of his artwork. However, it begged the questions – who was, and were there more burglaries?

Translated from the Twitter account of @BombinhoJuice: *'My women! Who stole my women! There'll be hell to pay! #BombinhoJuiceHalfPrice'*

It wasn't just Ricardo whose house was burgled, there were a whole spate of burglaries the previous day while Shyton United played away to West Bromwich Albion. It was looking quite suspicious and the players and the club itself were demanding answers and expecting Shyton's police force to capture the culprits immediately. Unfortunately, Shyton's police department were about as good as South Yorkshire Police so nobody was holding out too much hope. However, most had deduced that a team of criminals must've been behind it, as so many houses had been burgled, and due to the victims involved, maybe it had been an inside job.

Bob and I went to Maury's new house, (a castle with its own moat and drawbridge!) to get some answers from the man himself.
We were welcomed by Maury's faithful butler and shown into the magnificent 16th century castle. Maury was at his huge oak dining table, the kind you'd imagine at a castle. He was at the head of the table, ripping off a chicken leg then tearing off the succulent meat with his teeth. All he needed was a crown and a ceremonial robe to look like Brian Blessed.

**STANLEY:** Nice moat.
**MAURY:** There's salmon in that moat.
**STANLEY:** You have salmon in your moat?
**MAURY:** No, just a salmon. Well bits of a salmon, actually. I didn't like the salmon en croute and I threw it in the moat. No idea what the chef was thinking, I mean it's not the 1980s!
**STANLEY:** Were you one of the victims of the break-ins over the weekend?
**MAURY:** No, I have a moat.

The constant mentioning of his moat was starting to grind my gears, even if I had brought it up.

**STANLEY:** Could you tell me what's being done to protect the players? Not many players would fancy a transfer to Shyton United if it were deemed too dangerous for their Maseratis.
**MAURY:** Trust me, everything is being done to protect our players and staff from any further events. For example, every player's house

will have a moat built around it.
**STANLEY:** Moats are your solution?

Maury tucked into some more chicken. I liked chicken, though I was normally a fish man due to my Danish fisherman ancestry.

**MAURY:** Was I burgled? Burglars are like rabbits, they don't like to get wet. No criminal was getting into my home because of my moat.
**STANLEY:** Are you behind the new moating company?
**MAURY:** Yes, M.P.C. **www.MoatsPreventCrime.com**. Sales are up 100%! All the players will have them.
**STANLEY:** Which the club will pay for?
**MAURY:** Yes, the club will pay for the moats because we're a caring club.
**STANLEY:** And the money will go into your moat company?
**MAURY:** We're the only moat company in town.
**STANLEY:** Where were you during Shyton's game away to West Brom?
**MAURY:** I have a pedalo for my moat. Want James to take you around?
**STANLEY:** James? I thought you were calling him Jeeves.
**MAURY:** I prefer James, to Jeeves. And James can really speed round that moat.

Was he a new butler or not?

**STANLEY:** Since Alexander Kovich's takeover, many peculiar things have happened. Purely coincidental?
**MAURY:** Listen, this town honoured him with a statue and insisted the stadium be named after him.
**STANLEY:** My sources tell me that he instigated both those events.
**MAURY:** A man, nay, a god like him, who came from nothing and built up a £5.5bn fortune, deserves everything and more. And what the top man deserves, the man helping the top man deserves too.
**STANLEY:** That would be you?
**MAURY:** Right. James!

James came in within a second.

**JAMES:** Yes sir?

**MAURY:** Take Stanley around the moat on the pedalo. He's dying for a go.
**STANLEY:** No, I'm quite fine.
**MAURY:** Go, have fun! I love my moat.

Before I knew it, I was being pulled away and taken to the gate to get onto the pedalo. We went around about twenty times before I started crying and begging to go home. I fucking hate moats.

<u>**24<sup>th</sup> February, 2014**</u>

In light of the robberies, those bumbling police officers at Shyton police station had decided to interview Dwayne and Cheryl. Quite why they elected to interview them I had no idea. My cousin just happened to be a detective at that particular station and so I managed to get ringside seats for when Cheryl and Dwayne were interviewed.

DI Bud Davis was an ageing detective (not my cousin) who smoked one too many cigarettes, drank one too many Scotch's, had had one too many Gregg's iced buns, and modelled himself after Lewis Collins from the TV show *'The Professionals'*. He eyed Dwayne suspiciously, as Dwayne did the same to him.

**DI DAVIS:** What you staring at?
**DWAYNE:** What are *you* staring at?

DI Davis went around the other end of the table opposite Dwayne and Cheryl.

**DI DAVIS:** Did you notice anything unusual in the area over the weekend, Mrs Ford?
**DWAYNE:** Why you looking at my woman?
**DI DAVIS:** Because I'm speaking to her.
**DWAYNE:** You can speak to her and not look.
**DI DAVIS:** Is he always like this?

DI Davis averted his gaze.

**DI DAVIS:** Better? Or do you want me to go and get a blindfold?
**DWAYNE:** No need. Got one here.

Dwayne tossed over a blindfold he'd gotten from his pocket. DI Davis didn't take it and instead flicked through a report sheet on his clipboard.

**DI DAVIS:** Mrs Ford?
**CHERYL:** I didn't notice anything unusual.
**DI DAVIS:** In the report, Mr Ford, you've listed a number of items as having been taken, most of it surveillance equipment. Care to explain?

**DWAYNE:** Hobby of mine.
**DI DAVIS:** There was enough hi-tech equipment to fit out GCHQ!
**DWAYNE:** Anything wrong with that?
**DI DAVIS:** Why do you need so much?
**DWAYNE:** Can't trust anybody nowadays… and so it's been proved.
**DI DAVIS:** What do you need to surveil?

DI Davis gave Cheryl an 'is this guy for real?' look. Cheryl had the kind of legs that could wrap themselves around you and help bring home the bacon.

**DWAYNE:** You looking at my woman again?
**DI DAVIS:** No need to answer my question. Mrs Ford, you were home at the time of the burglary?
**CHERYL:** Yes.
**DI DAVIS:** You didn't see or notice anything?
**CHERYL:** I was having a nap.
**DI DAVIS:** They were that quiet?
**CHERYL:** I'm a deep sleeper.
**DWAYNE:** She is. Our bed's so comfy, man when I'm asleep I'm always out for the count. Nothing can wake me.
**DI DAVIS:** They only stole your surveillance equipment, right?
**DWAYNE:** Right.
**DI DAVIS:** Nothing else?
**DWAYNE:** Nope.
**DI DAVIS:** Jewellery? TVs?
**DWAYNE:** Just the surveillance stuff.
**DI DAVIS:** OK, I'll be in touch. Here's my number.
**DWAYNE:** Why are you giving us your number?

Dwayne shot up.

**DWAYNE:** Oh, I know your game. You're after my missus. Stick your number. Cheryl, we're going.

And with that, Dwayne led Cheryl out of the police station while DI Davis scratched his head and probably wondered what the hell just happened.

With the culprits of the Shyton United burglaries still at large and as likely to be caught as the South Yorkshire Police were likely to do the right thing, everybody in Shyton was on edge. And things were about to get edgier when I turned on my computer that morning and read on the BBC News website that beloved Shyton
United owner, Alexander Kovich had been killed in a car bomb attack outside his palatial home. Apparently, when he was blown up, there was blood, guts and rabbit fluff all over the place. The police had many suspects, and a lot on their plate. I didn't doubt that they'd need to call in extra police to help with the workload, I just hoped that they didn't ask for help from the South Yorkshire Police.

I made my usual trip to Maury's, hoping for some answers and expecting none. Under Maury's stewardship the club had gone through four owners since Sid Chesterton sold the club. Their last owner had been killed in Shyton, most of the team had had their houses burgled, and let's not forget the mysterious death of Shinji Takamoto. The way the club was being run, it was getting less and less appealing for any prospective transfer target. It wouldn't be long before players would prefer to play for Port Vale rather than Shyton United.

Maury was smoking a big, fat Cuban as I interviewed him in his own private massage parlour, where a young Thai man was massaging Maury's calloused feet. Maury only wore a towel around his waist and he had Sherwood Forest sprouting from his chest. It would be a quick interview.

**MAURY:** Obviously, our thoughts are with Alexander's family and friends at this tragic time. Shocking tragedy. Ooh, yeah that's good, Boon-Mee. We're all very upset about the untimely passing of Mr Kovich... Mm, pull that toe, Boon.

Maury didn't seem upset at all. And where the hell did Maury get Boon-Mee from?

**MAURY:** I can confirm that the club is up for sale. As usual, I'll be conducting a
thorough search for a new, reliable owner to steer this magnificent

ship. You so good, Boon-Mee.
**STANLEY:** Your record in finding reliable owners has been less than stellar so far.
**MAURY:** What was that?

Maury was very distracted. I had to get through this interview.

**STANLEY:** You don't have a good track record of finding suitable custodians for this great club.
**MAURY:** When I joined, we were the lowest of the low, scum of the earth and now look. Premier League, in the top ten, and Champions League qualification still within reach.
**STANLEY:** You've spent a lot trying to secure Champions League football. To balance the books you'll have to qualify for it every season. You're playing with the future of this club!
**MAURY:** You have to speculate to accumulate.
**STANLEY:** Aren't you worried that the bubble might burst? What if you don't qualify for the Champions League?
**MAURY:** No, not at all worried; as we don't live in a bubble. However, to allay the fans' fears, I myself have taken the lead and slashed my annual salary by 5%!
**STANLEY:** Last month you increased your salary by 700%.
**MAURY:** So 5% is a lot then, isn't it?

Talking to Maury was hurting my brain. I was pretty sure that each time I interviewed him I lost a few more brain cells. I left him alone with his Thai boy, who for some reason had a worried 'get me out of here' facial expression.

Bob and I had had a heavy night. We'd been up all night drinking, sharing stories and our worries about the future. We were both passionate Shyton United fans but we could only watch as our team went down a particularly dark and lonely alley that it hadn't been down before. Joe Meek had been with us, and so had some of his mates who were also Shyton United fans, and all expressed their worries that maybe things wouldn't be okay come the end of the season. It might not be this season that everything would go to shit, but next season was already giving fans nightmares. Who was Maury going to find to be the new owner of Shyton United? Who would remain with the team if Shyton United were without European football? A lot of the players that signed did so expecting to be in Europe next season, so we were sure that they all had clauses enabling them to leave if Shyton United didn't qualify. That would decimate the squad and leave us with a team consisting of K-Y, Jay Patel, and Li Bang. Hardly anything.

You would have noticed that one player was omitted from that tiny list. Yes, Tommy Gunn. Why hadn't I mentioned him? Well, the following morning once I had woken up with my head throbbing, and discovered that I was in a rather embarrassing position on the sofa with my head nestled on something else that was throbbing and belonged to Bob, we learned of wild rumours circulating that Tommy would be off to City in the summer. I tried making numerous calls to Tommy's house but I guessed his phone was off the hook. I then tried his mobile and wondered why I'd even tried his house as it was 2014 and who the heck still used landlines, but his mobile went straight to voicemail.

After a period of awkwardness in which Bob and I both agreed to never speak of that throbbing incident again, and once I'd wiped away something sticky from the side of my mouth, we went round to Tommy's place. We banged on the door. Tommy shouted from within.

**TOMMY:** Go away!
**STANLEY:** It's Stanley and Bob.
**TOMMY:** You sure? You're not the press?
**STANLEY:** No, we're the documentarians that have been following you around ever since the tail end of last season. We played crazy golf together.

**TOMMY:** You're not fans of Shyton?
**STANLEY:** Well, you know we're both fans of Shyton.
**TOMMY:** So you're not coming in.

I wasn't sure of the statistic about how much truth could be in a rumour, but I was a bit irked that it could be true and the Judas inside might well be off to City. Bob was a fair bit more enraged and did pack some heat in the form of a Swiss army knife. However, we were both rational men and wouldn't attempt anything if it all proved to be untrue.

**STANLEY:** Tommy, let us in!
**TOMMY:** Go away!

It was futile. Would've been nice to have put the rumour to bed, instead we'd have to keep one hand on our Swiss army knife and one eye on Tommy's back.
**1ˢᵗ March, 2014**

Chelsea were the visitors to Creek Alley Stadium. Chelsea were a team that Shyton United looked up to, certainly Maury did.

**MAURY:** Yes, I think Chelsea are the benchmark. If there's one team we'd like to emulate and become like, it's Chelsea. If we were like Chelsea we'd be able to sign anybody we want! As soon as we rejuvenate this town, get rid of the pollution, get rid of the current population, build better homes, have more boutique shops, improve education, get better weather, and finally, relocate Shyton to south west London then I feel it's definitely achievable.
**STANLEY:** Move Shyton?
**MAURY:** MK Dons did it.
**STANLEY:** Nobody cares about MK Dons anymore.

Shyton United were out on the pitch warming up. Tommy's name was read out over the PA system and was roundly booed by the Shyton fans.

**TOMMY:** I'll kill all of you!

Rumours continued to persist that Tommy Gunn would be sold in the summer to fierce rivals City. Despite the hatred and the animosity in the air between the Fudge Packers and Tommy Gunn, Tommy did not half put in a shift. Backed by the raging Jay Patel in goal…

**JAY:** C'mon, you bastards! Attack those sisterfuckers…

Just one of many streams of insults he slung his teammates', and the opposing team's, way. He was frightening.

With Tommy in irresistible form and driving his teammates on, and Chelsea not up for a dreary, drizzle-filled day in this part of northern England, it wasn't too much of a shocker when Shyton United emerged as 2-0 winners. Up the Fudge!

The downside to the victory, first time Shyton had secured consecutive wins since lord knows when, was that Oren was looking more and more like a capable manager. It was blatantly obvious that Tommy was the real driving force behind the upturn in results and that Oren had merely gotten lucky—like some other manager that season. It was something of a conundrum. Of course you wanted Shyton to win but in the long term, would it be better for them to lose a few now so that they could get rid of Oren Goldman and install a better manager who'd actually transform Shyton United? A dilemma if ever there was one.

Despite being the hero against the bankers of Chelsea, Tommy was still riled about being yelled at and called 'traitor', 'Judas' and 'gobshite' by the Fudge Packers. He invited me out for a drink at the local Fudge and Wrapper pub. He needed to unwind with a swift half and perhaps have a bit of a moan. Having a whinge now and again to get things off your chest was much better than keeping it all bottled up inside. Tommy was the kind of fella who'd bottle it up and only release it by head-butting something or someone. You had to wonder how he hadn't suffered serious brain damage yet.

The pub was half full with locals who called The Fudge and Wrapper their second home, and who the publican called leeches. Tommy and I approached the hefty, moustachioed barman with a belly any darts player would've been proud of.

**TOMMY:** Two halves?

Had to admire Tommy's professionalism and just sticking to a half of mild. Other footballers might have had a pint, not Tommy though.

**BARMAN:** We don't serve your sort in here.

That was directed at Tommy, not me. Documentarians with Danish ancestry were welcome everywhere. The rage built up inside Tommy like a house being flooded.

**TOMMY:** What?
Joe, dressed as ever in his Shyton United top, came over carrying a pint of Shyton's finest.

**JOE:** Get out, City scum!
**TOMMY:** I ain't going to City.

Joe slapped a *'Shyton Daily'* newspaper against Tommy's chest. Its headline: 'Gunn shooting off to City!' Oh dear. I had been in two minds whether to accept the Judas's invitation and I certainly didn't wish to be tainted by the same brush. Now I was the one that was like a house being slowly flooded.

**TOMMY:** That ain't true.

Or was it?

**JOE:** City scum!
**BARFLIES:** City scum!

The barman, Joe and the barflies tossed pork scratchings at Tommy and me. Great.

**STANLEY:** I'm not joining City, he is!

The pork scratchings were no longer directed at me.

**TOMMY:** I'll get all of youse.

Tommy made a hasty exit, head-butting the door open to leave. The door was a thick, old wooden door and not that moveable when using one's head. Tommy knocked himself out and collapsed to the ground.

**STANLEY:** Could somebody help me carry him to his car?

I drove Tommy to the hospital where he was revived, then I drove him home. He was fuming about what had happened at the pub and was fuming about the door.

**TOMMY:** I'm going to get that door.
**STANLEY:** You can't win, Tommy. It's a door!

Tommy stank of pork scratchings and did his best to rid himself by having a bubble bath and using a loafer to scrub himself clean.

**TOMMY:** Bloody pork scratchings! I win them the game, then they hurl fucking pork scratchings at me. Maybe I should join City, then they'll regret it.
**STANLEY:** The Shyton fans threw pork scratchings at you because they're so angry that you might leave. Their anger shows how much they want you to stay. The Fudge Packers love you.
**TOMMY:** I'm getting death threats! What kind of fans do that to their

hometown hero who's been with the club since he was a kid? Yeah, they love me!

Tommy's mobile rang.

**TOMMY:** Yeah? … I'm not joining them! Fuck off!

Tommy hung up his mobile then threw it and it landed with a plop into his toilet. Good throw.

**TOMMY:** Bollocks!

Brenda came in and, my word, I was speechless. To be honest, it took me a wee while before I realised it was Brenda. She looked… stunning! She was slim, busty and had the kind of body your mates would betray you for. Except, she was more Barbie than was natural – she'd need an umbrella if the sun came out. Tommy stared at me and I stared at Tommy. Her appearance was an obvious shock to him as well.

**TOMMY:** Bloody hell! I thought you were staying at your mum's!

Brenda forced an unnatural smile that would have made Posh Spice cringe. I would've left straight away but I had a PVC fetish and Brenda's skin was arousing me. Eventually I'd have to find out what Tommy thought of his new wife. At that moment he could do nothing but stare. Brenda left the bathroom and he and I went back to our shocked looks.

<u>**4<sup>th</sup> March, 2014**</u>

I had heard rumblings that something might be going down at Shyton United, that changes would soon be taking place on an industrial scale. Big changes and rumblings at Shyton United were not at all uncommon, as this was a club that this season had become like the British weather – constantly changing and making you as moody as a pregnant Welsh teenager.

We went down to the training ground and met up with Oren in the changing room. He was cleaning somebody's football boots, and doing a top-notch job in getting rid of the mud. Perhaps this would be his new job soon, as there were mutterings that after the untimely demise of Alexander Kovich, Oren would soon be shown the door.

**OREN:** No, no, I don't feel under-fire at all. Sometimes you go through difficult spells but we are in this together and we will fight together.
**STANLEY:** Why are you cleaning somebody's boots?
**OREN:** We must all pitch in together.
**STANLEY:** Right. Anyway, you don't feel you've lost the team's support?
**OREN:** No.

K-Y then came charging in… well, charging in as much as K-Y could charge in. He was riled.

**K-Y:** I want my place back! I should be number one, not Jay!

That was one area in which Oren had been quite strong. His stance on K-Y not being anywhere near the goal.

**OREN:** I'm sorry, it is not my decision.

K-Y pulled out a jar of Vaseline (no idea where he got that from), then got a big chunk of it and smeared it over Oren's face. K-Y turned and left, just like that. And what did Oren do? He calmly got up, went to the sink and wiped the stuff off with a towel. Could nothing anger this man? Ronnie then came stomping in and barged past Oren, knocking him off his feet.

**RONNIE:** Get the fuck out of my way. I've got business to take care of.
**OREN:** Banter.

Finally, Maury entered with two huge suited and booted men and pointed at Oren. The two heavies picked Oren up and carried him outside through the car park, then threw Oren into the street. Harsh! I wanted to ask Maury what he'd just done, but instead I was compelled to see if Oren was okay. The man was dusting himself down when he got a message on his mobile from Maury, which read, 'You're fired!' Tough way to go.

**STANLEY:** Are you okay?

Oren had a lost puppy look in his eyes and just nodded. He got up and went on his way, never to be heard of again. That last bit wasn't true but it sounded good.
**5<sup>th</sup> March, 2014**

With the departure of Oren Goldman, there was a huge amount of gossip over who would be his replacement. Hull City's manager, Barry Bloomer, was the favourite to succeed him in the flaming hot Shyton hot seat.

Needing to get out of Shyton anyway and get away from Bob with whom the level of awkwardness since the sofa incident had risen to Britney Spears *Toxic* levels, I made the journey over to Hull. I'd been ringing Barry Bloomer's phone all morning, and then eventually I got through to him. He explained over the phone that he'd been busy wheeling and dealing but could see me at his office at his club's training ground.

Barry Bloomer was your typical English manager. Rosy red cheeks, one too many fish pies, and would break out into a sweat when lifting his arm to drink a cup of tea. Despite his unfavourable appearance to any woman not needing financial support, he seemed to have a high opinion of himself, as his office was adorned with framed photos of himself, his favourite cars and his racehorses.

**BARRY:** Course, it's flattering to be linked with Shyton United, a great club and one of our closest rivals. I mean, my record stands up against anyone's so I can well understand the interest of Shyton. However, I just want to say, for the record, and categorically that I am 100% committed to... erm...

**STANLEY:** Hull.

**BARRY:** That's the one. I've got a four-year contract and I intend, as I always do, to honour it. I am a man of my word.

**STANLEY:** I understand that Shyton United have been throwing huge offers, astronomical salaries in your direction to try and tempt you.

**BARRY:** They can throw anything they want, Barry Bloomer ain't for sale.

**STANLEY:** Any words for the Hull City fans?

**BARRY:** Barry Bloomer will never go down the road to Shyton. I don't even know where Shyton is.

I had a feeling he wasn't too sure where Hull was either.

Barry was then kind enough to take me out. We got in his car and finally departed from the car park twenty minutes later. Barry had insisted on winding down his window and responding to every reporter's question about why I was in the car, whether he would stay loyal to Hull, and was he interested in signing such and such a player.

He took me to his home and I was introduced to his lovely wife, Sally. Sally and Barry, it just had to be. They showed me around their wonderful house, with views across Kingston-Upon-Hull and the Humber River. While I was taking in the sights, I had the unpleasant experience of being molested by their resident fur-ball.

**BARRY:** That's our cat. I love cats though I don't like calling her a cat. Her name's Daisy – she's so much more than a cat.

**STANLEY:** She's lovely.

I was tempted to kick the sexually-assaulting feline like a rugby ball and into the Humber River. Sally served us tea in their conservatory.

**STANLEY:** The rumours of you jumping ship are red hot. Is it true that you've received death threats from some of the Hull City faithful?

Barry laughed the kind of laugh that made you shiver and die a little inside.

**BARRY:** The only death threats I've ever received were from the wife when I didn't change Daisy's litter tray. No death threats and no chance of me leaving. My word is my bond.

From the blog, Fudge Packer for Life, Joe Meek wrote:
*'…Every football gossip site and fan page is saying that Barry Bloomer's gonna be our next manager. He's got a decent record but he's only won one cup in what, 25 years as manager? How's he going to make Shyton a winning team? Plus, he's never handled big name players before. How's he gonna cope with the Ricardos, the Bombalbos and the Bombinhos? He might be alright with the local lads, but he might struggle to be understood by the foreigners. If he does join, you gotta question his loyalty. If our team starts on the road to decline or if a better offer comes along, he'll jump ship quicker than a glory hunter whose team ain't winning.'*

<u>**6<sup>th</sup> March, 2014**</u>

Shyton United called a press conference and the usual people turned up for what had been expected ever since Oren Goldman got booted. Cameras went off, flashes lit the room as Maury introduced his fourth manager this season. He was getting to be an old hand at this. And who was the new manager that was beside him? Least shocking moment of the season, I'd wager.

**BARRY:** I'm delighted to be the new manager of Shyton United. With the amount of money spent, the club's underachieved. However I'm positive, with these players, we can still nab fourth place.
**TABLOID JOURNALIST:** At your previous clubs you always had a British core, how will you deal with the superstar foreign players at Shyton United?
**BARRY:** Well, obviously with foreign players it's more difficult. Most of them don't bother with the fly-fishing, or even go cheese-rolling. They don't even drink tea! Still, I'm sure they'll come around.
**TABLOID JOURNALIST:** How will you be able to get your views across to the foreign players? Multi-lingual managers such as Juan Lopez and Luis Jalapeno previously coached them, so they may find it a bit difficult to understand you.
**BARRY:** Listen, maybe some Johnny Foreigner don't speak the English too good, but if they've got half a brain they'll pick up the lingo.
**TABLOID JOURNALIST:** Any message for the Hull fans?
**BARRY:** The who fans? Look, I don't want to talk about some fantasy team. There's still plenty of points to play for and I intend to get every one of them. Are we done here? Alright, I've got work to do.

Barry departed as Maury thanked the press for gathering. So, Shyton had a new manager, but what about a new owner? I caught a quick word with Maury back in his office.

**MAURY:** We're not rudderless. We have time to find new owners…
**STANLEY:** Owners plural?
**MAURY:** Never fear, Stanley. Everything is going according to plan.

I seriously doubted that.

**STANLEY:** What plan would this be?

Maury tapped the side of his head.

**STANLEY:** Hull are pretty upset that you've poached their manager, what sort of compensation have you agreed?
**MAURY:** Don't worry, Stan, they've taken care of everything.
**STANLEY:** Who has?

Maury winked at me, patted me on the arm then headed away. Bastard. Somebody or some people were bankrolling all this, but whom? I was sure that soon enough, yet another press conference would be called and we'd discover Shyton's mystery backers.


## 8<sup>th</sup> March, 2014

It's Barry Bloomer's first game in charge of Shyton United and it's a tough away game at the Redbirds, Cardiff City. Cardiff City were another foreign-owned club, whose owner was the proud proprietor of 'The Hair Club for Men', which specialised in dyed black hair and dodgy moustaches for insecure men over 50.

With the team languishing in 7<sup>th</sup> place, noted tactical mastermind Barry Bloomer prepared his team. He was going for a typical 4-4-2 formation – the formation that had worked so well, sometimes over his entire career. He was, if anything, loyal to a system—if not to a team, or a city.

Making a welcome return to the line-up was Sonny Jackson, who had gone through rigorous counselling sessions and visited the best psychologist in Shyton. He was, by all accounts, a changed man and was much less of a chauvinist than before. Apparently, the psychologist had really gotten to the root cause of why he treated women the way he did and after the beating he had taken, had finally regained some measure of confidence to leave his home and play football again. His bruises had healed, and he was born again. It was noted that for much of his therapy he had hung out with K-Y an awful lot.

**BARRY:** Pass the ball and you know, score goals, and err, win because you're all diamonds! Off you go, lads.

The team trudged out, with Tommy leading the charge.

**TOMMY:** We'll fucking win anyway!

The players all filed out, leaving me alone with Barry.

**STANLEY:** Barry, you haven't had a great deal of time to prepare for this match. When did you come up with the tactics and formation?
**BARRY:** Sorted it out last night while lying in bed.
**STANLEY:** In bed?
**BARRY:** Yes, my son. I always work out tactics and formations in bed, it's something my missus and me have been doing for years. She's great to bounce ideas off, and for her valuable input.
**STANLEY:** Your wife helps choose your teams?
**BARRY:** She's gotta do something. She ain't going to want to whisper sweet nothings then have some rumpy pumpy with this ugly git, would she? Would you?
**STANLEY:** Not for a million pounds.
**BARRY:** Right, so got to do something before falling asleep, and talking football with the wife is a guaranteed way for one of us to nod off and the other to consider separation.

Uninspired as they were by Barry's uninspiring team talk, Shyton United were yet somehow all over Cardiff City. Though to be fair, if there had been turmoil at Shyton (and there had been plenty), there had been utter turmoil at Cardiff City. It showed too as Cardiff City played like a team without confidence, and with a 21-year-old Azerbaijani intern as the new head of recruitment.

Li Bang played a sweet cross to a seriously hefty-looking Bombalbo who, Zidane-esuqe à la Champions League Final 2002, swivelled and hit a rasping volley into the net. Bombalbo wobbled over to the Shyton United fans who were all dressed in fat suits in homage to Bombalbo.

**BOMBALBO:** Why are they dressed like that?
**TOMMY:** Because you're a fat fuck, you fat fucking piece of shit.

Poor Bombalbo. He sobbed immediately and had to be taken off because his feelings had been injured.

It stayed 1-0 despite constant pressing by Shyton United, and in particular the play by Ricardo and Bombinho. However, late on in the match, Tommy had to make a last-ditch tackle to prevent a Cardiff City striker from being through on goal. The referee deemed it to be a fair tackle, though the striker was injured and had to be stretchered off. The sound of booing was deafening.

**TOMMY:** Fuck off!

The game finished 1-0 to Shyton United and was their third win on the bounce. I spoke to Barry Bloomer about his first win as Shyton United manager, which moved them up to the dizzying height of 5th.

**BARRY:** Of course, I'm delighted. It's always a tough place to come but somehow I did it. I got the lads playing for me, and soon I'll be leading them to Champions League football thanks to me. Just goes to show that owners should have a bit more faith in British coaches named Barry.
**STANLEY:** Ricardo put in another scintillating performance.
**BARRY:** Yeah, my wife told me where to play him. She thinks about him a lot!

Barry gave me a disconcerting wink.

**BARRY:** Even I sometimes wonder whether I should play him or fuck him.
**STANLEY:** What's Bombalbo's current condition?
**BARRY:** Fat. Bombalbo's a fat tub of lard. The poor baby is sulking and will probably spend quite a few days on a reinforced treatment table stuffing himself with doughnuts. I've got no time for pansies.
**STANLEY:** Tommy Gunn made yet another bad challenge resulting in serious injury, even though the ref thought it fair. Will Shyton United take action?
**BARRY:** Stanley, c'mon! You said it yourself, ref thought it was fair and that's all that matters. It's a man's game, a contact sport. This ain't ballet! Besides, Tommy's a great lad and he's not that type of player.
**STANLEY:** That's not the first player Tommy's injured this season, which would suggest that he is indeed that type of player.

**BARRY:** Fuck off!

Barry was off. His ego was delicate for a man of the people.

Ronnie and Cheryl had been keeping a low profile for quite a while and hadn't made, as far as we were aware, any daring attempts to meet in public. We knew though, that Cheryl had been round Ronnie's gaff a fair amount of times, and we knew that Dwayne was becoming like the real life version of Sleeping Beauty. It was somewhat surprising then that Ronnie and Cheryl had arranged to meet at a high street café, though they were appropriately disguised.

Bob and I had been trailing them for a while and gotten enough footage and evidence to blackmail them if ever the need arose. With Ronnie having fleeced me a number of times, the desire to get some retribution (and some much needed cash back) grew, with interest, by the day.

Cheryl was wearing a headscarf and a ginger wig—and even in that she was sexier than Brenda. She poked her head into the café, scanned the area then popped in. What she didn't know was that Dwayne knew where she was and was watching her from the safety of an ice-cream van across the road. What Dwayne didn't know was that we were watching him watching Cheryl. It was all very MI6, espionage, Cold War, Tinker Tailor, James Bond, Chitty Chitty Bang Bang, double Dutch stuff… Of course, an ice-cream van was not the best choice of vehicle or 'Bugmobile' to use in Shyton, as Shyton's obesity levels were twice the national average and they loved their creamy goo. It wasn't long before what could've been a pre-teen or a massively overweight dwarf approached Dwayne in his ice-cream van.

**HUGE KID:** Can I get a choc-ice?
**DWAYNE:** No, they're all mine!
**HUGE KID:** Please, mister.
**DWAYNE:** You're fat enough. Go away!

The kid waddled off, crying to his mum. Was his mum's Brenda's sister? Would explain the size of the boy.

Cheryl joined Ronnie at his table. Ronnie was, rather bizarrely, signing autographs and posing for photos with adoring fans. I was positioned inside at a secluded corner table, whilst in the Bugmobile, Bob kept an eye on Dwayne. Cheryl spoke in a whisper, but as our microphones could pick up a pin drop in Burkina Faso, her whispering was useless.

**CHERYL:** Ronnie! Stop! People will talk.
**RONNIE:** What?

However, Ronnie showed no sign of letting up on signing autographs or of posing for photographs. Not only did it feed his ego, but with each autograph and photo, he gave them fliers of the latest goods he had for sale. He also sold them £1 watches for £2.50 a time. Cheryl soon got some attention and an adorable little girl approached her. The adorable girl was the kind you'd imagine turning up at someone's front door begging for food on a winter's day in Victorian London.

**LITTLE GIRL:** Can I have your autograph, please?

Cheryl signed it, putting a 'not' in front of her name.

**CHERYL:** Not Cheryl Ford. There you go.

She passed the autograph back to the delighted girl, who probably had aspirations to one day become a wife or girlfriend of some overpaid Premier League footballer. Those were lofty aspirations.

**CHERYL:** I can't keep drugging Dwayne. He's becoming suspect.

Ronnie stopped signing autographs.

**RONNIE:** Got some bargain laptops coming in tomorrow morning. Pop round. Cheryl, babes, don't worry. I'll take care of it. Nobody will know a thing.

Ronnie stood up and banged the table to get everybody's attention.

**RONNIE:** For 100% legit Ronnie Morrison merchandise and items not fallen off the back of a lorry, go to RonniesBargains.com! Cheryl Ford set up the website. She's right here!

He pointed at Cheryl who buried her head in her hands. I got a message that Dwayne was on his way. I re-joined Bob in the

Bugmobile. With Dwayne in the know, our plan to blackmail Ronnie and Cheryl had just died a death. We'd have to come up with some other way to reunite my money with my bank account.

**11<sup>th</sup> March, 2014**

Tommy rang me up and told me to get my arse down to Shyton's Magistrates' Court. I did and arrived just in time to witness Tommy coming down the court's steps, holding onto a visibly healthier Shannon and Luke. He looked pleased as Punch. I hated that character. Anyway, I thought it best at this time not to ask him about his possible move to City.

**STANLEY:** Got them back, I see.
**TOMMY:** Yeah, no one keeps my kiddies from me.
**STANLEY:** No conditions?
**TOMMY:** Got a social worker coming to stick her nose in once a week, and we've got to keep going to see a nutritionist person so we feed them proper. No more microwave dinners or oven chips and all that pig shit. Fresh veg, fruit and healthy food—easy cos I've hired a chef so Brenda won't be near the kitchen in future.
**STANLEY:** Where is Brenda?
**TOMMY:** She has to avoid sunlight.
**STANLEY:** Couldn't she do a Michael Jackson and just use an umbrella?

Tommy ignored me, and rightly so. This was a time to celebrate, and so I drove them to a local restaurant and waited in the car while they ate. I then drove them home where Brenda was waiting… inside I guessed.

**TOMMY:** Be back here tomorrow at 7am.
**STANLEY:** Yes sir.

Sir went inside with the kids… Wait, I wasn't his chauffeur! I threw the chauffeur's cap away and went home then relayed the story to Bob who laughed at me. He was right to laugh.

Later that evening, while at home and enjoying some fine port, I got a phone call from Dwayne.

**DWAYNE:** I know who it is.
**STANLEY:** You know who what is?

Of course, I acted innocently.

**DWAYNE:** The bastard that's been messing with my property.
**STANLEY:** Burglars again?
**DWAYNE:** I'm going to get him.
**STANLEY:** Get who?
**DWAYNE:** The bastard!

Dwayne hung up. Not sure why he decided to tell me, as if he did anything to Ronnie (if that was who he meant by calling bastard) then he had just incriminated himself. There were no interviewee-documentarian confidentiality clauses here. I got back to my port and watching the latest episode of Top Gear where the presenters had to cross yet another place in some old clapped-out bangers. Riveting stuff.


**<u>13<sup>th</sup> March, 2014</u>**

I was having coffee with Maury at his office in Creek Alley Stadium. He had bought (the club had bought) a top of the line, Italian-made deluxe espresso machine that did everything for you. All you had to do was turn it on, place a cup on the tray then press the button and hey presto! Hot, fresh coffee, and I must say that my cappuccino was better than any of the cafés along Shyton High Street. As I blew on my cappuccino after adding three sugars, Sheedy arrived carrying a document.

**SHEEDY:** Bad news, Mr Maury.

If the coffee hadn't woken him up, then Sheedy saying bad news definitely had.

**MAURY:** Inland Revenue?
**SHEEDY:** Bombalbo!

I leaned in. This was going to be a scoop. What was it? Had he died of a massive heart attack? Had he gotten diabetes? Had he been sold to a company that produced grease and lubricants? Sheedy slapped a document in front of Maury, whose eyes grew wider than Stewie Griffin's.

**MAURY:** He's 28!
**STANLEY:** Bombalbo's 28?
**MAURY:** Yes!
**STANLEY:** So?
**MAURY:** So? Everybody knows that you can't sign Brazilians once they're 28.
**STANLEY:** Why not?
**MAURY:** Ronaldo, Adriano, others… the list goes on. It's in Brazilian footballers' DNA that once they reach 28, their metabolism slows and they become a bunch of Neville Southalls. Sheedy, you've messed up. We're now stuck with an overweight footballer on a four-year contract who can't lose weight. This is a dilemma.

I drank more of my cappuccino. It was smooth and frothy, just the way a cappuccino should be. I got another cappuccino to go, whilst Maury and Sheedy discussed their fat problem. I went over to the Judas's house to find out once more about him moving to City.

He let his unofficial, unpaid chauffeur into his house. It was dimly lit, as the curtains were drawn. Brenda's condition must be very bad.

**STANLEY:** Why are we in the dark, Tommy?
**TOMMY:** Cos it's none of your fucking business if I move to City.
**STANLEY:** I meant the house.

So the traitor was off to City!

**TOMMY:** Oh. Well, Brenda's skin's a bit delicate, like I told you before.
**STANLEY:** Where is Brenda?
**TOMMY:** Oxygen chamber.
**STANLEY:** Right here, right now, just tell all the Fudge Packers everywhere and me, are you going to City?
**TOMMY:** Look, I ain't even spoken to anyone at City. I don't know how this got started, but it wasn't me.

So, you had it from the horse's mouth. Was Maury up to his old tricks?

**TOMMY:** So, stop going on about it and tell all those fans I ain't going anywhere. Now, you owe me.
**STANLEY:** What do you want?

I then spent the day driving Tommy and his kids around. If my career as a documentarian ever failed, then I was sure I'd easily get a new job as a chauffeur or a Shyton taxi driver as I knew these roads so well. I was sure as well to get a spiffing reference from Tommy.

From the Twitter account of @RonniesCheapGoods: *'Diamonds are a girl's best friend. Geezers, get your wallets out & treat your bird. Top quality merch from a man you can trust. #RonniesMerch'*

In Barry's first home game, Shyton United faced the formidable Newcastle United. Newcastle were a proper club, run the proper way, with the chairman riding roughshod over everybody and everyone. They were much like a company back in Victorian Britain whose employees were treated with the contempt they deserved and were frisked daily in case they had stolen a few crumbs. In fact, comparisons had been made that Newcastle United were the North Korea of the Premier League and that its chairman was the Kim Jong-un – not just due to his physical similarities but because he was a complete arse. Still, with the way Maury Git'a was running Shyton United, that unwanted label might soon pass to him.

Master tactician Barry Bloomer readied his troops with a stirring speech about his missus, his lack of nooky since 1988, and how it was no skin off his nose if Shyton did badly because he'd be sure to land a cushy job somewhere else down the line. This was because every club in the top two divisions had a go-to list of around eight managers, and Barry's name was pretty much near the top. Football looked after its own no matter the individuals' lack of success, notoriety, awful playing style, and abilities to relegate teams.

Barry's speech did the trick his tactics didn't. It didn't seem to matter too much, as Newcastle's notoriously leaky defence, combined with the lack of passion amongst most of their players helped Shyton stroll to an easy victory. Most of Newcastle's players were rather disenchanted, as they kept wondering how the hell they had gone from the wine regions, the Côte d'Azur, and the Alps of France to end up in Geordieland. Shyton United romped to a four nil win.

Strangely, Dwayne did not confront Ronnie and there appeared to be no animosity or sign that they'd been in an argument or fight. Either Dwayne was biding his time or he'd fingered the wrong man. How could he not know that it was Ronnie who was banging his prized possession? And if he thought it was somebody else, then who? I was sure we'd find out soon enough.

Here's Barry:

**BARRY:** Since I've come here, we've been playing out of our skin and I fully deserve to be rewarded because I'm so brilliant. It's down to me that we won four nil, it was almost like I was the one on the pitch scoring the goals and saving the shots. Tommy may have gotten a brace, and Ricardo the other two, but I had a hand in all the goals. It's because of me, really.

Barry's ego was big, was it Luis Jalapeno big?

**STANLEY:** Newcastle took another hammering, much like the old Shyton used to quite willingly receive in the glory days. Any words for them?

**BARRY:** Well, they've spent a lot of money this season and look where they are. When you spend that kind of money you've got to be challenging, haven't you? A lot of their players look as though they've come over here for a good payday and will swan off back home soon enough to live in their villas. It's not right. If I were managing them, I'd give them a right kick up their backsides and have them playing like Shyton have been.

Sounded as though he was offering his services to Newcastle should things go pear-shaped at Shyton. I'd had enough of chatting with Barry Bloomer and listening to his modesty so I went home, opened a tin of Heinz soup and settled in for a quiet evening watching *Star Wars*, episode 4 *'A New Hope'* – the best in the series.

From the Twitter account of @JoeMeek: *'Good win today. The Bloomer effect is already showing, instilling English grit. Englishman for an English team as it should be. #BloomersBoys #FPL*

<u>**16<sup>th</sup> March, 2014**</u>

There was yet another press conference and another set of new owners – the mysterious backers who'd been the driving force behind getting rid of Oren Goldman and appointing Mr Wheeler Dealer, Barry Bloomer.

To the left of Maury was a large, plump-faced fellow by the name of Randy Dicks. Randy had a white Stetson on, a bit like JR Ewing would wear on the TV show *'Dallas'*. To Maury's right was a podgy man by the name of Woody Fillet who wore a black Stetson. Wearing those black and white Stetsons reminded me of that myth about the Taj Mahal and how Shah Jahan had planned to build a Black Taj Mahal just across the river. This was much to Shah Jahan son's chagrin who considered his father mad and had him imprisoned in a cell that overlooked the Taj Mahal. I wondered if we could lock up Maury? Randy and Woody were in their 50s according to Wikipedia, and complete arseholes according to their Uncyclopedia pages.

**RANDY:** It's a real privilege to be one of the custodians of this super franchise.
**WOODY:** We want to assure fans that we are sports people, and being long time fans, we want the best for Showton.
**RANDY:** This means we'll honour the past but embrace the future. We're going to invest and rebuild. Starting with a super huge new stadium that I guarantee will be built at some point in the future.
**WOODY:** And unlike other clubs, there will be no debt put on the club.
**TABLOID JOURNALIST:** Can you allay fans' fears that you won't do to Shyton United what you did to Brazilian club, Pantheons?
**RANDY:** This is a completely different scenario. Those Brazilians just don't understand soccer ball. Not like you Brits.

After the press conference I tried to get a few words with the new owners, but Maury prevented me from doing so by physically blocking my path then ushering me over to a corner of the conference room. Swine. So, I put my questions to Maury instead.

**STANLEY:** A new stadium? Why does Shyton United need a new stadium? It wasn't so long ago Sid Chesterton completely upgraded and expanded the capacity of Creek Alley to meet the criteria set out by the Premier League. If these Yanks are serious then it's a complete waste of money.

**MAURY:** Stanley, you've become a bit of a negative Nancy. There's always room for improvement. Just imagine if we had a stadium like the Emirates.

**STANLEY:** Why would we need a stadium like the Emirates? That's around 60,000 capacity, we'd never fill it! The population of Shyton isn't even 60,000!

**MAURY:** Stanley, you've really become a bit of a pessimistic Pete. With Randy Dicks' and Woody Fillet's blessings and capital, we'll revolutionise Shyton itself and draw in the population—the workers and the residents—who'll then turn into fans of United. It'll be like how London soaked up all those towns and became such a huge mess. Shyton will do the same and be the London of the north. As *The Chemical Brothers* once said, it's time to 'galvanise'!

Maury left me, skipping away to be with his new American masters.

Translated from the Twitter account of @BombinhoJuice: 'I'll soon be reunited. Money can get you nice cars, house, women but not true happiness. *#MyAgentMustDie*'

After reading Bombinho's tweet, I then received a surprise message from Bombinho, asking me to visit him at his home. He had gotten quiet ever since his wife left him and took their child with her. Even though Bombinho was never alone, it seemed as though no amount of sexual gratification could replace the sexual gratification he'd gotten from Mrs Bombinho.

Bombinho wasn't the most sociable or active of chaps. Whereas Bombalbo had his food and his food blog, Tommy his family and his daily battles to keep them healthy and alive, Ricardo had himself and his mirror, Ronnie had his alleged stolen goods empire which included Dwayne's missus, Dwayne had Cheryl… to keep track of, Sonny and Li had their failing nightclub and Jay Patel, unknowingly, had his drug addiction (more on that later), it seemed that Bombinho didn't really have much, and was living a rather vacuous lifestyle.

Sprawled across his huge sofa with two big buxom, bikini-clad models curled up alongside him, I interviewed Bombinho with a Portuguese interpreter on hand. Bombinho only wore a gold-laced robe, I hoped he wore boxers underneath.

**BOMBINHO:** The heart isn't happy, the heart is weeping. You see this house, those cars, these women but my heart longs to be somewhere else. Every week I look at those numbers in my bank account and I worry about what to buy. Can you imagine that?
**STANLEY:** My heart is bleeding for you.
**BOMBINHO:** Yes, my heart is bleeding too. Bombinho Juice is suffering, and Bombinho is suffering. I cannot buy my wife or my child. Before they were in Malaga so I could go see them but now they're in Brazil.
**STANLEY:** Sounds like you want to leave Shyton.
**BOMBINHO:** Where?
**STANLEY:** The club you work for and the town you live in.

The women used their fingers to massage his nipples, going in a circular fashion. It was all very wrong and unsettling, even if he did have a body that K-Y would probably drool over.

**BOMBINHO:** This place you talk of, it's not for Bombinho. I need sun, beautiful women. I need my Brazil, my wife and son.
**STANLEY:** But you have a contract.
**BOMBINHO:** What's a contract?
**STANLEY:** The contract is a legally binding document.
**BOMBINHO:** It doesn't matter when the heart is dying.

The tanned woman on his left whispered something in his ear then licked his ear lobe. I coughed awkwardly but soldiered on, as any good documentarian should.

**BOMBINHO:** Excuse me for a moment. I need to empty my Bombinho Juice.

The interpreter and I shared a shrug of the shoulders. Bombinho led his two women away and upstairs. The interpreter and I waited even when the squeaks filtered down, then the love noises, then the groans and moans, the cracks, the anguishes, the spanking, the whipping… this carried on for a good two hours before the interpreter and I stood up and left.

<u>**22<sup>nd</sup> March, 2014**</u>

Shyton had a home game against Everton, the first match that was officially under the new stewardship of Randy Dicks and Woody Fillet. The fans without season tickets got a big surprise today when they discovered that match day tickets had gone up by 30%. And the fans with season tickets were in for a big surprise too. Here's Maury to explain another increase in prices.

**MAURY:** Yes, from next season our wise masters have decided that season ticket prices—for so long kept at League Two prices—will be increased by 45%.
**STANLEY:** Bit steep?
**MAURY:** Success and love doesn't come cheap. To be the best, you have to pay for the best.
**STANLEY:** What about all those loyal fans who can't afford yet another price hike?
**MAURY:** Loyalty comes at a price. For so long these wonderful fans have been seeing a great team on the cheap, now it's time for them to reward our loyalty by mortgaging their houses so we can pay higher wages and I can buy that chateau in Provence I've always wanted.
**STANLEY:** It wasn't so long! At the beginning of the season, prices went up, and now the loyal Shyton fans are being asked to pay through the nose again. With all that Premier League TV money, how can a club have such little regard for its fans?
**MAURY:** Is that the time? Well, Stanley, better go and make sure… err…

Maury fled. This man was despicable. And the fans knew it and were furious when they turned up at Creek Alley Stadium and went to the ticket office. Joe was one such furious fan.

**JOE:** This is a fucking outrage. How dare these Yanks do that!
**STANLEY:** You didn't mind the price increases before.
**JOE:** That was then, this is now. Once is acceptable to make us competitive but another? Yanks only been here 5 seconds. I blame that git, Git'a.
**STANLEY:** Maybe with the extra income the club can finally sign a good, clean goalkeeper?
**JOE:** Which we'd pay for by working our fingers to the bone.

**STANLEY:** You don't have a job.
**JOE:** Yeah, some poor foreign sod would have to graft, so I can get me benefits and buy my ticket so them bastard Yanks can play owner.
**STANLEY:** What will you do now?
**JOE:** You just see what I do!

Joe went charging in and bought a ticket. He glanced back at me.

**JOE:** Not missing Everton!

Yes, Everton was always the must-see game whenever that season's fixture list was released. I always pencilled in those dates.

So with many a disgruntled Shyton United fan in attendance, Shyton got the match underway to a bright new hamburger and fries era. The fans remained quiet throughout, even when Shyton scored a couple, whereas the American owners roared their approval like grizzly bears on Valium.

After the match, I tried to get man of the people Barry Bloomer's opinion on the ill feeling and tension between the fans and the owners due to the ticket price increases.

**BARRY:** Well, I'm a football fan like the people and I get where they're coming from. Times are tough for the working man. Food on the table, supporting the wife and kids, working 12-hour shifts down the mines, on the rigs, in the cinemas, theatres, casinos – it's a big expense. Luckily I'm a fantastic football manager so I don't have to worry about all that. Anyway, I understand the people. I am the people. But you know, I have as much business sense as my cat, Daisy. I can't even use a mobile phone, or a computer or an Etch-a-Sketch – I can't even read or write. I don't know when I was born, where I was born, who the fuck are you? I'm sure the owners know what they're doing like I know what I'm doing.

Barry left, with me scratching my head. No idea what he was on about and I was pretty sure that he didn't have a clue what he was on about either.

<u>**23<sup>rd</sup> March, 2014**</u>

At *The Fudge and Wrapper* pub, disgruntled fans had been gathered together by unemployed ringleader, Joe Meek. Pint in hand, Joe was preaching and ranting at the mob, I mean protest group.

**JOE:** Like you lot, I am deeply troubled by the takeover of our great club by these greedy Yanks. They promise no debt on Shyton and yet we're already 700 million in the red. Now I hear they've got the barefaced cheek to raise ticket prices.

After each rant the mob booed.

Joe grabbed a plastic bag and pulled out a brown and white striped scarf with Shyton United emblazoned on it.

**JOE:** From now on, we're going to hit them where it hurts. We're all gonna wear these colours at every game. That'll show them cowboys. Come, get your scarf and support your club!

A queue quickly formed as Joe handed out a scarf to a willing elderly recipient who wore a brown cloth cap – he looked like Andy Capp.

**JOE:** 5.99, please.

Andy Capp grumbled and gave Joe a look like he was a Nazi and it was WWII all over again.
**JOE:** Don't give me that evil look, granddad. Revolution ain't free.

Joe managed to flog all his scarves and the other merchandise he'd gotten 'wholesale' from Ronnie Morrison, and then riled up the mob once more.

**JOE:** Right, we're all ready. Next home game we're going to let them infidels have it. For now, we'll march to Creek Alley. Ready?

Infidels?

**STANLEY:** Joe, I don't think Randy Dicks or Woody Fillet are even in Shyton at the moment.

**JOE:** That git Git'a will be around. Come on lads.

Joe marched out, one arm raised with the mob following. Joe chanted,

**JOE:** 'Take your fuckin' debt, thanks, we don't want you here, Yanks!'

Had to admit, it was catchy. And there were others:

> *We pack fudge, yes we do*
> *Take your debt back home with you'*

> *'No more hikes, take a hike!'*

And my personal favourite,

> *'Fuck off you cunts!'*

To the stadium they marched and chanted, staying for a good few hours till teatime when the mob got restless and wanted to get home to watch Corrie. Bloody soap was on almost every day now!

<u>**26<sup>th</sup> March, 2014**</u>

I went round to Tommy's for a weekday snack and to collect my chauffeur bonus that he had promised me. The bonus was £150, plus a gift voucher from WH Smiths, which I was quite pleased with. That was more money than I'd ever made in a day! Would the other players need chauffeurs too? I could rope Bob in. I was sure he wouldn't mind the extra cash.

However, it wasn't all cash and Smiths' gift vouchers, as I was also there to document the latest in the saga that was Tommy's life. Brenda's face had a hard fixed look to it, like it wasn't turning into a frown or smile any time soon. It was like that famous Posh Spice smile that was never going to disappear. Sadly, and this was most tragic, the children were finding it hard to recognise their mother.

Her face was as supple as the oak dining table in Maury's castle, and could probably have been used as a substitute hammer. The sheen of her skin was something to behold, and she made me feel like I should go polish something. Poor cow was unable to make any kind of facial expression, and whenever she picked Luke up the youngster screamed.

**LUKE:** I want my mummy.

The other side effect was that Brenda was now less intelligible than Tommy, which was saying something. Her words came out slurred and mumbled and I had to ask her to write everything down.

**BRENDA:** I am your mummy.

Luke poked Brenda's new face in bewilderment. There was no give to it.

**TOMMY:** You don't look pleased that we got our kids back.
**BRENDA:** I am pleased.
**TOMMY:** What you say?
**BRENDA:** I am pleased.

This was painful. She pushed the words out like someone who was unwilling to apologise and did it through gritted teeth.

**TOMMY:** Why are you mumbling?

Brenda put Luke down and went to pick up Shannon who, having witnessed what Luke had been through, didn't want none of it; she tried to escape, and when she saw it was futile, bawled her eyes out.

**TOMMY:** Leave 'em alone. You're scaring them.

Brenda stood there a desolate lonely figure as Tommy comforted his two young children, taking them away from the scary monster. Liquid came down her face—couldn't be sure whether they were tears or if the lights were too hot and she was melting.

**STANLEY:** Boss, do you mind if I clock off now?

Tommy gave me a nod and I went back home to compile the footage. I also had to press my chauffeur's suit and hat.

Tommy had given me the day off from chauffeuring, and so I got Bob and a few other Shytonian filmmakers together to set up our chauffeur business. We decided to call our company 'Driving Mr Lazy' – Chauffeurs to the Footballers. We didn't have a fleet of cars yet, but the footballers had so many that they'd probably want us to drive theirs. We'd be on call like doctors. One of our crew, a real whiz when it came to gadgetry and stuff, went about creating an app for the footballers to use. It was all coming together nicely.

Unfortunately, Sao Columbus wouldn't be a client as he was no longer around – in fact nobody knew where he was. It was unfortunate because we had planned to fleece the forgetful bugger to the point that, by the time he was out of contract or to be sold we'd have taken most of his wealth. However, these remaining footballers either were incredibly generous with their money or just didn't understand the value of a pound, and so we gave them a fixed rate that was beyond the reach of a lot of wealthy people but not beyond the reach of a Premier League footballer with millions in the bank and less than hundreds in the brain cell department.

Dwayne hired us to drive Cheryl everywhere in a car with a specially fitted surveillance camera, to make sure he could watch her every move, as well as watch our every move in case we tried it on with her. I let Bob take on the Dwayne account. I myself kept Tommy and also sometimes drove Barry Bloomer, which was a bit of a pain. Every time we entered or left the training ground he insisted on winding down his window and talking to the press about possible transfers, tactics, football gossip, his views on the England manager's job and about every other facet of football, whether his opinion was wanted or not. Driving him added an extra hour or two but it counted when the bill was settled.

Yes, this was a nice little earner, a side business to our main goals as documentarians and filmmakers.

And, for me personally, getting to chauffeur them around (because sometimes we had to fill in for each other and drive each other's clients) was good as I got to hear some very juicy gossip and see where these footballers went. It wasn't always back and forth between home and the training ground, home and the nightclub, home and the brothel where the middle-aged grannies were. Sometimes these footballers requested to be driven to Shyton Caves, Huge Jack Off Studios, Crabbby Bridge, and even the park!

The best gossip we heard was that Dwayne only had one testicle, Tommy had a teddy bear called Snuff-a-lot, Sonny was a closeted homosexual and Ben Twaddle was a devout prat.

<u>**30<sup>th</sup> March, 2014**</u>

Shyton United faced a huge away game at Manchester City. Could they keep up their winning streak and win their 6<sup>th</sup> consecutive game? It had already broken all Shyton United records and was even more impressive when you considered the upheaval at the club; what with a new manager, and a previous owner being blown up. It was once again another example of true Shyton grit that no matter how much they got fucked they just gritted their teeth and bore it. Nothing was going to rock this apple cart!

However, they were up against some formidable foes with one of the form teams in the league. They were also up against Joe Meek and the rest of the Fudge Packers, who again planned to protest during the match at the 30<sup>th</sup>, 45<sup>th</sup> and 69<sup>th</sup> minutes. The 30<sup>th</sup> minute was in protest at the 30% increase in match day tickets, the 45<sup>th</sup> minute at the 45% increase on season tickets and the 69<sup>th</sup> minute as an extra protest to show how pissed off they were. At these minutes they were going to turn their backs and chant. Which chant they were going to use was anybody's guess, but I suspected my personal favourite.

Barry Bloomer fielded the same starting eleven as he had throughout his time at the club, and the same starting eleven every other Shyton United manager had fielded since the start of the season. This was a woefully small squad with many fringe players that nobody, even I, had heard of. They probably didn't even exist in this documentarian's mind.

However, despite the best efforts of Tommy, Ronnie, Ricardo and a lumbering, laboured, breathless Bombalbo, Shyton United came up short and lost the game two goals to nil. Bombinho was one of the few players worthy of a kick up the backside and Barry Bloomer was rightfully livid with him. Bombinho put in as much effort as a reluctant homosexual forced to make a baby the heterosexual way. He looked like a man lost, a man deprived of his smile, he was a shell of a man and he was about to get that shell kicked all over the place.

We managed to get into the changing room and capture the dressing down of Bombinho by Barry Bloomer.

**BARRY:** What the fuck was that? You're meant to be a footballer, aren't you? That was the worst performance by a player I've seen in 30 years!

Bombinho just sat there, head down as unresponsive as a corpse.

**BARRY:** You get paid a hundred grand a week and you can't be bothered, you're having a laugh! I'm not fucking having it. I'm not having you taking down Randy's and Woody's pants and giving them the old one two back and forth. No, you ain't playing at all any more till you buck up your ideas. People pay good money to see their team and you sulk like a five-year-old.

Barry spoke to me in the tunnel.

**BARRY:** With these foreign lads, it's tough you know? They're not used to the culture, the weather, the work ethic you've got to put in. They're too pampered. Tell you, it's so different from my day. We'll fine this lad a fortnight's wages and what, that'll be 200 grand? Some charmed life, ain't it?

Barry went off to be by himself. We went back to the changing room where there was a bit of a commotion as Bombinho was sobbing and letting it all out, including throwing football boots and football kits all over the place.

**BEN:** Be at peace, my son.

Mystic put a hand on Bombinho's shoulder, and then danced around him in a dance a pixie may have performed. It didn't have the calming effect Mystic was probably hoping for.

**BOMBINHO:** Stupid country, stupid weather, stupid football team! Stupid, stupid, stupid!

Tommy and Ronnie weren't having it and charged up to Bombinho.

**TOMMY:** You little ponce! Take that back or we'll send you back to where you came from!
**RONNIE:** Yeah!

Bombinho, in quite a gutsy move, stuck out his tongue at Tommy then blew a raspberry.

**BOMBINHO:** You stupid! I am Bombinho, I play for Brazil! You clean my boots with your tongue!
**RONNIE:** What a cry baby wanker!

Then, in a not unexpected move if you'd been following Shyton's story attentively, Tommy head-butted Bombinho. The Brazilian lad's head rocked back and forth like a Jack in the Box before he fell down in a heap.

**TOMMY:** Tosser.

There were gulps from some of the other foreign lads and a few mobiles being whipped out, with calls to agents asking if they could get a move straightaway as the team was full of xenophobic bastards. Still, Bombinho had it coming.

<u>**31<sup>st</sup> March, 2014**</u>

As soon as I felt it appropriate, which as you'd have noticed by the date was the next day, I went round to Bombinho's house to see if his mood had brightened. I had already been to Crabby Bridge to check for any recent suicides or suicide attempts. There was no sign of a below average height Brazilian amongst the recently fallen.

I rang his doorbell, not knowing whether he'd answer or even be in any mood to speak to me after the incident with Tommy. I had hoped that his bevy of beauties, his fast cars, his freedom to live how he wanted to live would soon make everything appear rosy again. Alas, I had no idea if that was the case, as there was no answer. I tried peering in through a gap in the curtains but couldn't see anything. Was he home? Who knew!

So, I made my way to Tommy's house. Not because he needed to be driven anywhere but because he needed to answer for what had gone down. I assumed the club would fine him. However, on his current wages, that wouldn't make much of an impression on him.

**STANLEY:** Tommy, even though Bombinho is a little girl, do you think your actions were acceptable?
**TOMMY:** Yeah.
**STANLEY:** Wouldn't a more sympathetic, 'arm round the shoulder, what's wrong, let daddy kiss it better' approach have been better?
**TOMMY:** No.
**STANLEY:** Do you think head-butting Bombinho and calling him a tosser is any way to resolve a situation?
**TOMMY:** Yeah.
**STANLEY:** Do you think by doing that it'll have a positive effect?
**TOMMY:** Yeah.
**STANLEY:** Do you care if you had broken his nose?
**TOMMY:** No.
**STANLEY:** Do you still need me to chauffeur you and Brenda to 'The Fat Mongrel' at 7pm?
**TOMMY:** Yeah.
**STANLEY:** Yes, boss.

I hurried away to prepare the car for Tommy's dinner date with

Polythene Pam.

<u>2<sup>nd</sup> April, 2014</u>

There was still no word on Bombinho. There were rumours that he had been checked in to a private hospital with severe concussion, or that he'd died in his home as a result of the head-butting and that his body was already giving off an awful stench, or that he was buried under a mountain of pussy, or that he'd done a runner and fled back to Brazil. All seemed highly plausible, except the first two. Although the first two were still more probable than the miracle that Bombalbo hadn't yet succumbed to heart disease. Bombalbo's large frame showed no sign of decreasing in ampleness, and his unwillingness to admit that he had a weight problem was a cause for concern. It was rumoured that his vision had already been affected by his coming obesity.

Dwayne was another who was suffering. Besides his paranoia (though quite well founded considering the carryings-on between Cheryl and Ronnie) and his insane jealously, he was starting to turn up late for training due to his oversleeping. Or should that be over-drugging at the hands of Cheryl – allegedly. It was now quite common during games to see Dwayne yawning. Fans and pundits alike wrongly assumed he was losing interest in playing for Shyton United, or worse yet, losing interest in the beautiful game. He was in fact losing consciousness and battling to stay awake.

Strange things were also happening to little mentioned Jay 'Beanie' Patel. Jay had found himself a pad in one of the rougher parts of Shyton. His three up two down house was once a squat, and when I visited, it still resembled a squat. I didn't fancy going there after getting used to the mansions of the rest of the team, and the castle of Maury. Even Tommy's old council flat was a million miles better than Jay's place. Jay didn't seem to mind, as he'd been plucked from the slums of Mumbai and anything in comparison to that was a veritable paradise.

Jay and I stood on his porch as kids played football on the street, neighbours fixed their cars with stolen parts, and family matriarchs shouted abuse at their husbands and children, all the while as local prostitutes solicited. It was quite the street and a grand place to be.

**STANLEY:** Sorry it's taken me so long to interview you. How are you

settling in?
**JAY:** It's super.

A football went flying past and smashed one of Jay's downstairs windows.

**STANLEY:** Crikey!
**JAY:** It's only glass, Mr Stanley. All these things can be repaired, the soul is more important.

He was sounding like Mystic.

**STANLEY:** Right. Having a bit of an acne problem are you?

Jay's face had more spots than a Dalmatian.

**JAY:** It is quite strange, Mr Stanley. And my balls are the size of coconuts.

I couldn't help but glance down at his crotch.

**JAY:** Would you like to see?
**STANLEY:** I'll pass for now.

Maybe K-Y would be interested? I left Jay and his gigantic balls, and went to meet with Sonny. I had been wanting to speak with him, ever since I heard rumours that he might be playing for the opposition. Sonny was at one of Shyton's newest spots, an all-male gym where guys could work out without being ogled by the local ravenous skanks.

Sonny was on a treadmill as I chatted with him. Sweat poured off his silky toned body. He was getting quite the attention.

**STANLEY:** All male gym, eh?
**SONNY:** Y-yo, dem wimin be checkin'. Safer...
**STANLEY:** Thought you'd love that.
**SONNY:** I I coming to work out, safe workout, yo know what I-I'm sayin'?

Sonny got off the treadmill and a skinny, well-hung lad in spandex came running up to him with a towel and started patting him down.

**STANLEY:** Finished your workout?
**SONNY:** N-no. Sauna time.
A young lad in spandex called out to Sonny from outside of the sauna.

**YOUNG LAD IN SPANDEX:** You comin'?

Sonny followed him in like an obedient puppy. It amazed me how radically different Sonny had become. Anyway, I left as I had no wish to conduct an interview in a sauna, especially if 'working out' was involved.

From the blog, Fudge Packer for Life, Joe Meek wrote:
*'To all Shyton United fans and other Shytonians, big game at home to Norwich this weekend and we need your support if we're to get the prices down so those of us on low incomes are not priced out. And if those Yanks don't budge on the prices then we need to budge them out of town. We ain't being ripped off any longer! Football's about passion and community, it ain't about profit! Shyton is for Shytonians, we don't need their money. Come along with your brown and white scarves—original Shyton United colours. If you don't have a scarf then you can order it here on my blog page. Only £5.99!'*

<u>**5<sup>th</sup> April, 2014**</u>

It's match day and Joe had organised for the fans to continue protesting before, during and after the home against the Canaries. With a megaphone in hand and standing on his soapbox much like John Major did so effectively in 1992, he tried to galvanise the disgruntled Shyton United fans. The few hundred Shyton United fans hung on Joe's every word whilst wearing their brown and white scarves. They were a gullible, stupid lot.

**JOE:** What do we want?
**SHYTON UNITED PROTESTORS:** Cheaper tickets!
**JOE:** When do we want it?
**SHYTON UNITED PROTESTORS:** As soon as reasonably possible.
**JOE:** What are we not going to do?
**SHYTON UNITED PROTESTORS:** Pay through the nose.
**JOE:** When are we going to do it?
**SHYTON UNITED PROTESTORS:** You haven't said!
**JOE:** No more hikes!
**SHYTON UNITED PROTESTORS:** Take a hike!

Joe was really into this. I hadn't seen him so pumped up and ready to do something since… ever. If he could apply the same effort and vigour that he did to this cause to his professional life, (if he had one), he could've achieved moderate success.

**JOE:** No more hikes!
**SHYTON UNITED PROTESTORS:** Take a hike!
**JOE:** Fuck off…
**SHYTON UNITED PROTESTORS:** …You cunts!
**JOE:** Everybody, remember what we're doing?

There were murmurs and nodding amongst the Shyton fans.

**JOE:** Now come on! Let's show those slimy Yanks what we think of them.

Joe went to a ticket office and approached the vendor.

**JOE:** One ticket.
**VENDOR:** £50, please.

Joe slid over a fifty pound note then took his ticket. He turned around, holding his ticket aloft proudly and shouted through the megaphone.

**JOE:** Revolution!

Inside Creek Alley Stadium and with the match a few minutes from getting underway, the Shyton United fans waved their brown and white scarves in the air and sang along to the tune of *'You'll Never Walk Alone'*.

**SHYTON UNITED PROTESTORS:** *Shyton, Shyton, with fudge in your hand/ And you'll never pack fudge alone, alone/ You'll never pack fudge, alone.*

In the director's box, Randy and Woody were less than pleased and their faces were red with rage. They looked like they had just had some of the hottest Texas chilli ever made and had it whilst sunbathing in a Saudi Arabian desert during the month of July. There were flailing fists and chewing tobacco spit everywhere.

**RANDY:** Stop this! Shut them up! This is our team, our stadium.
**WOODY:** How dare they, we own this franchise. We want respect!
**MAURY:** Yes, right away, my presidents.

I followed Maury as he left the director's box and went down the corridor into his office.

**STANLEY:** Where are you going Maury? What are you going to do?
**MAURY:** You'll see.

Maury took out a box from under his desk. The box had a lever and was connected by a wire.

**STANLEY:** What's that do?
**MAURY:** Look out the window and see.

Maury's office looked out to the pitch and you could see every section of the stadium. He pulled the lever and a huge black sheet unfolded from the top of the main stand and covered the protesting Shyton United fans. There were gasps and then silence. The fans had been put into their place; it reminded me of when you covered the eyes of a horse. Their protesting had stopped, and Randy Dicks and Woody Fillet could enjoy their soccer ball game again.

As this went on, Bob sent me word that Sao had arrived in the changing room. I rushed down there and saw it for myself. I was rather aghast, what was wrong with this chap? His Shyton United teammates were equally floored.

**RONNIE:** What you doing here?
**SAO:** Duh! We got a game, stupid.
**RONNIE:** You've been banned for 9 months, you bozo. You can't play.
**SAO:** Oh.

Maury directed the security to show Sao out.

**BARRY:** Alright now. Ronnie, big lad, you defend. Tommy?
**TOMMY:** What?
**BARRY:** You get the ball and go forward with it. Li, Sonny, Ricky, you whip the balls into Bombalbo.

Barry went over to Bombalbo, and put an arm around his belly.

**BARRY:** Tubby, you let the balls hit your stomach and let them bounce off into the goal.
**BOMBALBO:** Tubby?
While the team went through some warm-up exercises, Maury jammed a syringe into Jay's buttocks, which elicited a high-pitched moan from Jay.

**TOMMY:** Where's that whingeing pussy Bombinho?
**RICARDO:** I have not seen him for a while.
**RONNIE:** He's probably fucking around.

Dwayne yawned then said,

**DWAYNE:** He'd better not be fucking around with my missus.

**RONNIE:** Who would ever try to fuck around with your missus, Suspect? I mean, with your attention that would be suicide!
**DWAYNE:** Right…

Dwayne whispered but our mics picked up everything.

**DWAYNE:** But someone did.

Either Ronnie was being utterly foolish or he had more bravado and bigger balls than anyone that had ever existed. He even said it with a wry smile. I would've raised my hat to him, had I been wearing my fisherman's hat that day.

So, this was a new twist. Had Dwayne suspected Bombinho of being the one in the coffee shop that day? Bombinho was a known ladies' man, but then so was half of the Shyton United team. Was Cheryl Bombinho's type? Had Dwayne done something to Bombinho and was that why he hadn't been seen since Tommy had head-butted him? Lots of questions and no answers, yet.

The match got underway and even with the muffled support of the fans under that huge sheet, Shyton strolled to a comfortable two nil victory. Their march to Champions League qualification showed no signs of abating.

## 7<sup>th</sup> **April, 2014**

I got word that Bombinho was trying to get in touch with me and get in touch with me through Skype! Why Skype? Where was he? Was this an affront to FaceTime? I immediately logged onto Skype and waited for Bombinho to add me. He did within the time it took to make a cuppa, batter some fish, fry the fish, eat the fish, curse his name, and finish reading the first 'Flashman' book.

When Bombinho appeared in front of me on Skype, it looked a hell of a lot sunnier where he was. Very odd.

**STANLEY:** Wait a moment! You're not in Shyton!
**BOMBINHO:** No, I'm in Rio de Janeiro.

Shyton United wouldn't like that. Bombinho was in a hot tub talking to me on his iPhone and next to him was his curvaceous, sexually arousing, blonde bombshell of a wife. She made me feel funny. From what I could see, their hot tub was overlooking the sun-drenched Copacabana Beach. Lucky sods.

**BOMBINHO:** I was homesick, and I kept getting letters about my driving!

Bombinho had received so many penalty notices about various driving offences that he was at risk of being deported.

There was a huge smile across his face, though I didn't know whether that was because he was back home or because his wife's head had popped out of view.

**BOMBINHO:** I could not settle in England. It's so different to Brazil. Cold, wet, safe. I don't understand why so many poor Brazilians go to England. My life here is so much different.

What was Maury going to say? He'd be right pissed off.

**STANLEY:** But Bombinho, you do realise that you have a contract and at the moment you're in breach of it?
**BOMBINHO:** In beach? No, no, my house is over beach. See?

It looked a really fantastic location with many tanned honeys showing off their voluptuous goods. With my pasty Danish skin, could I ever be something they'd be looking for? They did say opposites attract. Or was I doomed to end up with a Sally Sedgefield, a chubby, 'sun-fearing' editor from a rival documentary company called 'Reality Docs'?

**STANLEY:** I mean, you won't be able to play for any other club and your salary will probably be withheld.
**BOMBINHO:** My agent Sheedy Dovani will make everything okay.

Sheedy had his fingers in everything. Just then a distressed-looking butler came rushing in.

**BUTLER:** Mr Bombinho, sir! It's Bombinholito. He's been kidnapped from school!

The iPhone was dropped into the hot tub and I caught a final sight of Bombinho's wife's head. Well, say what you like about England but kidnappings were rare.

<u>**8<sup>th</sup> April, 2014**</u>

I visited Maury the next day to discuss the Bombinho problem with him. What would Shyton United do? Would Shyton United twist the knife in or show some compassion as Bombinho's son had been taken? Sheedy Dovani was there, shadowing Maury. He was a creepy fellow, and if I hadn't been an atheist then I would've not been surprised if he had hailed from the deepest darkest depths of hell.

Maury was on his throne. He'd grown accustomed to the throne and I could see why. He had an electronic panel on the side with which he could control everything. He could summon butlers, order food, get something cleaned, notify the board that the club was up for sale, contact Sheedy, get his toe nails clipped – everything he could need. He didn't have to move an inch.

**MAURY:** Of course, Bombinho will be fined for every week that he doesn't report for training etc… He's already been fined a week's wages.
**STANLEY:** With his son having been kidnapped, I doubt he'll return anytime soon.
**MAURY:** Business is business and a contract is a…

Sheedy whispered into his ear.

**MAURY:** What? … How much?
**STANLEY:** What's he saying?
**MAURY:** He just told me a golfing story. Anyway, we will fully support Bombinho, and of course, we don't wish to look mean-spirited or inhuman in his time of need and desperation so we'll continue to pay his wages.
**STANLEY:** But you just said you wouldn't…
**MAURY:** You must stop holding on to the past, Stanley. What's most important is that Bombinho gets his son back and I get a portion of his salary. There, now I really must go and speak to Bombinho myself and make sure I'm looked after. Cheerio, Stan.

I left after being shown out by Maury's butler, then headed over to Barry's residence.

**BARRY:** It's a disgrace. I'm already short on players. I got one player who takes up two seats on the coach, got lads that don't speak English good. I mean, all they got to do is run around a bit and kick a ball. What's the game coming to?

**STANLEY:** In Bombinho's defence, his son takes priority over a game.

**BARRY:** What was he doing over there in the first place? He just up and left. He deserted us, like a coward. He won't be welcome back, regardless of what anybody says. I've got one striker left, Ricardo and the barebones of a team. Now if you don't mind, my missus and I need to sort out the team's tactics.

It's another training day and Barry had gotten the entire team doing some sprint exercises. Barry loved his team running around a lot and working on their fitness levels. His teams spent more time doing that than anything else, to a point where the ball itself became like a foreign object.

Bombalbo wasn't sprinting on his legs but in a wheelchair. He wasn't in a wheelchair because of injury or other some other medical condition (probably) but because using his legs was too tiring. He huffed and puffed and went up and down like the overweight cyborg he was becoming.

Mystic appeared in front of everybody, skipping merrily, and did a grand jeté to complete his entrance. Mystic had on a replica Bruce Lee *'Game of Death'* yellow jumpsuit. Why he wore that was anybody's guess. Then again, why he did anything and what he was still doing at the club was also a mystery. As Mystic began to open his mouth, Ronnie stealthily backed away and headed towards the changing rooms. Being a first-class documentarian it was important to know all and see all, and us Danish documentarians had eyes like chameleons.

**BEN:** My followers and sinners. Today I stand before you, with the force inside of me. I must say goodbye as I am returning to my spiritual home in Utah, USA to be with my kin. See you in hell... from heaven… or from the USS Enterprise.

Mystic skipped away like a ballet dancer who just couldn't cut it. So, that appeared to be the end of Mystic; hopefully. Barry had watched him give his speech and seen him leave and all I got from Barry was a shrug of the shoulders.

**BARRY:** He was useless. All he did was prattle on about nothing and tell us all to be like water and other useless shit. I don't think he helped select one team, or come up with one formation or set of tactics like my running towards the goal tactics. My wife was more help! Good riddance!

K-Y jogged over to the gaffer with a look of desperation and concern on his face.

**K-Y:** Boss, may I have a word?
**BARRY:** Sure, son.
**K-Y:** When am I going to play again?
**BARRY:** Listen, Jay's playing like a superhuman so I've got no reason to drop him.
**K-Y:** I need to play, boss.
**BARRY:** I know you do but, how can I put this… You're crap. My wife is a better goalie than you.

Barry put an arm around K-Y then patted him on the back and wandered off. I could see K-Y's heart sink. I think I could even feel it hit the ground. Poor lad.

An hour later and the team filtered into the changing rooms, including Ronnie who was acting all innocent and like he was one of the team… well, he was one of the team. Things were different. Things were missing!

**TOMMY:** I've been robbed!
**RONNIE:** Fuck me! They've taken something of mine!
**RICARDO:** Ricardo's penis enlarger!

I eyed Ronnie, who carried on the charade and went through his things like he had been a victim. I wanted to say something, but Ronnie had connections and I valued my testicles. The rest of the team checked their stuff as a call was made to the local police who'd probably be as much help as the South Yorkshire Police would be in policing a football match. Luckily, none of our equipment was laying around there and everything was safely locked up in the Bugmobile as well as at home.

Anyway, I was sure that it would only be a matter of time before Ronnie was eventually caught – by Dwayne for allegedly sleeping with Cheryl and by the police for allegedly nicking everybody's stuff. Hopefully that would happen after the last game of the season, because that would make a terrific ending to our documentary. Fingers were crossed.

Extract from Bombalbo's blog, Food with Bombalbo…

*'Last night I went to an Indian restaurant that is over one hundred metres from my house, so I had to get an Uber there — very long distance. It was not my first time to sample Indian food and I know from the beginning that Indian food is the favourite food of the English and the people of Shyton. Friends tell me that Indians come from India to eat the Indian food in Shyton! So, I went and I tried a speciality from 'Raj's Curry House', hoping to find something as good as Vatapá. I ordered a Vindaloo and I got something more local from Shyton called a Shytinaloo. The coxinha I ate before I left for dinner mixed with the Indian and it was a miracle that I made it home to my lovely toilet. I have bigger shits than I ever had even when I had a huge dinner in the Amazon. My shits were same colour as the curries I had! I think I also saw an onion bhaji. No more Indian restaurants for me. It's been seven hours and I'm still on the toilet. It's good that my toilet seat is soft and massages my butt cheeks.'*

With Bombalbo out as he still had the shits and Bombinho back in Brazil searching for his kidnapped son, Barry played Ricardo upfront with a couple of unknown youths drafted in to play on the wings.

Even with a squad lacking in depth, Barry was still confident that they had too much for Aston Villa.

**BARRY:** Aston Villa have been in woeful form for a while now. They're stagnant, there's something bad about the club, a depression. I feel sorry for the fans as there's a real lack of ambition about the place.
**STANLEY:** What will your tactics be?
**BARRY:** Well, the missus and I have come up with a solid game plan.
**STANLEY:** What's that?
**BARRY:** It's a bit complicated but try to bear with me. Ricky, he'll run towards goal, then Tommy and Dwayne, they'll run towards goal and then the wingers we've brought in, they'll do some more running and then when we've got the ball, we'll kick it at the opposition goal and score a couple. Two nil winners.
**STANLEY:** That's your game plan, is it?
**BARRY:** That's the game plan to success! Now, get out of my way.

Well, I didn't know how he did it but Barry's game plan that could've been devised by Wayne Rooney blew Aston Villa away and got them a comfortable three nil victory, with Tommy getting a brace and Ricardo getting the other with a sweet free kick. They didn't miss the Brazilians at all! Unfortunately, during the latter stages of the second half when Tommy was driving forward in search of his side's fourth goal, a bitter and mean-spirited defender with the playing style of Nobby Stiles, and who'd been given the run around all day by Ricardo and Tommy, performed a 'mistimed' two-foot tackle on Tommy. The tackle caused the crowd to gasp and make heaving noises as Tommy wailed in agony, writhing around on the ground like a mutilated worm. From the look of the tackle and Tommy's reaction, it wouldn't be a surprise if Tommy would be out for the remainder of the season. Quite rightly, the defender was given a straight red. I spoke to Barry about the tackle following the match.

**BARRY:** Well, it's that kind of thing we need to get rid of in the game.

We need to protect our talented players from blatant thuggery. I mean, it was shocking. If one of my players had done that, I'd have 'em out of the club.

**STANLEY:** One of your players has done that kind of tackle. In fact, Tommy performs that kind of tackle quite regularly and you don't say anything.

**BARRY:** I've never ever seen Tommy intentionally injure a fellow pro. Tommy's hard but fair, he's a man's man not some pussy that *you'd* probably like to watch play football.

Barry charged away. I hoped I hadn't damaged our relationship and that he'd continue to participate in our documentary. I was sure that he understood my journalistic nature and need to be objective even if I was a Shytonian, an avid Shyton United fan, and a Tommy Gunn supporter… and employee.

With that win, Shyton United were now on 66 points and looking good for Europa League football at the very least. Liverpool and Manchester City were leading the pack, with Chelsea following closely behind like an effeminate sniffer dog. These were exciting times, and everybody was looking forward to the next few games.

<u>**14<sup>th</sup> April, 2014**</u>

I visited with Tommy a couple of days later, not because he wanted me to chauffeur him anywhere, but just to check on his condition. I'd been busy recently, chauffeuring his wife and kids around instead.

Tommy was laid up in his huge, comfy bed with bandages around his leg.

**STANLEY:** Do you know how long you'll be out for?
**TOMMY:** I'll miss the rest of the run-in, that's for sure.

That was terrible news. Without Tommy, our third top goal scorer and our captain (I still considered Tommy to be club captain, not Ronnie), and with other players also missing, it was going to make successfully completing the season exceedingly difficult. The odds on Shyton United finishing in the top 5 let alone the top four was looking more and more remote. Tommy was the heart and soul of the club (as long as he wouldn't become the Benedict Arnold of Shyton), and without him driving us onwards and upwards then the chances of me winning my bet looked dire.

Tommy's mobile rang. It seemed to ring an awful lot when I interviewed him.

**TOMMY:** Hand me my mobile.
**STANLEY:** Yes sir.

I handed him the mobile. It amazed me how easily I went into servant mode.

**TOMMY:** Yeah? … I'm not joining City! … Who told you? … What!

He hurled his mobile at the wall. The rumour hadn't died, and with a couple or so months before the transfer window would open, the rumours didn't show any signs of stopping. The door opened. Of course we expected Brenda to come in, or perhaps one of the maids bringing with them some much needed refreshments like cups of tea and a few Hob Nobs. Instead, it was Sao. How he had gotten past security and managed to find his way in was anybody's guess.

**TOMMY:** What the fuck are you doing here?

**SAO:** What are you doing here?

**TOMMY:** I live here.

**SAO:** You don't live with me.

**TOMMY:** This is my house.

**SAO:** Get out of my bed!

**TOMMY:** Sao, look around. You see all those photos of me and my family?

**SAO:** Hey, guess who I saw?

**TOMMY:** Who?

**SAO:** Only Tommy's missus having lunch with Ronnie.

**TOMMY:** What?

There were moments in history when you got to witness something tragic about to happen: An explosion, a revolution, a mass catastrophe, a kettle boiling then blowing up – Tommy was that kettle. Tommy completely forgot about where he was and that he was injured as he shot up onto both feet then collapsed to the floor, knocking himself unconscious. If only I had filmed it.

**SAO:** What happened to your leg?

With Sao's eventual help after I had convinced him that he didn't live there and that his name was Sao Columbus and not Sally Hopkins, winner of Little Miss Chesterton, we got Tommy back into bed. I called Tommy's maids and explained the situation. I got out of there before Tommy woke and tried to either take out his frustrations on me or ask me to chauffeur him to find Brenda. If the latter then I was sure I'd be put into a very awkward position as they had a public barney. I instead went to one of Huge Jack's massage parlours for some light relief.

<u>**16<sup>th</sup> April, 2014**</u>

After a month of owning the club, I finally managed to secure an interview with Woody Fillet and Randy Dicks. They'd been rather elusive owners, though in some ways much more vocal and visible than Alexander Kovich – they didn't wear bunny costumes for a start. However, though they appeared to be hands on they'd rarely been in Shyton or in England. They instead spent a considerable amount of time stateside looking after their other franchise.

The interior of their office, previously occupied by Sid Chesterton, Chen Hu, Sheikh Abdullah, unknown owner (if he'd ever stepped foot in here), Alexander Kovich and now the Americans, had a much more different vibe going on. It was full on Americana with the walls being plastered with the heads of stuffed animals such as deer and buffalo, and without a rabbit in sight.

The owners were sat on huge leather sofas that must've been made from at least twenty animals apiece. Randy and Woody smoked cigars that would've put anything Arnold smoked to shame.

The pressing issue was the fans' displeasure about the rising ticket prices and their recent protests that had been suppressed at Randy's and Woody's insistence. Before launching into that subject I started off with some complimentary small talk to make them feel at ease – a tactic most good documentarians used.

**STANLEY:** I like what you've done to the place.
**WOODY:** This right here is genuine 100% American hide, straight from my ranch.
**STANLEY:** Very comfy.
**WOODY:** My hide is darn near the best hide you'll find.
**STANLEY:** Super.

It was odd how when I spoke with Woody and Randy I sounded even more English than usual. Like a pompous, snobbish, yet classy Englishman.

**STANLEY:** And the stuffed animals?
**RANDY:** We got a moose, a gator, a buffalo, lion – I killed 'em all. I

love killing like an asshole. Ain't they pretty?
**STANLEY:** Pretty dead...

Would've been prettier had they still been alive… as a documentarian, I needed to be objective.

**RANDY:** What you say?
**STANLEY:** Super!

I never said 'super'!

**STANLEY:** Settling in okay?
**WOODY:** Like hogs in slop. But you know, we love the Shyton people…

And their money!

**WOODY:** But we couldn't be here 24/7. The cold, the dreariness, the smog, the weird-looking gap-toothed gals, that's why we gotta shoot back to the land of sunshine, oranges and bikinis.

An image of the bloated Woody, hairy back and all, being given a rub-down by a hot young woman who looked like she was about to vomit all over the beached whale became persistent and wouldn't leave my brain. I'd need to spend a good couple of hours with Tiffany (she worked at one of Huge Jack's massage parlours) to help erase that memory—with a few shots of Jägermeister. Anyway, now was the time to grill these epic swindlers.

**STANLEY:** The fans have many grievances regarding your takeover and your subsequent actions; hikes in ticket prices for a fairly impoverished community in a town that had until recently been called the poorer cousin of Calcutta.
**RANDY:** Success don't come cheap. You want the best, you gotta pay the best. The fans should be thanking us we didn't charge more for their hotdogs and fries! Do we sell those?
**STANLEY:** We have pies.
**RANDY:** Key lime?
**STANLEY:** Steak and kidney.
**RANDY:** Steak and what?

**WOODY:** Heck, I just don't know why these fans are acting like a goat with a rifle pointed at its head.

**RANDY:** We already started plans for a slick new stadium that's gonna blow all others away.

**STANLEY:** I've already questioned Maury on this, but why does Shyton United need a new stadium? Creek Alley was renovated only recently and its capacity is sufficient for the town.

**RANDY:** Did he answer?

**STANLEY:** Sort of.

**RANDY:** So let's not run this mule again.

**STANLEY:** What about reports that because of your ownership, the club's debt now stands at £800m?

**RANDY:** That's a truckload of horseshit. The value of this franchise has doubled.

**WOODY**: If we hadn't come riding along like a couple of good ol' boys then this club would be running around like a hog on barbecue night.

**RANDY:** Yeah, we're like a couple of John Waynes.

They seemed more like a couple of John Wayne Gacys to me – a pair of evil clowns. I thanked them for their time and they departed, as they had to head home stateside to get some proper food.

From the Twitter account of @JoeMeek: *'All members of FPL, we're boycotting away game at Spurs. Enough is enough! #NoMoreHikes #FPL'*

In a further protest at Shyton United's pricing policy, a great majority of the Shyton United Supporters' Club, Fudge Packers for Life, boycotted the away game at Spurs, including principle fan Joe Meek.

Luckily for the Shyton United faithful, they didn't miss much as their team put in an awful shift. It was a dire performance by the away team, as the superior footballing side of Tottenham overran Shyton. Spurs' patient build-up play followed by lightning-quick counter attacks were too much for Shyton United, and left Barry Bloomer a frustrated plum-faced spectator on the side lines. Still, without their talisman in Tommy Gunn, not many had given Shyton United a prayer and it was no surprise when they found themselves two goals down by half-time.

The changing room at half-time was not a pleasant place to be. Barry was livid and I had never known a face to turn that colour or to emit that much steam. Angry sweat pinged off his brow.

**BARRY:** You bunch of no-hopers. My missus could've played better. Fuck, my mother-in-law could've done better. If you sacks of shit don't start putting in a shift then don't bother turning up for training. Wankers.

During the second half, Barry Bloomer raged at his players, before urging them on then taking it out on the referee whenever a decision went against them. To Shyton United's credit, they did up their performance level and started to play some decent football. The new lads that had been forced to come into the side did themselves justice and would undoubtedly be welcome at training, and be mentioned by name should there be any future books. Even Ricardo, who you'd have thought would've gone into his resplendent shell, played out of his skin—though you had to wonder if that was because he was playing for any scouts that might've been watching. Scouts tended not to visit Shyton because of its rampaging, ravenous dogs and its rampaging, ravenous women, so would only see Shyton United when they were playing in one of the more desirable parts of the country.

Despite the Fudge Packers' best efforts, Tottenham were able to contain them and keep Ricardo and the unknowns at bay. It looked as though Spurs were quite happy to take their 2-0 as they sat back and invited pressure. But they were sitting back a bit too much as suddenly in the final few minutes, a chance came Shyton's way. Li Bang whipped in a cross that just cried out for a fit striker to head home. Bombalbo strained and groaned as he leapt high into the air like a whale breaching, using a rather fragile and scrawny Spurs defender to enable him to get even higher. Bombalbo grabbed his chest in pain as the ball hit his head and smashed into the net. Shyton scored! Bombalbo fell back to the ground face down, landing on that unfortunate Spurs defender, who gave an agonised scream.

Barry was ecstatic, as were the rest of the Shyton United team and the few Shyton United fans who had made the journey to White Hart Lane. Could Shyton United get another and secure an unlikely draw?

Li Bang then noticed Bombalbo hadn't moved and went over to the massive lump who remained on top of that flattened Spurs defender. Li Bang poked at Bombalbo like he was poking Play-Doh. Li called the referee over and there was a hush around the stadium. It looked bad.

An hour later and White Hart Lane was empty. A mini-crane was driven onto the pitch to lift a lifeless Bombalbo up off the ground, and off the Spurs defender who had also perished. There was a crater-like hole in the ground and the Spurs defender's body was shaped like a U-bend. It was a sad day for football—a tragic accident that should hopefully warn people around the country about the dangers of eating out in Shyton. White Hart Lane's pitch would need extensive work done on it to get it ready for the remainder of the season.

I expected a few solemn words from Barry and some of the players.

**BARRY:** Well, it was terrible.
**STANLEY:** Yes, a truly horrid afternoon; a sad day for football.
**BARRY:** Abso-bleeding-lutely. A pathetic performance, I mean they were all running around like headless chickens. The only ones who emerged with any credit were the young lads I brought into the team. I deserve a lot of credit for doing that,. otherwise it wouldn't even be 2-1.
**STANLEY:** I was talking about Bombalbo.
**BARRY:** This is not the time to talk about that when the team just lost

a match! 3 points dropped!

Barry never took responsibility.

**STANLEY:** Shouldn't you shoulder some of the blame for the dismal first half performance?
**BARRY:** Me? What have I done? Did you see me out there? Fuck off!

Insensitive bastard.

From the blog, Fudge Packer for Life, Joe Meek wrote:
*'…What can you say? The fat tub of Brazilian lard was as mobile as a wheel-less mini and had the grace of Sylvester Stallone but he was a legend. Scored some important goals for us and will be a huge (in every way) loss. It's not shocking, there were fat alkies at the local Fudge and Wrapper who were fitter than Bomba, but you don't expect to see that when a player's going to head a ball. Thoughts for that Spurs player too – crushed by a Brazilian nut. Shit performance as well and those Yanks want us to fork out even more bread to watch 'em! Daylight fucking robbery.'*

After the devastating events of yesterday that left the whole of Shyton, Shyton United Football Club (except Barry Bloomer), and the world of football in shock, Bob and I spent a day compiling and putting together a little tribute to Bombalbo. 'Little Gordito' as he was affectionately known in some parts or 'Humpty Dumpty' as opposition fans knew him, was generally a universally-liked figure in the world of football. His heart was as huge as his appetite – yes, he had a gigantic heart. He often spent time in soup kitchens—even when he was not wanted there because he ended up consuming more than he served to those starving bastards. Even so, I always found him to be a self-effacing gentle soul and pretty much the complete opposite of his compatriot, Bombinho.

I got Bob to hack into Bombalbo's computer and we managed to go through his files in search of any last notes or blogs he might have been writing just before his timely death. We got lucky and found a folder entitled 'blogs' and saw his latest unpublished entry. It was a rather poignant, sad and personal blog that I doubted he would ever have published. It was dated the 18<sup>th</sup> April, just a day before his heart blew up, and here it is:

Extract from Bombalbo's blog, Food with Bombalbo…
*'Today I don't write about food, not even about the delectable Eggs Benedict I had for breakfast – so good, I had it twice. No, today I write because this morning I had bad pain in chest. I thought maybe I was hungry so I had some Crunch Corners, but then still I had pain. It got better after lying on sofa watching entire season of Hell's Kitchen but it made me worry. I went on scales and weighed myself. Is it true what everybody say about me? I was always bigger than most, but I thought big muscles not big fat—like Eric Cartmenez said. Now I think I should try harder and listen to horrible people at fat camp. After game with Tottenham tomorrow I speak with gaffer coach about it. I think he care about me and help me. I write this for me, I think I need to get my feelings off my tummy. Hope no one will read this. Come on, Bomba, you can do it. People jealous of your love cheeks. I must remember to get floor cleaner, and post my review of 'The Stuffed Hamster' restaurant. Memo to self – don't publish this.'*

Poor bugger. I'd like to think that they'd commission a statue of Bombalbo in his memory but I don't think they'd be able to afford it, or that there'd be enough bronze available to make it. Still, our video tribute to the man would be available on YouTube and that should be fitting enough. We made the video to Sir Mix-a-lot's *'Baby Got Back'* – very appropriate and touching.

Following the expected death of Bombalbo from a massive heart attack, Shyton United held a memorial service for him. His body had already been flown back to Brazil on an Airbus A380 (after an autopsy had been deemed not necessary), and his funeral arranged. Maury would attend the funeral on behalf of the club, though quite why he needed to spend another 9 days out there at a 5-star resort located on the Copacabana Beach at the club's expense was anybody's guess (not!).

The Shyton United team, Bombalbo's UK agent, bakers, chefs, fast food cooks, confectioners, butchers, grocers, a representative of the FDF (Food and Drink Federation), and the mini crane that had removed his body from the White Hart Lane pitch all attended the service. It was a solemn affair with a kind of wake held afterwards at the local Krispy Kreme's.

Tommy, Maury, Barry and Ronnie gave the eulogies – Maury did his via Skype from his hotel room in Rio.

**TOMMY:** I hardly knew the fatso. I guess he was alright, never had to head-butt him like I did some of youse. Ta.

Short and sweet, I guess you'd say.

**BARRY:** We'll miss Bomba. He was a good lad. Now, next game's at home to Hull. I'm told that they're my former team so you'd better win, you bunch of overpaid prima donnas!

Ronnie was next and he came up carrying a flute of champagne, and wore a t-shirt advertising **www.RonniesBargains.com**. He held the flute of champers aloft.

**RONNIE:** To Bomba! Now, check this crystal flute out. Top quality crystal, set of 24, yours for £19.99, can't say fairer than that. Speak to me afterwards. Remember, **www.RonniesBargains.com**. The best prices, no questions answered.

Finally, it was Maury's turn. Those of us in attendance had hoped that

Maury's eulogy would actually be better than the others and be an actual eulogy. Here was Maury:

**MAURY:** Thankfully, he passed his medical when signing and the insurance company had no idea that he had a heart condition. Therefore, we're quids in. Cheers, Bombalbo—we'd been wondering how to move you on. Forklift truck, someone said.

Well, I could only apologise to all Shyton United fans and the football public in general. That was all rather appalling. Anyway, now for those Krispy Kreme donuts that were made in honour of Bombalbo – a Bavarian-type donut filled with thick white goo.

**25<sup>th</sup> April, 2014**

The team were back in training, except for Tommy who was still on crutches. He was recovering well. Bob and I were in our BugMobile as we surveilled what was happening on the training ground and in the changing rooms. We spotted Ronnie head to the changing room, perhaps to get some more swag when a rather surprisingly mobile Tommy came up from behind and tapped Ronnie on the shoulder with one of his crutches. Ronnie turned around and got head-butted in typical Tommy fashion. Ronnie collapsed like a sack of Jersey potatoes.

**TOMMY:** Go near my wife again and I'll kill ya!

Tommy's mobile rang to the tune of Chumbawamba's 1997 hit, *'Tubthumping'*. Tommy had a confused look upon his face when checking his mobile.

**TOMMY:** Sao? What do you want? … No, Cheryl ain't my wife… What? Oh shit!

Tommy hung up his mobile. I had never seen him look sheepish before. Ronnie on the other hand had eyes filled with venomous anger, as blood trickled from his nose and into his mouth. He savoured the blood. Was he Beelzebub? He wiped away the excess vampire juice then rose to his feet, with Tommy awkwardly trying to help him whilst maintaining his balance with the aid of his crutches.

**TOMMY:** Sorry mate. Fookin' Sao. Look, fair's fair and you got every right to smack me one. Was an honest mistake.

Tommy was being remarkably decent for someone who was a certified nutter.

**TOMMY:** But you wouldn't hit a guy on crutches, would ya?

He would, and a scuffle broke out on the floor of the changing rooms. It took most of the squad to separate them, with both exchanging insults. Though it would've been an unfair fight due to Tommy's injury, it would have been fascinating to find out who would come out on top between those two. For Shyton United however, this was a disaster. If Tommy was the heartbeat of the team then Ronnie was something quite similar and if they were divided, it was difficult to know how Shyton United were going to get through the rest of the season. Tommy was already close to an exit, would Ronnie remain? If both left then it would be a complete disaster and you'd doubt that the other star players would stay. This was looking like the catalyst for complete doom at my beloved club. Was relegation the following season beckoning?

I needed a swift half to contemplate all of this. Though I was a documentarian, I was a Shyton United fan first and foremost. It was hard to witness the self-destruction of Shyton United.

Maury and Barry had come down to sort out the mess and get both Tommy and Ronnie back on friendly terms while I headed to the Fudge and Wrapper. Inside the pub there was a large gathering of fans in their Shyton United tops and brown and white scarves. The anti-Dicks and Fillet movement was sure gaining momentum.

Joe was holding a placard above his head which read 'Yanks Out!'.

Of course Joe and the rest of these fans had no idea about the scuffle that had broken out between the captain and vice-captain. The club didn't need this at this time.

**JOE:** It's time to get tough. Club's debt is now £1bn. Night and day we'll protest outside grounds with placards!

£1bn? No idea how he reached that number, though I knew that the club's debt was an astronomical figure. I downed my half of Shyton's best and admired the penmanship of some of the placards that were being held aloft. 'Shyton for Shytonians', 'Hands Off Our Fudge!', 'Yanks, No Thanks'. Joe shouted aloud.

**JOE:** We are Shyton United!

A huge cheer went up and Joe and the rest of the fans marched out of the pub. I went with them. I wasn't in the mood but it was my job as a fisherman with Danish ancestry to document all important events. They made the short journey to Creek Alley Stadium, led by Joe. Once they reached the stadium they got out a giant flag, set it alight and chanted:

**SHYTON UNITED FANS:** Dicks and Fillet out! Dicks and Fillet out!
**STANLEY:** Joe, which country's flag do you suppose that to be?
**JOE:** It's the American flag, innit?

Oh dear. The education system in Shyton wasn't the best.

**STANLEY:** It's actually the Liberian flag.
**JOE:** Stamp it out! Stamp it out!

That's what you got when you had somebody like Joe spearhead a campaign, no matter how righteous it was.

**JOE:** Fuck, we don't want to be upsetting Liberians!

I left the shambolic protest that was sure to get zero results and made a visit to Maury. He was now back home, but yes, you guessed it, he was in a new home. His tastes had somehow gotten more ostentatious, as his latest home was a bona fide palace—it was the equal of Buckingham Palace with fountains, sculptures and a driveway that wasn't much shorter than Stormont's.

After a few minutes of walking, I was shown into a grand hall adorned with chandeliers, and paintings of people I hadn't heard of. Maury was relaxing on a sofa that might have been the world's biggest sofa.

**MAURY:** The club's in great shape, never been better.
**STANLEY:** The club reported record losses.
**MAURY:** You know, the media are just scaremongering. The fans don't know the facts. I've seen the books, I know what goes in and out. And I can reassure everybody that I've never had it this good.

Maury showed me into his own tearoom, where we were served apple crumble and custard. It was rather scrumptious.

**MAURY:** More custard, Stan?
**STANLEY:** Absolutely!

My mobile vibrated with a message from Bob. I couldn't believe what he had just written.

**STANLEY:** Woody Fillet and Randy Dicks have sold the club?

Maury didn't look at all surprised or bothered and in fact kept pouring more Waitrose custard into my bowl. With all his money, couldn't his chef have made fresh stuff?

**MAURY:** That's old news. Happened this morning.
**STANLEY:** What? Why didn't you tell me?
**MAURY:** Didn't want to spoil your apple crumble.
**STANLEY:** I'm flabbergasted. What now? Keep pouring.
**MAURY:** Don't worry, we'll announce the new owners very soon. Your apple crumble's getting cold.

I finished my apple crumble and headed home. I was sure that Joe (his campaign had actually succeeded) and the rest of the Shyton support would be delighted. With the debt trebling under their ownership, death threats to their families and the stress of flying first-class between America and England once a month, it had obviously taken its toll on the loveable Yanks. Who would be the new owners this time? How many owners had there been since Sid sold up? This was starting to be quite the joke. My head hurt so I went home and took a long hot bath using sea salts I'd gotten from my aunt Joan for Christmas. It was a home game against Hull tomorrow, what else could happen?

<u>**26<sup>th</sup> April, 2014**</u>

It was a home game against Barry's former club, Hull City—not that Barry seemed to be aware they were his former employers. I turned up to the ground a good few hours before kick-off, after receiving a cryptic message from Maury, which I had assumed was telling me that I'd get to meet the new owners. Rumours had been circulating all morning on fan websites, Joe's blog, Reddit, and Twitter that new owners were already in place.

I made my way into the new owners' office, an office that had already been painted in gold leaf. Lavish! Seated in their splendid, shiny office were two well-known British personalities. Unlike the previous owners of Shyton United, these two had pedigree and were real football men. They'd danced the dance before, having owned a couple of clubs in the past with varying levels of success. One club had reached the league cup final and the other had yo-yoed between the Premier League and the Championship. They were also purveyors of hard-core and soft-core pornography and had numerous deals with Huge Jack (Their company, Bert's Silver Linings Inc., was the main distributor for Huge Jack Productions). It was no surprise that these two would go on to own Shyton United, as they'd been coming to Shtyon for years to check on the films being made by Huge Jack Productions, as well as make sure their stars were well-rehearsed. They had been occasional spectators of Shyton United's games as well, not just when Huge Jack became a club sponsor but before then as they'd been on friendly terms with Sid Chesterton.

The two new owners were Bob Silver and Bob Gilbert, the two Bobbies as they were affectionately known. They were both quite distinct, especially when they were standing next to each other because Silver was a tall, lanky fella with hair to match his name whilst Gilbert was hobbit-like (though some would fairly describe him as troll-like), with a voice like a gremlin.

**GILBERT:** First of all, we're lifelong fans of Shyton United so we're here for the long run.

This was of course quite untrue with regard to being lifelong fans. He'd made the same statement when they were being introduced as the new owners of the two previous clubs. Strangely, the fans always bought it.

**SILVER:** Lifelong.
**GILBERT:** However, we just can't believe the amount of debt this club is in.
**SILVER:** Incredible.

Silver brushed his beard and I caught a glimpse of his many gold rings. He'd put Ringo Starr to shame!

**STANLEY:** You're both successful businessmen, surely you would've thoroughly checked and done due diligence.
**GILBERT:** We took the club on in good faith but we're in shock. There'll be no transfers this summer.
**SILVER:** Not a sausage.

This was not a good sign. Shyton United was in desperate need of new signings because without them I feared that Shyton would be relegated the following season.

**STANLEY:** Not even a new striker? Shyton United desperately needs one of those!
**GILBERT:** Nope. We thought getting fourth would be nice but now it's bloody essential. I mean, what the club's spent on redecorating is more than the GDP of Greece.

I once again, with my keen fisherman's eye, surveyed the gold leaf-painted walls. Must've cost a pretty penny.

**STANLEY:** Is that real gold leaf on the walls?
**GILBERT:** Of course. We don't do things by half around here.

Shyton United had no chance. We had might as well pack up, go home and call in an insolvency firm.

The match was soon upon us, and as Hull City was Barry's former club despite his denials, I thought I'd get a few words from him. Would he approach the match any differently? He surely knew Hull City and their players so well that this match would make for an easy tactical battle.

**BARRY:** This'll be a tough game, there's no doubt about it. We're entering into the unknown here, foreign territory.
**STANLEY:** But they're your former club!
**BARRY:** Who? Most of their players are a bit foreign, never heard of them, can't even pronounce their midfielder's name. Elmo? Is that his name? Thought that was a character from the Muppets.
**STANLEY:** Sesame Street.
**BARRY:** Elmohandy? Amen Elmodandy? Never heard of him.
**STANLEY:** You signed him.
**BARRY:** No idea who they are or where they come from. They could be a bunch of Peles in that team, could destroy us.
**STANLEY:** Hull City's battling relegation.

Barry wasn't of this planet.

**BARRY:** Anyway, I have a team to get ready to take on Stoke. Move out of my way, son.

So, to the match and it was a dour affair for the Fudge Packers. If it wasn't for some outstanding saves by Jay Patel, Shyton United could've been trounced but they managed to scrape a 1-1 draw against the mighty Hull. Only a miracle could get them 4th now. The Shyton United team trudged off the pitch to boos from their fans. The gaffer wasn't best pleased either, booing them as well. Never in all my years documenting football and hamsters, had I seen a manager boo his own team… in public.

**BARRY:** Losers!
**STANLEY:** Booing your own team is hardly going to help matters.
**BARRY:** Did you watch the game? They were all dreadful. They're all to blame, not me! The missus could've done a better job than all of them.

I scuttled over to the post-match press conference, where the Bobbies were holding court. They didn't seem pleased and who could blame them?

**SILVER:** Terrible game.
**GILBERT:** After witnessing that, the whole team should be sold. Bunch of overpaid prima-donnas. You know how much some of these

guys get paid?
**SILVER:** £100,000 a week!
**GILBERT:** A week! These people live in a fantasy world.

This wasn't going to help team morale.

**TABLOID JOURNALIST:** Is it true that you're interested in buying French international striker, Jean-Paul Jones?

What the! That was news to me! The Bobbies had just told me that they wouldn't be purchasing anybody and would be closely holding the purse strings and now they're being linked with a move for a French international? Blimey!

**GILBERT:** It's true we put in a bid of £50m for Jones and offered wages of £200,000 a week. We believe this club can afford and should have one stellar performer.
**SILVER:** One stellar.
**GILBERT:** Now, we've got work to do if we're going to rescue this club.

None of this made sense. Didn't anybody give straight answers or answers that they'd honour anymore? This would need investigating. Where was Maury?

From the blog, Fudge Packer for Life, Joe Meek wrote:
*'Well, looks like our campaign to get rid of the Yanks paid off. Yeah, on the face of it, it was about ticket prices, and it was, but it was also to get those 'assholes' out of town. Anyone that calls the beautiful game 'soccer ball' should not own a 'franchise'. New owners are English, they'll get us and they'll bring the prices down I'm sure. No Englishman who owned a football team ever screwed the club, the fans and the town over...'*

Had to end the extract there. What a dollop of Shyton cottage cheese! I could think of a number of Englishmen who'd screwed over the clubs they owned or ran, look at… (Following names removed due to potential lawsuits… but they know who they are!)

<u>**28<sup>th</sup> April, 2016**</u>

Bob and I were in the Bugmobile outside of Dwayne's luxury mansion. He no longer allowed interviews, nor did he allow anybody to enter his home. He had tightened security even further once he'd heard about the kerfuffle between Ronnie and Tommy, groundless as it was. He hadn't heard however, who Sao had really seen Cheryl with, nor had he heard that Cheryl had been with anybody. Dwayne was an idiot. Could it be that he secretly didn't care whether Cheryl slept around or not? Bob and I had discussed this at length and that maybe he just enjoyed acting the prat while continuing to play a sleuthing game. If he'd dug any deeper then surely he would've known what most of us already knew, that Cheryl was cheating on him and was doing it with 'Del-Boy' wannabe Ronnie Morrison.

Despite Dwayne's best efforts to build a great wall of Dwayne around his prison, that didn't stop us from being able to see and hear everything that was going on inside. At that moment in the evening as most people were settling in and Sonny was being disciplined, Dwayne and Cheryl relaxed on a sofa watching the timeless classic, *'Sleeping with the Enemy'* – a film starring Julia Roberts.

Our equipment was so advanced that we could pick up a mouse sneeze. However, we hadn't bet on how sophisticated our equipment was when we heard someone speak and yet neither Dwayne nor Cheryl seemed to utter a word. From what we gathered after analysing the audio we had actually been able to pick up Dwayne's thoughts, his inner voice!

**DWAYNE:** She's mine. Tight in my arms… yes, you're mine forever. You like that baby? Nobody's going to come near you, not while I'm watching you. When you become a couple, you don't live a single life. Couple means two, always together, never apart. Ain't ever going to happen what happened to my family. My dad and uncles and grandad won't come near this place, not while Cheryl's my wife. Cheryl, every move you make, yes I know that Police song word for word.

Cheryl then actually spoke—for real spoke.

**CHERYL:** Drink, babes?

**DWAYNE:** No, no, I'm good.
**CHERYL:** I'm just gonna pop to the shops.
**DWAYNE:** What for?
**CHERYL:** Err… you know, I've run out of tampons.
**DWAYNE:** Oh, right.

That was the perfect answer to make the guy want to end the conversation quickly, as well as make him feel super uncomfortable. He wouldn't have a clue about Cheryl's menstrual cycle.

**DWAYNE:** Don't forget your tracker.

She tapped her ankle and soon left the house, pulling away in her cute sports car. Incredibly, and maybe this killed our theory, Dwayne pulled away in his customised black Hummer. He was on the trail, and we were on their trail. Maybe this was going to bring an end to the story.

The drive was short, as Cheryl just went down her tree-lined street to another tree-lined street. All these rich footballers lived in close proximity to each other because the affluent residential area of Shyton was incredibly new and small. Cheryl pulled up to the kerb and got out of the car with her skirt riding higher than Beyoncé heights. She went to an extravagant, over-the-top, blinged-out house that was either owned by a rapper with no taste, or Sonny Jackson. As we'd been to see Sonny before, we knew exactly where we were.

Dwayne parked a little further away from Cheryl's car, and we parked a bit further back still. We had a good vantage point to see everything that Dwayne was doing, and anything that Cheryl might do when greeting Sonny on his porch. But why was she at Sonny's? Was this a new secret meeting place for Ronnie and Cheryl? Surely Sonny wasn't going to risk anything after his beating at the hands of that woman? Sonny had been much changed since that altercation. He'd rarely been seen anywhere except for when he had to honour his contract, playing for Shyton. He was a shell of his former self and we feared for him at the hands of any woman. Unless he'd turned into a masochist, this wasn't going to end well.

Sonny answered the door and stepped back a few steps. Cheryl smiled a gleaming smile that exuded confidence. Confidence that anybody would feel when you were in the presence of somebody like Sonny who feared you and your kind. Dwayne didn't hang around, however. He revved his engine, burned rubber and screeched away like he had just committed a robbery. Cheryl turned, she was well aware of everything… the sly minx. As soon as Dwayne was out of sight, Cheryl smiled at Sonny again and skipped away from Sonny's and back into her car, leaving Sonny scratching his head. Bob and I did the same. What was all that about?

Once Cheryl was dust, I went up to Sonny's house and rang his doorbell. He eventually opened the door. He had a dressing gown on, and was trembling so much that it was like his nerves had been shot. He stammered when he spoke.

**STANLEY:** What did Cheryl want?
**SONNY:** I-I d-don't know.
**STANLEY:** Hmm, alright.

I raised my hand and Sonny staggered back, protecting his head, reminding me of Gollum when he feared being hit.

**SONNY:** Dontcha hurt me!

Sonny closed the door. It would be interesting to see what would happen tomorrow at training.

We arrived at the training ground early the next morning waiting for the guaranteed altercation between Dwayne and Sonny. It was starting to look clear that Dwayne just fancied getting into situations with the wrong party. He probably got off on it, the sick bastard.

Sonny arrived, looking shaky as he timidly went inside the entrance of the training ground. Dwayne came tearing up, flying out of his car like a whirlwind of jealous rage. He was on the warpath like a juiced up Tony Blair, and jumped Sonny from behind. A part of me was starting to feel sorry for Sonny, as it looked as though he had given up his chauvinistic ways. There was a brief one-sided scuffle with Sonny cowering, trying to protect himself and muttering inaudible things. Ronnie sneaked out of the changing rooms and hid behind a white pillar. The smug git had a look upon his face that wasn't smug this time, it was a confused why-hadn't-he-copped-on-it-was-me look.

It was Li Bang and K-Y who eventually managed to pull Dwayne off of Sonny. Sonny appeared to have emerged out of the kerfuffle without much damage being done. Had Dwayne thrown any punches? Was this just for show? I went in for a closer inspection as Sonny remained on the ground. There were some superficial scratches to Sonny's face, but nothing major and nothing to what he'd experienced at the hands of that righteous woman.

**DWAYNE:** What you been doing with Cheryl?
**SONNY:** Wh-wh-what you chatting 'bout, playa?

Sonny didn't even have the confidence to look at Dwayne in the face.

**DWAYNE:** I ain't the playa, you the playa!
**SONNY:** N-n-no. I did nothing. I don't mess with other playa's bitches, I swear, dawg.
**DWAYNE:** You calling her a bitch, now? Look at me!

Dwayne was enjoying this, having such dominance and power over another human being – I bet it felt good. The smugness was obviously contagious and he'd caught a whole load of it from Ronnie… maybe via Cheryl like an STD. I stood with K-Y and Li Bang who had let go of Dwayne after he brushed them off like lint from a T-shirt.

**K-Y:** Women can be so problematic.

I wondered how K-Y would know. Dwayne towered over Sonny, who looked as though he had the fear of god in him.

**DWAYNE:** Why was my Cheryl at yours last night?
**SONNY:** Please don't hurt me!

It amazed me how Sonny's speech had gotten less hip-hop since his beating. He was now intelligible.

**DWAYNE:** Answer the goddamn question or I'll kick your arse!

Sonny broke down in a flood of tears that were biblical in proportion.

**SONNY:** I don't know! I DON'T KNOW!

Sonny wailed, and everybody believed him. Ronnie sneaked off back to the rock he'd crawled out from, and Dwayne pretended to storm off like a man on a mission to discover who his wife's secret lover was. It was baffling. One quick search on OldFlamesReunited.com would've yielded the answer he was looking for.

K-Y and Li-Bang helped Sonny up and they headed to the changing rooms.

The players trained, put through their paces as only Barry Bloomer could do. He made them run and run, and taught them a new tactic of running towards the opposition's goal and shooting when there was an opening. It was a brave new tactic from the footballing mastermind that was Bloomer.

Sonny though was clearly not up to it and, with permission, headed back to the showers early. K-Y soon joined him out of frustration because of how bad Jay Patel was in training. Bloomer ordered K-Y to the showers to help clear his mind and perhaps get the hint that he should tell his agent to find him a new club sharpish.

The tactics and training of Barry Bloomer were boring me as it was like a typical schoolboys' training session that could've taken place anywhere across England, with little emphasis on anything other than winning and playing out of your skin. I joined K-Y and Sonny in the showers, which meant I spied on them in a completely non-perverted, non-Korean way. The only time I would consider same-sex relations would be if I were stuck on a fishing boat lost at sea and the only company were a bunch of horny Danish fishermen.

The steam rose out of the showers, and gave the changing room a feel of a sauna. For some reason K-Y was pointing at Sonny's crotch. Was this going to be the moment when all would be revealed and Sonny would complete his transformation? If it hadn't been for the fact that Sonny was showering, I could've sworn that he was sweating. He was nervous being around K-Y… he was nervous being around everybody at the minute.

**K-Y:** Whoa, what's that huge thing?
**SONNY:** Y-yo, wh-why you staring dere, playa?

Sonny backed away.

**K-Y:** Look, what is that?
**SONNY:** M-my mamba?
**K-Y:** Nah, the thing on your mamba.

Now even I looked harder as I hid behind a locker, doing what Ronnie had done earlier. K-Y was right. Sonny lifted up his mamba like he was lifting up a headless shovel.

**SONNY:** Th-there ain't no thing on my m-mamba. Yo dawg, stop looking… it's just love bites.
**K-Y:** Love bites? Right! You should get it checked out.
**SONNY:** W-what you be knowing 'bout dis shizzle?

With every spoken word, Sonny inched farther and farther away.

**K-Y:** I've seen a lot of mambas.

Sonny backed away until he was out of sight.

**K-Y:** Hi Stanley.

I backed away until I too was out of sight. No matter how curious I was about the whole business and my temptation to experiment for research purposes I decided it wasn't the right time. And I was sure that the answer to the Beatles song 'Girl' was that pain wouldn't lead to pleasure.

I had backed away so far that I witnessed Dwayne charging at Ronnie! What the fugu! Dwayne pummelled Ronnie with a flurry of fists that would've made some very good boxer proud. Ronnie tried getting in a few words but his mouth was busy getting the shit beaten out of it. Dwayne had finally worked it out, or perhaps he'd known all along and had been merely playing games, luring Ronnie into a false sense of security. He was the spider and Ronnie was the unsuspecting fly. Dwayne sure did pick his moments.

**DWAYNE:** Why you sexting Cheryl?

A foolish move indeed! Ronnie must've known that Dwayne would bug Cheryl's mobile. For fugu's sake, we'd even tapped her mobile and had many a pleasurable evening servicing ourselves looking at pictures of Cheryl—pictures that would've put Jennifer Lawrence's to shame! But it did beg the question, how long had Dwayne known this? It was highly doubtful that Ronnie had been 'sexting' with Cheryl only recently. What was Dwayne playing at? Bob would need to confront him!

**BOB:** Eh?

Through a bloody and gurgling mouth, Ronnie responded.

**RONNIE:** I didn't, I swear. Bruv, you got it all wrong!

Unlike when Sonny was being attacked, nobody tried to separate Dwayne and Ronnie, which I took to mean that nobody cared for the wheeler-dealer bastard. I certainly wasn't going to come to his aid, especially as my bank account was dangerously low on funds, and the Rolex watches he sold me had been duds that I couldn't even give away.

Ronnie was crying like a little baby. Dwayne rose up off of him perhaps out of pity. It was, let's admit it, hard to know who to root for here. Both those plebs were certainly no fisherman's friends. They were both utter arseholes and made the case that hot women *were* attracted to bastards and why I was single.

**DWAYNE:** You're not worth it.

Dwayne then rugby-kicked Ronnie in the ribs proving that his statement hadn't been true and Ronnie was worth it.

**RONNIE:** My ribs!

Dwayne spat at the ground and stormed off like a pissed-off, stubborn tornado that refused to be typical and went off in a straight path. With at least one of Ronnie's ribs bruised or cracked, would Shyton United be able to field a team to complete the season? Barry Bloomer came rushing over and he tended to Ronnie. He called over the physios and the team doctor.

I went after Dwayne, who grabbed his gear from the changing rooms then headed straight to his car.

**DWAYNE:** I'm done with this club. Too many playas want my woman.
**STANLEY:** Only one, I think.

Dwayne stopped in his tracks. A wee bit of urine seeped out of my Johansen.

**DWAYNE:** You trying to be funny? Hated this club from the first minute I stepped foot in this wannabe Oldham.

Dwayne made a call on his mobile.

**DWAYNE:** Sheedy… Tell the gaffer I'm outta Shyton. Find me a non-threatening club, like Swansea or something, or see if Arsenal Ladies are interested… Yeah, miserable and dangerous working conditions… Perfect way out…

**STANLEY:** Was this your plan all along? Did you want this to happen so you could get out of your contract?
**DWAYNE:** I completely reject the accusation and…

Suddenly, a blacked-out SUV pulled up and some heavy-set men in FBI-like suits raced out and bundled Dwayne into the back of the SUV. It sped off and away from the training ground. I turned to Bob in astonishment, mouthing 'what the fugu just happened?'

FUGU: A pufferfish, eaten as a delicacy in Japan. Prepared incorrectly, it can be deadly. Fugu was my fish of the day.

I was woken early by a ringing in my ears which I then realised was my phone ringing. I answered, and to my surprise it sounded like an awful Michael Jackson impersonator.

**STANLEY:** K-Y, is that you?

There was high-pitched breathing. I didn't even know that was possible.

**STANLEY:** K-Y? Do you know what time it is?
**MYSTERIOUS VOICE (PROBABLY K-Y):** No, it isn't James. Jay's been done.
**STANLEY:** Been done?
**MYSTERIOUS VOICE (DEFINITELY K-Y):** Drugs in his house. Lots of them. Police station. You don't know me. Bye.
**STANLEY:** Bye K-Y.
**MYSTERIOUS VOICE (BET THE HOUSE IT'S K-Y):** Bye, Stan.

The line went dead. I made a quick call to a contact I had at Shyton police station and sure enough, Jay Patel was in jail for his alleged involvement in the distribution of class A drugs. I popped down to the police station and was taken to Jay's cell. He cut a pathetic-looking figure. I asked him if the allegations were true and of course he denied it. However, my contact showed me photos of the interior of his rundown two up, two down house and it was filled to the rafters with white powder. There was more white powder in there than in a washing detergent factory.

My contact told me that Jay kept telling them he'd been framed but he couldn't say by whom. No one had been seen sneaking into Jay's house and it was looking like Jay had either been royally stitched up or he was the biggest distributor of cocaine since Pablo Escobar. If it were the latter, then that would represent quite the achievement for a guy from a small irrelevant town somewhere in northern India.

<u>**1<sup>st</sup> May, 2014**</u>

The hits just kept on coming. With Jay being charged with multiple counts of drug trafficking, dealing and distributing, training today had a rather weird atmosphere. However, K-Y was rather sprightly and eager to impress, as it looked like he was once again Shyton United's number one. Another notable absentee from training was one Sonny Jackson. Where was he?

Calls were made but he couldn't be reached. We went round to his house and nobody answered the door. We had a strange feeling of déjà vu that he'd done one like Bombinho before him. Except which country would he escape to? Maybe he was in desperate need of a psychiatrist.

K-Y performed admirably in goal. He only let in a couple of dozen howlers from Shyton's reserves, while what was left of the first team were getting massages.

**BARRY:** Jay's as fucked as a turkey leading up to Christmas. Would be a miracle if he's able to be back in time. So, we've got no choice but to let K-Y back in the team. We've got him on a program so intensive he should be like Peter Schmeichel when we're done.
**STANLEY:** So no replacements coming?
**BARRY:** Are you kidding me? And let that clown K-Y back in between the sticks? We're allowed an emergency loan signing if we're short. We're just waiting to hear back from the FA.


From the blog, Fudge Packer for Life, Joe Meek wrote:
*'Don't look as though ticket prices are gonna come down. Tried to get talks with the owners but they ain't returning our calls. If anything, with what they're saying, ticket prices might be going up again. Can't trust these guys. They're shadier than Huge Jack.'*

<u>**2<sup>nd</sup> May, 2014**</u>

For once, Joe Meek wasn't far off. There were allegations today in *'The Shyton Daily'* of bribery and corruption aimed at Bob Silver and Bob Gilbert. Their purchase of Shyton United was coming under scrutiny, as well as their dealings with Huge Jack. I did my usual visit to Maury's, who was out on his own private golf course practicing his putting.

**MAURY:** Bogus charges.

Maury swung his club. He'd been putting the hours in.

**STANLEY:** Where are Messrs. Gilbert and Silver? No one's been able to reach them for comment since the story broke.
**MAURY:** Did you know this palace has its very own dungeon?
**STANLEY:** What about Tommy Gunn? Rumours continue to persist that he's off to City in the summer. Have you secretly done a deal to sell him?
**MAURY:** They say inquisitive people were tortured down there.
**STANLEY:** Are you threatening me, Maury?
**MAURY:** Look at my swing.

I saw Bob back away.

**STANLEY:** Tommy Gunn?
**MAURY:** A lot of the equipment is still down there.

I then backed away as well. Maury was getting to be a right prickly pear.

We made our way back home in the Bugmobile, making a quick stop at the newsagents. Bob and I almost suffered simultaneous cardiac arrests when we saw the headline on *'The Shyton Daily'* newspaper:

*'SONNY JACKSON DEAD!'*

Bob was speechless! I read on.

**STANLEY:** Cause of death, unknown disease. Crikey!

Of course my immediate thoughts were who would fill the left back role in Shyton's last two games. Shyton barely had a team anymore!

<u>**3<sup>rd</sup> May, 2014**</u>

In their penultimate game of the season, Shyton United were away at West Ham United.

Barry gave a team talk to a bunch of mostly unknown Shyton United players that even I didn't know the names of.

**BARRY:** Seeing as Jay's stuck in jail waiting to be deported (probably), Sao banned, Tommy injured, Bombalbo and Sonny dead, Dwayne missing and Bombinho still in Brazil searching for his son, we're short. Now, we have enough players from our reserve team to cover Bombalbo, Sonny, Tommy, Sao, Bombinho and Dwayne but who can be our goalkeeper, seeing as we haven't found an adequate replacement?

K-Y was beaming. Surely he'd be back in goal for this game.

**BARRY:** Ronnie, could you play in goal?

Right there I witnessed the death of a man, spiritually. K-Y's face sunk like the Titanic, and he was crushed. There's nothing like a man whose life, whose essence had been sucked out like somebody had stuck a Dyson down his throat. He was more deflated than one of Huge Jack's faulty sex dolls.

The Shyton United team trotted out, whilst K-Y had to be dragged out – lifeless as he was. The Shyton United away section cheered passionately for their team—they had decided to return, seeing as there was an outside chance that they could still get fourth and qualify for the holy grail that was the Champions League. Bubbles were blown all around Upton Park. A cracking game would surely follow.

Ronnie did a magnificent job in goal, repelling every shot that came his way like he was repelling offers that were well below his asking price. K-Y didn't notice, as he was in a trance-like state… Had he slipped into a coma? Should I have alerted the medical staff? Nah, sure he was fine.

Despite the fact that Shyton fielded a mostly inexperienced team, they played exceptionally well with real fight. Though a dying cat could've looked as sprightly against a woeful and lacklustre West Ham side whose players were more interested in what excuses to come up with for the missus when taking a girlfriend away for a dirty weekend.

The only goal of the game was a rather laughable affair, with Ricardo playing a one-two with Li then hitting a hopeful, looping shot that somehow sailed over the mentally-preoccupied West Ham keeper.

I caught up with Barry after his team deservedly won 1-0. Having said that, a team of Bobs could've won against that West Ham side. Despite what Bob might say, he was a worse footballer than Robert Rosario.

**BARRY:** Well, I was magnificent. The way I led my team to victory. Playing Ricardo on the left wing, touch of class.
**STANLEY:** Ricardo always plays on the left wing.
**BARRY:** Any tinker man would've been tempted to switch him and put him up front. Not me – stick to what works.
**STANLEY:** You fear change?
**BARRY:** Don't be a wally.
**STANLEY:** Rather fortuitous victory considering how the Hammers already had one foot on the beach and one hand holding a piña colada.
**BARRY:** Why should that bother me? That's for their gaffer to sort out. All I care about is me winning. If you ain't got nothing interesting to ask I'll be off.

Barry left in a bit of a huff. There was something very Luis Jalapeno about Barry Bloomer. Luis was an arrogant numpty which was clear as day but Barry, he was just as bad despite the man of the people image he liked to portray.

<u>**5<sup>th</sup> May, 2014**</u>

The sun shone down on a headstone, which bore the name Sonny 'Doughboy' Jackson, aged 25 years – beloved son, brother, mentor to Li, nightclub owner and wannabe G.

Good news: Tommy was no longer on crutches and was expected back imminently!

The remaining members of the team gathered for the funeral, except Dwayne who still hadn't been heard from, not that anybody had tried to locate him.

According to the Shyton coroner who had done a rush job on Sonny as he'd already booked his holiday to Benidorm, it turned out that they weren't love bites on Sonny's penis but some unknown venereal disease that was now named 'Sonny Jackson's Disease'.

Out of all the mourners (and there weren't many), the one guy most upset appeared to be Li Bang. Aside from him, Brenda looked incredibly upset on this most glorious of days when the sun made a rare appearance in this glum part of England. I hadn't even realised that she and Sonny had any form of relationship. She patted her face dry, as tears appeared to be streaming down her face.

**TOMMY:** You alright?

With the amount of surgery Brenda had done she was now as intelligible as a mumbling, still alive Sonny. Her mouth could barely open and none of the muscles in her face seemed to work. A crack team of code breakers deciphered the following dialogue as uttered by Brenda.

**BRENDA:** Hardly knew him.
**TOMMY:** What?
**BRENDA:** It's the sun. Too bloody hot.
**TOMMY:** What? Why you crying?

Something went off in Tommy's head like he was Sherlock Holmes and just cracked the case.

**TOMMY:** Sao was right… but wrong! You did fuck him! You bastard!

Tommy dived head first onto Sonny's coffin and head-butted it
repeatedly. He knocked himself out on the third head-butt. If Tommy
didn't have a boxer's brain then he must have the strongest skull ever!
When he awoke in hospital some hours later, he demanded he and
Brenda get tested for Sonny Jackson's disease. Both were cleared and
Tommy had to sleep on the sofa.

<u>**7th May, 2014**</u>

A couple of days later and I got a call from Tommy. He had patched things up with Brenda for the umpteenth time, though that wasn't the reason why he was calling. He was calling for a whole other reason that he wouldn't divulge over the phone. Instead he demanded that I come and pick him up then take him to Creek Alley Stadium. He told me to be quick about it, as he wasn't paying me to sit on my fat arse. Yes, those were his words.

Even though it was close to midnight, I did as instructed because my fledgling limo business couldn't afford to turn away clients and these Shyton United footballers were our bread and butter. I got down there sharpish and Tommy climbed in the back. He was dressed in a black SAS-like uniform, which raised my suspicions.

**STANLEY:** Tommy, what's going on?
**TOMMY:** I pay you to drive, not ask questions.
**STANLEY:** I am a documentarian. Asking questions comes second nature, first nature being fishing.

Tommy wasn't talking. By what he was wearing, where we were going and at the time we were going there I suspected that Tommy was going to do something Maury would've been proud of. Sometimes you had to fight fire with fire.

**STANLEY:** If I'm right and you're going to do what I think you're going to do then don't you think this is the worst possible car to go there in?
**TOMMY:** A car's a car. It's black, innit?
**STANLEY:** Well, no, it isn't black. I don't know how you didn't notice, because this car's visible from the moon as it's painted in gold. Remember, you asked me to get it re-sprayed in gold? I think your exact words were, 'get the car done in the *blingiest* colour, get it done in *Goldfinger* gold so that every fucker knows I'm coming from a mile off and can get the fuck outta my way', sir. We're driving in a car so bright that we don't need to use the headlights at night. Sir, people have reported this car to the authorities claiming that the apocalypse is coming.
**TOMMY:** Keep your gob shut.

We arrived at the stadium. Tommy bunged the security a couple of fifties each. We headed to Maury's office. I wasn't quite sure why I had gone with Tommy, as I was now an accessory but I was curious to know what Tommy would discover.

**STANLEY:** Is any of this wise? Breaking into Maury's office?
**TOMMY:** I gotta find out what's going on. I don't trust him.

Somebody not trusting Maury? That was a first! Tommy flicked through the files in a filing cabinet and spotted a folder labelled 'transfers'. He pulled it out. There were a bunch of Shyton United players named on there, alongside their overinflated transfer fees. It was truly shocking how much Shyton had blown – enough money to build and run a hospital! Then there was a document entitled 'proposed outgoings' and on it was one name, Tommy's, and his proposed transfer to City for £50m. Also on the paper was a contact at *The Shyton Daily* and their phone number.

**TOMMY:** I knew it!

As we'd suspected, Maury had been behind the rumours all along.

**STANLEY:** What are you going to do about it, Tommy?
**TOMMY:** I don't know.

I believed him. I took him home, along with a photocopy of the evidence. I would've dreaded to be Maury at that moment. You didn't want to be the target of Tommy's head.

I took a walk around Shyton town centre. It was just a few days before the big game against Crystal Palace. Should Shyton win by a landslide and their respective rivals for fourth get thrashed, then Shyton United, SHYTON BLOODY UNITED, would qualify for Europe for the first time in their history. And not just qualify for Europe but for a chance to play in the Champions League no less! A remarkable position to be in for a club deemed relegation favourites by the commentators, no-hopers by the media and tossers by opposing fans. Shyton, with a population rivalling Haringey, were now cemented as one of the top-sides in the country and by far the most controversial. There had hardly been a day gone by that they hadn't been in the papers or websites for their footballing success, for the deaths, for the allegations of fraud and for the unpaid transfer fees. It had been a real rollercoaster of a ride and on Saturday it would all come to an end. Either Shyton United would finish fifth, which would still be an incredible achievement and would qualify them for the dreaded Europa League or they'd nab fourth in the most unlikely turn of events since Cheryl inexplicably agreed to marry Dwayne Ford. By the way, there had been no news of Dwayne's whereabouts and local authorities still couldn't give a fuck.

There was a noticeable tension in the air. Huge Jack's Studios had closed down production; the high street was filled with nerves and questions. Could it actually happen that Shyton play host to Barcelona or Rubin Kazan? At the local butcher's, grocer's, baker's and confectioner's – otherwise known as Tesco's, Shytonians gathered, much like their grandparents would've done in actual local shops, to gossip about this monumental game that was fast approaching. They got together and nattered until security told them to buy something or bugger off—true Shytoninan hospitality.

As I wandered the streets of my beloved hometown I passed Homeless Bill—the resident Oscar the Grouch; a tramp who resembled Worzel Gummidge and still stank of Versace's Eros cologne since Bombinho had spotted him one day and ordered he be drenched in the stuff. While I meandered I met Joe Meek, bottle of beer in hand, in a contemplative mood much like I was. Joe was nervous, he trembled as he drank his bottle of Shyton Best, trickles of beer escaping down his stubbly chin.

**JOE:** Who would've thought it, eh? I've been opposed to most things this season but never in my wildest dreams could I have dreamt that we'd be on the cusp of Champions League qualification. It's a footballing miracle. I don't know how we've almost got there with all the problems this team's had, and I don't know if we can do it because we're relying on some major results going our way. Results, which, let's face it, are as likely to happen as Tommy Gunn leaving Shyton United; but the footballing gods have put Shyton in a position of 1000/1 to make it to the Champions League.

I left Joe as he kept on wandering aimlessly, somehow finding his way into one of Huge Jack's blue movie houses and massage parlours—one of the few places where there was no tension and if there was, it could be relieved. As for myself, I kept looking for others to interview. Shops were selling Shyton scarves—both the old and the new ones—there was bunting everywhere, posters of Shyton's heroes like Tommy Gunn, Ricardo Bombalbo, Ronnie Morrison and Jay Patel. Shops sold Bombalbo fat suits in homage to the late, great striker. There were even T-shirts with 'Where's Dwayne?' printed on them in the style of 'Where's Wally?' Excitement was in the air, and it was a wonder to be in this great town, as Shytonians came together in unison.

I stopped off at the Fudge and Wrapper where all the meals had been named after the footballers and their associates. There was Toad in the Hole, renamed as Toad in the K-Y, Bangers and Mash – Li Bang and Mash, Shepherd's Pie – Cheryl's Pie, Spotted Dick – Sonny's Dick, the 'All-You-Can-Eat' buffet – the Bombalbo, and so on. It was quite impressive yet depressive.

I ordered the Ricardo Carbonara, al dente (wasn't quite sure of the relevance of that dish to Ricardo – could see the relevance if it had been called K-Y's Carbonara with extra cream), and a couple of pieces of Ronnie (bread). I washed it all down with a pint of Shyton Best and remembered that in a couple of days Shyton United had a home game against the mighty Eagles. I should've felt happy either way, but the thought of us playing the big guns of European football made it feel like a do or die game, as if to lose would be a disaster. How were the players feeling? Were they packing it as much as I was? After finishing my meal, I headed over to who else? Tommy Gunn. He was a Shytonian and if anybody would be packing it, it would be him.

He was looking pretty chilled, relaxing on his huge leather sofa. His legs were again wide apart like he was going to give birth, and he looked resplendent in his Union Jack boxers. He rubbed his Stiles a couple of times whilst watching some daytime TV. Brenda was nowhere to be seen, and the kids were being looked after by a nanny. His injured leg looked pretty fine and he was not suffering any obvious discomfort. Would he be ready for the Palace game?

**TOMMY:** Nah, I'm pissed off.

Oh right, the Maury situation.

**STANLEY:** Surely that can be put to one side for the time being so that we can try to secure Champions League nights?

Even I, for that moment, no longer cared how we, or should I say Maury, had gotten us to this position where we were one win away from making history. Tommy wasn't talking.

**STANLEY:** I guess all you can think about is the Palace game, eh?
**TOMMY:** Nah, all I can think about is the amount of pain I'm going to give to that piece of shit. I'm gonna give him the butting of a lifetime.
**STANLEY:** Tommy, that can come after. Now, about the Palace game, any screamers lined up?
**TOMMY:** That bastard made my life a nightmare. Own fans turned against me, even my family stopped talking to me. I'm going to break his nose into a thousand pieces.

This was getting me nowhere so I tried slinking off.

**TOMMY:** Where you going? Kids gotta go playgroup or sumink… Take 'em.

I died a little inside.

**STANLEY:** Yes, boss.

After taking the kids to their playdate, I went home and worked with Bob through the night to get ready for the final game of the season. Heady times lay ahead.

<u>**11<sup>th</sup> May, 2014**</u>

Excitement was in the air as Tommy made his return from injury in what could be his last game for Shyton United, as they took on Crystal Palace in their final game of the season. It was one of the games that would decide 3rd, 4th and 5th places and who would get Champions League football and who would suffer the Europa League—the most hated tournament of Premier League football managers (behind the League Cup… and that other one).

Of course, the return of Tommy was big news, and rumours were still rife that his departure was imminent. However, all that was small fry to the ramifications of a win for Shyton and a shock loss for both Arsenal and Chelsea. Those two teams would need to suffer losses by at least 3 goals apiece, with Shyton United needing to win by 6 goals. If any of that were to happen, it would be the biggest shock in history until two years later.

In the changing room amongst the well-known first teamers of Tommy, Ronnie, Li Bang, K-Y, and Ricardo were six nondescript football players whom I shan't waste my time on, as they'll do nothing for the narrative. Us Danish fishermen have no time for small fish.

**BARRY:** Now, I'm one win away from securing us fourth place and playing Champions League football next season. Tommy, you're captain. K- Y, you're back in goal.

K-Y leapt into the air with joy, like a dolphin out of water.

K-Y back in goal for this fixture? I was well aware that it was only Crystal Palace, the sixth or seventh best team in London, but they had been FA Cup finalists in 1990 in which they had almost beaten a Manchester United team containing Lee Martin. That was a brave move by Barry Bloomer after the previous brave move of having Ronnie Morrison in goal. Could goalkeeper James 'K-Y' Black be a better option than central defender, Ronnie Morrison?

**RONNIE:** I'm captain!
**BARRY:** Not for this game, son.

Justice there. The sunshine was beating down onto the pitch like one of Huge Jack's moustachioed male stars beating down on one of the female starlets from Huge Jack's sadomasochism movie, '*Whore Wars: The Cock Awakens*'.

To the match, and Shyton needed to do the impossible. Only an act of god—or something far more logical with a slew of conspiracy theories following—could make the impossible possible and see the Fudge Packers beat the Eagles by six goals, and their rivals lose by the requisite amount. No Fudge Packer, me included, should've had a sleepless night, because that was not going to happen.

The first bit of action saw Tommy power forward, driving into the box. It was like he'd never been away. As he powered on into the box, he had his heels slightly clipped in the slightest of challenges that only the most delicate of creatures, or a Michael Owen, would've gone down under. And yet:

**STANLEY:** Penalty! And he's off! The defender's remonstrating with the referee as are all his Palace teammates, but the ref's having none of it and has sent him off for the most innocuous of challenges. Blimey!

I had assumed commentary for this match, recording it specially for the Shyton United end of season review, DVD/digital download.

**STANLEY:** Ricardo's going to take the penalty. He's assumed duties from Tommy. He takes the ball in hand, places it onto the penalty spot as is the norm, stares into the goalie's eyes and the goalie looks back. What's going on? Ricardo looks evermore, and he's given the goalie a cheeky wink. Why, I never! The goalie shies away…blushing? No. Ricardo strides up to the ball and lashes it home. Goal!

The Palace goalkeeper later told me he had been sure that Ricardo was coming onto him.

**STANLEY:** A very controversial beginning to the game!

And the controversy wouldn't end there. Minutes later and this happened:

**STANLEY:** Another penalty! Another player off! Goal! Less than ten minutes gone and Shyton are two up and playing against 9 men! This is a dream start for Shyton!

While the match was on I couldn't help but glance at Maury and see him rub his hands in glee.

**STANLEY:** As every other Fudge Packer in the stadium, and across Shyton, I also have my ears glued to the two matches involving Chelsea and Arsenal. We really are living in a wonderland as both those sides are currently 1-0 down. This is incredible!

And it was incredible and things only got better, to the point that I was rather speechless throughout the rest of the commentary. There were goals, there was even more controversy, there were nail-biting moments, and when there was a minute left, complete and utter jubilation. News filtered in from the other two matches involving Shyton United's rivals. Both Arsenal and Chelsea had inexplicably lost 3-0 and, amazingly, Shyton United had completed a feat thought as likely as the second coming of Christ, and beaten the mighty Eagles 6-0! What a game! What a season! What unfathomableness!

At the end of the match, fireworks were set off, one of which went rogue and blew up Darren's house—a known meth lab. (Darren had featured heavily in this documentary until being thoroughly omitted—except for that one instance.) The team and the fans were all jubilant, and even I shed a tear. In the changing room, champagne bottles were uncorked and the contents overflowed as the team celebrated.

Tommy then elected to pour a bottle of champagne over me and shouted:

**TOMMY:** Tosser!

For some reason, despite his man of the match performance, Tommy was much angrier than usual and seemed to want to take it out on me. Shouldn't he have been one of the happiest of all? I hightailed it out of there and to the safety of Maury's office. In the stadium, the fans continued to celebrate and refused to leave – who could blame them? The Shyton police, wanting to get home, used tear gas in an attempt to disperse the crowd and make them go—it had no effect. Years of pollution from the factories making those plastic switches had made Shytonians a resistant bunch.

Maury was downing a glass of champagne. Perhaps in his drunken, weakened state I'd be able to get some straight answers from him about this most strange of days, and yes, the strangest of seasons. Being soaked in champagne left me feeling rather uncomfortable. Sticky trousers and pants did not a happy documentarian make... or something like that. Anyway, sticky pants were not going to stop me.

**STANLEY:** Shyton United have qualified for the Champions League for the first time in their history. Yet, even at this early stage with the final whistle having only come less than an hour ago, there's a flurry of controversy.
**MAURY:** Rival clubs are just jealous of our success. They'd been planning this for ages, in case an unfancied side like us managed to snatch fourth. The powers that be don't like it when an outsider breaks up their little club. You of all people Stanley should be pleased as punch and glad that a minnow became a... mannow...
**STANLEY:** I'm as pleased as the next Shytonian; but being a documentarian, I have to be cynical and question everything. Everybody else will do the same. I mean, you thrashed Palace 6-0, thanks to six penalties and three Palace players being sent off.
**MAURY:** What you trying to say? That I bribed the ref? I refute that!
**STANLEY:** Well, I didn't say that. However, that's now firmly lodged in my mind... Isn't it also odd that the other two teams fighting for fourth suffered scandalous decisions, each losing 3-0?
**MAURY:** As Jimmy Greaves once said, it's a funny old game.
**STANLEY:** Bizarre red cards and penalties. Players suddenly being off-form.
**MAURY:** Not my problem. Speak to the FA or UEFA. Human errors are a part of our game, and long may it continue. Relax, Stanley, and enjoy the gravy train of success.

Maury raised his glass, he was indeed in high spirits. I reluctantly raised my empty hand as I had not been offered a glass of champagne by the tight-fitted so and so.

**MAURY:** To me... and the team I represent... for now.

Maury's mobile rang to the tune of *Eye of the Tiger*.

**MAURY:** Yeah? … Who is this? … Wait!

The line went dead. He tried calling someone in a panicked, sweaty hurry. More and more he reminded me of a sweatier, less ballsy version of Tom Cruise's character in *Tropic Thunder*.

**MAURY:** Damn it Sheedy, answer!
**STANLEY:** What's the matter?

Maury stared at me as though he didn't recognise me at all.

**MAURY:** Get out! Out! Out!

He started pushing me out, then gave up and rifled through his filing cabinet, binning every document. I personally would've shredded then burnt them, perhaps Maury was showing his inexperience. Suddenly, and without warning, two uniformed police officers burst in along with DI Bud Davis, who stank of Bell's whiskey and Silk Cut cigarettes. And he reminded me of that character, Tosh from the TV show, *The Bill*. A lot of things reminded me.

**DI DAVIS:** Maury Git'a. You're under arrest.
**MAURY:** Err… what? For what?
**DI DAVIS:** For fraud, trafficking women…
**MAURY:** I thought that lorry was carrying cheap Romanian liquor, not cheap Romanian women.
**DI DAVIS:** …Blackmail, and for being a first-class prick.
**MAURY:** You can't charge me with that!

The two police officers handcuffed Maury.

**DI DAVIS:** You have the right to…
**MAURY:** Where the hell's Sheedy? Stan, get my solicitor!
**DI DAVIS:** How could you do this to Shyton? This town gave you everything!
**MAURY:** This town? I despise this town.

With good reasons too. The first reason was because his wife was killed in Shyton town centre. One evening there was a stampede at the local kebab restaurant, when it was falsely reported that they had run out of gyros. The locals weren't happy and the poor unfortunate Mrs Maury, who had been passing the kebab restaurant at the time, just happened to be in the wrong place at the wrong time. She was crushed like an eyeball in a vice.

The police officers took Maury away, though Maury struggled and fought like a petulant child throwing a tantrum.

**DI DAVIS:** Come on, Git.
**MAURY:** Don't call me that! It's 'Geeta'.

That was the other reason. Shytonians could be rather cruel and often referred to Maury as 'Git' – though, to be fair, he was.

*'The Shyton Daily'* journalist was outside the ground snapping away, as Maury was put into the police car. Questions should've been buzzing around inside my head wondering who had tipped off the police but I already knew. Tommy was behind this and I had to tip my hat off to him. Though it was hardly a genius move to simply present evidence to the police or the paper (however he had done it); it was still something that I had never thought Tommy would be capable of. Oddly, though this might well lead to the temporary destruction of my beloved club, it might also be the catalyst for change, good stewardship and ultimately long-term prosperity and health. As Patrick Swayze's character 'Bohdi' said in the buddy-cop surfer classic *'Point Break'*, *'It will sting a bit but it's for your own growth.'*

It was imperative I spoke to Tommy and got his views. However, I doubted he'd utter a word, as real smarts and proving that people's perceptions about you being a dimwit were misconceived were keeping your mouth shut; no matter how tempting it was to shout from the rooftops and proclaim that it had been your idea from the start—à la David Beckham when he intentionally got himself booked all those years ago.

<u>**12<sup>th</sup> May, 2014**</u>

The next day, I popped round to Tommy's gaff.

**TOMMY:** You're early.
**STANLEY:** Come again.
**TOMMY:** I booked you for later. Take me to the stadium for the press.
**STANLEY:** I received no booking, sir.

As soon as he started speaking to me in a client-to-paid-chauffeur kind of way, I immediately donned that cap and responded in the appropriate manner. I didn't literally don the cap.

**TOMMY:** I booked it through the new app.
**STANLEY:** App, sir?

Had one of the other chauffeurs/documentarians gone behind my back and created an app for our service without telling me? The rascals! Anyway, I needed to get back to the subject I came here to discuss.

**STANLEY:** I guess you know all about Maury.
**TOMMY:** What if I do?

He was being cagey, rightfully so.

**STANLEY:** Tommy…
**TOMMY:** Sir!

He thought I should remain in chauffeur character when he hadn't realised that I had transitioned back to documentarian.

**STANLEY:** I was with you when you took the documents, the very same documents that incriminated Maury and were the basis of his arrest.

Tommy took a step closer and his bulging forehead came into crystal clear view. Was I to be another victim?

**TOMMY:** Let's go to Creek Alley.

I duly drove Tommy to Creek Alley, where he was going to give a press conference to reassure fans once and for all of his status. A throng of media outlets, and one Joe Meek, were there as Tommy read a pre-prepared statement.

**TOMMY:** I love Shyton United. This is my hometown club and I never had any intention of leaving. All those rumours were unfounded, my heart's in this town and in this club. The only way I'd leave is if none of you wanted me here.

The Shyton United fans, well just Joe, chanted Tommy's name.

**TOMMY:** Me? I'm Shyton for life.

Well, that was us reassured. Joe and I, being the sole supporters there, embraced and would've embraced Tommy but for our fear of a tremendous butting.

The press tried asking him questions but Tommy got out of there pretty sharpish.

And that was really the zenith of it all. Maury was finally being investigated and would no doubt soon be behind bars. Tommy had insisted he'd be at Shyton till the porn stars came home. Shyton would (unless the authorities said otherwise) be playing in the qualifying stage of the Champions League next season, which meant their key players had no reason to leave—unless Shyton got kicked out of the Champions League and relegated due to financial irregularities that were sure to be revealed once Maury had made a plea bargain. That really was the peak, and now it was all about to go downhill.

<u>**15<sup>th</sup> May, 2014**</u>

The plan had been to visit all of the Shyton United players and sort of have a review of the season. Obviously that wouldn't have taken long, what with all the tragedies and disappearances that had affected the first team since the start of the season. However, there were enough players remaining to get a clear picture of their thoughts of Shyton United's successful first season back in the top flight. We decided to begin with one of Shyton's big summer signings and one of the few success stories, despite his personality. Unfortunately, when we got to Ricardo's, there was a slight problem. The paramedics were there, along with Ricardo's agent Sheedy and the Shyton United team doctor. They were in deep discussion trying to work out what to do and whether it was safe to move Ricardo. Ricardo was standing naked, posing in front of one of his many mirrors and had become so transfixed he wasn't budging.

**RICARDO:** So beautiful and rip. Can't move.
**STANLEY:** Ricardo?

Ricardo didn't respond. Just his eyeballs did the talking now.

**STANLEY:** He's almost catatonic. Doctor, what's wrong with him?
**TEAM DOCTOR:** Transfixia Narcissism Excessivia. First I've ever seen of it. Potentially first case ever. There had been mumblings amongst team doctors that it existed but we thought that it was an urban legend. There had meant to be a case of it at Manchester United a few years back.
**STANLEY:** What is transfixia narci…
**TEAM DOCTOR:** Transfixia Narcissism Excessivia. It's a condition in which the patient cannot stop looking at their reflection.
**STANLEY:** What if he does stop?
**TEAM DOCTOR:** If they do they could suffer a massive cardiac arrest.

Ricardo's eyeballs were going from side to side at a hundred miles an hour, yet remaining fixed on his reflection.

**STANLEY:** Is there any known cure, doc?
**TEAM DOCTOR:** Unfortunately, medical science hasn't come that

far yet. There's a lack of funding, a lack of cases and a lack of willingness to help the patients who get it.

**STANLEY:** Who normally gets it?

**TEAM DOCTOR:** Top level footballers.

**STANLEY:** Oh dear.

**TEAM DOCTOR:** The only hope is that one day he'll get bored of looking at himself.

I doubted that would ever happen.

**TEAM DOCTOR:** It could be years before Ricardo moves again.

I left Ricardo's house as they attempted to lift Ricardo onto the gurney whilst making sure he could keep looking at his reflection. They needed an upright gurney like the one used on Hannibal Lecter in the movie, *'The Silence of the Lambs'*.

With that being a rather wasted trip, I popped round to Tommy's place, where there was more bad news. Tommy was at Brenda's bedside, along with a fine-looking nurse and an atheistic priest. Brenda couldn't move, much like Ricardo, but rather than literal narcissism, it was a case of indirect narcissism due to way too much cosmetic surgery.

**ATHEISTIC PRIEST:** Through this *holy* anointing that's as sure to work as I am to ever do a real job, may the imaginary *Lord* in his hippie-like love and mercy help you, with the grace of the alleged Holy Spirit. May the Lord Krishna or Yahweh or the flying teapot, who frees you from sin… pfft, what sin? Save you and, blah blah blah. Who buys this bullshit?

The priest stormed out, slamming the door behind him. He'd chosen the wrong profession.

**STANLEY:** I'm so sorry, Tommy.

I put a comforting hand upon Tommy's shoulder then swiftly removed it when I could see that it was an unwanted gesture.

**TOMMY:** Silly cow.

Tommy then broke down. I had never seen Tommy cry before, and knowing that I could neither comfort him or… whatever the other option was, I left and let him and the nurse get on with it.

Brenda died later that evening, and Tommy was to regret that the last words Brenda heard from Tommy's mouth were 'silly cow'. Soon after she fell into a deep, bitter unconsciousness never to awake, no matter how hard Tommy tried to shake her awake to apologise.

<u>**18<sup>th</sup> May, 2014**</u>

Maury had spilled his guts, I assumed for a more lenient sentence, and had revealed the full scale of the corruption and fraud committed at Shyton United. It was the biggest news of the season, and had thrown the English game into disarray. How had Shyton United gotten away with it? Unpaid transfer fees, bribery, match-fixing, money laundering, the alleged murder of a Japanese footballer, you name it and it was committed. Shyton United football club was destroyed and the town would surely never recover. It was like the town and club had been hit by a Hurricane Katrina, the tsunami that hit Japan and the tsunami that had hit Thailand all in one go. Somebody might need to get that priest back to perform the last rites for the club and town. It was a horrible time.

From the blog, Fudge Packer for Life, Joe Meek wrote:
*'…Well, that's it then. The club's utterly fucked. Maury rolled over and got his belly tickled more than an effeminate, needy puppy. He squealed louder than Henry Hill and now Shyton is so deep in shit the only way out would be a journey 100 times longer than Andy DuFresne made. I can't believe how fucked we are. None of the top-earners are going to stay, the only one who might is the keeper and that's because he's got no choice. It's gonna be a long hard road back, much harder than any Shytonian experienced before. We've been fucked in the arse before, but this is bigger, stiffer and longer lasting than any previous fuck. Fuck! Why should us fans suffer? It wasn't us! If that Maury ever gets out, he'd better go in some kind of FBI-like protection program cos otherwise he'll be our regular go-to bitch. Fuck!'*

Joe was right to be livid, and I felt pretty much the same way. I paid a visit to the gaffer. He'd been unavailable previously, and to be honest, I'd been too depressed to visit any of the players or management in case more horror stories would be revealed. Besides, my depression brought on by the club's situation made it difficult to rise in the morning.

**BARRY BLOOMER:** We're really up shit creek.
**STANLEY:** Any news from Bob Gilbert and Bob Silver?
**BARRY BLOOMER:** Don't make me laugh. They disappeared faster than Houdini.
**STANLEY:** What will you do now?
**BARRY BLOOMER:** Well, of course I'm loyal to this club so my

first concern is them. It doesn't matter that we've been barred from participating in Europe and relegated to League Two. I want all... err...
**STANLEY:** Shyton...
**BARRY:** United fans to know that I'm with you 100%, come rain or shine.
**STANLEY:** That's great to hear. If you stay, steering the ship, that might persuade others to stay. This club needs some stability.

We exchanged smiles. Maybe I'd misjudged Barry Bloomer. Perhaps he had some integrity after all.

<u>**19<sup>th</sup> May, 2014**</u>

I awoke to the news that Barry Bloomer had quit the club and joined arch-rivals Coventry City. The bastard! The rat!

This was all so thoroughly depressing, so I went to the light amidst all the darkness and visited Cheryl Ford. Of course she'd no doubt be in mourning or frantic with worry for her missing husband. Regardless of her emotional state, her beauty was enough reason for me to pester her and cheer myself up. When I went round to hers she wasn't there so I tried Ronnie's, as I wasn't stupid. Sure enough the two of them, rather brazenly I thought, were strolling around his lush, green garden, hands in each other's back pockets like the inseparable lovebirds they had always been.

**STANLEY:** It's been a while since Dwayne's mysterious disappearance...

Cheryl started to weep what were probably crocodile tears. Even so, Ronnie put an arm around her.

**RONNIE:** It's still a bit delicate. Cheryl and me were gutted when Dwayne went MIA.

**STANLEY:** Still landscaping?
**RONNIE:** What?

There was a mound of fresh earth with a bunch of compost bags around it, a wheelbarrow and a couple of shovels.

**STANLEY:** What's buried there?
**RONNIE:** Unwanted merch. Now get your mince pies off of my business…

Just then DI Bud Davis and those same two police officers were shown in by one of Ronnie's freaked out, illegal Filipino servants.

**DI DAVIS:** Ronnie Morrison?
**RONNIE:** Shit, it's the filth.

Ronnie used Cheryl to obstruct then threw her towards them. He legged it, with the police officers in chase.

No matter how hard he tried to evade the police, Ronnie was soon arrested and charged with burglary, dealing in stolen goods and named chief suspect in the disappearance of Dwayne Ford, a charge that was later dropped. Dwayne Ford has never been found… nor looked for.

<u>**22<sup>nd</sup> – 25<sup>th</sup> May, 2014**</u>

After discussing it with Bob, and feeling that I wasn't actually getting any work done because of my depression, I decided to get away from Shyton for a little bit. The place was just the definition of misery, and it had become even more of a dump than it had ever been. It was so bad that local councillors were pondering whether they could rename the town 'Grimsby II'. There was even talk of abandoning ship altogether and letting it become a landfill site.

Whilst I was away, big things had happened for Li Bang. After Sonny's death, Li had decided to close down their nightclub and put all his efforts into a music career. When not training or playing, he'd been making records with DJ Yuichi, and upon Shyton United's demotions released a dance hip-hop fusion track that the kids loved, called *'(I Wanna) Pump Ya Booty'*. It was such a catchy song with its repetitive lyric,

> *'Pump ya booty, pump ya booty, yeah, yeah, I wanna and I'm gonna, pump ya booty…'*

Even I found myself singing it. Wherever Li Bang went he was mobbed, it was like Beatlemania all over again—though they called it 'Bangmania', and his female followers labelled themselves 'Bangers'. Youth pop culture of today. Couldn't help feeling that women lib of the 60s and 70s had since done a massive U-turn.

During my time away I rented a cottage deep in the Cotswolds, far away from everything, including Tommy's persistent bookings through the app that I had not approved of. It was a lovely quaint cottage, with a thatched roof, a fireplace and no Premier League footballers in sight. Despite this, after a day of doing nothing but get through a box of tissues and eat an unusual amount of pork scratchings, I got a phone call from Bob who was in hysterics. He told me that K-Y had decided to retire from football. Whether K-Y retired or had actually been released I was not certain. Anyway, I wasn't sure how that was funny, as it sounded like quite a sound idea to me. Bob then got to the punchline: K-Y had decided to take up basketball and had immediately been appointed captain of Great Britain.

I found out when the British team's next training session would be and, to my delight, it wasn't a million miles away. I finished off my last packet of pork scratchings and prepared to go and visit K-Y.

<u>**26<sup>th</sup> May, 2014**</u>

I caught the British basketball team in the middle of a training session at the country's top basketball arena. Playing point guard was my old pal, K-Y. As you could guess, every time a ball was passed to him it was dropped. I detected quite a bit of anger in the faces of the British team whose members had once dreamed of being able to compete with the likes of Lithuania and the Philippines. Those dreams were now up in smoke.

Upon his 'retirement', K-Y was voted the league's worst goalkeeper since Bobby 'Couldn't Catch a Cold' Jade. I had to admire K-Y that despite humiliation after humiliation he still went out in public, and never shied away. I caught a few words with him courtside, as he let fly with a shot that flew miles wide.

**STANLEY:** Have you actually retired from football?
**K-Y:** Absolutely. Too much machismo, too much preferential treatment. It's not like how it used to be. I didn't decide this overnight, it was something I had thought about for a good long while and decided what would be best for me. I think I've found my calling in basketball.
**STANLEY:** You won't ever return?
**K-Y:** Well, never say never Stan. A club might come calling tomorrow.
**STANLEY:** And the British basketball team might win the Olympics.
**K-Y:** Exactly.
**STANLEY:** So, you weren't actually released then?
**K-Y:** Don't know what you mean.
**STANLEY:** Things are going well with the basketball?
**K-Y:** Yes, with me in the team, we've risen from 131st to 130th in the world!
**STANLEY:** Excellent. How about your personal life?
**K-Y:** Yeah, great. Let me introduce my new special someone.

Since when had K-Y broken up with his previous partner?

**STANLEY:** I didn't know you had someone new. I didn't even know you had broken up with the last.
**K-Y:** Well, you were preoccupied with all the craziness going on at Shyton and probably too busy to notice.

K-Y called out.

**K-Y:** Honey? Come over.

There were a bunch of people scattered around and I wasn't sure who he was calling over. A figure in the distance started coming forward in answer to the call. It had long blonde hair, tallish… An errant basketball flew my way and smashed me in the face, knocking me out cold. I woke later in the changing room with the team doctor by my side, and an ice-pack over my eyes and forehead. Of course K-Y and his partner had already left.

After a visit to the hospital, I was later released and went back home to Shyton.

The gloom hadn't lifted yet from Shyton. It was like a thick blanket of smog made up of depression, despair, fraud, lies, shock and porn. Smog much thicker and heavier than Beijing could ever hope to produce.

I drove around town, a town that was now a ghost town. More and more shops were boarded up, as were the homes of the famous footballers that once plied their trade for this most unfancied of teams. Though the remaining players couldn't leave just yet till the transfer window opened, many hoped they would be transferred and therefore relocated anyway. If they didn't secure moves then they'd probably just refuse to play. There weren't too many Alessandro Del Pieros and Gianluigi Buffons nowadays.

I eventually got the courage to go to Creek Alley Stadium, where chains and padlocks were on the gates, fastening them close together— if only they could do that to Shytonian lasses' legs. The rate of teenage pregnancy was hitting Swansea levels.

I shook the gates and mouthed to myself, 'Is this the end of Shyton United?'

**SAO:** What's going on?
**STANLEY:** Sao, what are you doing here?
**SAO:** Where is everybody? Wait... this isn't Liverpool.

Sao walked away. How was he still alive? How hadn't he been run over, electrocuted, or had a main artery accidentally severed while preparing lunch? He reminded me of the joke of the blonde wearing headphones while getting a haircut. Joe Meek came round the corner and joined me. Not a word was uttered, as we stood in silence and just looked forlornly at our beloved club. Nothing needed to be said.

<u>1<sup>st</sup> June, 2014</u>

It was rather surprising to me that there was yet one more nail available that could be hammered into Shyton United's coffin. Yet somehow another nail was hammered in to further shut a coffin that was pretty airtight as it was. The nail in question was Tommy Gunn.

A press conference had been called and it wasn't to be held at Shyton's Creek Alley Stadium. The conference was being held at arch-rivals City, a club historically and accurately bigger than Shyton United.

There was another media throng, another slew of reporters, another bouquet of microphones, another bunch of supporters representing the supporters' club and Joe Meek, a relic of the past. Tommy held aloft the shirt he'd be wearing, the blue of City—the traitorous bastard. It was hard to be impartial, even as a well-respected documentarian.

**TOMMY:** I'm pleased to be joining City. It's been a lifelong dream to play for them and I can't wait to get started.

How long had this transfer been in the works and how long had Tommy been aware of it, and perhaps, even pushed for it?

Naturally, Joe was less than pleased, jeering Tommy throughout and calling him every insult under the sun, stars and moon. He then shot up and started throwing everything he could get his hands on, mainly his ciggies.
Security tried to restrain Tommy but only so much muscle could keep a deranged lunatic down, and Tommy threw himself at Joe. Tommy gave the unemployed slob the head-butting of a lifetime—and it was indeed of a lifetime. Firstly, the whole moment was like it was in slow-motion—and I'm talking Scorsese's *'Raging Bull'* here. Joe's shocked, frightened-white, gob wide-open face the target of Tommy's raging, maniacal, throbbing head. Tommy's head came at Joe's in a whirlwind of flash bulbs and pure anger. Then boom, bash, two worlds collided and the crack was heard around the globe as two lowlife titans collapsed.

<u>**1ˢᵗ July, 2014**</u>

A month had passed since the infamous head-butt, and I was standing before yet another gravestone in an area of Shyton cemetery reserved for Shyton United players and their families. The grave belonged to Tommy, and his epitaph read, 'One head- butt too far'.

Tommy Gunn. Local bad lad who rose from the gutter to achieve his dream of playing in the Premier League. This was the end.

I joined Joe Meek at the Fudge and Wrapper for one last pint before I too left Shyton to resume my normal life away from the pain and misery. The pub was reminiscent of the town – it was dead. Joe remained, though I sensed he wouldn't stick around for too long, despite him saying the contrary.

**JOE:** We'll be back. Whether it's as Shyton United, AFC Shyton, FC United or Titi Telecommunications Ltd FC. This club will never die. Its spirit will live on and grow, even if it means starting from the very bottom tier. Fudge Packer for life!
**STANLEY:** Do you hold any grudges in respect to Tommy?
**JOE:** Nah, I won't speak ill of the dead. What's done is done. Can't change any of it, can I? It's time for rebuilding.
**STANLEY:** What about Maury?
**JOE:** Don't speak his name! Hope the bastard rots.

Maury's upcoming trial was sure to shed more light on the murky world of top-flight football. It was going to be one of the trials of the century, that was for sure. Anyway, that was for another book.

# EPILOGUE

Shyton's population was down to double-digits, the town was bankrupt and it had become known as the Detroit of England. The few hold-outs remaining were eternal optimists, then there were those that had gotten accustomed to solitary confinement in previous lives, then there were people who had been homeless elsewhere and now weren't, and the remainder? Well, who could say what their reasons were. The town had been selected for demolition to make way for anything that might be needed in the future, such as the biggest car park in the world. Even Huge Jack's Productions had relocated – there was nothing left. It was like a nuclear bomb had gone off. So tragic from how things were just a year or so ago.

And where had the bulk of Shytonians gone? India, no less. An Indian company by the name of Titi Communications had read of the plight of Shytonians and offered to relocate them, as well as offer them jobs at a huge industrial estate in Bangalore. Titi Communications were the number one mobile phone network in south Asia. Shytonians were manning the phones and computers at the Titi Communications call centre, handling calls from irate Indians and having to convince them that they really did keep up-to-date with popular Indian soap opera, *Diya Aur Bati Hum*.

In another twist, who should be the Titi Communications manager to all those Shytonians? None other than Jay 'Beanie' Patel, and he was no slacker. Apparently he carried a whip and was not afraid to use it.

Maury was sentenced to twenty years in the most one-sided case known to legal history. If not for his testimonies incriminating others, then he could've gotten an even longer sentence.

I did indeed return to Manchester and I began a new project entitled *The Art of Hamster War*. Bob was no longer by my side and had instead elected to try his luck in London. I heard he's doing quite well directing television adverts for Lynx deodorants.

I settled back down, acting and feeling as if nothing had happened. Upon learning that Shyton United as an entity was no more, I decided to get to work on the project that became known as Shyton United, the film, and the book that you've just finished reading. I thank you for your time, and hope that if you're ever in the north of England and in need of a parking space you'll think of Shyton.

Best,

Stanley Gobsen
Available to document weddings, birthdays, and fishing excursions.